An Impetuous Bride

Julie Caille

ZEBRA BOOKS
KENSINGTON PUBLISHING CORP.

This book is dedicated to special friends

Sharon Schulze
and
Brenda Barber

with thanks for being you

ZEBRA BOOKS

are published by

Kensington Publishing Corp.
475 Park Avenue South
New York, NY 10016

First printing: September, 1991

Printed in the United States of America

AN INNOCENT WIDOW

"Halt the horses for a moment," he said. He watched with approval as she slowed the phaeton exactly as he'd taught her to do, then he took the reins from her hand.

"Look at me," he commanded, and when her head turned, he bent and kissed her on the mouth.

"Mr. Deveaux," she choked, pushing against his chest, "what are you doing? We are in the Park, for God's sake!"

"I beg your pardon," he said with sudden stiffness. "You did not seem to be objecting overmuch."

"Well, I do object!" she said fiercely. "This has all been a ruse, hasn't it? You let me believe you were my friend when all you truly want is to dishonor me!"

"Nonsense," he replied, taken aback. After all, what had it been but a kiss? She had been married, hadn't she? "You're making a great piece of work over a trifle," he added irritably.

"Yes, I daresay it *is* a trifle to you," she accused. "Well, I am much more worldly than you think, Mr. Deveaux. I know all about men like you!"

Derek caught hold of her wrist, his voice smooth as cream. "Worldly or not, my sweet, you know nothing about me."

Chapter One

Miss Stacia Amaryllis Ashcroft had it all reasoned out. If an unmarried young lady from the wilds of North England chose to come to London under false pretenses, why, whose business was it but hers? Indeed, she could think of no reason why anyone would discover her deception, for who in the world would question a lady's claim that she was a widow?

Having satisfied herself yet again on this point, Miss Ashcroft's attention returned to the other passenger in the southward-bound, rather antiquated coach that had been her father's. The gentleman was slim and fair, and though his features were unreservedly masculine, no one could have denied that he bore a strong resemblance to the lady. At the moment he was engaged in loving contemplation of his newly acquired Wellington boots, but Miss Ashcroft did not hesitate to continue the conversation which had briefly been allowed to lapse.

"To be sure, I shall have to be careful," she said, in her low, soft voice. "But Edwards is a common enough name, after all, and who is likely to make an inquiry? No one, I am convinced. The important thing is that for the first time I can live as I choose, without having to submit to horrid restrictions. As a widowed lady I will have absolute *buckets* of freedom."

The gentleman, who happened to be her half brother,

5

gave a lazy yawn. "Mind you don't forget what I said," he warned. "Even widows must conform to the rules of propriety." He glanced down at the large silver buttons on his new coat, and added, "And you'll need to be twice as careful when you draw money from the bank. Old Farquhar knows very well you ain't married."

Stacia chewed her lip for an instant. "Frankly, I do not see that as a problem, Marco. Naturally when I deal with Mr. Farquhar I must do so as 'Miss Ashcroft.' And when I am finished, I will simply go back to being 'Mrs. Edwards.' I do not think it can fail."

Marco shrugged. "I still think it's a bird-witted scheme. Dash it, you're unmarried, and you ought to be presented as such. Your birth is as good as any of the other chits being puffed off by their mamas. It could still be done, y'know."

"At my age?" she countered, a little impatiently. "Even if I were willing—which I am not—who would you have do the 'puffing off'? You know there is no one except Papa's disagreeable aunts and uncles, and none of them ever go to London at all."

She stared into space for a moment, then said with finality, "You will be my protector, my dear. I daresay that will be quite sufficient." Her slim hand brushed back a recalcitrant curl. "Anyway, we are both of age and may do as we please."

Marco's sole response was another yawn. It was obvious that he was tired of the subject, so Stacia nestled back into the squabs and stared out the window at the passing scenery.

She really could do as she pleased, she mused. Thanks to Uncle Travis she was a wealthy woman now, for he had left her his entire fortune—ninety thousand pounds of it—and she had still not recovered from the surprise. Again and again, she'd wondered why he had singled her out in this fashion. She'd only met her father's brother a few times, and those visits had been enough to convince her that Uncle Travis was nearly as cold a man as Papa. Was it possible that he'd been fonder of her than she'd realized? Or had he merely left her the money out of pity? It was something she would never know.

Briefly, she wondered what Uncle Travis would have thought of her pretense. Likely he would have understood it no better than Marco, but that was because she would never have allowed him to suspect her true motivation. Desire for freedom was the excuse she had offered Marco, and though she did want freedom, the underlying reason was more complicated than that. The truth was that the thought of making her debut as a single girl at the age of three-and-twenty made her cringe. She was too old for that now. At the very least, it would cause talk and raise a few eyebrows, while at the most, at the worst, people might guess the humiliating truth. They might guess that her father had not bothered to give her a Season at the proper age because he had not loved her enough. Or to be more honest, that he had not loved her at all.

And, to own the truth, the idea of masquerading as a widow sounded rather exciting—there was something about the word *widow* that spelled sophistication and refinement. To be sure, the scheme had seemed excessively daring when she had first hit upon it, so daring in fact that her hands had actually begun to shake. That was foolish and weak, of course, but when one had never been permitted to do anything very much in one's life, any sort of adventure was as alluring as food to the starving.

Resting her chin on her hand, Stacia mentally reviewed the past she had invented for herself. She had christened her fictitious husband Frederick Edwards and given him the meritorious occupation of soldier. Like so many others, poor Frederick (named for the duke of York) had gone bravely off to the Continent to fight against Boney and been killed at Waterloo in 1815. She had mourned him for nearly two years—a more than dutiful period—but had now put off her blacks in preparation for a sojourn to London. Yes, the story seemed quite satisfactory. There should be no reason

7

why anyone should doubt it.

Stacia's brown eyes grew a little more distant. In truth, she *had* just put off her blacks, but her mourning had not been for any husband. Her father, Sir George Ashcroft, had passed on to whatever fate awaited him just one year ago last month. Ironically, it had been on the anniversary of Papa's demise that they'd learned of Uncle Travis's death. It seemed that Uncle Travis, who had been so busy making his fortune in the West Indies that he had never married, had died on the island of Antigua, beating his brother to the grave by some three weeks. The news, of course, had been a long time in reaching them—his niece had been a wealthy woman for a whole year and not known it.

Stacia's brows wrinkled suddenly. How foolish to think of death when it seemed her life had just begun afresh. Without further ado, she turned her thoughts to her stay in London. She was certain to enjoy it a great deal more as a widow than as an unmarried young woman without a sponsor, she reflected. Of course, even a widow could benefit from a sponsor, but that was something upon which she preferred not to dwell. Somehow it would all work out, she told herself firmly.

The important thing was that she could avoid all contact with her father's relatives, all of whom looked down their noses at her as though she were some sort of insect. It was because of Mama, of course. They all thought Stacia would do something shocking, and as chaperons they would have done their utmost to prevent her from having any enjoyment at all.

Her present plan precluded that dreadful scenario. At long last she was free to leave Ashcroft Manor and the bleak, cloistered existence she had suffered there, and she meant to see that nothing interfered. For an instant, her lips tightened to an unyielding line. Perhaps if she had been of a retiring nature, if everything in ˙her character had been less defiant and willful, perhaps then she might have been content with the lot she had been dealt. But that had not been the case.

8

And so there was a great deal of favor to be found in her deception. As "Mrs. Edwards," she could bypass those rigid rules of propriety invented solely for unmarried girls, for a widow required no watchdogs or chaperons— though of course she must conduct herself with breeding and dignity. Out of respect for Marco's wishes, Stacia had agreed to hire a companion to lend her countenance, but the companion she envisioned was probably not what he meant. What Stacia had in mind was someone worldly enough to offer advice, yet young enough to be a friend. She would have no dried-up disapproving old spinster to impede her freedom—Marco would discover that in time.

Stacia's thoughts drifted down this path as the gently swaying coach filled her with drowsiness. But when sleep finally cast its mesmerizing net, it was of something far more pleasant than freedom that she dreamt.

Sir Marco Ashcroft gazed pensively at his sleeping sister, wishing he felt as comfortable with this madcap scheme as she did. He might not be as worldly a fellow as, say, Reggie Denchworth, but he dashed well knew up from down. And there were one or two things that were becoming increasingly clear to him.

First of all, with nearly a plum to her name, little Stacia was bound to be the target of every fortune hunter in town. To add to this, she might well draw notice of her own account, for she was really quite a passable-looking girl. As accustomed as he was to Stacia's appearance, Marco realized he had never paid her physical assets much heed. His own tastes ran to more sultry types, but as he studied his young half sister carefully, he was assailed with a stab of misgiving. Some men, he thought uneasily, might find that reddish hair of hers attractive. Moreover, he had just noticed that her figure was good. Quite good, in fact. And the combination of good looks and Uncle Travis's fortune was certain to attract a deal of attention.

On the other hand, the poor girl really did deserve to

have some fun. He had never thought about it much, but he supposed that the sheltered life their father had forced her to lead must have been devilish boring. He frowned. Had she ever had any friends? He could not remember any, but he'd been away at school so much of the time he'd probably just missed meeting them.

His curiosity stirred, he studied Stacia's fine features speculatively. Father had never taken much of a fancy to her, had he? A pity, of course, but the old man hadn't cared much for women. On this count, at least, Marco was prepared to be indulgent, for who could blame the old codger? After all, his own mother had been a sickly creature, unable to survive childbirth, while Stacia's mother had eloped with a lover a bare year after her daughter was born. Doubtless a betrayal like that soured a man's opinion of the fairer sex, he reflected.

But, devil take it, the old man really ought to have done his duty and found his daughter a husband! Despite his selfish ways, Sir Marco Ashcroft held his half sister in very genuine esteem, and faulted their father a great deal for his omission.

Mayhap this "widow" scheme was not as mad as it seemed, he thought drowsily. After all, as Stacia had pointed out, she *was* a little old to join the debutantes. This way it would not appear as though she'd been left on the shelf. Of course, he had argued against the scheme at first, until eventually it had dawned upon him that his determined young sister did not need his permission and, indeed, meant to go off to London with or without him. It was then that he had given in. And what real damage could her little deception do? A bit of town bronze was just what she needed.

With this comfortably sanguine belief firmly entrenched in his mind, the young baronet nodded off to sleep. In truth it suited him very well to go to London, for he had a bit of fun in mind for himself as well. A far too angelic smile curved Marco's lips as he slept.

*   *   *

"My dear Derek, I fail to understand how you can take either that tone or that attitude with me!"

Lady Winifred Deveaux glowered at her only son, wondering uneasily whether tears or anger would serve her purpose better than the wheedling remonstrances she had been employing.

"'Tis outside of enough," she continued, "that I must come begging to you for my resources, but that you should refuse me—!" Tears seeming the more persuasive weapon, she searched for her handkerchief. "A viper! That's what you are." She sniffed and dabbed aggrievedly at her dry eyes. "And when I think of the affection I have lavished upon you all these years, I could positively weep. Your coarseness of feeling does you no credit, my son. No credit at all."

Mr. Derek Deveaux's bored gaze had been sweeping the tiny sitting room, but at this, he slanted a look at his mother. "Spare me the homily, Mama," he replied. "The answer is no and that is final."

Lady Winifred studied his hard, handsome face, noting resentfully that he had never even bothered to sit down. Indeed, her son had the effrontery to appear perfectly at ease, his tall, lithe body lounging in what she considered a highly disrespectful pose. Why, his hands were even in his pockets, she thought indignantly.

Her voice became a little shrill. "And when I ask you to wait upon me at your nearest convenience, I do *not* mean after a week or more has slipped by. For all you knew, I might have been in the direst need. I might have been upon my deathbed for all you cared."

"Something assures me that if that were so I should have heard about it," he retorted with strong irony. "However, balls and ballgrowns scarcely constitute dire necessities, do they? You know I do not have the ready for such nonsense." He pushed away from the wall. "Is there anything else you wished to say?"

Two bright spots of color entered Lady Winifred's cheeks. "Certainly there is!" she answered. "Since when is it proper to call upon your mama dressed in such rough garb? Very pretty behavior, Derek, upon my word. What your father would have said I'm sure I do not know."

"Neither do I. I will leave you to speculate upon it without me, however. I have an engagement to go riding."

"Yes, and I can guess with whom!" she cried, goaded by his indifference to unleash another grievance. "I'll take leave to tell you that *that* is another source of humiliation for me! My only son, the child of my body, fraternizing with the most notorious whore in London!"

Derek's black brows rose a fraction of an inch. "Fraternizing, Mama? Such a delicate word for such an indelicate meaning. I own I am surprised at you."

"And I am ashamed of you," she snapped. "That woman is not fit to scrub your floors much less—" She broke off, her lips compressing in sharp disapproval.

"Much less share my bed?" he suggested softly. "I think, dear Mama, that you concern yourself unduly in my behalf. As it happens, the liaison to which you refer is drawing to its inevitable close, but that, ma'am, is nothing to do with you. Who told you, by the way?"

For the first time, Lady Winifred looked flustered. "Oh, how can I remember now?" she said angrily. "All society knows. Your doings are no secret."

Her son sneered. "It was that fool, Duncan, wasn't it? I'll have a word with him about this."

"You will do no such thing!" she cried. "Sir Cuthbert told me nothing that every other fool in town does not know!" Too late, her own words registered. "And he is not a fool," she insisted. "He is simply not . . . not *learned*, Derek, which can hardly be considered a grave imperfection."

He laughed harshly. "Learned? The man's lucky he can remember his own name. But what the devil do I care? Marry the man, if you will. If you can," he added, in a heartless tone.

Lady Winifred tossed her dark, greasy ringlets. "Indeed I shall. I will have him in the end, you will see. And when that happens, my son, the shoe will be upon

12

the other foot. Do not come begging to *me* for money. I shan't forgive your cruelty."

"*If* it happens," he returned, "I will be the first to wish you happy. You'll have all the money you want, and a half-witted dolt to bind to your apron strings. You won't need me anymore, will you?"

Her eyes darkened with unnamed emotion. "You were never bound to my apron strings," she choked out. "You never needed a mother. I've known that since you were a tale-bearing brat of five. You never loved me! You've never loved anyone but yourself."

For a few splintered seconds her son stood utterly immobile. Then, without a word, he turned and strode from the room, leaving a bleak, oppressing emptiness behind. Lady Winifred stared after him, wishing desperately that she had held her tongue. But it was many years too late for such regrets. She heard the front door slam shut, and for a long time after it echoed in her mind.

Twenty minutes later, Derek found his mistress sitting beneath an oak tree, its shade shielding her porcelain complexion from the sun. He did not dismount, though he knew by the coy way she was gazing up at him that it was her wish. He made a curt greeting and gestured toward her horse, but instead of rising, she seemed to settle farther into the grass.

"Oh, Derek!" She murmured his name softly, her tone full of reproach.

"Come, Dominique," he commanded. "Get up. I've no mind to sit upon the ground." She had tried this trick on him before, and it was even less amusing than the first time.

She presented him with her most inviting pout. "You are ungallant, sir, not to mention surly. You might at least offer to give me a leg up. You know I cannot mount without assistance."

"Then you should have stayed on your horse," he said unsympathetically.

Nevertheless he did dismount and, with an ease that spoke well of his strength, tossed his mistress into her saddle. As he swung back onto his gray hack she urged her mount closer to his.

"You're not angry with me, are you?" she whimpered.

Shooting her one of his unfathomable looks, Derek spurred his mount to a trot. "No," he said in a forbidding tone.

He was in one of his black humors, which he knew would irk her, mostly because she had no understanding of what caused them. Though he comprehended her only too well, he was ruefully aware that she—in common with every other woman he had known—hadn't a clue to how *his* mind worked. To be fair, he did not expect it, for, beyond her primary function in his life, Dominique and the others of her kind played but a minor part, and no part at all in his eternal quest for peace of mind and soul.

"Do you like my new riding habit?" she inquired, adroitly bidding his attention to the sleek body it encased.

Derek's green eyes swiveled, then stayed to linger just where she'd intended. "That depends," he answered suavely. "Did I pay for it?"

"If I said no you would be angry," she teased. "For that would mean some other gentleman had done so, wouldn't it?"

She was thrusting her bosom forward, and vivid memories of how that delightful bosom looked unclothed brought a swift surging to his blood. He had not been to her in several days and, to his annoyance, Derek felt his body respond.

"True," he answered flippantly, "and then I'd have to beat you, my love, for being unfaithful. And you wouldn't like that at all."

She flashed him a startled look. "You would not really do that, would you?"

"Oh, would I not," he told her grimly.

"No, no, you must be teasing. I don't like it when you do that, Derek."

The whine in her voice reminded him of his mother.

"Do not try me, Dominique," he warned. "I have no more mind to share my light o' love with another than I do to frolic on the grass with her in the middle of Hyde Park. Where anyone might see," he added meaningfully.

That was what she was trying to do—to entice him to make love to her, albeit quickly, in the Park in broad daylight. She'd mentioned it once in the darkness of the night, but he'd thought it to be a jest until he learned otherwise. Amused he might be, but it was not a desire he shared, especially in his present, damnable mood.

For a while, they walked their horses along the banks of the Serpentine, while Dominique cast him overt glances, full of entreaty and pique. Derek paid her no heed, his awareness focused upon the cries of the gulls and carrion crows, and the bittersweet scent of spring wildflowers. Better to concentrate upon the whispering wind than on his mother's vicious recriminations. His eyes shifted to the dark blue water, where a variety of waterfowl nested and fed. Better to think of herons and mallard ducks than her endless demands for money that he had every intention of putting to better use.

"I do not know why you will not speak to me," complained his mistress. "I do not understand you at all, Derek."

He glanced at her and sighed. "I am being a beast today, aren't I?" he remarked.

She had a face to capture any man's eye, a countenance worthy of odes and sonnets. When he had first met her, he'd felt as though he could never look his fill. "You're looking well, Dominique," he added.

It was an understatement and he knew it, but he never made fulsome compliments—and particularly not to beautiful women. If a female was beautiful, he thought cynically, she already knew it. She did not need a man to tell her so.

"And you, Derek, are looking as cross as a bear," she returned, quite sulkily. "I wish you would let me cheer you up."

15

"You are cheering me up, my dear. By God, that habit yields its price in the pleasure of the view. But aren't you cold with nothing underneath?"

At once her fair head tilted, her dimples quivering with eagerness. "Yes, but 'tis the fashion, you know. Half the ladies in London do the same, after all, and I am never behindhand when it comes to what is à la mode."

He smiled sardonically. "But that hardly applies to riding dress. What if you should take a spill?"

Dominique's light laughter tinkled on the breeze. "Then you, sir, may take as long a look as you can manage whilst I scramble to my feet!"

Perhaps, he reflected, the liaison could be allowed to go on a few days longer. Though he had not anticipated it, his earthy little mistress was actually diverting his mind from his difficulties. True, they were now supplanted by a baser need, but his self-control was far stronger than Dominique suspected. At one-and-thirty, he considered himself well past that callow and rather embarrassing age where one could be swept away by ungovernable lusts. Well, at least not by a fully clothed female in the middle of the Park, he amended.

"Should you like to dine at the Pulteney this eve?" he said abruptly. "I don't believe you've yet done so. I may, of course, be mistaken."

Her head jerked in surprise. "Do you mean it?" she asked, her bemusement ill-concealed. "Do not toy with me, Derek. 'Tis cruel of you to make the offer if you do not mean it! *Do* you mean it?"

"I should not have said it otherwise, Dominique."

His ill humor had already returned, but, unaware, her hand crept boldly out to caress his thigh. "You are so good to me," she murmured, batting her lashes coquettishly. "I must think of a way to repay you, but what can I possibly do?"

Derek surveyed her with unconscious dislike. "I'm sure you'll think of something," he said dryly.

*　　*　　*

Stacia awoke slowly. Eyelids squeezed shut, she tried to recapture her dream, the elusive, marvelous dream which had brushed so close to her deepest, most secret desires.

Since she had been a little girl, Stacia had lived in the world of the imagination. She had cherished one fantasy in particular and, now that she was grown, it lingered on in her memory to tantalize and tease her.

She was at a ball, and she was the most sought-after girl there. She cast all the other females into the shade, not only because she was the most beautiful, the most elegantly attired, the most graceful and witty, but also because there was one particularly handsome, charming gentleman who could not take his eyes off her the entire evening. And though all her partners were gallant and attentive, this one special gentleman was different.

He was her Romeo, her Lochinvar, her Prince Florizel. He was the man who would claim her as his own, who would love and cherish her above all else, above all his worldly possessions. He was the one who would treasure her more dearly than the costliest jewel, more dearly than life and even what lay beyond.

To be loved. That, of course, was the salient part of her dreams, the keynote around which they all revolved. Freedom was but a path to that love, a means to unearth the golden treasure chest she so desperately sought. And Uncle Travis's fortune was giving her the chance to pry it open.

Perhaps she was only castle-building. Perhaps she was really quite ordinary, and there would be no prince waiting at the end of the road for her arrival. But instinct told her otherwise. Long ago, her beloved governess had told her that there was someone for everyone and that each person must strive to find his or her own heart's desire. And that was what Stacia intended to do.

She would cling to her dream.

Chapter Two

Derek had intended to return to his lodgings, but instead he found himself heading for upper St. James's Street and his favorite gentlemen's club. Wearing a slight frown, he halted his match-geldings directly in front of White's famous bow window and handed the curricle-and-pair over to his groom.

He had always appreciated the atmosphere at White's, partly because an encouraging portion of its members agreed with his politics and partly because it provided him with a sanctuary from members of the opposite sex. With a single exception, the females in his life had been sexual rather than romantic partners, and that exception had taught him a great deal about the wiles of women. He had learned, too, that such liaisons were best kept short-lived, for though he tried his best to treat his mistresses as human beings, by and large they seemed determined not to grant him the same courtesy. Such relationships were inevitably a compromise, but he was a sensual man whose passionate nature required an outlet. And since the odds of finding a woman whom he could love, admire, and value—and who would make an effort to understand and love him in return—seemed very small, he had formed the habit of suppressing his emotional needs. As for companionship and sensible conversation, he relied on members of his own sex for that.

Not that he was at all sure he wanted to converse, for

18

Dominique's expert "gratitude" had left him perversely cross. Conversation, however, was what he was destined to receive, for one of the first people he happened upon was Lord Andrew Carisbrooke.

The younger brother of His Grace the Duke of Wight, Lord Andrew was a tall, attractive man with a thick mass of light brown hair, a high-bridged nose, and humorous lips. He had been with Derek at Oxford and though they saw each other seldom, he ranked as one of Derek's few, true friends.

The two men exchanged greetings, and Derek pulled over a chair, saying, "The last time I saw you, Drew, you were conducting what looked like a damned serious flirtation with the latest Incomparable. Recovered from that ailment, did you?"

Lord Andrew smiled. "Has it been that long? Gad, I'd almost forgotten about Eve Marlowe. A pretty, elegant girl, she was. Just my style. And now she is Lady Frome," he added, on such a note of regret that Derek's brows flew up.

"Never tell me she refused you?" he inquired in an idle tone. He thrust his long legs out before him and cast the other man a quizzical look.

There was a sigh of mock gloom. "I never made the offer. And now I suffer for my want of resolution."

"Despite her fading presence in your memory," said Derek dryly. "'Fess up, Drew. You're as leery of leg shackles as I am."

Rather to his surprise, his friend took the statement seriously. "Not really. 'Tis only that I have not found the right woman. I did consider Miss Marlowe though. She had a reserve I found interesting."

Derek found himself smiling. "Poor Drew. Did she admire your fortune more than your *beaux yeux?*"

Lord Andrew fluttered his lashes. "Hard to believe, isn't it?"

"On the contrary, I find it very easy to believe. Now if you were me, you'd not have that problem."

"Of course not," Lord Andrew agreed, his tone very

bland. "Your own emerald orbs being so remarkable."

Derek's eyes gleamed. "Devil take your raillery, Drew. You know that's not what I meant. 'Twas to my lack of fortune I referred. Don't try to make me out a coxcomb." His gaze shifted to rove about the room. "Speaking of coxcombs, is that fool Duncan here?"

"Sir Cuthbert?" Lord Andrew regarded him curiously. "Not to my knowledge. Is it true he's dangling after your mother?"

Derek grimaced. "True enough. God's blood, Drew, can you see that mincing Tulip as my stepfather? His waistcoats alone are enough to turn a man's stomach. Have you seen the one embroidered with pink roses and yellow hummingbirds?"

Displaying an annoying lack of sympathy, Lord Andrew grinned wickedly. "Tut-tut, Derek. I fear you do not fully appreciate your own enviable position. If you play your hand carefully he may offer to teach you his way of tying a neckcloth. A variation on the Oriental, I am told. No one else has succeeded in copying it."

"The man's a fool," said Derek unemotionally. "And I've no patience with fools, male or female. Between my estates and my mother's debts, I've enough to my worry about."

"Perhaps you ought to get married. Someone with a nice fat portion to her name."

The light suggestion drew a scowl from Derek.

"God forbid." His booted foot pulled an adjacent stool closer. "All I need is to be saddled with a spoiled twit with nothing on her mind but frivolity and fashion." His lip curled. "Dominque's allure has already waned, so I can envision how fast a mewling little heiress would pall. That sort of woman would bore me in a week."

Lord Andrew eyed him for a long moment. "You know, you really do surprise me," he said delicately.

"Oh? Why?"

His friend shrugged. "Merely that beneath that chilly exterior I know you to be a warm-hearted man. A generous and tolerant man, even. The sort who cares

20

about his fellow human beings."

Derek's left eyebrow shot up. "Egad, Drew, you flatter me. A little old to be turning toad eater, aren't you?"

Ignoring the remark, Lord Andrew shifted the conversation ever so slightly. "Do correct me if I'm wrong, but was it not you who lectured me so sternly upon the pitiable fate of climbing boys? Was it not you who said that children ought to be educated and not exploited? Strange views indeed from the man who"— gone was the delicate touch—"is said to have a number of by-blows stashed away in the country."

Lord Andrew did not add that he found the *on-dit* ludicrous, but his gray eyes probed Derek's face for clues to the truth. He was destined to remain in the dark, however, for Derek's cool rejoinder neither refuted nor explained the rumors.

"Never listen to gossip," was all he advised. Reaching into his pocket, Derek drew out a small enameled snuffbox and flipped it open with his thumb. "As for the employment of four and five year olds to clean chimneys nearly as narrow as their frail bodies," he continued, "I meant every word I said, Drew. It must stop."

Accepting a pinch of proffered snuff, Lord Andrew said in a placating voice, "It *is* illegal to apprentice a child younger than eight to a master chimney sweep."

"Yes, and what the devil good is that when the law is not enforced? The Commons is ready to pass a bill prohibiting the use of climbing boys entirely, but the damned Lords will defeat it unless someone persuades them otherwise. But I've no seat in the House of Lords, and no knack for making pretty speeches." His tone grew suddenly deliberate. "Your brother has both."

"Touché." Lord Andrew sighed. "For your sake, Derek, I will ask the duke to address the issue. And in return," he added in a slightly pained voice, "do try to be a little easier on the ladies, eh? They are not all as superficial as you would make them out."

Derek smiled derisively. "No? Find one that proves otherwise and I'll be happy to meet her."

"Ah, but if I do perhaps I'll want her for myself," teased his friend. "Find your own true love, Deveaux. It will do you good." He paused, then added carefully, "My cousin, the Lady Claire, has recently expressed distinct regrets where you are concerned." His eyes dropped to study his boot tassels. "I promised her I'd mention it to you."

The name brought a wintry look to Derek's features. "The Marchioness of Telford made her choice long ago," he said roughly. He hesitated, then surged to his feet. "I'll take my leave of you now. I only came by to see if Duncan was here."

Lord Andrew surveyed him sadly. "No doubt I'll see you again soon."

"No doubt," was the unpromising response.

Derek was halfway to the door before he turned. "Oh, the devil! Dine with me tonight, Drew, at the Pulteney, at nine. I'm taking Dominique there. Don't ask me why."

Lord Andrew Carisbrooke dipped his head in acknowledgement. "As gracious as ever, I see," he murmured. "Aye, I'll see you there, of course. At nine."

Quitting White's in a fairly positive frame of mind, Derek considered the problem of Dominique. He knew well enough that he ought not to flaunt his mistress in such a respectable place as the Pulteney Hotel, just as he knew what had provoked him to invite her. Sheer pique. It was infantile, of course, but there it was. He wanted to wound his mother. Since it pleased her to make a fuss over every piece of gossip she heard about him, then by God he'd give her something to fuss about.

Pushing the matter aside almost savagely, Derek made up his mind to deal with Sir Cuthbert Duncan. It was, he realized, an errand likely to prove more exasperating than onerous, and he wanted to get it over with as quickly as possible. Twenty minutes later, he successfully tracked down his mother's cicisbeo in one of the smaller cardrooms of Boodles.

Several onlookers nudged each other when Derek entered the room, it being common gossip that Sir Cuthbert was dangling after Lady Winifred Deveaux. That the lady's son did not approve his mama's choice was evident from his ominous look, or at least it was to everyone but Sir Cuthbert himself. Indeed, upon being apprised of Derek's presence, Sir Cuthbert appeared quite gratified to see him, and even went so far as to put down his cards to make his blustery greeting.

"Why, hullo there, m'boy," he bellowed. "What's to do? Care to join us for a bit of faro? My luck's in, I should warn you, but you're welcome to stay. The more the merrier, eh?" Forced by his extremely high shirt points to rotate his entire body halfway around, Sir Cuthbert thrust out his chest like an overstuffed peacock, his beringed fingers fiddling with the many fobs and seals which hung from his waist.

These actions were plainly designed to draw attention to his magnificence, and the smile which curled Derek's hard lips grew decidedly sardonic.

"No, I think not," he answered. He surveyed the preposterous dimensions of Sir Cuthbert's neckcloth with contempt. "But I would like a word with you," he said in a deceptively soft voice which warned others in the room that trouble was brewing. "If I may," he added, even more softly.

Far from being alerted, Sir Cuthbert preened under Derek's examination. "'Tis my own creation, m'boy," he boasted, gesturing at his cravat. "A variation on the Oriental. Daresay you couldn't tie it yourself. Takes years of practice, y'see. Her la'ship likes it. Her la'ship likes to see me looking up to snuff. 'Sir Cuthbert,' she tells me, 'how you contrive to always look the veriest Pink of the Ton I'm sure I don't know!'"

Quite able to envision his mother making just such a foolish remark, Derek's face darkened. "A word, Sir Cuthbert," he repeated. "In private, if you please."

Sir Cuthbert stared at him in surprise, then shrugged his padded shoulders. "Why, certainly, m'boy, certainly." He rose to his feet as gracefully as his tight lacing would allow. "Anything to oblige her la'ship's boy. 'Pologies, gentlemen."

When they were well away from the others, Derek's manner grew even less polite. "I'll not waste time on civilities, sir. It has come to my attention that someone has been repeating vulgar gossip about me to my mother. Was it you?"

Sir Cuthbert turned pink around the jowls. "Not me," he protested. "Never repeat gossip. Never repeat anything that ain't true," he added, with dogged simplicity.

"Commendable," murmured Derek, his brows drawing downward. "Nevertheless, in the future you will do me the favor of keeping the more sordid tales you hear about me to yourself. In particular you will refrain from coupling my name with any courtesan's in my mother's presence. My affairs are not her concern." He paused meaningfully. "Nor yours, I might add."

Sir Cuthbert's understanding being less than tenacious, he did not fully perceive that Derek's manner and tone were unfriendly until the end of this speech.

"Uh, certainly," he said nervously. "Anything to oblige." He clapped Derek familiarly on the back. "What your mama don't know won't trouble her, eh? All right, then. *I* understand!"

Derek stepped back with a fleeting scowl. "Good," he said curtly. "I trust no second reminder will prove necessary."

A minute later, when Sir Cuthbert swaggered back into the cardroom, he was still feeling a dash unsettled. That young cub of Winifred's certainly had a devilish nasty temper, he mused. He couldn't put his finger on exactly why, but those piercing Deveaux eyes gave him the chills. He hadn't done anything wrong, of course, but one had to tread cautiously with such prickly fellows. No more gossip to Lady Winifred. All right, then. He could remember that.

"Promised young Deveaux I'd show him the Oriental,"

he explained, in answer to the inquiring looks from his fellow card players. He shook his head and lowered his splendor carefully into his chair. "Not the variation, of course. Too difficult. Warned him not everyone has the knack for these things. 'Takes years and years of practice,' I said."

Those within earshot exchanged knowing glances and went on with their cards and conversation.

Stacia examined her apartment at the Pulteney Hotel with a thrill of satisfaction, reveling in the knowledge that it was one of the best hotels in London. Marco had labeled all such establishments as devilish dull, but in the end they had both agreed upon Pulteney's, it offering the happy combination of pristine respectability and an excellent view of Green Park across the way. Limmer's was actually far more to Marco's taste, but as it was known as the dirtiest hotel in town and frequented by all manner of sporting individuals, some of them quite vulgar, he had rejected it (not without regret) as being wholly unsuitable for his sister.

On the whole, Stacia found her apartment quite magnificent, each room furnished with the utmost attention to style and detail. Axminster carpets adorned the floors, crimson brocade graced the walls, and the severe, neoclassic furniture proved more comfortable than it looked. A huge, four-poster bed dominated the bedchamber, its crimson and gold counterpane and hangings so rich that Stacia felt she had strayed by accident into a chamber meant for a princess.

Her clothing barely filled half of the room's huge wardrobe, and she made a mental note to begin purchasing additional and more fashionable gowns as soon as possible. Of course most of what she had brought with her was recently acquired, since her inheritance had enabled her to replace the unflattering black dresses from her period of mourning. The frocks made by her Lancashire dressmaker, though not as smart as she could have wished, had the merit of being well cut and new, and it was with pleasure that she anticipated donning one of her pretty evening gowns for dinner.

Stacia sighed wearily, wishing Marco had not gone out. He had an acquaintance from Cambridge he wished to look up, and it was typical of her brother that he must do so at once, rather than wait until the following day as she had suggested. She did not object to his leaving her, of course. It was only that her rooms were so large and quiet, and she was feeling small and just a little lonely. How unfortunate, she reflected, that she did not even have a lady's maid to keep her company. That was yet another matter to be rectified on the morrow.

Stifling a yawn, Stacia pulled the pins from her hair and frowned into the handsome gilt mirror. She had never known quite what to make of her own looks. Was she anything beyond the common? Would the gentlemen find her pretty? She honestly did not know.

She had no memory of her mother, but Papa had once told her that she was nothing in comparison. It had made her sad, and for a number of months she had dreamed wistfully of a beautiful mother, a mother she did not resemble and would never know.

However, she'd eventually decided that she really wasn't *that* bad. After all, she wasn't too tall or short, too fat or thin, nor was she baker-kneed or pockmarked or anything like that. She was simply herself, she thought prosaically. Her red-gold hair was probably her best feature, but she had never seen anything amiss with her eyes either. They were only brown, but at least they were widely spaced and functioned perfectly. And her teeth were straight, which must be considered an advantage. The only real trial was her nose, she thought critically. It tilted at the end, and there was that unfortunate dusting of freckles across its bridge which no amount of Denmark Lotion or vinegar seemed able to discourage.

Oh, but what did it matter, anyway, when there was no one to see her?

Stacia's loneliness intensified. Why had Marco left her

26

like this? In an effort to divert her mind, she walked to the window to gaze out upon Piccadilly and the fair prospect beyond. Green Park looked very lush and inviting, and if she had had the energy to do so she would have chosen to explore it then and there. However, three days of traveling had left her feeling drained, so it seemed wise to postpone the stroll until morning. A rest was what she needed and the sensible thing to do was to nap so that she might be wide awake and refreshed when Marco returned.

Marco. Stacia had always adored her half brother, and though she was wise enough to know that he was not the most selfless of people, she also knew that in his own way he loved her too. He might be selfish, but he was the only one left who cared what became of her.

She would do anything for Marco.

Stacia's nap lasted rather longer than she expected. When she awoke it was dark and it took a few groggy moments for her to remember where she was. London. The Pulteney Hotel. Marco. Her confusion gave way to puzzlement. Where was he? If he had come back, he would surely have awakened her by now, for he must be as hungry as she.

Groping her way about the dark room, she managed to light the candles and shiver her way into an evening dress of pale green. She then sat down at the dressing table to arrange her hair into a semblance of order, all the while listening for sounds from the set of rooms across the hall. Unfortunately, the only noises she heard were the mutterings of her own empty stomach; Marco must either have been detained or lost track of the time.

To verify this, she stepped quietly out into the corridor and knocked at the door opposite her own. Just as she had feared, there was no answer. It seemed very strange, to say the least, and she could not help wondering if some accident had befallen him. The moment this entered her mind, Stacia became uneasy. How would she ever find him in this huge city? What would she do? Who could she turn to for help?

As always, her very active imagination was conjuring up the worst possible scenarios. Marco was dead. He had been attacked by cutthroats and was even now lying in a gutter somewhere, bruised and beaten and bleeding. He had been robbed and knocked insensible, and was wandering through the streets, calling her name . . . Or perhaps he had been impressed into the Navy! He could be lying bound and gagged somewhere in the belly of a ship, helpless and confused, needing her. An unpleasant, hollow feeling that had nothing to do with hunger churned in her stomach.

Oh, this was nonsensical! No doubt he had found his friend Mr. Denchworth and they were presently on their way to the hotel, inventing excuses for their tardiness which they would try to foist upon her. She must cease her worrying and act sensibly.

A more logical solution was that Marco *had* returned, but that when he had knocked at her door she'd been sleeping too soundly to hear. If that were the case, he might well have decided she would sleep until morning and that he would go down and eat by himself.

Relieved, Stacia straightened her shoulders and made up her mind to go down to the dining room and search for him. What a foolish creature she could sometimes be, she chided herself.

Yet when she descended to the ground floor, there was still no Marco. There were a few people standing about in small groups; voices, both male and female, echoed in the long, narrow lobby. For the first few moments Stacia could only stare at their grand clothing and sophisticated appearance, momentarily quashed by a feeling of inadequacy. Then, forcing herself to be bolder, she went in search of the dining room.

It proved easy enough to find. However, in the few seconds she stood in the doorway, her anxious brown eyes perusing the diners' faces, she became the object of a number of curious glances. Some were only idle, several

28

(from the ladies) seemed a shade inhospitable, while one or two of the gentlemen gave her far too insolent an inspection.

Backing hastily away, Stacia was filled with frustration. How irksome this was! Here she was, positively starving, and no Marco! And now people were looking at her as though she had no right to be here, she thought indignantly. It was almost too much to bear. Very much in a huff, she whirled around—and walked straight into a warm and disconcertingly solid male body.

"Oh! I beg your pardon!" she gasped, then broke off just as suddenly. Aloof green eyes gazed so coolly down at her that any further apology died in her throat. To make matters even more embarrassing, she discovered that her hands had instinctively flown up and pressed themselves to a very elegant waistcoat. Appalled, she drew them away as if they were burnt, then flushed at the theatricalness of the action.

The man's expression changed, and what might have been a flicker of amusement crossed his dark, handsome face.

"On the contrary, it is I who must beg pardon, ma'am," he said. "I should have stepped aside and did not. Pray accept my apologies."

He was accompanied by a lady and another gentleman, Stacia observed. She noticed the lady most, for she was very fair and exceedingly beautiful, save for a tiny, peevish puckering at the corners of her mouth. Her fingers curled like ivy around the green-eyed gentleman's arm, while her muslin gown clung to her figure in a way that was positively indecent.

Quite abashed, Stacia was about to retreat when a familiar voice floated down the room from the entrance foyer.

"There she is! There's my li'l shister. Shweet li'l filly, ain't she?"

Stacia whirled in dismay.

Her brother had obviously been drinking. Supported by another gentleman, he only just managed to stagger

29

across the lobby to her side, grumbling as he did so, "Now, Dench, do let go! I'm quite cap'ble of walkin' by m'shelf. Don't want li'l Stacia to shink I'm in m'cups, do you?"

Stacia had never been so mortified. Marco's voice was vulgarly loud and this, combined with the moronic expression upon his face, so incensed her that she momentarily forgot their audience.

"Where on earth have you been?" she blurted, her soft voice trembling with emotion. "I've been sick with worry about you and here you are, for pity's sake, thoroughly foxed!"

"No, no," objected Marco, oblivious to her anger, "only shightly dishguised. No one'll know if y'don't go blabbin' it to everyone. Do y'know m'friend Dench? Don't shink I ever brought him home wish me. Dench, thish is Stacia, my *widowed* shister. Ain't she pretty? Rich, too! Going to make shome lucky fellow a fine wife!" he added, heedless of Stacia's blushing attempts to hush him.

Marco's friend made a correct little bow. "Reginald Denchworth, at your service, ma'am," he said. "And a thousand apologies for your brother's condition. Didn't realize he was drinking on an empty stomach until it was too late. I would have let him sleep it off but . . ." His shrug seemed more careless than sorry. "He would come back to see you, ma'am. Nothing else would satisfy him."

"Gotta take Stacia t'dinner," announced Marco to the world at large. "She ain't had a shing to eat shince noon." Jerking suddenly out of Mr. Denchworth's grasp, he grabbed hold of Stacia and slung his arm heavily around her shoulders.

His weight made her knees buckle, and undoubtedly they both would have fallen had not the green-eyed gentleman intervened. In a trice, Marco's weight was removed, Stacia's balance was restored by a steadying arm, and Marco was once again deposited in Mr. Denchworth's embrace.

"Take him upstairs and hand him over to his valet,"

30

her rescuer ordered Mr. Denchworth. Then that green gaze, so impossible to read, was swinging back to Stacia. "Which room?" he inquired.

"Room?" she echoed, a trifle blankly. "Oh, the one on the right on the . . . the third floor overlooking Piccadilly. But there is no valet, I'm afraid. We . . . he has not—I mean, my brother's valet has not yet arrived." Flushing hotly, she avoided those shrewd eyes and addressed Mr. Denchworth, who was already dragging Marco toward the staircase. "Never mind, I will show you, sir. I must go up anyway, for I cannot dine alone."

"Wait." A firm hand on Stacia's arm made her pause, and her heart gave an odd little flutter.

"Derek, darling." The lady spoke at last, her vibrant voice pettish, her warmth aimed solely at her escort. "I should very much like to sit down. The woman has found her brother. There is no cause for . . . us . . . to interfere."

At first, it seemed the tart reminder was successful, for the hand fell away. Yet those green eyes still glittered down at her, an enigmatic expression in their depths.

"Tell me your name," was all he said. "I'll have them bring a tray up to your room."

It was such an admirable solution, Stacia could only marvel that she had not thought of it herself.

"It's Mi—Mrs. Edwards," she responded, unhappily aware that her cheeks were still quite pink. "A tray would be most welcome, sir. Thank you very much." She gave him a shy smile. "My room is directly across from my brother's," she added softly, quite unaware that her meaning could easily be misconstrued.

The lady's blue eyes flashed. "You mistake, madam. The gentleman already has a—" Before she could complete the sentence, strong fingers clamped so tightly around her wrist that she winced with pain.

To Stacia, the gentleman's action was as incomprehensible as it was disturbing. "I'm sorry," she said awkwardly. "Perhaps it is too much trouble—?"

"Hardly," retorted the gentleman, a dry nuance to his

31

tone. "Run along now, Mrs. Edwards. Your dinner will arrive shortly, I promise."

Stacia found herself obeying the unmistakable dismissal, though she was not at all certain she cared for being ordered about in such a domineering fashion. It was very much like being dictated to by Papa, she thought, as she followed Mr. Denchworth and Marco up the stairs.

Feeling absurdly cross, she paused near the landing, glancing back at the trio below. To her surprise, they were still in the same place she had left them. From where she stood, the green-eyed gentleman's face looked cold and very harsh, while the lady's looked drained of color, as though she had just received a very great shock. However, the second gentleman was gazing rather speculatively up at Stacia, a small smile on his lips. Flustered, Stacia turned and hurried away, wondering whether they were having a quarrel, and if so, whether she had been the cause of it.

The green-eyed gentleman was not a kind man, she decided with a shiver. She felt rather sorry for the lady.

Kind or not, Stacia soon found she could not put him from her mind. When her dinner tray arrived ten minutes later, she was still brooding over the episode, a small preoccupied frown creasing her brow. It was bad enough, she reflected, that he had witnessed Marco's disgraceful behavior, but she could not quite discard the notion that she, too, had somehow made a fool of herself. And for some inexplicable reason, she did not want that man to think she was a fool—though why she should care tuppence what he thought was a complete mystery!

Immersed in thought, Stacia did not at first espy the folded slip of paper tucked beneath her silverware, but when she did, her breathing went all at once unsteady.

The message was brief, written in a heavy black scrawl that looked as arrogantly bold as its author.

Dear Mrs. Edwards,
Pray accept my apologies. We will dine together
another night.

Derek Deveaux.

For the space of several seconds, Stacia simply gazed at
the note, completely at a loss to understand his meaning.
Did he think she had wanted him to ask her to join his
party? Or could he possibly think she would dine with
him . . . alone?

The very notion made her cheeks go scarlet. How
could he think she would do so? And how very
presumptuous of him to have written a note at all! At
least, she suspected it was presumptuous, but perhaps in
London such a gesture was considered acceptable?

Frowning over this, Stacia smoothed the paper and
began rather absently to eat her dinner. Well, he had
offered his apologies, so he must have thought he had
something to apologize *for*. What could it have been?
Was it because he had not invited her to join his friends?
Surely he could not be referring to their collision—that
had been entirely her fault and scarcely required another
apology on his part.

No, she was certain he meant something improper by
it. Perhaps Marco's performance had led him to believe
they were persons of low breeding, she thought glumly.
Perhaps he even thought she was a woman of loose
morals. Feeling absurdly depressed by the possibility,
Stacia took a sip of the light wine that had come with her
food.

Yet how very attractive he had been. She had not been
granted many opportunities to meet members of the
opposite sex, but certainly none of Marco's friends had
been nearly so . . . well, so manly! Of course, his eyes
alone would have set him apart, but that raven black hair
and those clear-cut features were equally striking.
Stacia's eyes closed as she tried to recall his image. He
had seemed to tower over her, so he must have been taller

33

than Marco, and his physique had certainly been more muscular. Beyond this, however, there had been a forceful quality, an authoritativeness that told her more clearly than words that Derek Deveaux was used to being obeyed.

In a flash, Stacia's frown was back. Yes, he was very attractive, but had she not already made up her mind that he was also a little cruel? How brutally he had seized his lady's wrist, she remembered. Why would he have wanted to hurt her? What could she have been going to say that he so disliked?

With a long sigh, she picked up her fork and slowly continued with her meal. The last thing she needed was to involve herself with someone as hardhearted, as cold, and as insensitive as Papa, and she would do well to remember it.

Out of the blue, she recollected the other gentleman, the one who had stared at her when she had looked down from the top of the stairs. She wondered why he had smiled so strangely, as though he found the whole situation excessively amusing.

There was nothing at all amusing about it, she reflected. She had been embarrassed by her brother, ogled by the people in the dining room, and insulted by this Derek Deveaux. And now, to cap it all off, she was alone again. She felt like bursting into tears.

"You've amazed me yet again, my cool friend."

Lord Andrew sipped his drink and gave his dinner companion a considering look. "First, where other men would choose a more discreet moment, *you* have the outrageousness to cast off your mistress in a public place! You were damned lucky she didn't screech down the Pulteney's highly respectable walls. Or did you know she wouldn't dare? Was that why you chose to do it here?" Receiving no answer, he glanced around the hotel dining room thoughtfully. "Then," he went on, jabbing the air with his fork, "the moment the fair but furious

Dominique is gone, you have the bloody nerve to write this new lady a note. On the basis of three minutes' acquaintance, no less." His voice was full of amused incredulity. "Mrs. Edwards evidently made quite an impression."

Derek shrugged, his handsome face noncommittal. "She's got grace and manners, despite her brother. Probably a merchant's daughter. And if it's true that she's a rich widow . . ." He let the words dangle in the air.

Lord Andrew put down his fork. "No," he said firmly.

For the first time, Derek looked a little nonplussed. "No?" he responded, his brows shooting up. "What the devil do you mean?"

"I mean that the role of fortune hunter does not become you. Forget what I said before. I was only jesting." Met with silence, he went on, "Need I remind you of your own sentiments?"

"Which are?" The question appeared to be indifferent; Derek was concentrating on his dinner.

Lord Andrew smiled. "A mewling little heiress would bore you in a week. Your own words, my friend."

"And so she would," Derek retorted, reaching for his wine. "But what makes you think I mean marriage? You go too fast for me, Drew."

"*I?*" Lord Andrew guffawed. "On the contrary, it is you whose mind darts about so fast that the rest of us mortals are left agasp. What the devil else could you mean? How else could her money benefit you?"

Derek shot him a frowning look. "'Twould be pleasant to have a mistress who is not always whining for money."

"A novel experience, indeed," agreed his lordship, after a few startled seconds. "So you wish to make that pretty little creature your new *chère-amie?* Is that what you expect me to believe?"

"Believe what you like. I make no decisions until the size of the lady's fortune is established."

Lord Andrew's eyes narrowed. "A man with such a keen social conscience should not be making that sort of statement. 'Tis deuced peculiar."

Derek speared his beef almost viciously. "You're an idealist, Drew. I'm not . . . despite my 'social conscience,' as you so quaintly put it."

"Ah," said Lord Andrew, watching him carefully. "So you will make the lady a declaration only if her fortune is large enough to suit you?"

"Why are you so curious?" Slowly, Derek put down his fork. "You want her for yourself, perhaps?"

Hearing the slight edge to his friend's voice, Lord Andrew's eyes gleamed with mischief. "As a matter of fact, the notion had occurred to me," he lied, summoning an apologetic tone. "One can never be too wealthy, you see."

"Now that's coming it too strong. You wouldn't wed a merchant's daughter and you know it. You're too damned high in the instep."

"Alas, you know me better than I thought," admitted the duke's brother with a grin. "No, I wouldn't wed the daughter of a cit, but what if she's not a cit? What if she's a lady of unblemished reputation and unimpeachable birth? *Then* I might consider it."

Derek looked at him. "In that case," he said unhesitantly, "you just might find you had a serious rival."

"A great many of them, perhaps," suggested Lord Andrew slyly. "She was very pretty, wasn't she?"

For a moment, Derek made no answer. "Yes," he said, rather curtly. "Yes, she was."

Chapter Three

Golden April sunshine tiptoed into Stacia's bed-chamber, veering past the undrawn curtains to spill over the coverlet of the Pultency's huge four-poster bed. Absently raking her red-gold curls from her face, Stacia rose up on one elbow and blinked, engulfed in a euphoria as potent as sap rising in a tree. For five glorious seconds it lasted, before it was dashed to bits by memories of yestereve and Marco's muddleheaded behavior. Her first whole day in London, she thought dejectedly, and Marco was probably going to sleep through most of it.

With a short sigh, she padded barefoot to the window to gaze rather wonderingly upon the broad thoroughfare below. Yesterday she had thought Piccadilly the busiest street imaginable, but at this hour the activity was somewhat reduced. There were carts and wagons aplenty, of course, but the smarter conveyances driven by the upper classes were considerably less in evidence. Perhaps their owners were like Marco, she thought cynically, and were merely occupied with recovering from whatever addlepated amusements of which they had partaken the night before. Doubtless they would be doing their part to jam up the streets by afternoon.

Palms pressed flat upon the sill, her wistful gaze slid over to Green Park. Beyond the shrubbery, she could see an enticing glint of blue just visible over the tops of the yews. It must be the reservoir, she mused. She had read about the reservoirs of the Chelsea waterworks in the guide book she had borrowed from the vicar.

Feeling slightly irritable, Stacia worked open the window sash so that the fresh air might seep in and clear the cobwebs from her head. Green Park looked the perfect place for a stroll, she thought, but dare she venture there alone? When one was country-bred, an early morning walk was an acceptable part of one's regime, but perhaps the more fashionable members of the Ton did not so indulge themselves? Would it be considered seemly? As this concern nipped at her conscience, a cool wafting of air delivered an invigorating mixture of scents to her nose. At once her scruples fizzled. Why should she try to resist the urge to explore? It was for precisely such freedom that she had decided to be a widow.

Propelled by eagerness, Stacia hurried into her clothes, her brown eyes shining with determination. Explore was what she was going to do and that was all there was to it. Sparing a quick glance for her appearance in the mirror, she wrapped a shawl about her slender shoulders and headed for the door.

Pausing outside Marco's room, Stacia listened to her brother's snores. They were loud and heavy, confirming her suspicion that any effort to wake him was likely to be useless. Last night had not been the first time she had seen him drunk—she knew from experience that his mood would be vile when he awakened. Marco would not thank her for disturbing him, she assured herself, and could therefore scarcely complain if she took a walk without him.

The air outside was brisk but refreshing. The nearest park entrance, she saw at once, was at the gatekeeper's lodge opposite Clarges Street and it was to this site that she directed her steps. Beyond, the shimmering waters of the reservoir beckoned her forward and her mood lightened as a gentle breeze stirred the feathers on her bonnet. Stacia smiled to herself. Yes, it was definitely right to come here alone, she thought contentedly. In his

38

present state, Marco would only have put a crimp in her pleasure.

Humming a soft tune beneath her breath, she wandered along the walkway encircling the long, oblong-shaped reservoir. Ahead, the sun had finished creeping above the rooftops of the elegant mansions edging the park, its rays lending iridescence to the rippling, greenish blue waves. Strange, she thought suddenly, how all that glittering brilliance made her think of Derek Deveaux's eyes . . .

Her humming ceased as the disturbing fancy caught hold. Until now she had been fairly successful at barring him from her thoughts, but the temptation to mull it over here, in these peaceful surroundings, was ridiculously strong. Gingerly, she allowed Derek's features to form in her mind, but with his image came uninvited remembrance of his height and solidity and the spellbinding way he had looked at her, a sort of aggressive sizing-up that was every bit as disturbing in retrospect as it had been at the time.

Dismayed, she told herself that this experiment in self-indulgence had gone far enough. Already her serenity was gone, destroyed by memories of a cold-faced man with eyes the color of frozen emeralds. She quickened her pace with a shiver, scolding herself quite roundly for behaving like an impressionable ninny. She told herself that Derek Deveaux was as arrogant and unfeeling as Papa, that he was a man who would aggravate rather than soothe, and that any impact he might have upon her life must be one of chaos and hazard. There could be no doubt that he was a man she ought to avoid.

Downcast by the conclusion, Stacia fell into a brown study so deep that she reached the end of the reservoir before noticing the young female on the bench. The girl was shabbily dressed and completely alone, giving every appearance of being equally lost in melancholy reflection. She was sitting with head bowed and shoulders hunched, one elbow braced upon her knee so that her chin might rest upon the palm of one hand, the other plucking

39

nervously at her skirt.

There was something forlorn about the posture and as Stacia hesitated, she heard a muffled sob that touched her heart. Tossing aside her reluctance to intrude, she left the walkway to approach the young woman.

"Good morning—" she called out, breaking off as the girl started violently.

Stacia looked at her in mute astonishment. She was gazing at the loveliest, most breathtaking creature she had ever seen, or, indeed, could ever have invented within her colorful imagination. Even knowing it was impolite, she could not prevent herself from staring at the girl's face, with its frame of ebony curls, violet-blue eyes, sooty lashes, cherry lips, and dainty, perfect nose.

Beautiful as an angel's smile, she thought in bemusement. Surely she had read that line somewhere in a poem? The description was apt, for this girl was certainly the closest thing to an angel she was ever likely to see. But angels shouldn't cry, as this one so obviously was doing.

"I . . . I do beg your pardon," Stacia went on, swallowing her amazement. "I did not mean to startle you, but I could not help noticing your distress." She searched through her reticule for a handkerchief. "Are you perhaps in some sort of trouble?" she asked. "Is there something I can do to help? Here, take this." She shook out the crumpled square of lace-edged muslin. "Only if you wish to, of course," she added with a bolstering smile. "It's quite clean, I assure you."

The angel accepted the offering and daintily wiped the moisture from her eyes. "You are very kind," she said with an unsteady sniff. Her well-bred voice was lower than Stacia expected, but pleasant and remarkably even for one suffering such emotional tumult. "I do not normally indulge in such bouts," she added, blowing her perfect nose in the gentlest fashion conceivable. "'Tis only that life has lately treated me so abominably."

Stacia watched in fascination as the young woman repaired the "damage" to her face. As if by magic, the

40

handkerchief erased all evidence of weeping. Nothing remained but flawless beauty—no red nose or eyes, no mottled complexion, not even any hiccups, as Stacia always managed to have after even the nearest brush with tears.

Stacia's sympathy was touched with awe. "I am sorry to hear it. Do you require assistance, then? I will help you if I can." She took a place on the bench next to the young woman. "Allow me to introduce myself. My name is Stacia . . . Edwards." She cleared her throat. "I am a widow," she added, for no reason at all.

At this, the angel seemed to brighten. "Ah, we have something in common, then," she stated, with a sad sort of pride, "for, alas, my treasured husband was killed at Waterloo." She pressed Stacia's handkerchief lightly to her eyes. "I would not be sitting here now if Algie were alive. He would have taken care of me and none of this would have happened."

In the face of such genuine distress, Stacia could not quite bring herself to embellish upon her own less truthful history. "I am so sorry," she repeated, a shade hesitantly. "Is that why you were crying?"

The angel sighed. "Actually, no," she confessed. "Other trials have recently beset me. You see, ma'am,"—she clasped her hands to her bosom—"I have been . . . abandoned."

Stacia blinked. "Abandoned?" she echoed. Somehow it was not at all what she had been expecting to hear.

"By a man," finished the angel darkly. "We were to have been married this very morning."

"Why, how perfectly odious of him!" Stacia looked indignant. "Do you mean to tell me he simply left you? Here in this park?"

The angel frowned the tiniest frown. "Actually, no," she admitted, giving Stacia an oddly assessing look. "I will tell you the whole if you swear to keep it a secret. You see, the truth could damage my reputation."

"I see," said Stacia, a little blankly. "Very well, then. I promise not to betray you."

The angel leaned forward, her manner confidential.

41

"He told me he had purchased a special marriage license. We arrived in London last night and he was supposed to take me to his godmother's house." Her eyes held Stacia's captive as she spoke. "Well, there was no godmother, and no special license, either. Wilfred had been lying all along. He intended to set me up as his mistress, you see."

Stacia was appalled. "Gracious, what on earth did you do?"

"I hit him over the head with a coal shuttle."

"You what?" Stacia stared at the angel, who suddenly looked a trifle less angelic than she had a moment before.

"I am sorry to shock you, but it was either that or submit to his horrid embraces. You have been married, Mrs. Edwards. You know what men can be like."

"Er, yes," agreed Stacia, who had not the least idea. "Did you . . . did you injure him?" she inquired in a cautious tone.

The angel shrugged. "I did not remain to find out." She did not sound in the least repentant. "I do not think he was dead."

"Good gracious, I hope not! Then what happened?"

"I left him lying on the floor. The house was in one of those streets over there." She gestured vaguely toward the east end of the park. "I have been sitting here ever since, trying to decide what to do."

Again, Stacia was scandalized. "You have been sitting here on this bench all night?" She reached out and caught up one of the angel's slender hands. It was stiff with cold.

"You must come with me," she said with decision. "I am staying at the hotel across the street. You need food and a good rest, and I am going to see that you get it."

"Oh, how good of you, Mrs. Edwards," she said, on a soft, gentle sigh. "I fear I have no alternative but to accept. I have spent the night racking my poor tired brain, but to my sorrow I have no acquaintances nor family in London. There is no one whose generosity I can importune, not even the remotest kin I can call my own." Her eyes fell to the grass at Stacia's feet. "I shall be obliged to find employment of some kind as soon as possible," she added sadly.

At these words, the idea which had been germinating in Stacia's head burst into bloom.

"You have found it already," she said on impulse. "I am in urgent need of a companion, you see. You are ideal for the position, as I am looking for someone young and gently bred to bear me company and . . . and uphold my respectability, as my brother phrases it. I will pay you one hundred pounds per year"—a trace of uncertainty entered Stacia's voice—"if you choose to accept, of course."

Stacia smiled to cover her embarrassment, for she knew her tumbling speech had ended on an anxious note which the angel could hardly have missed. Somewhat to her surprise, however, her offer did not receive immediate acceptance. Instead, the violet-blue eyes lifted and stared, filled with a mingling of disbelief and some other, naggingly familiar emotion. It was almost like the look Marco would have when he was thinking of telling lies but was not quite sure whether he could get away with it.

"How very kind you are," replied the angel, after a period of rather curious silence. "Of course I will accept, and with heartfelt gratitude. I . . . I knew it was right for me to pray. I don't do that very often." For the first time, her voice shook ever so slightly. "You astound me, Mrs. Edwards. You are willing to rescue me from the consequences of my own folly. Few women would do even that, let alone with such a generous offer."

"That cannot be true," objected Stacia, thinking this nonsensical. "I am doing what anyone in my position would do."

In answer, that exquisite head shook a swift negative. "On the contrary. Do you realize that I have not even told you my name? Certainly I have given you no reason to believe me qualified for this position. You have asked for no references. For all you know, I may be a murderess."

Feeling a trifle put out by this allusion to her

43

negligence, Stacia retorted, a bit crisply, "Well, we will make inquiries about this Wilfred of yours, if only to set your mind at ease. I do not require references and as for your name, tell me what it is and that will settle that objection."

"Angeline," said the angel in a quiet tone. She smiled, a queer little flicker that vanished almost at once. "Angeline Greaves."

Hours later, Stacia tapped at her brother's door and, receiving no response, tried turning the knob. She had reached the end of her patience and was determined to wake him if necessary.

Marco lay curled atop a four-poster bed as elegant as her own. He was on his side, his mouth shut, a seraphic smile curving his lips. To her disapproval, she saw that Mr. Denchworth had done little more than remove her brother's boots. For gracious sake, he might at least have thought to put a blanket over him, she thought indignantly.

"Marco." She shook his shoulder gently. "Wake up." Nothing happened.

She shook him again. "Marco, do you hear me?"

Although Marco's smile vanished, he only turned over and started snoring.

"Marco!" Exasperated, Stacia raised her foot and gave him a sharp jab in the derriere. "Wake up!"

Much to her satisfaction, this did the trick.

Her brother uttered a sharp yelp and, one at a time, screwed open his bloodshot eyes. "What the devil—! Oh, it's you," he muttered. His voice was croaking and irritable. "Good God, Stacia, what the bloody hell time is it?"

"It is well past noon," she responded, ignoring his profanity. "Time for you to wake up. I have been waiting for you for hours and hours. It was a great deal too bad of you to go and get yourself foxed last night."

Shaken by vague memories of his inebriation, Marco

44

made a valiant effort to raise himself to an upright position. His clothes were sadly crumpled and a full day's growth of stubble covered his chin.

"Dash it, Stacia, what's the rush?" he got out just as the nausea struck. His head dropped to his hands, but after a few more moments he managed to mumble, "Can't a fellow have a bit of a lark without his sister raising a dust?" His muffled voice held an acerbic note.

Stacia pulled over a chair and sat down, regarding him with a mixture of sympathy and dismay. "I do not mean to raise a dust, Marco. Truly I don't. And I am very sorry you do not feel well. Does your head hurt as much as usual? If your excesses yield such painful results I am surprised you wish to pursue them."

Her brother cast her a darkling glance. "You wouldn't understand. You're a girl."

Stacia folded her hands. "I see," she said, rather doubtfully. "Well, there is nothing I can do about that, is there? Shall I ring for a maid?"

"What for?" he muttered.

"To bring water so that you may wash and shave, of course." Her head cocked consideringly. "Would you like some food as well?"

"The only thing I want," he told her bluntly, "is to use the chamber pot."

Taking the hint, Stacia rose to her feet. "Very well," she said, calmly refusing to take umbrage. "Do you think you can make yourself presentable in half an hour? I have someone I want you to meet."

Marco raised his head. "Who?" he said suspiciously.

His expression compelled her to explain. "I have hired a companion," Stacia replied, at her most dignified. "I met Mrs. Greaves this morning in Green Park. She is young, but seems entirely suitable, a war widow . . . like me. A respectable person, of course."

"A respectable person?" Marco looked pained. "How the devil do you know she's respectable? And you shouldn't have gone walking alone, Stacia. It ain't at all the thing."

45

"I was perfectly safe," she countered.

Allowing this to pass, Marco adopted a patronizing tone. "In any case, you little twit, you don't just hire people off the street. I suppose it did not occur to you to ask for references?"

Stacia bristled. "You do not understand. There can be no doubt that she is of gentle birth. Her grandfather was a vicar, she told me. And as it happens she is in trouble, so my offer will benefit us both."

"Trouble?" Marco snorted. "Aye, and I can guess what sort. Did she cry upon your shoulder? When's the brat due?"

Stacia stared. "What brat?"

"She didn't mention it? What an innocent you are, Stacia, to be so taken in." Her brother swung his legs over the side of the bed, grimacing horribly as he stood up. "Ten to one the wench is expecting a child," he added in a disparaging tone.

A little shocked, Stacia glared at her brother. "What an odious thing to suggest! This is just the way you behaved last time you were foxed, and I refuse to discuss the matter until you can be pleasant about it." She stalked to the door. "Whether you know it or not, *I* am the wounded party here. You failed me last night, Marco. It's no thanks to you that I got any dinner at all. Your conduct was inexcusable. And I have no great opinion of your Mr. Denchworth either!"

And with this Parthian shot, Stacia swept from the room.

At Stacia's insistence, Angeline continued to rest upon the spare bed in her benefactress's dressing room, so that when Marco presented himself thirty minutes later, he was unable to catch a glimpse of his sister's companion. Stacia was still a little vexed about his behavior, but his promptness in heeding her request did much to mollify her. And since she had been secretly wondering if she was expecting too much of her brother, who had (she argued)

46

a perfect right to pursue his male pleasures without sisterly interference or censure, she made sure to greet him with no hint of her earlier displeasure.

"Now that is much better," she approved, giving his clean shirt and trousers a warm look. "I trust you are feeling more the thing? I do hate to see you indisposed for such a nonsensical reason."

Marco, whose recollections of the previous evening were disquieting at best, found himself unequal to the task of explaining to his sister just how very indisposed he was beginning to feel.

"Oh, ah, yes," he lied. "Much more the thing. Quite capital, in fact." His voice was only a shade too hearty as he followed her into the sitting room. "About last night," he went on, managing to look charming as well as rueful, "I really am sorry. I . . . well, the devil's in it that I don't remember too much, but tell me . . . *did* you ever get your dinner?"

Stacia took a seat. "I had a tray sent to my room," she informed him. "And I am sorry I ripped up at you about being foxed." Having no wish to discuss Derek Deveaux, she swiftly changed the subject. "But as for the other matter, I do need a female companion, Marco, and when you meet Mrs. Greaves, I think you will agree that she will suit the purpose admirably."

Her tactic did not work. "That may be so," he retorted, "but what I want to know is this: who the blazes was that tall devil I saw you with last night? The fellow with the black hair. I may have been drunk as Davie's sow, but *him* I remember."

"She is very lovely," Stacia continued chattily. "I do not think I have ever seen anyone like her. She is quite young—"

"I remember his voice—"

"And she has the prettiest eyes! They are almost violet in color. Truly extraordinary, I think you will agree—"

"Cold," corrected Marco, staring reminiscently at the opposite wall. "As cold-eyed a devil as I've yet seen. Felt queer as Dick's hatband when he looked at me."

Stacia began to feel cross. "I daresay it was the consequences of drink which made you feel queer, Marco, and not Mr. Deveaux! I do wish you would forget him. Here I am trying to tell you about Angeline and all you can talk about is that horrid man."

"Horrid, was he?" jumped in Marco with righteous wrath. "By gad, do you tell me he had the bloody gall to introduce himself to your notice? Did he *trifle* with you?"

"Don't be absurd! The gentleman simply prevented *you* from knocking me to the floor, that is all. And he was not horrid. I said that only because . . . oh, because you are making such a fuss over him."

Marco looked wounded. "I? Make a fuss? Come off it, Stacia. I'm simply trying to determine that all was well with you last night. That you were, uh, safe from unwanted attentions." That this pompous sentiment was a little late off the mark dawned upon him at once. "Well," he went on, flushing guiltily, "I daresay it's a good notion to hire a companion after all." He positioned himself before the fireplace, his voice stiff with fortitude. "Go ahead, summon the female. I will try to be fair."

Despite everything, Stacia's lips twitched at this heroic display. "Very well. I will go and fetch her."

Nearby, Angeline Greaves awaited the summons with inward resignation. She was still exhausted, but until she knew her mistress better she had no intention of being anything but submissive and biddable, prepared for any request this Stacia Edwards might choose to make. Dame Fortune had bestowed one of her rare smiles—with a well-placed nudge, of course—but Angeline knew better than anyone just how long it was likely to last. Thus far, Mrs. Edwards's motives for hiring her were unclear, but such unwonted kindness was bound to carry a price. There *had* to be some ulterior purpose, she reasoned, for what woman in her right mind would go out of her way to be cast into the shade? And by her own companion, no less?

She waited quietly, knowing Stacia was talking to her brother. Doubtless the brother would feel his superior gender gave him the right to gainsay his sister's choice, but it should not be difficult to persuade him otherwise. Angeline's mouth tightened to a contemptuous line. Gentlemen, she thought, were easy enough to sway, for they never looked beyond a woman's exterior to see what lay beneath. Her hand crept up to touch her cheek, stroking its fine, soft texture with dispassion. No, she reflected, 'twas usually the ladies who cast a spoke in the wheel.

When Stacia entered the room, she was smiling.

"Come," she said in a friendly manner. "My brother wishes to meet you. Despite being a baronet, he is not at all top-lofty, I assure you. I have already explained the whole to him, and he has promised to be open-minded." She hesitated. "He may ask for references, but if you cannot produce them I have made up my mind to stand firm on this matter."

"It is good of you," murmured Angeline, her sidelong glance full of puzzlement, "but I wish I might understand the reasons for your adamancy."

Stacia gave her a laughing look. "Oh, my reasons are purely selfish. I need a companion to lend me countenance and it suits me very well to hire someone young."

Anticipating that Marco's reaction to Angeline would be well worth witnessing, Stacia watched her brother carefully as they entered the sitting room. Her instincts proved correct. Under her fascinated gaze, Marco's mouth sagged open and a look of glazed stupefaction crept over his normally handsome features. It was as if, she thought, he were gazing upon a sight unmeant for mortal eyes and been struck dumb as a result, like an erring character in some ancient epic. But even though his fishlike gape caused her a ripple of mirth, she was also conscious of her splendid brother's sudden and rather awkward resemblance to a dressed mackerel.

"Ahem." Stacia frowned pointedly. "Marco, I should like you to meet my companion, Mrs. Greaves. Angeline, this is my brother, Sir Marco Ashcroft."

Angeline murmured a response and curtsied gracefully, while at the same time Marco bowed and found his voice.

"Mrs. Greaves," he repeated, sounding dazed. He cleared his throat in an obvious effort to collect his scattered wits. "Welcome, ma'am," he went on, tugging at his cravat. "My sister tells me she has, uh, hired you as her companion."

"Yes, sir," replied Angeline, fixing him with her huge violet eyes. "But if you should object, Sir Marco, I will gladly leave." She faltered slightly, her eyes clinging limpidly to his. "I do not know where I would go, but I daresay there are inexpensive places where a respectable female could find lodging—?"

Marco looked askance. "Good gad, no," he protested. "Nonsense, Mrs. Greaves! My sister is free to choose whomever she likes as her companion. If it's you she wants, then as far as I'm concerned the matter is settled." He rocked nervously on his heels, unable to do anything but stare.

"But I have no references," she confessed in a whispery, remorseful voice.

"References?" scoffed the young baronet, as if he had never heard the word. "Who needs 'em? I never worry about such paltry stuff. If my sister likes you, then what possible objection can I make?"

"My sentiments exactly," put in Stacia with a twinkle. "I knew you would come about, Marco. Mrs. Greaves and I will rub along together perfectly well, which will leave you free to pursue your own activities."

As if by magic, her words jolted Marco out of his bemused state. As it happened, his activities the previous evening had been of far too celebratory a nature, a fact which he had come to realize while dressing. He and Mr. Denchworth had gone to a cozy little gaming hell off St. James's Square, where, if his hazy memory served him

50

correctly, he had proceeded to lose nearly two thousand pounds at French Hazard before Dench had dragged him out of the place. It was money he could ill-afford to lose, for his inheritance, though not contemptible in size, was small in comparison to Stacia's.

The trouble was, he really had thought he would win. He'd *believed* he would win and, by George, when it came right down to it, he still could, couldn't he? Fortunes were won and lost every day of the week, and nobody but a Johnny Raw would allow the loss of a mere two thousand to throw a rub in his way.

The instant this stimulating notion entered his mind, Marco made a decision. "I've got to go out," he announced. "And I don't know when I'll return. If you wish to eat without me, do so."

"But where are you going?" asked Stacia in bewilderment. "We have so much planning to do, Marco. Is it about a house?"

"A house?" For a moment, Marco looked perplexed. Then his brow cleared and he chucked his sister under the chin in a brotherly fashion. "Oh, aye. I'll find you a house to live in, never fear. We won't have to stay in a hotel for long." He moved to the door, then paused, looking as though there was more he would say. "I'll be finding lodgings of my own," he said finally, with a significant look at Stacia's ethereally lovely companion. "You have Mrs. Greaves now."

Somewhat startled, Stacia stared at him, but decided against arguing in front of Angeline. "I see. Very well, then," she replied, concealing her dismay. "I'll see you later. Do not worry about us. And . . . be careful, won't you?"

Marco smiled his most charming smile. "I'm always careful," he soothed, and left the room.

He might have added that it would take more than care to win back all the money he had lost. It would take a clear head and a devilish run of good luck.

51

Chapter Four

Four days later Stacia left the Pulteney Hotel for the elegant house Marco had found for her in Upper Grosvenor Street. Back in Lancashire, Marco had promised that they would live together, but that, she learned, had been based upon his assumption that she would choose an older, spinsterish sort of lady to bear her company. According to Marco, Angeline's youth and beauty precluded his sharing their residence, particularly as Angeline had confessed to being only one-and-twenty (an age which could hardly be considered either "old" or "spinsterish," no matter how one looked upon it). It was with some reluctance that Stacia at last conceded to his reasoning, but without Marco she felt rather like a boat set adrift without an anchor.

On the other hand, Marco was only too eager to visit, so it was not as though she'd really lost him. He came, of course, to gaze at Angeline, a circumstance his sister found rather tiresome. It was not that she objected to his infatuation, but she did dislike the manner in which he chose to display it. What little time he did not spend in Mr. Denchworth's company he now squandered in her front parlor, his mouth hanging open in a moonlinglike fashion. To add to this, he was looking hollow-eyed and hagged, but this she attributed to his ardor, which was obviously of a violent and unpredictable nature.

As much as she adored him, after several consecutive days of this, Stacia was growing annoyed. She was only beginning to comprehend the disadvantages of having a companion who was not only two years younger than herself, but considerably more beautiful as well. Not, of course, that she was regretting her impetuous action. To be sure, it *was* disconcerting to have her brother casting sheep's eyes at Angeline, but Stacia Amaryllis Ashcroft was not about to go back on her word.

And when it came right down to it, she had already grown attached to her companion and did not want to give her up. She was pleasant, intelligent, keen-witted, and well-read, which reenforced the impression that she was a Person of Quality fallen upon hard times. But while Angeline was willing and able to speak upon almost any subject, the details of her past remained shrouded in mystery.

For example, since their first meeting Stacia had wondered repeatedly about the perfidious gentleman who had so wrongly tried to seduce Angeline, but each time she tried in a discreet fashion to broach the issue, Angeline merely turned the matter aside as if it were no longer of any account.

However, on the morning of their fourth day in the house in Upper Grosvernor Street, Stacia fixed upon a more straightforward approach. Whether she admitted it or not, the possibility that this Wilfred had suffered a serious injury must trouble Angeline, and ought therefore to be investigated. And the proper inquiries could scarcely be made until her companion revealed more details.

"Now, Angeline," she coaxed, setting aside her futile attempt at embroidery without a trace of regret, "I thought you wished to learn whether or not you had inflicted any lasting injury upon this man? You said he was unconscious when you left him. You must have struck him quite hard, you know." She tried to make her voice encouraging. "Don't you wish to learn whether he is alive or . . . I mean, alive and well?"

Angeline pursed her lips. "Oh, he is perfectly well, never fear."

"I do not know how you can be so certain."

The violet-blue eyes raised from stitchery which was every bit as impeccable as Stacia's was mangled. "I am sure because I saw him."

"You did?" Stacia gave her a searching look. "When? You didn't mention it."

"I did not think of it," Angeline said coolly. "I saw him when we were out shopping yesterday."

"Oh? Well, that must have been a relief to you," said Stacia. "I am relieved to hear he is well. Did he see you?"

"No."

Stacia sat back and surveyed the other girl. "Well, I am surprised you did not tell me. I was worried about it, even if you were not."

Angeline's needle stabbed into her embroidery. "I beg your pardon, ma'am. I did not mean for it to cause you anxiety."

Stacia watched her gravely. "How shocking to think that a titled gentleman would behave so intolerably." She hesitated. "I know you have suffered a severe disappointment and it may pain you to hear this, but if the gentleman is so dishonorable I am sure you are very well rid of him."

"Indeed," agreed the other girl. "All men are swaggering, egotistical beasts, but gentlemen of the aristocracy are the very worst. They think their privileged birth gives them the right to bully, to betray and seduce without care or apology, to promise all and deliver nothing. Men are deceivers, Mrs. Edwards. So be warned."

Taken aback, Stacia stirred uneasily. Where was the shy, hesitant girl of a few day before? Was Angeline really what she seemed?

Once more, Angeline's needle dipped in and out. "Of course, few people are really what they seem," she

54

continued, unwittingly answering the question. "We all have two faces, don't we?"

"Yes, I suppose that's true," agreed Stacia, thinking of her own deception. Naturally she fully intended to confide her true marital status once she knew the girl better. "Did you love him very much?" she inquired with sympathy.

"Love who? Oh, you mean Wilfred?" Angeline's fingers stilled and her lips folded into a scornful smile. "Good gracious, no, Mrs. Edwards," she said, almost lightly. "What in the world makes you think that?"

They had had several unconventional conversations over the course of the past few days, every one of them leading Stacia to speculate with interest about her beautiful companion's background. Having every respect for the other girl's privacy, however, she resolved to pry no further. After all, she knew only too well what it was like to have secrets. Angeline would confide when she was ready.

The latest and darkest of Stacia's own secrets was her unaccountable preoccupation with a certain black-haired gentleman. She had not seen Derek Deveaux again, a circumstance that made it all the more difficult to explain why she still thought of him. She told herself over and over that no one but a wet-goose would attach so much value to so fleeting an encounter, but such reproaches were in vain. Though she pretended otherwise, it was much more than idle interest that drove her to scrutinize every crowd and every carriage she saw. This continual search was automatic as breathing, a purely reflexive action that proved impossible to resist. Because of Derek, each day stretched out with powerful possibilities and each night swirled with disturbing dreams.

However, after seven nerve-racking days of this, Stacia was growing cross. Why in heaven's name had he bothered to write that note if he did not mean to seek her out? And since she had already convinced herself that he was callous and cruel, why did she care? It was probably only her overzealous imagination that made him seem so fascinating in retrospect. It would be far better to get the meeting over with so that Mr. Deveaux could either establish himself as her admirer or set her mind at ease by proving himself unworthy of her notice.

Instinct warned that she ought to concentrate upon meeting other people and forget him, for intermingled with Stacia's propensity to dream floated a hard core of common sense. Doubtless there were many gentlemen who would be only too willing to facilitate her initiation into the Ton by making her the object of their gallantry. As for Mr. Deveaux, if he had cherished any real intention of becoming her suitor he would have found her by now and made some effort to gain a proper introduction.

Still, she mused, mayhap she was giving the man too much credit. Was it not within the realm of possibility that he had been searching for her high and low and had simply been unable to discover her whereabouts? She had been about town a good deal, but only on the footpaths of Green and Hyde Park in the mornings and in the ladies' shops and the circulating library in the afternoons.

Or perhaps he needed a reminder. After all, both Papa and Marco had always mislaid things and forgotten promises; gentlemen did not seem to possess truly organized minds. Perhaps if she were out where he could see her . . .

Papa's old traveling coach was to blame, she decided arbitrarily. It was simply too cumbersome to use in the Mayfair streets, besides being completely closed so that no one could see who was within. What she needed was a dashing town vehicle of her own so that she might jaunt around with the rest of the beau monde. Then he would be able to find her without difficulty.

"I wonder where one goes to purchase a phaeton?" she said aloud. A fresh sparkle entered her eye as she contemplated this daring new course of action. "Do you know, Angeline?"

"A phaeton?" Angeline glanced up, mildly interested. "I do not know. You might ask Sir Marco."

"Yes, he would know, of course." Stacia reached for the bellpull, her expression thoughtful. "But so should my servants," she added.

Thanks to Marco and Mr. Denchworth, Stacia had acquired a full retinue of experienced domestics. The two men had culled some names from a rather erratic perusal of the advertisements in the newspapers, and had eventually managed to compile a list of qualified candidates. Stacia herself had conducted the interviews, an unfamiliar task she was pleased to think she had handled quite creditably.

Her butler soon answered the summons.

"Ah, there you are, Challow," she said with a smile. "Tell me, where does one go to purchase a phaeton?"

Challow, a tall, ruddy-faced man of dignified bearing, composed his features into a wooden expression. "A phaeton, madam? Why, one could do so at Tattersall's, certainly. They sell horses, carriages, coach-harness and the like."

"And where is Tattersall's, please?"

Her butler hesitated. "It is situated near Hyde Park Corner, but"—he gave a discreet little cough—"surely madam would not consider visiting such an establishment herself?"

"Indeed I would. Is there a reason why I should not?"

"Forgive me, madam, but Tattersall's is not a place for ladies. It is"—he paused, plainly at a loss—"somewhat of a gathering site for sporting gentlemen and other persons involved in the, er, business of the turf."

That her butler found this a sufficient explanation was obvious, but under her father's authority Stacia's life had been one long prohibition after another. Having escaped all that, she had no patience to waste upon new restrictions and rules that doubtless would prove as needless and senseless as the old.

"Do you mean gentlemen like my brother?" she said, deliberately misunderstanding. "I do not see why that would be so very bad."

"Not bad, madam," murmured her butler apologetically. "Simply improper."

"Oh, stuff," said Stacia, glancing at Angeline. "We shall take a footman with us. I have a fancy to conduct my own business in this matter. Marco did well in choosing a house, but when it comes to carriages, I have a feeling he will not understand exactly what it is I have in mind."

Or appreciate it, she added silently.

The three-year-old filly nickered as Lord Andrew ran his hand over her smooth, dun-colored flanks. A few feet to the side, Derek stood with arms folded over his broad chest, an aloof expression masking his thoughts. He was done assessing the horse and had fallen to studying the creature's fat, foppish-looking owner, who had positioned himself a discreet distance away in an effort to appear indifferent. Derek knew his inspection was making the fellow nervous, but he didn't give a tinker's damn. Anyone who would part with a horse like this for any reason other than necessity was a fool who didn't deserve to own it in the first place.

At length Lord Andrew signaled the stableboy to return the horse to her stall. "How much would you say she's worth?" he asked Derek in an undertone.

Derek lifted a shoulder. "Less than the asking price, perhaps, but not much. She's prime blood, Drew, there's no disputing that. You'd race her, of course." He spoke quietly, so Hatherleigh wouldn't hear.

His friend's mouth quirked. "Naturally," he responded. "At Epsom Downs. You haven't had second thoughts about selling Palatine, have you?" Not waiting for the negative he knew he'd receive, Lord Andrew sauntered over to the filly's owner, exchanged a few words, and returned.

"She'll go next auctioning day unless I meet Hatherleigh's price," he told Derek. "It's damned high but I'm going to think it over."

Leaving the stables, the two men entered the spacious auctioneering yard of Tattersall's Repository. Being Tuesday, it was not a sale day, but their purpose had been merely to look, and to keep abreast of current dealings in horse barter. They had each singled out Hatherleigh's filly at a glance, but it was only Lord Andrew who could afford to buy.

As it happened, it caused Derek only a small pang to forgo a horse he would have loved to have owned. He had Palatine, after all. Palatine was the jewel of his own contriving, the result of careful hand breeding between his only stud and a feisty mare he had won in a card game. The sire had been too temperamental a stallion to race, but its offspring was a horse in ten thousand, a miracle of flesh and blood and bare, blind chance. In Palatine lay Derek's sole hope of recouping his fortune and implementing the plans closest to his heart. The sire stallion was gone now, dead of a heart attack, so Palatine was the only road to fortune he had left.

Unless he married an heiress, of course. Derek's brooding gaze wandered to a boisterous group of military types lounging against the wall of the next stable. They were all staring at something, but Derek was too lost in introspection to bother to turn and look. An advantageous alliance, he was reflecting, could save him a great deal of time, trouble, and worry. It was a perfectly rational option.

Well, and why not?

Derek's right hand balled into a hard fist, his habitual response to tension and duress. Why the bloody hell should he *not* repair his finances in so logical a manner? Curse it, half the noble houses in England owed their precious hides to such cold-blooded marriages, and no one but him appeared to find it the least offensive. He could wed an heiress, and racing Palatine could become but a pleasant diversion, an aristocratic pastime designed to relieve an aristocratic gentleman from his aristocratic boredom.

Struck by the incongruity of the notion, Derek's lips twisted into a mirthless smile. He doubted he could do it. When push came to shove, he doubted he could force himself to wed for such a soulless motive. With his luck he would end up with a shrew like his mother, a spoiled, demanding little wife who would expect him to buy her clothes and jewels and carriages she did not need, a cold and passionless whiner who would be stiff as a corpse in bed. Even worse, far worse, was the chance that such a creature might dislike children. His children. God's blood, the very notion made the bile rise in his throat.

He did not want such a wife.

He thought then of Claire—beautiful, mercenary Claire, who had declined to marry him because he was not rich. After five years he could barely remember why he'd wanted her so badly, and as for the hurt, it had long since been buried. His lip curled slightly. He did not need a wife at all.

Yet somewhere deep inside his head a taunting voice protested.

And what of that pretty little widow with the liquid brown eyes? She was not really mistress material, was she? Only a cabbage-head would think otherwise.

Derek's fist jammed into his breeches pocket. He'd thought of her countless times these past few days, but each time he'd repressed his desire to see her, regretting the impulsive note he'd written. Yet even now, despite all resolution to the contrary, his thoughts kept skittering back to Stacia.

Stacia.

It was a soft, pretty name, he thought idly, suitable for such a soft, pretty creature. Short for Eustacia, perhaps?

"Good God, I must be dreaming."

Lord Andrew's tone jerked Derek back to the present, while the sight which met his eyes brought him stock-still in shock. How she had come to be here, at Tattersall's, was temporarily a moot point; what swept him into the most towering rage he had ever known was the sight of Stacia in converse with one of the most notorious profligates in London.

"Hell and damnation!" Derek's muttered expletive hissed out, and his teeth clamped tightly shut. "What in Satan's name does she think she's doing?"

From the moment they'd entered the auctioneering yard, every eye had been riveted upon the two women. Talk had halted almost in midsentence, heads had swiveled, and several mouths had gone foolishly slack. Later, there would be those who insisted that only a loose screw like Sir Joshua Croxton could have mistaken the ladies for bits of muslin. The presence of a footman in full livery, they would protest, beyond doubt proved them to be gentlewomen, and any less flattering conclusion was quite absurd. Still, no one would ever deny that the entire scene was exceedingly awkward.

The first silence had already passed, replaced by a hum of outrage at the unprecedented invasion of a purely masculine sanctum. A few gentlemen shuffled their boots in the dust and politely pretended they'd noticed nothing, several eyed the two women in a surreptitious manner, while the rest simply goggled like gapeseeds at a fair.

Stacia's courage was wobbling as the depth of her solecism began to sink in, her consternation accentuated by the knowledge that she had been warned. She swallowed nervously, aware that both Angeline and her footman were looking to her for guidance.

What was she to do?

To retreat was too cowardly a course to contemplate,

yet to proceed seemed equally rash. Oh, *why* had she not taken her butler's advice? Even Angeline had expressed misgivings at the wisdom of visiting Tattersall's on their own, but no, Stacia Amaryllis Ashcroft had been in one of her headstrong moods.

"Over here, my pretties," called a voice in the distance. "We'll help you find whatever you're looking for."

Stacia raised her chin as a crack of coarse laughter rolled on a gust of wind. Her footman was clearly at a loss as to what to do, although he took a menacing step forward, as though the barrier of his body could somehow prevent the whispers and stares from reaching his mistress.

Stacia wished the ground would open and swallow her up.

"Good God, what a stunner!" gasped a nearby gentleman, who had apparently not grasped the significance of the footman. His eyes were glued to Angeline. "An Incomparable among Cyprians, by Jove. Where the blazes has she been hiding?"

His companion, a swarthy, dissolute nobleman of approximately forty years, raised his quizzing glass to study the two women. "Now that I cannot answer, Matravers, but I have every intention of finding out." Glancing neither to left or right, he approached them purposefully, circumventing Stacia's footman as if he did not exist.

"I bid you good afternoon," he drawled. "Is there something I can help you two ladies find?" His bow was distinctly mocking, but Stacia affected not to notice.

"Good afternoon, sir," she said hesitantly. "Indeed, perhaps there is. Can you tell me how one goes about making a purchase in this place?"

"A purchase?" He looked amused. "What sort of a purchase, my dear?"

The muddy, heavy-lidded eyes made her skin crawl, but Stacia had no choice but to brazen this out.

"A phaeton," she replied, more stiffly "Perhaps you could direct us to where they are housed."

Instead of answering, the man put up his quizzing glass and submitted her to a long, sneering appraisal. "Now what would a pretty little piece like you want with a phaeton?"

Stacia's mouth dropped open. "I beg your pardon?" she said in speechless indignation.

He laughed, a thick, unctuous sound that sent shivers down her spine. "Don't put on airs with me, little dove. I can see the soil on your wings." To her horror, his hand seized her arm, the other shooting out to coil, snakelike, round her waist.

Stacia's footman found his voice. "'Ere now, 'ere now, guv'nor, let me mistress be!" Before the servant could act, however, Stacia launched her own, rather makeshift attack.

"How dare you!" she cried, swinging her reticule at the nobleman's face. By sheer luck she struck him square on the nose, and from somewhere nearby a few cheers arose. In the next instant, Angeline joined in with such vehemence that Stacia's loathsome assailant yelped.

It was the last sound he made before Derek Deveaux's fist crashed into his face.

Chapter Five

While several onlookers cheered, Stacia regarded
Derek with a mingling of awe and fascination. His hat was
askew and his straight black hair disheveled, yet he
appeared unconscious, even uncaring, of the appearance
he presented. Indeed, at that moment he looked the
epitome of her romantic dreams, looming over the other
man like a warrior of old, his hand curled in a fist that
might just as well have held a sword. Yes, a sword would
have made it quite perfect, Stacia thought dreamily.

She adjusted her bonnet and stepped forward.

"Th-thank you, Mr. Deveaux." Dear God, her voice
was actually shaking, and so, in fact, were her knees.
Embarrassed, she cleared her throat and summoned what
little dignity she had left. "I cannot think what can have
possessed this . . . this *person* to behave in such a caddish
fashion," she went on. "I had believed it quite safe for a
lady to walk about town in broad daylight with her
footman . . ."

Her defensive little speech faded to silence, for Derek
was paying her scant heed. To her astonishment, in fact,
he had the amazing incivility to spare her no more than a
cursory glance before returning his gaze to her would-be
assailant. Her breasts heaved indignantly as her romantic
images crumbled. She had wasted days thinking of him,
but for all the notice he gave her, she might as well have
saved herself the trouble!

"Get up, Croxton." The order was curtly voiced and unromantic in the extreme. "Can't you recognize a respectable woman when you see one? I suggest you apologize at once."

Looking as though he would spit, the man called Croxton struggled ungracefully to his feet. From his expression, Stacia expected him to say something quite nasty, but instead he bowed in her direction.

"My apologies, *ladies.* I will leave this *gentleman*"—his sneer was firmly back in place—"to repair the damage to your sensibilities. He's rumored to be very good at it."

He touched a hand to his jaw, his ugly glance sweeping the crowd. Then he elbowed his way through the surrounding throng and disappeared.

Still scowling, Derek eyed the crowd. "Let's give the ladies some air," he suggested, his tone rather short.

Fortunately this was met with almost unanimous agreement. There were a few mutterings and head-shakings, but the assembly, being largely composed of upper-class gentlemen, seemed willing to conduct themselves in a gallant and chivalrous fashion. All but one— the same brown-haired gentleman from the Pulteney— wandered away.

To Stacia's indignation, Mr. Deveaux seized her peremptorily by the elbow. "Coming here was a mistake," he said. "I will escort you back to your carriage. I assume you have one?"

His cool assumption that she would obey banished the last traces of Stacia's gratitude. "Of course I have one," she snapped, "but I have not yet concluded my business in this place—"

"And what business is that?" he cut in. His dark head bent close to hers, his breath hissing out to graze her cheek. Very softly, he said, "In case you don't realize what I have just done, allow me to explain it to you. To save your reputation, my girl, I have just planted another man a very public facer." For an instant, his gaze dropped to her bosom and his voice took on a velvet quality. "You *are* a lady, I presume? Now is the time to correct me if I am laboring under a misconception."

Stacia gasped at his effrontery, hot color sending quick sensation to her face. "You are insulting, sir. If my brother were here it would be you sprawled upon the ground, I can assure you!"

The hard lips curled. "So it is as I thought. Well. With a little clear thinking, we should be able to prevent this blunder from becoming the *on-dit* of the Season." The remark was for the brown-haired gentleman, but his next words were solely for her. "And the way to do that," he said, directly into her ear, "is for you to take your extremely delectable backside out of here as quickly as possible." He angled a look at Angeline. "Who the devil is she?"

"She happens to be my companion," Stacia said angrily. "Not that it is any concern of yours! I am perfectly capable of conducting my own affairs without your assistance, Mr. Deveaux. I had the situation quite under control before you swashbuckled over to turn things into a common brawl. And if you don't let go I shall scream. You are hurting me."

Without argument he released her, watching expressionlessly as she reached up to rub her arm. "Very well, ma'am," he replied, "It shall be as you wish. I've better things to do than waste my time rescuing ungrateful little shrews from—"

"Oh, for lord's sake, Deveaux, don't be such a dull stick," drawled the other gentleman, evidently deeming it time to step in. "There's no rule that says a lady can't come to Tattersall's. It's simple a tad . . . unconventional."

A gentleman to his fingertips, Stacia's defender executed an impressive bow. "Permit me to present myself, since this surly fellow here has forgotten to do so. Lord Andrew Carisbrooke, at your service, ladies." He looked at Stacia. "Proper introductions were overlooked at our first meeting, though perhaps you do not recall the occasion."

Still smarting from Derek's cavalier treatment, Stacia

66

responded with a graceful curtsy. "Of course I remember, sir. I am happy to make your acquaintance." She favored him with her prettiest smile, hoping to show Derek Deveaux exactly what his shabby behavior had cost him. "And this is my companion and friend, Mrs. Greaves," she added. She stepped closer to Angeline, who was looking a little pale. "This is her first visit to London."

She noted with approval that Lord Andrew did not gape like a moron at Angeline, although he did favor her with a rather deep bow. He was obviously more worldly than Marco, she thought thankfully. As for Mr. Deveaux, if he had noticed Angeline's loveliness, he certainly showed no sign of it.

"Welcome to London," Lord Andrew said gravely. "However, if this"—his gesture encompassed the stableyard—"is one of your first impressions, Mrs. Greaves, we shall have to work hard to make recompense."

Stacia, herself rather impressed, was quite shocked when Angeline barely acknowledged the statement. "We really ought to go, ma'am," she voiced. "Your brother can purchase the phaeton for you. We really should not be seen in such a place."

"You cannot purchase a phaeton today," threw in Derek. "Sale days are Monday and Thursday, and Monday only during the summer. Is *that* why you're here?" He spoke quite neutrally, yet Stacia had the oddest feeling he was surprised.

She toyed with the notion of giving him a firm setdown, but decided against it. Just because *he* had the manners of a country bumpkin did not mean that *she* ought to be anything but civil.

"As a matter of fact it is," she replied with dignity. "I presume one is permitted to *view* on the other days of the week? Else why would all these gentlemen be here? It seems quite a popular place."

Lord Andrew smiled. "Quite right, ma'am." He gave her a conspiratorial look. "Well, as long as you're here, it seems rather a shame not to have a look about. Eh, Derek? Why don't we show the ladies what Tattersall's has to offer?"

Deciding that Lord Andrew was as charming as Derek was unromantic and boorish, Stacia gave him a dazzling smile and accepted his proffered arm.

"I should like that very much, sir. However," she added, gazing demurely up at him through her eyelashes, "there is not the least occasion to trouble Mr. Deveaux with my concerns. He has better things to do."

A queer sound came from Derek's throat, but whether it signified annoyance or some other emotion was impossible to ascertain. Stacia glanced over her shoulder, but saw that he was offering his arm to Angeline, a circumstance which afforded her far less satisfaction than it ought. If he was put out by her remark, he certainly managed to conceal it quickly enough, she thought in disgust.

Fifteen minutes later, Stacia's opinion of Derek Deveaux underwent a further decline. He made no effort to be pleasant, his sole object being, in her view, to make her feel as unsophisticated and self-conscious as possible. He made several cynical remarks, and when she almost stepped in some horse dung (of which the whole place reeked), he was unamiable enough to remark that she would have seen it if her nose were not so high in the air. And while Lord Andrew patiently explained the finer distinctions between carriages, it was only Derek who was uncivil enough to suggest that she was far too inexperienced to make an intelligent choice. And when she finally did find one she liked—a dashing racing phaeton whose small, wine-colored body towered high atop huge springs—Derek Deveaux actually had the discourtesy to laugh.

"Yes, and how long do you think you'd be alive to drive it?" he demanded in a mocking tone. "That rig is meant for a man. You'd kill yourself in the first ten minutes."

Stacia put up her chin and smiled sweetly. "If I did, I

have not the least doubt that you would gloat. You could then have the pleasure of telling all your acquaintances that you knew it would happen."

Unfortunately, she had chosen to cross swords with a master. "Well now, ma'am," he responded, with infuriating composure, "if it's my pleasure that concerns you, there are far more interesting things you could do than go out and break your silly little neck."

Stacia stared at him in outrage, but before she could form a suitably scathing reply, Lord Andrew again intervened.

"I fear he is right," he explained. "In his own cloddish way, the poor fellow does have a point. You see, ma'am, high-perch phaetons have a tendency to overturn rather easily. Contrast this carriage with the next, if you will. Observe its low body and do, pray, consider how much simpler it would be to enter than this one. That is a park phaeton, you see, and very popular with the ladies."

"You can even climb into it without providing the world a view of your ankles," was Derek's sardonic contribution. "Though I'm not at all sure that that recommends it."

Teeth clenched in irritation, Stacia surveyed the park phaeton. "What do you think of it?" she asked, turning to Angeline. "Is it dashing enough to suit the purpose?"

Angeline appeared startled at having her opinion solicited. "I fear I must agree with the gentlemen about the higher carriage," she said in a constrained voice. Her delicate complexion heightened as she added, "The other seems dashing enough, and looks a great deal safer."

"And what deep, dark purpose do we cherish?" inquired Derek. "Or need I ask?"

Stacia turned her back on him. "Yes, my lord, I think perhaps the park phaeton might answer. Now tell me how one goes about making a purchase, if you please."

Lord Andrew bowed, his eyes full of mischief. "If you like, I can act as your agent in this matter. Perhaps I may call upon you to discuss the arrangements in, er, greater detail?" His eyes rested thoughtfully on Angeline.

Stacia hesitated. "Are you quite certain? I really do not wish to put you out"—something in that brief glance made her alter her speech—"but it would make things a great deal easier," she finished gratefully. "Thank you so much."

"'Tis an honor to assist you," Lord Andrew declared. He reached for Stacia's hand and pressed it to his lips. "'Tis always a pleasure to assist a beautiful lady," he added with exaggerated gallantry.

Too conscious of Derek, only inches away, Stacia took small notice of his lordship's magniloquence.

"Well, I think it is very kind of you to offer," was all she said. "You have certainly been excessively obliging, sir." She bestowed her warmest smile upon Lord Andrew, making sure to place the slightest emphasis on the word *you*. "I may decide to purchase a matched pair as well," she added thoughtfully, "but I think my coach horses will serve for now."

"Why the devil doesn't that brother of yours make himself useful? He could have done this for you."

The sharp question came from Derek, and seemed deliberately intended to provoke her beyond endurance.

"I daresay he could have," she flashed, "if I had requested it. I hardly think I need justify such things to you, Mr. Deveaux."

He surprised her by laughing, a deep, rich sound that sent a curious thrill up her spine.

"That's right, you don't," he mocked. "If you were accountable to me, ma'am, you'd be back in Upper Grosvenor Street by now." One side of his mouth curved unpleasantly. "But you've chosen the right sleeve to hang on, my dear. You're clearly more up to snuff than you appear." His eyes shifted to Lord Andrew, who was looking extremely pained. "Before you fork out any blunt," he advised, "I'd be damned sure she's able to repay it—in one way or another."

His insufferable speech complete, Derek Deveaux

turned on his heel and strode off, leaving Stacia to stare after him in speechless, consummate rage.

Lord Andrew sighed. "Oh dear," he murmured, quite inadequately. "That was not very well done of him, was it?"

"The conceited, condescending, self-centered, arrogant *oaf!*" Her hands clenched into small fists, Stacia stalked up and down the length of her sitting room, pouring forth the full sum of her outrage into Angeline's sympathetic ear. Her temper had been simmering ever since Tattersall's, but she'd somehow kept it contained until they reached home.

"As though I were the sort of ingratiating, toad-eating person," she continued, "who would try to . . . to *insinuate* myself into Lord Andrew's good graces merely because he is . . . *oh!* It simply makes my blood *boil*, Angeline. I really, really think that I loathe him."

"You think?" Angeline studied her with slightly raised brows. "Good gracious, ma'am, how could you do otherwise? The man treated you quite abominably."

"Yes, he did! But *why?* Why should he intimate that I might try to trick his lordship into purchasing a phaeton I could not pay for myself? What would give him such an opinion of me?" Stacia made an angry, sweeping gesture with her hand. "We only met the one time and—" She stopped suddenly, remembering. "My God, Angeline, he *knew!* He knew all along where I lived!"

"And you thought he would pay you a visit?" guessed Angeline shrewdly. "That type doesn't bother with the preliminaries, ma'am. When he's ready, he'll go straight for the throat."

Stacia stared at her companion. "You mean—?"

Angeline nodded gravely. "I fear so, Mrs. Edwards. He is exactly the sort of man I warned you about. And I'd beware of the other one, too."

"Lord Andrew?" Too agitated to think clearly, Stacia

pressed her hands to her cheeks. "Oh, no. I'm sure you are completely off the mark *there*. Lord Andrew is a gentleman, Angeline."

"Why, yes," agreed her companion coolly, "he is that. But these so-called gentlemen are the worst because their gallantry makes you feel you can trust them. And that is what you cannot do. Never trust a man, Mrs. Edwards, gentleman or no." She said the words so bitterly that Stacia left off her pacing and sat down, her anger cooling as she took in Angeline's expression.

"What happened to you, Angeline?" she asked quietly. "What makes you speak this way?"

For at least half a minute Angeline did not speak. She appeared to be studying her hands, but when her eyes rose they were blazing, vivid and fierce, containing an intensity that Stacia had never seen.

"Nothing happened to me," she replied, her voice very low. "But someone I knew—someone I loved very dearly—was deceived and ruined by a man like Lord Andrew Carisbrooke. Someone I knew bore a bastard because of a suave, smiling nobleman like him. And I have learned from her misfortune."

Stacia's hand raised, as if she might touch the other girl, but the distance between them was too great. "I am so sorry," was all she said.

Angeline's moist eyes shone like sapphires. "I did not mean to tell you that. Have I shocked you?"

"A little," Stacia admitted. "You are younger than I, yet you have so much more experience of the world. It makes me feel quite strange."

"You feel deceived in me, I suppose. You are beginning to realize that you have taken an adventuress into your home, and are wondering what you ought to do about it." The lovely face held a trace of defiance. "I don't blame you. 'Tis natural to feel thus."

"I'm not sure what I feel," retorted Stacia honestly. "*Are* you an adventuress? Is that how you see yourself?"

For the first time, Angeline looked uncomfortable. "Perhaps," she answered, shifting restlessly in her chair.

"But not by choice."

Some instinct told Stacia her companion was done making confidences, so she guided the subject into a less awkward channel. "Tell me," she said slowly, "do you think I was wrong to permit Lord Andrew to arrange the purchase of my phaeton?"

The perfectly shaped lips curved. "Gracious, no, ma'am. To own the truth, I thought 'twas prodigious clever in you. You achieved so much, and all in one stroke."

Stacia blinked. "I did?"

"Yes, you did." Her air brisk, Angeline ticked off what she termed "achievements" on her fingers. "First, you now have a competent person to deal with the business. Second, a gentleman of obvious wealth and rank has promised to pay you a visit, and that is something you can use to your advantage. And third," she added, a little slyly, "you managed to give Mr. Deveaux the come-uppance he so richly deserved. He was exceedingly annoyed."

Stacia could feel the warmth returning to her cheeks. "Well, I am glad he was annoyed!" she exclaimed, her vexation now oddly divided between Derek and herself. "I was equally annoyed, no, *incensed!* He has the manners of a pig. As for Lord Andrew, despite what you say I think him very kind and obliging, though I am not at all sure I would wish him to *make up* to me. Oh dear, how very vulgar that sounds. He really is charming and I suppose I would not object if he wished to . . . to flirt."

She realized suddenly that she was babbling, but it had served to fill in an awkward gap. This was certainly not the time to tell Angeline her suspicions regarding Lord Andrew. After all, she had nothing more to go by than that one covert glance, but feminine instinct told her she was right. Despite Angeline's almost churlish behavior, she had effortlessly attracted the first handsome aristocrat who crossed her path. No doubt this was but a taste of things to come, for the girl was simply too beautiful not to be noticed. But what of Derek, she wondered suddenly. Had he been affected as well?

Angeline misinterpreted her pause. "A mere visit does not mean he's paying court to you, ma'am. Far from it. But as long as you are wary, you can use him to ease your way into society. Unless"—she paused, her face hardening—"unless his reputation is unsavory, in which case he can do you no good. That is something we had best discover."

Before Stacia could come up with a reply, a noise from below heralded what they both knew was the arrival of Sir Marco. Stacia's brother had fallen into the habit of appearing just before teatime, for her cook had a way with cakes and pastries and Marco possessed a ravening sweet tooth. Thus far, he had always been accompanied by Mr. Denchworth, but upon this occasion he was alone, his face set in so somber an expression that for a moment Stacia feared he had gotten wind of her excursion to Tattersall's.

"Stacia," he said, after a rather strained greeting, "I must have a word with you." His eyes went to Angeline and for once did not glaze over. "My apologies, Mrs. Greaves," he added with a small bow, "but this is a private matter. Hope you understand."

When Angeline was gone, Marco threw himself moodily onto the settee and withdrew a snuffbox from his pocket. He then proceeded to fiddle with the object in his hands for so long that Stacia grew impatient.

"What is it, Marco?"

She regarded him nervously, her hands gripped together. Had he discovered that Derek Deveaux had insulted her? Was he about to rip up at her for venturing to Tattersall's on her own?

Marco glanced up and suddenly slammed the snuffbox onto the table beside him. "I'm in a bit of a pickle," he announced rather jerkily, "but I didn't come here for a raking-down, so if you have any affection for me you'll spare me that. I know I've been a fool. I don't need you to tell me so."

Stacia eyed him in alarm. "Tell me at once what is

wrong!" she begged, casting about in her mind for something dreadful enough to warrant such despondency. "My God, Marco, you have not killed someone, have you?"

Marco refused to return her look. "Worse than that!" was his gloomy prognosis of the matter.

Her eyes widened. "Gracious, what could be worse? Marco, are you quite yourself?" she said anxiously. "Have you been drinking?"

He shook his head. "I'm sober as a judge at the moment, though I can't say I don't sometimes—" He broke off, drawing a breath. "As to what I've done, well, I've lost the devil of a lot of money, that's what I've done."

Flooded with irrational relief, Stacia found herself asking, much more calmly, "How much?"

"Nearly six thousand," said Marco morosely, his chin sinking into the folds of his cravat.

Her calm vanished. "Six thousand!" she echoed, gripped with shock. "*Pounds?* You mean six thousand *pounds?*"

"Aye," sighed Marco. "And the devil's in it that I can't pay. At least I'd be devilish hard pressed to do so. Most of *my* fortune is tied up in Papa's estate, y'know."

Several seconds passed while the significance of this statement sunk in. Then Stacia said hopefully, "Can you not explain this to the person you owe? After all, it is not like a *real* debt. Perhaps he will be willing to—"

"Gaming debts are real, Stacia," Marco said sullenly. "A debt of honor has to be paid."

Her soft brown eyes grew troubled. "I see," she replied. "Well then, what are you going to do?"

"The only thing I can do. Cast myself on your mercy. You've got enough blunt, for God's sake. You'll never miss it." He saw her expression. "Confound it, I'll pay you back!" he cried, leaping to his feet. "Like Dench says, a fellow can't lose all the time! Sooner or later I'll—"

"Sooner or later!" Stacia looked appalled. "Do you mean you plan to continue gambling?"

"Yes, but with a clear head so I don't get scorched!" He prowled the room once, then stopped by the fireplace to stare down into the empty grate. "Trouble is," he continued, his shoulders hunched, "these places keep trying to ply you with drink. I was winning at first. I was ahead by two thousand, and then I took that first sip. The next thing I knew I was dipping under and then I just kept falling further and further under the hatches."

Stacia rose and went to him. "Don't look so, my dear. Of course I will give you the money. By rights, some of it should have been yours anyway. I cannot think what could have been in Uncle Travis's head to leave it all to me." She hesitated. "But you really must take better care. I don't mean to scold you, but you did say you knew you had been foolish—"

"Foolish to let drink cloud my judgment!" he corrected. "It won't happen again. Something will turn up trumps."

A discreet tap on the door proclaimed the butler's arrival. "A letter for you, madam. It was delivered this instant."

"Thank you, Challow." Stacia took the letter with studied unconcern, yet one quick glance was enough to assure her that the handwriting was not Derek's.

And what possible reason would he have for writing? mocked an inner voice. Mr. Deveaux had made it very clear that he despised her as much as she despised him.

"Who's it from?" Now that his problems were a fair way toward being solved, Marco was willing to be cordial. "Who do you know in London?"

Stacia broke open the wafer and scanned the contents curiously. "It's from someone called Lady Crackenthorpe," she said in mystification. "She wishes me to call upon her at one o'clock tomorrow, but states no reason." She glanced up. "I don't know who she is. Do you?"

Marco smiled crookedly. "Aye. She was a great friend of Uncle Travis's. Well, well, I wonder what she wants with you?"

Chapter Six

Lady Crackenthorpe proved to be as singular as her name, though this was not discernable from any peculiarity in her appearance. Her dovelike prettiness had lasted well into her forties, but it was, rather, her excessive generosity which set her apart and earned her the genuine approbation of everyone she knew. Within her sphere of influence her kindness was legend, while her tendency to bear malice toward none, no matter how great the provocation, protected her from the few spiteful creatures who were jealous. As it happened, she was a widow (Lord Crackenthorpe having succumbed to an ailment of the lungs more than a dozen years before), and in consequence had received several offers to fill his shoes. Remarriage, however, was not Lady Crackenthorpe's objective; she had refused them all, but in so kind-hearted a fashion that each of her swains had gone away mollified, convinced that it was enough simply to keep the best-humored woman in the world as his friend.

"Oh, you dear child!" were the lady's first words when Stacia was ushered into her presence. "Poor, dear child! Come and let me have a look at you." Her outstretched hands grasped Stacia's in a light squeeze, her Dresden blue eyes glowing with sympathy. "You are as lovely as your mother," she continued, urging her toward an elegant Sheraton couch. "How marvelous to meet you at last! I would have written to you sooner but I caught a chill a fortnight ago, and am only now feeling well enough to receive visitors. You see how red my nose is!" She smiled. "Now come and sit down and tell me all about everything."

Stacia sat obediently. "I do beg your pardon, ma'am, but I am not perfectly sure how it is that you know me. Are you perhaps one of my mother's relations?"

"No, my dear, I cannot claim that honor." Lady Crackenthorpe smiled again, very gently. "I knew your Mama only slightly. Eustacia came out the year before I, in the spring of '96."

"Did you?" Stacia's heart leaped. "Oh, will you tell me a little about her? That is, if you do not mind? You see, I was told next to nothing when she . . . when she left, and it would mean a great deal to me."

Lady Crackenthorpe regarded her sadly. "Alas, I know so little. I know that she was a gay creature who loved to dance and flirt, and that your father adored her in the beginning." There was a pause. "She was not always as kind to others as she might have been. I know Sir George never forgave her for eloping with Peter Dorney. Travis told me how it was."

"You knew Uncle Travis?"

"Oh, yes. I knew your uncle very well. In fact, he asked me to marry him." She laughed at Stacia's expression, a merry sound that chased the shadows from the room. "Dear Travis," she added fondly. "How I miss him."

The butler entered at that instant, carrying a tray laden with refreshments so that the conversation temporarily ceased. Stacia accepted a cup of tea and a trifle, and after taking a sip and a nibble, she remarked. "So, ma'am, you invited me here because—?"

"Because Travis asked me to do so. You see, he wrote to me before he died. He knew he was sick, and he was . . . taking care of things. He was very fond of you, Stacia. He told me he had left you his fortune, and that if you came to London you might need a little support and guidance." Her eyes twinkled a little. "Perhaps I had better explain that. You see, my dear, I have the felicity of being what is known as shockingly good Ton. I am on terms with all the patronesses of Almack's, as well as anyone else you care to mention. Travis thought you would *take,* as the saying goes, and asked me to do all I could to smooth your way—which, I might add, I would be delighted to do, for your sake as well as for his."

Stacia absorbed all this with a slight frown. "I beg your pardon, ma'am, but I cannot help thinking it rather strange." Her voice faltered a little. "Uncle Travis never *seemed* fond of me, so this comes as a bit of a surprise."

Lady Crackenthorpe sighed. "Well, the man did have trouble expressing his feelings, I'll grant. I'm afraid some men are like that, my dear. Many times it's due to their upbringing. They keep everything locked inside until they're fit to burst."

"I do that myself, a little," Stacia confessed. She sipped her tea reflectively. "Though perhaps it is only because until recently I'd no one to talk *to.* Except Mrs. Hanson, our housekeeper, of course. And Cook."

Lady Crackenthorpe's eyes grew moist during this prosaic speech, but when she finally replied, after a pause of some three or four seconds, her voice was brisk with decision.

"Well, at least you are finally here and we may mend *that* situation," she said. "Now then, you must set me straight upon one point, my dear. I received a very proper letter from Mr. Farquhar at the bank informing me of your arrival, which is what Travis had instructed, you understand. But Mr. Farquhar referred to you as Miss Ashcroft, and, well, I'd heard the oddest rumor that someone called 'Mrs. Edwards' had inherited Travis Ashcroft's fortune." Her brow wrinkled sightly. "My dear girl, have I been misinformed? Is it possible you are married?"

Stacia stalled by taking another bite of trifle and nearly

choked on a crumb. "No, I'm not married," she mumbled, after a quick swallow of tea. "Uh, no one mentioned that I was widowed?" To her own ears, the attempt to avoid a direct reply had a terribly feeble sound.

"Widowed!" Lady Crackenthorpe set down her teacup abruptly. "Good gracious, you poor girl, and you so young. What on earth happened?"

"Well, ma'am," Stacia said cautiously, "I quite meant to tell people that poor Frederick died at Waterloo. It had such a heroic sound, I thought."

Lady Crackenthorpe looked taken aback. "Oh dear. And what *did* happen?"

The older woman's gaze was so direct and brimming with compassion that Stacia found she could not lie.

"Well, the truth is, ma'am," she said, embarking upon a rather stumbling explanation, "that I am not wed. I thought to tell people I was because . . . oh, because I did not want all the fuss that normally accompanies an unmarried girl's introduction into society—for which I am too old, anyway. And also because I wanted my freedom. I have not had much of that, you see, and I thought . . . well, I thought that if I were a widow . . ." She lifted her hands in a helpless gesture. "I do hope you are not too shocked."

To Stacia's relief, Lady Crackenthorpe showed no disposition to break into hysterics.

"Perhaps you are more like your mother than I imagined," was her curious pronouncement. "Though I hope that is not true in all respects. Eustacia was an impulsive woman, and if you'll pardon my saying so, wholly unsuited to be a mother." She studied Stacia's face. "I think it might be better if we talked of her on another occasion. Today I want us to spend time becoming acquainted. If I promise not to give you a scold, will you tell me more about your plan? It sounds a trifle injudicious, and I owe it to Travis to be sure you do not land yourself in a predicament."

Stacia flushed. "I fear I already have, ma'am. Only yesterday in fact."

Under Lady Crackenthrope's inquiring eye, Stacia found herself relating the previous day's events. Explaining the episode at Tattersall's proved a difficult feat, particularly when she reached the point where Derek Deveaux entered the picture.

"You say *Derek* knocked Sir Joshua down?" There was a hint of incredulity in Lady Crackenthorpe's tone, along with some other emotion Stacia could not interpret. "I find that rather amazing."

Stacia shifted nervously. "You are acquainted with Mr. Deveaux, then?"

"I should rather say so. I have known Derek since he was born. He is my godson." She reached for the teapot and refilled both their cups, saying casually, "And why should he have done such a violent thing, I wonder?"

"I'm sure I do not know." Stacia replied. "Perhaps he is in the habit of knocking people down?"

Her ladyship's head shook. "Not to my knowledge. Except, perhaps, in one of those sporting establishments where the gentlemen go to box. In the general way his inclinations run to verbal severity. Derek can be blunt to the point of harshness, though he is usually pleasant to me." She paused. "There *are* reasons why he is so," she added enigmatically.

Stacia raised her chin. "I thought him very arrogant."

"Did you, my dear?" Lady Crackenthorpe sipped her tea and considered this. "Yes, I can see how he would seem so. He is always courteous and considerate to me, but I have heard him speak to others in a manner which I must admit caused me pain." She sighed. "Do go on with your story, Stacia. What happened next? I assume my godson was not . . . tactful?"

"Tactful?" Stacia arched a disdainful brow. "No, ma'am, he certainly was not tactful. But Lord Andrew Carisbrooke did his best to make amends. What an amiable gentleman *he* is." She went on to finish the tale, adding, "So Lord Andrew will arrange the purchase of my phaeton. He is to call upon me soon to discuss it."

"And that pleases you?"

"Well . . . I suppose it does," she replied in confusion. "He is very nice."

"Nice?" Lady Crackenthorpe looked amused. "Lord Andrew is the Duke of Wight's brother, my dear—one of the most eligible bachelors in the realm. He is renowned for his gallantry, his fortune, and his handsome countenance. Unmarried ladies and ambitious mamas are forever laying traps for him, though so far he has avoided stepping into one."

Stacia could not help smiling. "Gracious, ma'am, you make him sound like a rabbit." She tried to recall Lord Andrew's face, but it had faded to a blur in her memory. "I suppose he is handsome. I did not notice particularly."

"But you noticed Derek," guessed her ladyship. When Stacia only cast down her eyes, she went on, "My godson is not renowned for his gallantry, my dear, nor does he possess a large fortune or even a title. Nonetheless, he is by no means penniless, and as for his birth—I daresay he is related to half the nobility in England. On the whole, I think 'twould be fair to say he is as sought after as Lord Andrew. Perhaps even more," she added pensively. "Women find him fascinating, I am told."

Stacia tossed her red-gold curls. "I cannot imagine why," she declared. "His manners are perfectly detestable."

Lady Crackenthorpe seemed to choose her words with care. "I agree there is seldom a good excuse for bad manners, but if anyone has an excuse, it is my godson. He had a very trying childhood, Stacia, and his mother, Lady Winifred, treated him with what I can only call cruel indifference. Yet there is nothing uncaring about Derek. You will discover that yourself."

At these words, the image of a sad-faced little boy flashed in Stacia's head, but she hardened her heart and said, rather colorlessly, "I beg your pardon, ma'am, but such a discovery seems unlikely. Mr. Deveaux has nothing but contempt for me. He made that quite clear."

"I see." Lady Crackenthorpe crossed her plump ankles and surveyed her guest with a calm, tolerant eye. "But then I quite fail to see why he came to your rescue. For that is what it amounts to, isn't it?"

"You know, I have been thinking about that," Stacia said in a low voice. "I think it may have something to do with my companion. Angeline is the most excessively beautiful girl you could ever imagine, and I . . . that is, all the gentlemen seem dazzled by her. Even Marco is besotted. In fact, I shouldn't wonder if they will make a match of it. At this very moment, he and Mr. Denchworth are driving her in the Park."

"Gracious, Stacia, what will you tell me next? Why in the world would you hire a girl like that? How old is she?"

Stacia studied her fingertips. "One-and-twenty," she answered in a subdued tone. "I own she is young, but she is a widow. A *real* widow," she added, flushing slightly, "and a vicar's granddaughter. I know someone older would have been more appropriate, but she needed work, ma'am, while I needed someone who would be a friend, not a . . . a watchdog. And I like her."

Lady Crackenthorpe's head tilted thoughtfully. "Not so much like your mother after all," she said unexpectedly. "Eustacia would never have tolerated a rival." Her voice was rather dry. "And you think Derek is attracted to the girl?"

"Who would not be? When you meet her yourself you will understand. I thought her an angel myself."

"I suppose I shall." Her ladyship reached across the space between them to give Stacia a motherly pat on the arm. "Tell me," she said, "what is it you want? Do you know?"

Stacia met the guileless blue eyes squarely. "Of course. I want to enjoy myself." She answered almost by rote, giving the speech she had uttered to herself a hundred times, at every hour of every day for as long as she could remember. "I want to meet handsome gentlemen and make scads of friends. I want to become fashionable and attend balls and soirees and such. I want to dance and play cards and wear beautiful clothes—"

"And how long will all this keep you happy?" interrupted Lady Crackenthorpe.

Stacia's voice faltered. "How long? What do you mean?"

"I mean how long will such diversions be enough? I know your father kept you a virtual prisoner at his estate, my dear, so that you are starving for all these frivolous activities. 'Tis natural, and I do understand. But when all these things begin to pall, as they inevitably will, what will you do then?"

"I . . . I don't know. *Will* they pall?" Stacia was doubtful.

Lady Crackenthorpe nodded. "I think for you they will. For some, no. The social whirl goes on year after year, and they never see beyond it or themselves. I won't say more on that head, for it would be vastly uncharitable, but you, Stacia, are different. I sense it. You are going to need something more substantial than pretty clothes and compliments. You are going to need a husband."

"Am I, ma'am?"

"Yes." Her ladyship paused, studying Stacia with an approving air. "Not just any husband, however. *That* was your mother's mistake and you must not repeat it. Lud, what lovely eyes you have, especially when you open them wide and look at me so! Between your prettiness and Travis's fortune, you are going to receive a great many offers, I think." She smiled at Stacia's startled look. "No, in your case, achieving a respectable match is not our difficulty. Our real challenge is to find you the *right* husband." At this, her voice grew adamant. "You need to make a love match, my dear. I had a husband who loved me, and I know there is nothing and no one who can ever replace him. Ever."

This discussion of marriage, the first she had ever had with another woman, left Stacia feeling shy and breathless.

"I would like to marry," she ventured, "If I fell in love . . . if he were warm and gentle . . . and if I were certain he loved me in return . . ."

Lady Crackenthorpe had thought of something else. "It's just occurred to me that your companion's beauty may be a blessing in disguise. 'Tis a pity you are *so* wealthy—we'll have the fortune hunters to contend with—but if your Angeline is as beautiful as you say, it may be a very good thing."

"How is that, ma'am?"

"'Tis my theory," she went on, "that if a man is going to fall in love with a woman, he will do so despite all odds, and nothing is going to prevent it. But if a man is *not* going to fall in love, or if his love is not as solid as it should be, well, that man can easily be led astray by a pretty face. Do you catch my meaning, Stacia?"

"I'm not sure, ma'am," said Stacia weakly.

"I'm saying that *true* love cannot be led astray by the beauty of a rival. There are those who will disagree with me, I'm sure."

"How will I know he's not in love with my fortune?"

"Ah, yes, your fortune. Well, I should be able to guide you in that province. I have a pretty fair notion which gentlemen are on the lookout for a rich wife. Such things are generally known."

Some inner devil prompted Stacia to ask, "And your godson? You said he has no fortune. Is he looking for a rich wife?"

There was a short silence. "I should be very much surprised," Lady Crackenthorpe said finally, "if Derek married for any reason other than love. He has had very little of it in his life, but . . . I think he knows his lack." She let out a short sigh. "But him I fear I cannot guide."

"That I can readily believe," said Stacia tartly. "I'm afraid I have nothing but pity for the poor woman he chooses to wed. A more difficult man to please I cannot imagine." She saw Lady Crackenthorpe's frown. "Oh, I *do* beg your pardon, ma'am! I should not have said that. I know you hold him in affection. Do please forgive me."

"No, no, there's nothing to forgive, my dear. I have always valued honesty." The lady sighed again. "But I am sorry you have taken Derek into such aversion. I had hoped to introduce the two of you at the ball I am giving two weeks hence." She made a small gesture. "The cards are already written. I would like to invite both you and your brother—"

"And we will be happy to attend," put in Stacia hastily. Having no wish to offend, she paused, rather embarrassed by the question she'd been longing to ask for the past half-hour. "So, ma'am, am I correct in assuming that you will countenance my deception? You will not give me away?"

"Of course, I will not! Gracious, Stacia, what business is it of mine if you choose to tell people you are a widow? That's not to say I approve of it, of course, but I daresay 'tis too late to change the story now. Yes," she added, reading Stacia's expression, "I see that I am right. Well, I think it a mistake, but you have already chosen your path. When you marry, of course, you will be obliged to tell your husband the truth."

"Must I?" Stacia bit her lower lip. "Yes, I suppose I would have to, wouldn't I?"

"Yes, my dear," said Lady Crackenthorpe gently. "I really think you would."

Marco, meanwhile, was tooling Mr. Denchworth's curricle on a roundabout course through the Mayfair streets, having finally persuaded his friend to take the groom's seat and allow him to handle the ribbons. During their entire drive in the Park it had been Marco who'd occupied the groom's perch, which had certainly not been part of his plan as Dench dashed well ought to have known! Being wholly unused to playing second fiddle, Marco had responded by plunging into a fit of the blue-devils.

Nothing was going right in his life, he thought sullenly. He'd wanted to woo Angeline, and how the deuce was that possible when it was Dench sitting beside her? He'd complained, of course, but instead of offering to change seats with him (as agreed upon at the outset) Dench had pointed out that it was *his* curricle, and that Marco was a cow-handed whipster who could scarcely handle a gig, much less a dashing and elegant racing curricle. That Dench had been so ruthless as to mention this in front of the woman Marco adored, the woman he had every intention of making his lawful wife, had put him into a passion from which he'd not yet recovered. Even now that he had finally taken his rightful place at Angeline's side, he was still fuming with indignation. The knowledge that he had lost another two thousand at faro the previous evening further exacerbated his ill humor and made him even more careless than usual.

"Dash it, watch out!" growled Mr. Denchworth as Marco made a last minute decision to turn into Half Moon Street at the same instant a high-perch phaeton was emerging.

Angeline uttered a cry as the curricle rounded the corner at what was obviously too wide an arc to avoid the other vehicle. Mr. Denchworth swore and made a grab for the reins, which Marco was jerking wildly, but there was nothing he could do. Fortunately, the driver of the phaeton proved as expert as Marco was inept, and managed to swerve just enough so that the two carriages did not collide. However, both sets of horses lost control and plunged about in their traces, terrified whinnies tearing from their muscled throats.

Mr. Denchworth leapt from his perch and ran to their heads, while the other driver's groom did the same. Within seconds, the two pairs of horses were steadied, but it was apparent that Mr. Denchworth's turnout had not emerged from the incident unscathed. In fact, its front right wheel had struck a lamppost and was slanted at a very unpromising angle.

Mr. Denchworth was suffering paroxysms. "Devil take it, Marc, what the deuce did you think you were doing? Look at what you've done to my curricle! Just look at it! My new curricle! It's ruined! Ruined!" He threw his hat on the ground and pulled his hair in frustration.

Acutely mortified, Marco climbed out of the vehicle and bent down to survey the damaged wheel. After an uncomfortable silence in which he listened to more despondent ranting, he said, "The axle looks solid, Dench. It's only the linchpin that's broken."

While this was going on, the driver of the phaeton had descended to the ground, but neither Marco nor Mr. Denchworth paid him any heed until they heard him speak.

"Mrs. Greaves, are you unharmed?"

Marco whirled to see an elegantly attired gentleman at least half a dozen years his senior assisting his beloved out of the carriage. Very much chagrined by the knowledge that he had actually forgotten his angel, he stepped forward with a possessive glare. "I say, ma'am, do you know this fellow?"

The gentleman bowed slightly. "Lord Andrew Carisbrooke, at your service, sir. And yes, Mrs. Greaves and I have been introduced." He raised his quizzing glass and gave the damaged wheel a brief, disinterested scan. "Might I inquire whether you have ever driven a curricle before?"

Marco flushed scarlet. "Of c-course I have!" he stuttered. "Dozens of times! Anybody might have such an accident. I daresay you know that as well as I!"

Lord Andrew inclined his head. "To be sure," he agreed. "I trust you will take no offense, however, if I suggest that in the future you refrain from driving females. If you wish to kill yourself, of course, it is your prerogative, but someone as lovely as Mrs. Greaves"—

he gave Angeline an oblique look—"hardly deserves such a fate."

Marco bristled, but during the small interval in which he attempted to formulate a suitable reply, Lord Andrew had the audacity to reclaim his beloved's attention.

"Dear me," he remarked to Angeline, "we seem to be attracting another congregation of spectators. This shows signs of becoming a tedious pattern in our acquaintanceship." He offered her the crook of his arm. "Come, let us leave these two gentlemen to their devices, ma'am. I would be happy to escort you to whatever destination you care to name."

Angeline's sooty lashes lowered for an instant, then she glanced from Marco to Lord Andrew. "Thank you," she murmured. "I would very much like to return to Upper Grosvenor Street as soon as possible."

Powerless to prevent his angel from departing with Lord Andrew, Marco grit his teeth as she accepted his lordship's arm.

"I'm devilish sorry, Mrs. Greaves," he said miserably. "I'd be happy to take you myself if I—"

"Oh, no, you don't!" jumped in Mr. Denchworth with wrath. "You're going to help me walk these horses back to the mews! Look at it, Marc! Just look at it!"

Marco gave Lord Andrew a menacing look. "Very well, sir. I assume," he added meaningfully, "that she will have no cause for complaint while in your company."

Lord Andrew looked amused. "My dear sir—What did you say your name was?"

Marco drew himself up to his full height. "Sir Marco Ashcroft," he said in a dignified voice. "At your service."

"Ah yes, I thought you looked familiar," said his lordship, somewhat obscurely. "Well, Sir Marco, let's just say that if Mrs. Greaves has cause for complaint, I will meet you when and where you like. Swords or pistols," he added gently. "Your choice."

Marco swallowed. "I daresay that won't be necessary,"

he admitted in a grudging voice.

"No, I daresay it won't," agreed Lord Andrew.

Angeline's rescuer urged his grays into a trot and glanced down at her stiffly averted profile. He studied the perfect features, wondering what secrets that rigid expression hid. Dare he attempt a little light flirtation? She was the brightest diamond he had ever seen, but she would obviously require a light hand and a gentle rider. Three or four witticisms crossed his mind, but each of these he eventually discarded in favor of a more serious remark.

"I don't know if you realize it, ma'am, but you truly did have a narrow escape." He paused, but she said nothing. "You could have been thrown out of the carriage," he added. "You could have been killed."

She looked at him then. "Don't you think I know that?" she answered in a low, repressed voice. "Do I look like a fool to you?"

Half-peeved and half curious by the response, Lord Andrew tried a different approach. "No, my dear ma'am, you *look* like a goddess," he said lightly. "Surely you cannot be unaware of that." But what was meant to be teasing won no response from the lady.

"So you accuse me of vanity, my lord. How very noble."

"Good God, you're as prickly as a gorse bush, aren't you?" He smiled slightly. "Or a porcupine, more like."

"I use what defenses I have," she replied. "I think that is fair."

He slowed his horses a little and surveyed her with growing interest. "What makes you think you need them? Do I look like a villain to you?"

"What does a villain look like?" she responded, quite levelly. "Missing teeth? No hair? The word *scoundrel* emblazoned on his chest?"

"Well, ma'am, I haven't *seen* one who looks as you

90

describe." He glanced down at her, a laugh in his eye. "For argument's sake, let us assume you are correct. I am a villain and a scoundrel, despite the fact that I have somehow managed to retain my teeth. What next?"

Angeline looked a little disconcerted. "I haven't the faintest notion what you wish me to say."

"Say anything you like," he said promptly. "I must listen since I can't run away. Ask me a question."

Angeline's jaw tightened. "Very well. How old are you?"

"Thirty," he replied, glancing down at her with a slight frown. "Pray continue."

"And where did you live when you were ten?"

"An odd question," he said. "In Dorset, mostly, when I wasn't at school. The Isle of Wight during the summers. Why?"

He found her shrug as unconvincing as her reply. "No reason. This is a foolish game we play."

"What makes you call it a game?" he said curiously.

Those gorgeous violet-blue eyes swiveled to his face. "Isn't that what it is?" she said cuttingly. "The Carisbrookes have always enjoyed games, have they not?"

"Now what the devil is that supposed to mean?" he demanded.

"It means, my lord, that I am no milk-and-water miss to be taken in by a few blandishments. Nor am I impressed by your pedigree."

His eyes narrowed. "Good God, I should hope not! Upon my honor, you don't mince words, do you?"

She stared down at her clenched hands. "I beg you will mind your horses, sir. We are going far too slowly."

Lord Andrew shook his head in confusion. "What the deuce have I done to incur your displeasure?"

"You and your family represent everything I most deplore," she answered frostily.

"Is that so?" he said in astonishment. "Well, let me tell you something, Mrs. Greaves. I didn't have to rescue you just now. I did so because I saw a woman in distress, a woman I had every reason to suppose might be grateful for my assistance. I shall not make that mistake again, I assure you."

When Angeline made no answer, his voice turned scornful. "If you think to arouse my interest with this ploy, you've got the wrong sow by the ear. The matchmaking mamas have already tried every trick. Marriage is the furthest thing from my mind, my girl."

"I am very well aware of that," she lashed back. "Carisbrookes never marry beneath them, do they? All the world knows that." Despite the fury in her tone, she seemed to shudder.

They turned into Upper Grosvenor Street and rolled to an abrupt halt in front of number twelve. Lord Andrew sat immobile while his groom assisted Angeline out of the carriage.

"Do not bother to thank me," he said coldly. "But if it suits your fancy, ma'am, I beg you will inform Mrs. Edwards that I will wait upon her Monday next to discuss the purchase of her phaeton."

"I shall do so." Angeline's reply was equally chilly.

His face set in a haughty expression, Lord Andrew Carisbrooke sent his grays the signal to continue. The phaeton rolled forward over the cobbles, turned down Park Street, and disappeared.

Angeline stared after him for a long time, then turned and walked into the house.

Chapter Seven

Monday proved damp and chilly, so that when Lord Andrew Carisbrooke mounted the puddled steps of her house, Stacia was curled up near the fire with a book in her lap. She had been anticipating his arrival—Angeline having dutifully delivered his lordship's message—but to suggest that Stacia was cast aflutter by the honor would have been a vast exaggeration. Except for a visit from Marco she had been alone the entire day, and that brief visit had effectively shattered her peace. During the hour since Marco's departure she had done nothing but stare into the flames, brooding over her brother's alarming genius for losing money. Her worried expression did not completely abate when Lord Andrew was announced.

Being aware of the slight awkwardness in having no female in attendance, she made sure to explain Angeline's absence to her aristocratic caller. Mrs. Greaves, she told Lord Andrew, was suffering from a sick headache and had retired to her bed for the remainder of the day.

For a reason not quite clear in her mind, Stacia had expected Lord Andrew to exhibit concern, but beyond a response of the most perfunctory nature he displayed no visible interest in the state of Angeline's health. Perhaps he had not been as taken with the girl as Stacia had thought, for not only did he appear completely indifferent, his expression grew almost chilly when Angeline's name was mentioned. As soon as the topic of conversation switched, however, he grew animated, so that after a few minutes Stacia found him as entertaining as before.

The phaeton, he reported with a smile, had been purchased without a snag and was soon to be delivered to the same mews in which she kept her traveling coach. Stacia found the ensuing half-hour delightful, Lord Andrew being so obliging as to aim the full brunt of his charm in her direction. She could not help but be flattered by his attentions, for in her entire life no one had ever exerted himself to such a degree in her behalf. His behavior was too correct to qualify as flirtation, yet he managed to make her feel attractive and amusing, and that was very nice indeed after the way Derek Deveaux had treated her.

After he took his leave, Stacia sat quietly for a spell, ruminating upon the complexities of human nature. How strange, she thought, that Angeline had taken his lordship into such a dislike. Angeline did not care for Mr. Deveaux either, but, oddly, her dislike for Lord Andrew seemed much stronger and more focused.

Stacia sighed and glanced regretfully toward the rain-streaked windows. She had hoped the rain would cease before five o'clock, but at this stage of the day it hardly seemed likely. Lady Crackenthorpe had invited her for a drive in her barouche at the fashionable hour, but this was evidently not to be.

To escape her worries, Stacia rested her head on the back of the settee and began to reconstruct her favorite daydream, the one in which she was at a ball and all the gentlemen were vying to dance with her. Her dance card was full, and each of her partners was wearing the same maudlin expression that Marco wore when he looked at Angeline. Best of all, hovering in the background was that one special gentleman, the one who stood by the wall and gazed at her with his heart and soul in his eyes.

Stacia frowned suddenly. Until today this dream lover

94

had always been blurred and indistinct, but somewhere along the line her subconscious had filled in the haze. He now had a face and name, as well as the most unforgettable pair of green eyes she was ever likely to see.

Derek.

Her spirits sank as she reflected on the unsuitability of the choice. *He* would never look at her in such a way, she thought forlornly. But the notion was mesmerizing and for a few moments she allowed herself to play with it, to imagine that handsome, sardonic face softened with longing and passion. In her mind's eye she pictured the green eyes filled with tenderness, the hard lips curving into what she fancied would be an utterly heart-stopping smile. And in her imagination she met his gaze across the ballroom and knew his desires, knew exactly how it would feel when he held her in his arms and pressed his mouth to hers . . .

Stacia's eyes flew open as she realized the path her thoughts were taking. Physical love was something upon which she had never dwelled, but one could scarcely live in the country without being aware of certain facts. She knew very well that mating was something that all creatures did, but somehow when it came to human beings her imagination had always fallen short. When she was fifteen, Mrs. Hanson had told her that men had "needs" and women didn't, and that it was best for Stacia to understand this *just in case.* The warning had been uttered in such ominous accents that Stacia's curiosity had been roused. In case of what? she had longed to ask the reticent housekeeper, whose firmly sealed lips revealed the futility of such a question. In case she ever escaped Ashcroft Manor long enough to meet someone of the masculine gender?

"Oh, blast the odious man anyway," she muttered. Very much annoyed with herself, Stacia jumped to her feet and began to pace.

It ought to have been Lord Andrew she put into her fantasy, or even that handsome Mr. Matravers. She had met Mr. Matravers at the lending library the other day and had liked him well enough to accept his invitation to walk in the Park. And at least *he* had the courtesy to come to call, she thought indignantly, which is more that Mr. Deveaux had ever done.

Indeed, what had Derek ever done to deserve her notice? Oh, she was willing to concede that he had arranged for her dinner to be delivered to her hotel room, but knocking that man Croxton to the ground had been completely unnecessary. And why had he bothered to do so when he so obviously held her in contempt? It made no sense at all.

As much as she would have liked to mull the whole thing over a few dozen more times, Stacia had more pressing worries than Derek. Marco had requested that she lend him another four thousand pounds, and against her better judgment she had yielded to his pleas. Since his departure, however, she had been wondering whether she had made a mistake. It was easy enough for Marco to say he loved her and if their situations were reversed he would do the same for her, but their situations were *not* reversed!

Crossing to the fireplace, she sank down and stared into a blaze as restless as her emotions. In the end, of course, she knew she would give him the money, but the whole business made her extremely uneasy. She had always believed she would do anything for Marco, but this wanton gambling away of a fortune—*her* fortune—could scarcely be called a necessary sacrifice. She had to make him stop.

Despite the fire's heat she shivered, her hand sweeping across her brow in a gesture that was all at once desolate. Marco was the only person in the world who loved her, the only person on whom she could rely. He was all the family she had. If he asked for more money, would she have the strength to deny his request? And would she lose his love if she did?

* * *

Some time later a sound from outside the house made her glance toward the window. Surely it could not be Marco again? Weary of her own company, Stacia rose and went to look out. Directly below, a curricle-and-pair stood alone in the street, but its driver had already disembarked and she could see no one but the groom standing guard over a pair of black geldings. Was it someone for her?

A moment later sounds from the ground floor confirmed the fact that another caller had arrived. Feeling absurdly pleased, Stacia smoothed her hair and ran through a mental list of her new acquaintances. She had enjoyed a pleasant chat with a Mrs. and Miss Cotleigh in the lending library; she had also met a very friendly woman named Mrs. Lempster and her two daughters in Hyde Park. It might very well be either of them, for they had both promised to call. And then, of course, there was Lady Crackenthorpe, who might have taken it into her head to drive out despite the weather. But no, she remembered suddenly, only gentlemen drove in curricles. Then perhaps it was Mr. Matravers.

Stacia's nerves did pirouettes as both butler and visitor mounted the stairs. She knew her butler's dignified shuffle, but the caller's tread was firm and confident, and did not sound like Mr. Matravers. No, it belonged to some other gentleman, one who was large, sure-footed, and perhaps a trace impatient. And then Challow announced him, and Stacia stood quite still, gazing warily into Derek Deveaux's mocking green eyes.

"Good afternoon, ma'am."

The politeness of the greeting was belied by an appraising expression as he sauntered forward and bowed. He was simply dressed yet looked superb, his dark blue coat fitting his shoulders perfectly, his doeskin trousers clinging to his thighs and hips. He was completely and shatteringly masculine, with a presence that eclipsed everything and everyone that Stacia had ever known.

His dark brows climbed at her failure to reply. "You

97

look astonished to see me," he said. "Is it really so surprising that I should call?"

Stacia swallowed. "It is, actually. After the way you behaved I can think of no reason why you should visit me, Mr. Deveaux."

"Can't you?" he murmured. "I can."

He moved closer, his dark head tilting to look down at her intently. "I should have come sooner," he added. His hand went out to touch her arm in the exact place where he had gripped it so tightly at Tattersall's. Stacia froze, unable to move, her eyes on the faint grooves at either side of his uncompromising mouth.

"I hurt you the other day." He spoke the words softly, his thumb brushing the area where, beneath her long-sleeved gown, finger-shaped bruises smudged her flesh. "I came to apologize. It was not . . . intentional."

Awareness rippled through Stacia at the seductive contact, breaking whatever spell had kept her paralyzed. She took a small, outraged step backward, at the same time recalling Lady Crackenthorpe's words.

Women find him fascinating. Had she meant it as a warning?

"And that is why you came?" she asked in a haughty voice. "To beg forgiveness for your intolerable conduct?"

The twist of his lips did not quite qualify as a smile. "Not entirely, ma'am. May I sit? Or do you mean to throw me out upon my ear?"

"Yes, you may sit," she answered. "As it happens, I was about to ring for tea. I will not lie and say you are welcome, but you may join me if you like." Except for the drumming of her heart Stacia was in command of herself now, and demonstrated this by giving him a straight, toneless look.

His expression now intensely sardonic, Derek inclined his head, yet he had enough courtesy to wait until she was seated before disposing his tall frame onto the settee.

He cast a look about the small but elegant sitting room.

"You've settled in, I see. How do you like London?" The commonplace inquiry contained an oddly challenging note.

"I like it very well," she retorted, on her mettle. "Do *you* like it?"

His gaze flashed back to her face, his eyes narrowed slightly. "Yes, I like it well enough," he said shortly. "I've an estate in Suffolk which commands a great deal of my attention, but I come down to the city occasionally."

There was an awkward silence.

"I've come from Lancashire," she offered.

"Yes, I know." He draped a negligent arm along the back of the settee. "My godmother told me about you. You're Travis Ashcroft's niece and heiress." He studied her closely, his voice noncommittal. "Odd he left nothing to your brother."

"There is nothing in the least odd about it," she said defensively. "Marco has my father's estate and title." Without knowing why, she added, "Nor does my brother begrudge me my fortune, if that is what you are implying."

"I'm not implying anything." His green eyes fixed on her a shade less casually. "But if rumor is correct, Mrs. Edwards, your brother has lost money in half the clubs in London. Are his pockets as well-lined as that? Gambling is an expensive and dangerous habit. I have good reason to know."

Stacia's hands twitched at his mention of Marco's losses. "I would not dream of answering such an impertinent question," she retorted, "nor can I think of any reason why it should concern you."

"Ah, but it does," he said, an odd laziness in his tone.

"Then I suggest you ask him yourself."

"Perhaps I will." He shifted slightly. "Lord Andrew tells me your brother ran a curricle into a lamppost yesterday. Your companion was a passenger."

"Again, I cannot see why that would interest you," she said coldly.

99

Beneath the heavy brows, his eyes gleamed. "And I can only assure you that it does."

They each fell silent as Challow entered with the tea tray, deposited it upon a large ottoman, and ceremoniously poured them each a cup. Accepting hers, Stacia took a small sip, at the same time noticing the look which Derek gave his own cup of steaming black liquid.

"You don't like tea," she observed. "Would you prefer something else? I haven't done much toward stocking the cellar, but I can offer you some sherry."

She thought he looked mildly startled. "No, but I thank you for the offer, ma'am." He smiled then, a real smile that crinkled his eyes and made him appear years younger. "Save your sherry for my next visit."

Dismissing her butler with a nod, Stacia latched onto these last words. "I am still unsure what the purpose of *this* visit is, Mr. Deveaux." She sipped again at her tea, and added incisively, "Is it merely to pry into things which are none of your affair?"

Her waspish remark failed to rile him, yet some other emotion flickered across his face and his smile vanished.

"On the contrary," he baffled her by replying, "I never pry into things which aren't my affair—in one way or another." Ignoring her look, he proceeded with what she was beginning to think of as an inquisition. "Drew tells me the arrangements for your phaeton are complete. So now that you have it, tell me, do you have any notion how to drive it?"

"Not yet," she admitted, with growing resentment, "but I assure you I am quite capable of learning. You look skeptical, Mr. Deveaux, but I've seen many ladies handling even more daring conveyances than mine. I daresay I can handle a simple park phaeton."

His short laugh mocked her heated riposte. "And who is going to teach you, my sweet? Your ham-fisted brother? He scarcely sounds the ideal tutor."

"And I suppose *you* are?" She threw the words at him

with flashing eyes and heaving bosom, as angered by his form of address as by the insult to Marco.

"Let's just say I've never driven into a lamppost, drunk or sober," he said smoothly. "So I've come to offer you my services, Mrs. Edwards. *That* is the other reason for my visit."

She was thrown completely out of stride. "You are offering to . . . to teach me how to drive my phaeton?" she stuttered.

His brows lifted. "That was my meaning," he retorted in a very gentle voice. "Unless you require my tutelage in some other domain?"

Even to one as naive as Stacia, the innuendo was clear.

"Get out." Surging furiously to her feet, she pointed a trembling finger toward the drawing-room door. "I refuse to sit here and be insulted, Mr. Deveaux. Please leave this house immediately."

Derek rose, but instead of heading for the door he came over and captured her wrists. "It was not my intention to insult you," he said with a docility that seemed utterly foreign to his nature. "Please forgive me. I should not have said what I did. It was a jest, a jest that fell flat on its hapless and miserable face. I apologize."

"Please leave," she repeated, more out of pride than of any real wish for him to do so.

"But I haven't finished my tea," he protested. "You could not be so cruel."

She glared up at him, knowing herself a prisoner in his grasp. "You haven't even tasted your tea! And I should not forgive you, Mr. Deveaux. You are behaving badly and you know it." As he drew her infinitesimally closer, she tried to pull away. "Let go of me! I am not some common tart you can kiss and cuddle when you will it."

Derek's lips twitched. "One need not be a tart to be kissed," was his incorrigible answer. "I know a great many ladies who like it very well. Some of them even like to be, er, cuddled."

101

Stacia's cheeks flamed. "Well, I am not one of them!" she snapped. "I wish you will stop this flummery and let go of me!"

He was holding her so close the tips of her breasts grazed his waistcoat.

"What flummery?" he asked in a seductive voice. "I've done nothing yet. Nothing to warrant such vehemence, at any rate. But I'd like to very much. Would you like me to, Stacia?" His manner was coaxing, his gaze fastened persuasively on her mouth.

Stacia could scarcely breath. With a stab of alarm, she realized how near she was to saying yes. As appealing as Lord Andrew had been, Derek's sexual charm was far stronger, and far, far more dangerous. It pulled at her like a magnet, beguiling her to forgive him, to press against him, to humiliate herself by offering him her lips. Instinctively, she knew that with the smallest encouragement he would kiss her and more, and a small, lonely part of her ached to know how it would feel. But then that contemptuous expression would return to his eyes, the look that was sure to mean that she was nothing in comparison to other women he had known. All her old insecurities raised their ugly heads, and, appalled by her own weakness, she gave a yank so sharp he let go.

"If I had a fancy to be pawed," she gasped, "the last person I would choose to do it is you! As far as I am concerned, you are nothing but a vulgar libertine with an inflated opinion of himself. I'd as lief be mauled by a . . . a pig than be kissed by you." Stifling a sob, she added, "You are no better than that beastly man at Tattersall's and I wish to heaven you would leave."

Derek stepped back. "Very well," he said, his voice cold as winter ice. "Forgive me, then, if for a moment I thought otherwise. There was that in your face that led me to—" He broke off, silent for a moment. "In truth, I am nothing like Sir Joshua, Mrs. Edwards. I hope to prove that to you eventually."

Stacia's legs were shaking. "Based on your conduct

thus far, I sincerely doubt your ability to do so, Mr. Deveaux. You seem very much like him to me."

To her astonishment, he seemed to flinch, though later she would wonder if she imagined that infinitesimal jerk or the stiffness in the muscles of his jaw.

Still, it was enough. Her self-doubt struck hard and ruthless, the eternal distrust in her own instincts sinking its claws into her ever-foundering confidence. Perhaps she had been too severe, she worried. He'd obviously thought she was willing and as Mrs. Hanson said, men had their needs. What Mrs. Hanson apparently hadn't known was that women had needs too. Stacia had been convinced of this for some time, and when Derek had held her so close she'd known it for certain. Had her shameless longing shown in her face? Is that what he had been about to say? If so, it was infamous to place all the blame on him.

Determined to play fair, she said in a trembling voice, "Perhaps, Mr. Deveaux, if you made the least effort to be nice to me—"

"Nice?" he repeated. "And what does that mean, little widow? To sit here all agape and feed your vanity with pretty compliments? Is that what you want? Do you expect me to say that you are lovely and desirable, and then keep ten feet away?"

Rendered practically speechless, Stacia stared up at him in hurt and bafflement. "No, I don't wish you to tell me lies, Mr. Deveaux. It's obvious you don't like me and"—when his expresson changed she went on hurriedly—"and I assure you the feeling is quite mutual. As for your offer to teach me to drive, I am sure you must wish to withdraw it, so—"

"No," he said curtly. "My offer still stands, if you choose to accept. If you've a talent for the ribbons, I will teach you to drive well enough to cast all the other females into the shade."

Stacia eyed him doubtfully. "That is generous of you, Mr. Deveaux. After what has just passed between us

103

. . . I'm not sure whether I should or could accept."

He shrugged, evidently thinking her objection foolish. "Think it over," he advised. "As for my not liking you, ma'am, you have it the wrong way around. There's a great many things I like about you."

"Including my fortune?" Stacia could have bitten her tongue off, but the words were already out.

He gave her a peculiar look. "Including your fortune," he agreed.

Later, back at his lodgings in Bruton Street, Derek scowlingly reassessed the results of the interview. Well, he needed no one to tell him he'd botched the whole bloody business. He'd told her the truth. It hadn't been diplomatic, but then diplomacy had never been his long suit. In fact, anything to do with tact or prevarication had always been completely alien to his nature. Tiptoeing around what he wished to say was impossibly difficult; he could neither appreciate nor simulate such delicacy.

He slouched in his old leather chair, one booted foot propped against the corner of his desk. On the other hand, he reflected, though the encounter had been more battle than banter it had been no waste either. He'd learned even more than he'd hoped about Stacia Edwards.

The first thing he'd learned was that, of the two breeds of widow, she was undoubtedly of the proper and respectable variety. In fact, if he hadn't known she was a widow, he might even have said she was a virgin. But there weren't too many virgin widows wandering around these days, especially not ones as attractive as Stacia Edwards. Even when the husbands proved inadequate in their conjugal endeavors, he thought cynically, the majority of women usually found an accommodating replacement. He'd been the accommodating replacement enough times to know.

The second thing he'd discovered was that she'd

known all about her brother's gambling losses. Shaking his head in disgust, Derek reached across a pile of papers for his low tumbler of whiskey. Generally speaking, he didn't give a bloody rush if the brother lost his inheritance at the gambling tables, but there were other considerations.

For instance, whose money was he losing?

He took a large gulp of whiskey, absently sloshing it around his mouth as he thought. There would always be country greenhorns who came to town and lost every penny they had in the Pall Mall hells. Some even shot themselves as a result. Nine times out of ten the poor fools had fallen prey to some damned ivory turner, a person whose black-hearted purpose was to lead the Gullible into the Dens of Vice to be fleeced of everything but the shirts on their backs. He despised such practices even as he pitied their victims, but his altruistic inclinations did not run to bailing them out. He hoped the rumors regarding Sir Marco Ashcroft were false, though they were probably accurate if Stacia's reaction was anything to go by. The young ass had obviously been dumping his troubles in his sister's lap.

Derek's frown deepened. Under normal circumstances he'd not have mentioned it to her either; however, if what he suspected was true, she ought to be warned. He'd always thought it ironic that the men who incurred the debts refused to tell their families until it was too late, never mind the fact that half the time it was the money their wives brought into the marriage that they were losing. The prevailing opinion was that the settling of debts of honor was best left to gentlemen; ladies did not discuss such things and were better kept in blissful ignorance of anything dealing with money. Well, in a way he could understand the convenience of the attitude. His own mother had made his father's life a living hell after she'd learned he was gambling.

Derek tossed off the remainder of his drink, pushing aside the unpleasant memories as the fire burned a track down his throat. Immediately, his thoughts flew back to Stacia. He could easily envisage her delicate features and delectable form, while the sparks that flew from those misleadingly soft eyes nearly took his breath away. The girl certainly had spirit, he mused. He liked that in a woman, though he was singularly unthrilled at the aspersions she had cast upon him. To be likened to that whoremongering Croxton was more an insult than she could ever have realized; the fact, however, that she had a sharp tongue was no new discovery.

No, the third thing he had learned about Stacia was that, despite her almost prim respectability, she'd wanted him to kiss her. In fact, she needed kissing very badly. He was, after all, familiar enough with women's bodies to recognize the signs. And there was no doubt in his mind that he wanted to be the one who did it. In fact, he'd come within an amesace of doing so despite her protestations.

Perhaps he *would* marry her, he mused. His sweeping statement about "mewling little heiresses" hardly seemed applicable to such a soft little spitfire. He couldn't imagine being bored with her, though of course there was plenty of time for that malady to develop.

He sighed deeply. Very likely she was just as spoiled and foolish and shallow as every other society twit—but she *was* rich. He'd verified that through his godmother.

There was one other rather amazing particular to the entire issue. It struck Derek at the exact moment he reached to pour himself another whiskey, and was startling enough to make his hand pause in the air six inches above his glass.

For the first time in his life, the notion of binding himself to a woman in legal wedlock did not seem completely and utterly unendurable.

Chapter Eight

"I warned you about him, didn't I?"

Having listened to Stacia's account of Derek Deveaux's visit, Angeline studied the mingling of emotions in her employer's face with less dispassion than usual. Until now Stacia had been an enigma to her, but where Derek Deveaux was concerned the girl was as transparent as glass.

"It's because you're a widow," she added pityingly. "He knows you have tasted the so-called pleasures of the marriage bed. Men think women miss that sort of thing. They think we cannot resist the temptation they offer."

With a surge of surprise, Angeline discovered that she was trying to be kind. It struck her as odd, to feel this tug of sympathy for one of her own sex; even odder, she was actually growing fond of Stacia.

In fact, thus far the suspicion that she'd been hired for an ulterior purpose appeared to be groundless. Stacia Edwards was ridiculously generous, but her generosity seemed to be without design, inspired simply by good nature and a genuine compassion for Angeline's needs. She had given Angeline a month's salary in advance and five new gowns of a finer quality than she had ever owned in her life. And she even seemed willing to look upon her brother's infatuation with a benign eye, and *that* was truly unusual!

"Well, I *must* learn to drive my phaeton properly," Stacia went on in a reasonable tone. "Else there is no sense having it. And I do think Mr. Deveaux is right about Marco. My brother is a bruising rider, but put him into anything with wheels and"—she made a resigned gesture—"well, you know what happened. Of course there is Papa's coachman. I suppose I could ask Old Sam to teach me. . . ."

Angeline cocked her head. "But you don't want that, do you? You are looking for a reason to accept Mr. Deveaux's offer."

Stacia's eyes were troubled. "Am I? Perhaps that's so. I don't know how it is possible to be so furious with the man and at the same time so . . . so . . ."

"Fascinated?" put in Angeline dryly. "Therein lies the danger, ma'am. Some men have that quality. They're like flaming candles, while we are the poor fluttering moths who fly too close." Beneath the calm in her face, there was a ripple of pain. "The nearer you go, the more your wings are singed."

Stacia shivered at the metaphor. "You are so cynical, Angeline. What made you this way?"

Angeline felt the familiar welling of bitterness in her chest. "Life has not been kind to my family, Mrs. Edwards."

Instead of accepting the brief answer as she had in the past, Stacia moved to the end of the settee closest to Angeline's chair. "Would you care to talk about it?" she asked. "Perhaps it might help."

A thin layer of Angeline's reserve melted at the offer. "In truth it would be a relief to speak," she said slowly. "I have not done so because I felt you could not understand. I felt, too, that you might terminate my employment if you learned the truth about my history. I believe I misjudged you in that, ma'am." She paused, drawing a deep breath. "I told you I was an adventuress. That's not quite true. Adventures hold no allure for me. All I want is a home, and to feel safe and to be respected

108

by those around me. And despite what I have said to you about men there are even times when I would like a husband of my own."

Stacia nodded. "And you should have one. You are too beautiful to live alone all your life."

"Too beautiful." Angeline repeated the words bitterly. "Like my mother. I told you already that my mother was a vicar's daughter. She lived in the village of Exbury, in the southernmost part of Hampshire near the Channel. She was promised to the local squire, a gentle man who I think must have loved her in his way. But she was too beautiful, and rumor of her extraordinary beauty spread for miles." She paused significantly. "Eventually, it even drifted across the Solent to the Isle of Wight."

"The Isle of Wight!" Stacia echoed the words sharply. "But that is where . . ."

Angeline nodded. "The Duke of Wight was a rake of the first order, Mrs. Edwards. My mother met the present duke's father along the side of the road as she was walking into the village. She refused his advances and he left, but he came back a day later. My mother was completely innocent, Mrs. Edwards, and the duke was an attractive man. He seduced her in a field of clover, she told me, then climbed on his horse and rode off without a backward glance. It was only the once, you understand, but once was enough. Two months later my mother found she was with child."

Stacia looked aghast. "What on earth did she do?"

"She confessed the truth to her father, who in turn went to the squire. The squire was willing to wed her immediately and give the child his name, but I'm sure the local folk must have realized the truth. Unfortunately Squire Lambourn died a year after the marriage. My mother was with child again by that time. The squire's, of course." She eyed Stacia's face and was amazed to see no horror in her gaze. "You are wondering which child I was."

"You are not . . . the duke's daughter, are you?"

Angeline paused for several seconds, toying with her options. Then she let out a sigh. "No," she confessed. "My half sister, Sarah, was the result of the duke's seduction. Sarah died when I was eight. My mother remarried, again with unhappy results. He was a sea captain and a drunkard, but she loved him, God knows why. He died at sea. When I was fourteen my mother succumbed to an inflammation of the lungs and I went to live with Squire Lambourn's sister, a spinster in Southhampton. Unfortunately, she was one of those dreadful people who are only happy when everyone else is miserable. She said my mother got what she deserved. She was glad she was dead."

"Oh, my poor Angeline!"

Angeline smiled at Stacia's distress. "You see why I am bitter? My life with my aunt was one of drudgery, but even that I could have borne. It is this wretched face of mine." She gestured. "My aunt hated me even more than she'd hated my mother. I was very stupid. It took me a long time to realize her hatred sprang from sheer jealousy. She used to slap me, just to see my cheek turn red.

"When I was seventeen I ran away. I had some money saved and was willing to do anything but prostitute myself. I won't bore you with the details of a long, tedious story, but I will tell you that I did eventually find honest work with an eccentric woman who painted portraits in her leisure. She hired me as her housekeeper and part-time model, and for a while the situation seemed ideal." Despite Angeline's desire to remain impassive, a trace of sarcasm crept into her voice. "That lasted until her suitor, a local landowner of respectable lineage and prurient interests, attempted to rape me. She prevented him and even forgave me for 'enticing' him, as she phrased it, but her forgiveness had a price. She'd grown tired of painting only my face, she said. She wanted to paint all of me, without my clothes, and in what I can only call immodest poses. It was then that I made the decision to leave."

Stacia shook her head in disbelief. "Good God, I don't blame you! But why London?"

Angeline decided to be brutally frank. "To be honest, ma'am, I was going to pretend to be my half sister and put in a claim with the Carisbrookes. I'd discovered that the current duke resides in Grosvenor Square during the Season. He wouldn't have received me, of course but he might have given me money. I'd be such an embarrassment, you see."

"But of course you changed your mind."

Angeline smiled at Stacia's matter-of-factness, as though such a dishonest act could not possibly be carried out. Her employer was naively prepared to give credit where none was deserved, an attitude Angeline would normally have derided. Instead, she found such blind faith endearing.

"Yes, but not for the reason you believe," she said. Her dark lashes lowered. "My pride was actually what interfered. And I began to realize that he likely wouldn't believe me anyway because I've no proof. And even if he did, he likely wouldn't care two straws. The old duke's by-blows are probably strewn all over England."

"What a contemptible man he must have been!" Stacia said indignantly. "To father a child so casually and then to go off as though it were nothing! It is the act of a fiend." Then her mobile expression changed, shifting back to perplexity. "But wait, Angeline, you have not explained how or when you met your husband, Captain Greaves."

Suddenly ashamed by the number of lies she had told, Angeline flushed. "There was never any Captain Greaves," she said with difficulty, "any more than there was any Wilfred. They were both sheer fabrication. I came to London on the common stage and . . . I have never been wed."

By the following afternoon the sun finally broke through the clouds, a happy circumstance that prompted

111

Mr. Matravers to visit and to beg the honor of Stacia's company for a drive in the Park. Though she was in no mood to talk, Stacia accepted the invitation, partly because she had been chafing to get out and partly because the gentleman seemed so nonthreatening. In itself the drive proved enjoyable, but her thoughts were so taken with recent occurrences that she found herself replying automatically to his determined efforts at flirtation. Afterward, she could not recall their conversation, except for the moment when she'd realized he was talking about Derek.

". . . I could scarce credit my eyes when he knocked poor Croxton into the dust," he remarked. "The Deveauxes are all such a crotchety bunch. Jettington is no better, though a good sort of a fellow when you get to know him."

It was his first sentence that caught Stacia's attention. "You mean you were at Tattersall's when—" She blushed deeply.

Mr. Matravers patted her hand and smiled. "Yes, ma'am, but I beg you will not regard it. *I* knew you were a lady the moment I clapped eyes on you. In fact, it was when you hit poor Croxton on the nose that my heart was smote. You are a woman in a thousand, ma'am, and I adore you!"

"Now Mr. Matravers," she said reprovingly, "you must not talk like that. It is most improper and I do not like it."

At once he'd professed himself corrected, apologized profusely, and then gone on flirting with her for the remainder of the drive. She had no idea what she'd said in response, but since he'd driven away with a smile on his face there was obviously no cause for worry. There was enough on her mind without that.

Stacia was tired. She had not slept well during the night, for the more she'd tried to relax, the more her problems had seemed to magnify. Her thoughts had spun for hours at full tilt, revolving from Derek to Marco to

Angeline to herself with dizzying, exhausting incessancy. And when she'd finally slept, she'd dreamed that Derek was seducing her in a field of clover while a woman in black painted their portrait. It had left a bad taste in her mouth.

And after all that, the only definite conclusion she'd been able to reach was that something needed to be done to provide for Angeline's future. Some action *had* to be taken, for the girl was of the gentry and by rights should be given the chance to make a respectable marriage. Moreover, Angeline's extraordinary beauty made her even more vulnerable than she would otherwise be. She clearly needed a husband to protect her, and (contrary to Stacia's initial hopes) Marco was definitely not the one to do it.

With abrupt decision, Stacia made up her mind to visit Lady Crackenthorpe. Likely her ladyship would have some notion what could and should be done for Angeline, and at the same time, Stacia could discover what Derek's godmother thought about her godson's offer to teach her to drive.

As she ought to have predicted, Lady Crackenthorpe deemed the offer generous. "You see, my dear? Derek is not such an ogre, is he? In fact, he has some very fine qualities." She said it fondly, while refilling both their teacups. "In my opinion, you would be wise to let him instruct you. Derek was offered membership in the Four-In-Hand club, though of course he turned it down. That sort of thing is not at all his style, I'm afraid, but it does show you how skilled he is. Only the very best whips are elected."

"I see," Stacia murmured. Sipping her tea, she suddenly recalled the rest of what Mr. Matravers had said about Derek. "Tell me, ma'am, do you know of someone named Jettington? Can you tell me who he is?"

To her surprise, Lady Crackenthorpe seemed reluctant to answer. "Jettington is the peerage name of the Deveaux barony. The person to whom you refer is

Rupert Deveaux, Derek's uncle. He is . . . not a good man, I am sorry to say. At present, he holds the title to which Derek is heir presumptive, but his many indiscretions and excessive lifestyle have done nothing to dignify his rank. Thus far he has no son of his own, though poor Lady Jettington has tried repeatedly to supply him with one—to the detriment of her health, I might add. It is very sad. Fortunately he is in Paris at the moment so you will not be obliged to meet him." She paused. "I am sorry, my dear, but this subject distresses me so . . ."

"Then I apologize for bringing it up," Stacia said instantly. "Tell me, ma'am, shall we be able to drive out later today? I have already done so once today and enjoyed it excessively! The sky is so blue and the birds are singing!"

"By all means!" agreed Lady Crackenthorpe, catching her enthusiasm. "I shall send my barouche around to your house at a quarter to five. Will you bring Mrs. Greaves?"

"As to that, ma'am, I have been meaning to discuss Angeline with you." Setting down her teacup, Stacia proceeded to outline the plan which had been forming in her head.

Lady Crackenthorpe listened with a thoughtful air. "I think that is very generous of you, my dear, but I want you to be sure. Once you embark upon this scheme, you know, there will be no going back."

"I understand that, ma'am."

"Then I think it will serve the purpose very well. And by the bye, I mean to ask Derek to escort us. I do so enjoy his company. I trust you do not object—?"

"Not at all," answered Stacia in an uncertain voice.

Lady Winifred Deveaux tapped her foot and glanced at the ormolu clock upon the mantelshelf. She was more impatient than anxious; doubtless Sir Cuthbert had either forgotten the time or was absorbed in perfecting his neckcloth. Or both, she thought, on a faintly exasperated sigh. If one wished to espouse a dedicated dandy, it seemed one had to put up with a great deal. She was loath to admit it to others, but the man really was the most dreadful slow-top in existence. The plumpness of his pockets made up for it, of course, and in Lady Winifred's book, birth and wealth were everything. And there was no denying he was good-natured, in a dull sort of way, which was more than she could say about her first husband.

Her marriage to Richard Deveaux had been arranged by her parents, the Earl and Countess of Worthmere, and though Richard had been the younger son, they had deemed the match adequate for their third and plainest daughter. Winifred had been willing enough to marry the handsome Richard, but unfortunately Richard had taken her into immediate dislike. It had been, she recalled, a daunting and depressing way to begin a marriage. Her husband's attitude toward her had never altered, nor had he made any effort to conceal his feelings. He'd kept a mistress from the first, and had been disobliging enough to object when she'd filled the void in her life with frivolous pursuits and lavish entertainments. Worst of all, he'd been hypocrite enough to raise a dust when she'd taken a lover, a quiet man who'd given her, if not love, at least something nigh to it. It was the closest she had ever come to real happiness, and she blamed her own son for its ruination.

Her mind fluttered back to the time, so long ago, when five-year-old Derek had stumbled into her boudoir and seen them together. She had begged him to forget, but her hysterical threats and promises had served no purpose—the child had told his father anyway. Lady Winifred's lips twisted bitterly, but before she could nurse her grievance to its full height, she was brought back to the present by her butler's announcement of Sir Cuthbert's arrival.

115

Sir Cuthbert Duncan entered the room with his customary pavonine strut. In his usual fashion, he peered at her through his quizzing glass before speaking, surveying every detail of the costly (and as yet unpaid-for) ensemble she was wearing.

"Afternoon, m'dear. That's a very fetching shade of pink," he finally pronounced. "Very fetching indeed."

Next, as was also part of his usual routine, he wandered over to scrutinize the pristine folds of his cravat in the mirror above the fireplace. He touched the starched folds here and there, puffed out his chest, and said, "What a dashed fine couple we make, eh, Winifred?"

It was not his usual remark. Her heart beating fast, Lady Winifred pulled her lips into a fatuous smile.

"La, sir, what a charming thing to say when all the world knows that *you*, Sir Cuthbert, are quite unsurpassed in elegance." She pressed her hand to her bosom and said, "I vow I am quite giddy to hear you link our names!"

Fixing happily on her first statement, her swain nodded at his reflection. "'Tis true, ain't it? Y'know, Winifred, this arrangement took me over two hours to achieve, but, dash it, it was worth it! I mean, look at it! When it comes to fashion," he added, "I fancy Sir Cuthbert Duncan is slap up to the rig. And I fancy you could ask anyone in town and they would tell you the same."

"Indeed, you always look the first style of elegance," she agreed quickly. "Everyone says so. It is an honor to be seen in your company."

At this, the baronet turned, a crease between his brows. "Y'know, that boy of yours don't like me, Winifred."

"Derek?" Lady Winifred licked her lips. "Yes, Derek has always been difficult. But 'tis just his way—you must not regard it when he says disagreeable things. I daresay he is motivated by jealousy," she added resourcefully.

116

Sir Cuthbert's frown vanished. "Aye," he remarked, preening a little, "that's likely the case. Y'know, the young 'uns these days just ain't what we were. No quality. No manners. No style. Perhaps I ought to drop a hint in the boy's ear. Ought to let him know just how to go on."

Lady Winifred eyed him in horror. "Good gracious, you could not possibly be so stu—" She broke off, swallowed rapidly, and readjusted her expression. "Oh, my, just look at the time! We had better go now, sir, else we may as well not bother."

"Go?" Sir Cuthbert looked at her vaguely.

"To the Park," she reminded with indefatigable patience.

The Pink of the Ton clapped a hand to his brow. "What a memory you have, Winifred," he said admiringly. "By Jove, a woman like you is just what an absent-minded fellow like me needs."

True to her word, Lady Crackenthorpe's barouche joined the rest of the beau monde that day in its five o'clock junket toward Hyde Park. The collapsible top was down, affording its three passengers—Stacia, Angeline, and her ladyship—an unhampered view as they rolled along the Mayfair streets. Stacia's composure, however, was significantly imperiled by Derek's presence.

Indeed, they were sitting practically face to face, for he rode beside them on a large gray hack, and she and Angeline were occupying the rearward-facing seat. Of course, she reflected, he might have nudged his mount forward so that their eyes could not meet so easily, but no, Mr. Deveaux was perverse enough to keep the gray precisely abreast the barouche. And since pretending he was not there seemed ridiculous, Stacia instead took the opportunity to study him during an interval when his gaze was elsewhere.

Perhaps because they were not currently engaged in a

117

verbal skirmish, she could more fully appreciate his athletic form and the hawkish contours of his face. His nose had a patrician curve she found oddly pleasing, while his cheeks were lean, and his chin smooth but for a tiny, crescent-shaped scar. His mouth was as hard as always, yet somehow it did not look quite as set and rigid as she had sometimes seen it. And he was well-proportioned, she noted, with nicely shaped hands, and legs long enough to match the broad muscularity of his upper body. In addition, he sat his horse as though he'd spent his life in the saddle, controlling his mount effortlessly, his guidance virtually undetectable.

Though Stacia's inspection lasted but a few seconds, Derek's head swiveled just in time to intercept her look. One black brow arched in response, and his eyes delved hers just long enough to bring a tide of color to her cheeks. He knew she'd been looking him over, she realized in chagrin.

Nevertheless, as embarrassed as she was, she could not seem to tear her gaze from his. Their eyes linked in a manner that was almost physical, a bonding of mind, and of heart, and of the very air which separated them. Sounds faded—the clopping of horses' hooves, the rumble of wheels, the distraction of human voices—it all melted away, leaving Stacia floating in a disconnected sea with nothing to cling to but her all-consuming awareness of the man on the horse. And during those suspended seconds, she knew a surge of feminine self-assurance as old as time itself. He wanted her, his look said. He wanted her in a way that put a queer, butterfly flutter into the pit of her stomach.

Yet as soon as she looked away she was unsure. Had it simply been her well-developed imagination working overtime?

Feeling absurdly alone, Stacia gave herself a stern mental shake. Why would Derek want her, especially when someone like Angeline was within view? He had glanced at her companion at least seven times since they

118

had left Upper Grosvenor Street, and though his face held none of the callow bemusement Marco displayed, still, to expect him not to notice the other girl's beauty was ridiculous. After all, simply because he concealed his reaction did not mean the man was blind. And what were plain brown eyes and reddish hair compared with eyes the color of shimmering sapphires and hair as black as the midnight sky?

Stacia turned and stared at the passing trees, aware of the mixed-up, muddled state of her emotions. What was she to do? Winning Derek's respect was fast becoming the most important thing in her life, but there was more to it than that. To understand it and deal with it, she was going to have to sort it all out logically. It was the only way.

All right, then, so what specifically did she want?

Well, for a start, she pondered, she wanted him to regret all the uncivil things he had said and to apologize. She also wanted him to visit her, not because she was rich or because he thought she might kiss him, but because he found her company stimulating and her conversation satisfying. And she very much wished to see those hard lips curve in a genuine smile, a smile she could answer with a smile of her own, an expression of spontaneity and joy.

Engrossed, Stacia studied her fingers, feeling the gentle sway of the barouche as it rolled its way into the Park. And if all of this came to pass, she mused, would it be enough? Would she be satisfied? Lifting her head, she gazed intently at Derek, absorbing the aura of forcefulness that sat his shoulders like a mantle. And then the realization hit, spilling into her conscious mind like water through a break in a dam. She wanted more than an apology or a smile.

She wanted to conquer his heart.

Stacia's breath drew in sharply, the air assaulting her lungs in the searing shock of self-discovery. Was what she wanted possible? She had failed to win her father's love, a failure that had hurt so terribly that just remembering drove a fist of anguish into her chest. She fought the pain, breathing slowly, focusing on the clear spring day and the comforting sound of Lady Crackenthorpe's voice as she spoke with Angeline. Could she survive another rejection? What if her first impression of Derek had been right? What if his heart truly was as cold and unyielding as Papa's?

Casting him another swift glance, Stacia acknowledged that she had little choice in this matter. Her own heart demanded that she give him another chance. She would accept his offer to teach her to drive and see what transpired.

Lady Crackenthorpe's voice drew her from her reverie.

"An heiress always creates a stir," she remarked, addressing the issue she doubtless believed to be on Stacia's mind, "especially when she is as pretty as you. If we meet any of the patronesses of Almack's I shall be sure and introduce you, and *that*, my dear, should set the seal upon your social success. The rumors of your fortune have been circulating, so I daresay everyone will wish to make your acquaintance. And as for Mrs. Greaves—I beg your pardon, Derek?"

"I said nothing, ma'am. Pray continue your speech."

Derek's brusque tone perplexed Stacia. A moment before, she could have sworn he was at ease but now his posture was as stiff as buckram. Observing his unbending expression, Stacia's spirits plummeted. Did this man even possess a heart? Was her ambition hopeless?

"You have some objection to my being a social success, Mr. Deveaux?" she inquired. She made her voice pleasant, hoping he would respond in like manner, but all he did was shrug.

"By no means," he answered. "If that is all you desire, ma'am, I daresay your wish will be granted." The flippancy in his tone suggested he found such a wish unworthy of serious consideration.

"It is *one* of my desires," she responded with a hint of

120

frustration, "and I can see no reason why you should look so cross about it. It can hardly signify to you if people like me, can it?"

He cast her a sardonic look. "Wealth attracts false friends," he pointed out, "just as beauty attracts false lovers. I trust you and Mrs. Greaves can deal with that."

Stacia's exasperation was growing, but before she could form a suitable reply Lady Crackenthorpe intervened.

"Hush, now, here are Lady Stafford and Lady Carlgate." Her voice lowered to a whisper. "Derek, I beseech you to be on your best behavior! For Stacia's sake, my love."

To Stacia's surprise, these simple words wrought an amazing change in Derek's behavior, transforming him into what (for him) seemed a virtual pattern card of affability. She watched in bemusement as he exchanged polite greetings with everyone they met, smiling dutifully or nodding soberly, depending on the nature of the conversation. He paid one very plain damsel a pretty compliment upon her attire, and endured with true stoicism an elderly duke's lengthy recitation on the boons and benefits of paregoric draughts. Of course, Stacia knew that he did it to please his godmother rather than herself, but at least it proved that he could behave well when the occasion required.

As Lady Crackenthorpe had predicted, they soon encountered two of the patronesses of Almack's riding in a barouche similar to their own. Of the pair, Stacia thought Lady Cowper the more good-natured, for everything Lady Jersey said seemed to hold a double meaning. Lady Crackenthorpe introduced them, and Stacia found herself subjected to a barrage of impertinent questions concerning the size of her fortune and the fate of her Uncle Travis. Angeline's presence did not merit as much notice and beyond inspecting the girl with raised brows and uttering the words, "How do you do?" in rather a cold tone, Lady Jersey appeared far more interested in needling Derek.

"I understand you may soon have a new papa, eh, Mr. Deveaux?" No one could have missed the mischief in her voice and Stacia saw the heads turn in nearby carriages.

"I have heard nothing to support that supposition, ma'am," was Derek's sole response, and though it was spoken with courtesy, the familiar, clipped quality had returned to his voice. However, Lady Jersey, far from taking offense, merely laughed and twirled her parasol.

"Lud, boy, Sir Cuthbert Duncan has been dancing attendance upon your mama these past four weeks! Never tell me you have not noticed! Or perhaps you have merely been occupied with more serious matters?" Her bright blue eyes darted slyly between Angeline and Stacia.

Derek bowed slightly. "As you say, ma'am."

"You know," continued Lady Jersey with another little trill, "I've been hearing some mighty shocking rumors about you, Mr. Deveaux." She gave him an arch look, her finger wagging playfully. "And if what I hear is true, sir, then you are as wicked and naughty a rogue as your uncle! With such stories afoot, I don't think we shall be able to grant you vouchers this year. Do you agree, Emily?"

"Now, Sally—" began Emily Cowper gently, before Derek cut her off.

"By all means save your vouchers for someone more deserving," he stated. "These three ladies, for instance." The implication was that vouchers for Almack's ranked extremely low on his list of wants, but Lady Jersey affected not to notice.

"If *I* were a young lady who valued my reputation, *I'd* take mighty care around this particular gentleman," she announced to the world at large. "My poor Lady Crackenthorpe, you have all my sympathy. I don't know how you can bear the humiliation."

Derek's godmother looked unhappy. "Why, I'm sure I don't know what you mean—"

"I beg your pardon, ma'am," Stacia blurted out, her eyes flashing, "but Mr. Deveaux has been nothing but a *paragon* of gallantry for our entire acquaintanceship! And it is very, very wrong of you to call him wicked, for indeed he is no such thing. He has been everything that is amiable and obliging from the moment we met."

For a long moment no one spoke, and then Lady Jersey broke the silence.

"Why, Mr. Deveaux," she said in sour amusement, "you appear to have made another conquest. How *do* you manage it, I wonder?"

Chapter Nine

"Bravo, Stacia!" exclaimed Lady Crackenthorpe, after the two patronesses had driven on. "You said exactly what I should have said myself if I had had my wits about me." She made a small, condemnatory cluck with her tongue. "Honestly, Sally Jersey can be the most provoking creature. They call her 'Silence' you know, because of her inability to keep a secret. The woman is such a gossip."

"Only think what she will say *now*," remarked Derek. There was a glint of unholy amusement in his eyes. "A paragon of gallantry, Mrs. Edwards? Shame on you for telling lies. Only yesterday I was a vulgar libertine."

Stacia blushed scarlet. "I may have done it a shade too brown," she said tartly, "but someone had to stand up to the woman. How could you just sit there and allow her to insult you?"

He raised a negligent shoulder. "I've never cared what people said of me, and I don't intend to worry about it now. If they wish to talk, then let them. It fills their narrow little minds with something other than space."

Angeline coughed. "I thought it a noble gesture, ma'am. The gentleman should show more gratitude."

"It would have been far better for your mistress if she had held her tongue," Derek retorted. "She does not know what she defends."

Prompted by his censorious tone, Stacia said rather crisply, "Mrs. Greaves and I have agreed not to mention the fact that she is my companion, Mr. Deveaux. As far as I am concerned, she is my friend come to visit me for the Season. I must ask that you address her with that in mind."

Derek's eyes narrowed. "You have a generous nature, ma'am. Perhaps a great deal too generous."

Stacia was startled. His remark was almost too perspicacious, as though he somehow knew that she had, against every particle of her better judgment, sent Marco a draft for four thousand pounds that very morning. But of course there was no way that he could know that.

Angeline interpreted his remark differently. "I do not deny that I am Mrs. Edwards's companion," she said in a affronted voice. "Nor, sir, do I ask for special favors."

"I'm very glad to hear that," responded Derek, his voice soft with meaning. "I should dislike to see anyone take advantage of your *friend*. There are those in this world who are very good at playing on the sympathies of others."

"Indeed?" Angeline's beautiful face flushed with anger, making her look like a goddess whose ire was aroused. "Are you suggesting that I am one of them?"

Stacia glanced from Angeline to Derek, disturbed by the animosity that flowed between them like a living thing.

"Leave her alone," she said shortly. "Angeline does not need to explain herself to you and neither do I."

"She is right, Derek," concurred Lady Crackenthorpe quietly. "You are stepping out of line. You have other matters to attend to right now." She gestured at something ahead of them. "I think you had better brace yourself."

Stacia's head turned in curiosity, so that she was just in time to see an elegant vis-à-vis maneuver its way around a pair of landaulets whose occupants were conversing. It proceeded in their direction, its gorgeously liveried coachman directing its equally gorgeous pair of chestnut-colored horses past several other vehicles. The beautifully appointed equipage looked like a miniature coach, for it was so small and lean it could hold no more than its two occupants—a man and a woman—and they were sitting face to face.

"Now, Derek, love," murmured Lady Crackenthorpe in an undertone, "he really is harmless, you know. There is no reason why your mama should not wed him if she likes."

Stacia's ears pricked up. Was Derek's mother the lady in the vis-à-vis? As the carriage drew closer, she could see the woman was stylishly attired in pink figured muslin, while her lavish headdress, a French bonnet, sported flowers and a curled ostrich plume. The lady also looked as though she might be very haughty, an impression which was confirmed by the lady's height of manner as she greeted Lady Crackenthorpe.

"Good afternoon, Constance. What a pleasant surprise." Apparently, however, her top-lofty tone concealed nervousness, for her next words were spoken in shriller, more wavering accents.

"I did not expect to see you, Derek." She cleared her throat and prodded her gentleman companion. "Look, Cuthbert, here is Derek. You must say hello."

The gentleman responded by poking his head as far out the window as his neckcloth would allow, his eyes rolling around to peer at Derek with all the cautious unenthusiasm of a woodpecker peeping from its hole. One look at Derek's sardonic visage was enough to make him pull back.

"I see him, Winifred," he complained in a frenzied whisper. "And he sees me. But, dash it, he's got that nasty look on his face again. I *don't* think he likes me!"

Derek's mother hissed something that no one could hear, while at the same time Lady Crackenthorpe, with her usual grace of manner, went ahead and performed the

126

introductions as though such antics were a commonplace occurrence.

This time it was Lady Winifred who leaned out the window. "How charming to make your acquaintance, Mrs. Edwards." She gave Stacia what was meant for a smile, then looked down her nose at Angeline. "What family did you say you were from?" she inquired in a condescending tone.

"I did not say," said Angeline with dignity. "I was raised in Hampshire, ma'am."

"I see." Lady Winifred's expression conveyed her low opinion of such undistinguished origins. "And how is your health, Constance?" she said, diverting to a more worthy target. "Have you quite recovered from your ailment?"

Lady Crackenthorpe had no chance to reply, however, as Sir Cuthbert chose this moment to interrupt. "Are you the new heiress?" he asked Stacia with interest. "If you are, then I've heard about you."

Taken aback, Stacia's lips twitched. "Well, I—"

"*I'm* rich too," he confided pridefully. "Only a baronet, of course, but I've got more gingerbread than most of 'em. Inherited one fortune from an uncle and another from my grandmother!"

"How . . . how fortunate for you," Stacia told him, her eyes twinkling. She heard Lady Winifred choke.

"Fortunate," repeated Sir Cuthbert, his head bobbing eagerly. "Aye, a fortune is a dashed *fortunate* thing to have. Ha! That's pretty amusing, eh, Winifred?"

"Very witty," agreed Lady Winifred dryly. "Derek, did you receive the letter I sent yesterday?"

Stacia watched Derek curiously, observing the cool detachment with which he regarded his mother. "Which one?" he inquired, sounding bored. There was no sign of affection, no evidence that these two were bonded by anything other than blood.

"The *only* one!" she snapped. "I asked you to call upon me this morning. Did you bother to read it?"

"If I did, I don't recall," he replied in callous tones. "What did it say?"

Lady Winifred looked furious. "If you'd read it, you would know!"

"He's got a devilish nasty temper," Sir Cuthbert informed Stacia from behind his hand. "Her la'ship says he's jealous. Not everyone can tie the Oriental, y'know. Too difficult."

"Oh, good God," said Derek, rolling his eyes in disgust. "Very well, then. I'll wait on you tomorrow, if you like. Just be sure you're alone."

Lady Winifred compressed her lips, then bestowed a spurious smile upon Stacia. "Do not look so distressed, my dear. He's jesting, of course. My son and I have a rather unconventional relationship, as you will no doubt discover." She paused significantly. "The woman he weds will have to be very patient."

Stacia's eyes flew to Derek, whose distinctly satanic gleam dared her to agree.

"And intrepid," she added, sending him a saucy smile.

"And rich," struck in Sir Cuthbert, anxious to be helpful. "Don't forget rich."

Stacia was soon to see that day as the turning point in her London career and the end of her life of near anonymity. Though society's doors would doubtless have opened to her eventually, Lady Crackenthorpe's introduction oiled the hinges and rotated the knobs that much more quickly. In effect, Stacia became an overnight sensation, the latest novelty in a world which thrived on formality, manners, and fashion. The afternoon following her drive in the Park, Stacia's drawing room overflowed with ladies and gentlemen from the upper reaches of society, a collection of names and titles who had taken their cue and come prepared to welcome her, albeit cautiously, into their ranks. But while Stacia smiled and answered their questions and

128

talked of nothing in particular to everyone in general, her thoughts kept flitting back to Derek, who seemed to be the only person in London who was absent.

Lady Winifred and Sir Cuthbert were among the second day's throng, arriving just in time to claim the last two seats in the room. Beyond a few desultory statements, however, Derek's mother was unable to say very much to Stacia, largely because she was obliged to keep turning back to Sir Cuthbert, who kept plucking at her sleeve in an effort to recapture her attention. In common with the majority of those present, Stacia regarded this performance with amusement, but it was evident from her expression that Lady Winifred did not.

On the third day, vouchers for Almack's arrived in the four o'clock post. There were two of them, Lady Cowper having been kind enough to include one for Angeline, but, oddly, it was a triumph which Angeline did not appear to share.

"We did it, Angeline," Stacia exclaimed, waving them joyfully. "They've accepted us both!"

"You really want me to go, don't you?" Angeline's expression, devoid of the delight Stacia would have expected, was instead a curious mingling of amazement, exasperation, and gravity. "Do you truly wish to go through with this scheme to introduce me to the Ton?"

"Of course I do." Stacia eyed her in surprise. "Don't you wish to?"

"Oh, yes," answered Angeline nodding. "The advantages for me are obvious. But for you there is a disadvantage."

Stacia sat down abruptly. "I am not as pretty as you, you mean," she said bluntly. "They will all be looking at you. I do understand that." A faint sigh escaped her lips as she took in her companion's mesmerizing beauty. "Except the fortune hunters, such as Mr. Matravers. Lady Crackenthorpe warned me about him."

"I do not try to draw their stares," insisted her

companion, a little defensively. "To own the truth, there are days I cannot abide the sight of myself." Her lovely angel face was somber, her ebony curls caressing cheeks as soft and delicately tinted as a nectarine. "Sometimes I wish I were ugly, just so I might walk down the street unnoticed."

Appalled, Stacia protested these sentiments. "Oh, no, Angeline, you must not say that. Your beauty is God's gift and you must value it. To do otherwise would be very wrong. Surely you must know that."

A reluctant smile tugged at Angeline's mouth. "You know, ma'am, you are the oddest woman I ever met. I like you for it though. In the beginning I thought you had some scheme brewing. I thought you wanted something of me, that your kindness would have its price. But I was wrong, wasn't I?"

"Good gracious, Angeline, I want nothing from you but friendship. Except perhaps—"

"Yes?"

"You will not fall in love with Mr. Deveaux, will you? Promise me you will not, for I don't think I could bear it if—" Stacia broke off, hot color staining her cheeks.

Angeline was frowning at her fingertips. "There's little chance of that, ma'am," she said dryly. "Mr. Deveaux does not like me, nor I him." Then she looked up and saw the blush. "Good gracious, ma'am, you cannot be in love with him yourself?"

"I . . . I don't know, Angeline. How could I be? I scarcely know him, after all." She could never confess that she had vowed to win Derek's heart. Angeline would scoff at such a goal. "But he disturbs me and, well, I find myself thinking about him quite often. Too often for comfort."

Angeline's face filled with consternation. "Do not be taken in by his charm, ma'am!" she begged. "Oh, I'll grant you he is pleasing to look upon, but his behavior toward you has been anything but amiable. Do but recollect his conduct at Tattersall's! I am convinced his motives for seeking your company are dishonorable. To put it plainly, he wants your fortune. After all, did not Lady Crackenthorpe say that he was poor?"

Stacia's chin lowered in dejection. "She did. And the oddest thing is that he actually acknowledged that my fortune was of interest to him. I did not know what to make of such an admission."

"What audacity!" the other girl exclaimed. "The brute! He is so set up in his own conceit that he dares to tell you that? Only think how he would treat you if you married him. He is a scoundrel and a rake, ma'am."

Suddenly very irritated, Stacia's jaw set in a stubborn line. "Good gracious, Angeline, you cannot possibly know that. For aught I know, the remark may have been in jest. I do not know him well enough to judge."

"That is farradiddle, ma'am, and you know it. The man is so arrogant he thinks he may say what he likes. He thinks we females have merely to gaze upon his face and we will swoon like idiots." Angeline's hands gripped the arms of her chair so hard her knuckles went white.

Stacia had had a nagging headache since breakfast, and it chose this moment to crescendo, a roiling pain in her head which set her teeth on edge.

"You may be right," she said curtly, "but we may also be making a piece of work out of nothing. I refuse to judge him on so limited an acquaintance. I've decided to accept his offer to teach me to drive. I shall see how he behaves."

Angeline bowed her head. "I beg your pardon, ma'am," she said. "I spoke out of turn."

The hurt in her tone was evident, and Stacia's annoyance receded. "Oh, Angeline, forgive me. I did not mean to sound ungrateful for your concern. It is only that I have to make my own decisions in this matter. I have to make my own mistakes, do you see?"

Angeline rose. "That's exactly what I'm afraid of," she

murmured. "If you will excuse me, ma'am, that gown you wore this morning needs a few stitches. You must have caught the hem."

Lured by the vision of a soft bed and a cold compress for her head, Stacia soon followed her companion out of the room. As she mounted the stairs to the second floor, it crossed her mind that this would be her last peaceful evening, for tomorrow there was Lady Crackenthorpe's ball, and after that, it was only a matter of choosing which in her rising pile of invitations to accept. Since Lady Crackenthorpe had approved her plan to sponsor Angeline's presentation to the Ton, she had been introducing Angeline as her friend rather than as her companion, so all the invitations were for them both.

However, in her present mood Stacia was finding the notion of appearing next to Angeline at every social function a bit dispiriting. She supposed that did not speak very well for her character, particularly as she really was very fond of the girl. It was only that Angeline was so excessively, extraordinarily beautiful! Of course, it was entirely within the realm of possibility that Angeline would become betrothed early in the Season—if only she could overcome her prejudice against men, that is. Lady Crackenthorpe had spoken of the famous Gunning sisters, two Irish beauties who had made splendid marriages despite their penniless state. If they could do it, then so could Angeline.

Perhaps because of her pounding headache, Stacia's head filled with more niggling concerns. She must tell Derek to be more polite to Angeline. Doubtless he would be at his godmother's dinner party tomorrow evening, she thought, but how would he behave? Would he be pleasant? Above all things, she wanted to understand him, for without understanding how could she possibly hope to win his heart? She knew he was fully capable of respectable, well-bred behavior when he chose to

132

exercise that talent. In fact, he could be amazingly charming when he was not looking like a thundercloud. For Lady Crackenthorpe's sake, Stacia hoped that he would be in one of his pleasant humors, but if he were not, she was determined to do her best to bring out his good side. Helping to make the dinner party a success was the least she could do to thank Lady Crackenthorpe for her kindness.

That resolution made, Stacia's thoughts slid on to Marco, who was to escort them to the party. Where had he been these past few days? The question brought a resurgence of worry that would not be dismissed. Did he stay away because he had lost more money and was afraid to tell her? She had written him a letter, reminding him of the party, but thus far he had not answered it.

Ringing for her maid, Stacia eased down on the bed and rubbed her aching brow.

Maisie appeared immediately. "Yes, mum?"

Stacia explained about her headache, and the maid's tongue clucked in sympathy. "Here, now, mum, you just lie still while I fetch a nice cool cloth dipped in lavender." She went over to draw the window curtains, stating, "This ain't the time to say it and it ain't my place to complain, so I won't mention it now, mum, when you're feeling poorly. But when Certain People undertake to usurp my duties . . ."

"What do you mean?" Stacia murmured without much interest.

Maisie turned around. "'Tis Mrs. Greaves, mum," she said, planting her hands on her hips. "Taking it upon herself to mend your gown. I was aiming to fix that torn flounce myself this very night, mum, but she's already at work on it. I reckoned you ought to know."

"Angeline means no harm, Maisie. She only wants to be useful."

Maisie sniffed. "Ain't nothing useful about having a charmer like her in the house, mum. Trouble, that's what she is." She went toward the door, adding, "I'll be back in

133

a wink with that cloth."

However, when the maid reappeared, it was with the tidings that another visitor had arrived. "Challow put her in the Yellow Saloon," she informed Stacia with exasperation. "I told him I'd ask you if—"

Stacia sighed. "Who is it, Maisie?"

"Lady Winifred Deveaux, mum. But if you don't feel up to snuff, I'll go back and tell Challow to—"

Stacia sat up. "No, no, I'll see her. Help me make myself presentable again, will you?"

Composing her features into a welcoming smile, Stacia entered the Yellow Saloon to find Derek's mother standing with her back to the door. Her head was tilted downward, and when she turned, her gloved hand was clasping a small statuette that Stacia had purchased a few days before.

Ignoring the trespass, Stacia greeted her visitor with conscientious politeness.

"Good afternoon, Lady Winifred. What a pleasure to see you again so soon." Despite her headache, the statement had its measure of truth, for anything to do with Derek was of compelling interest.

Restoring the china shepherdess to its place on the table, Lady Winifred drew up her lips and pulled off her gloves.

"I trust you will forgive my calling so late in the day, Mrs. Edwards," she gushed. "I simply *had* to visit you again so that we might become better acquainted." She cast an admiring glance about the room. "What a pretty room this is. And so much snugger than your drawing room! There were so many people in there yesterday I vow 'twas impossible to converse with you, my dear. How excessively popular you have become."

If her voice held a grudging note, Stacia made a determined effort not to notice. "I have been very fortunate," she replied, her head throbbing painfully.

"Lady Crackenthorpe's introduction has worked wonders. Won't you sit down?"

They sat, Lady Winifred laying her gloves next to the china shepherdess. "You are so young," she remarked, her sharp eyes pinned to Stacia's. "Do you have children?"

The bluntness of the question caught Stacia by surprise. "Gracious, no," she stammered. "Certainly not." Her visitor looked inquiring, so she continued, "My, er, husband was killed before— I mean, Frederick and I were married only a few days before he was to report for duty. I never saw him again," she added, with what she hoped was a grieving air.

Lady Winifred displayed a startling lack of sympathy. "Ah, well, it is much to endure, but I daresay you are better off without him," she stated. "I have heard that he was a mere captain in the Life Guards. Now that your expectations have changed, you are in a position to make a more advantageous marriage. One must look to the future, you know."

"Er, I suppose so, ma'am," agreed Stacia, wondering which gossip had created her husband's rank. "But I had not thought of marrying again so soon."

The lady's greasy black ringlets bounced with her nod "Very prudent of you, my dear. Men can be the most thoughtless creatures, always doing what you *least* want, and never doing what you *do*." Her voice took on a complaining note. "My son, alas, is no better than the rest of his sex. Worse, in fact. He knows I cannot live upon my jointure, yet he refuses to help me pay my bills. Can you conceive of such ingratitude? A lady must dress, after all, and those wicked tradesmen simply will not let one alone. They are such vultures."

"But I expect they really do need to be paid," ventured Stacia, a trifle timidly.

Her guest lifted her nose. "Nonsense, my dear. They make a great deal too much as it is. They only want my money so they can imitate their betters and foist their upstart daughters into shabby-genteel marriages. If only I could convince Derek—"

She broke off as Challow arrived with refreshment, and while Stacia poured, Derek's mother squinted fussily at the steaming liquid in her cup.

"That is not green tea, is it? Green tea gives me tremors and palpitations. Even vertigo, on occasion. I hope you never suffer as I do, my dear. I have *so* much to bear." Her wispy sigh suggested travails too numerous to mention.

"Sugar?" said Stacia faintly.

The ringlets bobbed. "Thank you. A little more . . . yes, that's it. So, tell me, my dear, do you like my son?"

"Like?" Seized with a sudden urge to fidget, Stacia floundered for an answer. "Er, I do not *dis*like him, ma'am, though his conduct toward me has been somewhat . . . erratic. He has offered to teach me how to drive my new phaeton," she added, as an afterthought.

"Indeed." Lady Winifred looked pleased. "How obliging of him. Perhaps he has formed a partiality for you. I confess I would be glad if he has."

"Oh?" said Stacia helplessly.

"I always wanted a daughter," remarked her visitor pointedly. "My son is just as arrogant as his father, alas, and no comfort to me at all." In a sudden, dramatic gesture, she clasped her hands to her bosom. "If only my dearest Cassie had lived! Then you would not see me thus afflicted!"

Wondering why the woman was telling her this, Stacia said, "You did have a daughter, then?"

"Three," answered Lady Winifred proudly. "Cassie, Beth, and Maria. None of them survived infancy, however." Her voice fluctuated, then climbed in ferocity and pitch. "Only Derek thrived. My girls were so sickly, but *he*"—Stacia was shocked to hear the bitter note in her voice—"was as sturdy as a workhorse. While each of my precious daughters wasted away, Derek was howling his lusty lungs out in the nursery. I should have been grateful, I know. But I wanted my girls to live. They would have been mine, you see. Derek was my husband's from the moment he was born."

Stifling her disapproval, Stacia forced a compassionate response. "But, ma'am, Derek *is* yours. Surely you and he can share a love that is as special—"

A sharp gesture silenced her. "Love," repeated Lady Winifred almost dully. "My son has no love for me, Mrs. Edwards. It should have been Cassie who lived. She was such a beautiful little thing. She would have made a splendid marriage and taken care of her mama. Then I would not have to wed that foppish fool." She searched in her reticule and drew out a handkerchief, which she immediately applied to her eyes.

Watching, Stacia bit her lip. How tragic that Lady Winifred should feel like this, she thought. And how much more tragic if she had let Derek guess.

Knowing some comment was expected of her, she said awkwardly, "I scarcely know your son, ma'am, but from our short acquaintance I have the impression that he conceals his true feelings. Lady Crackenthorpe says some men are like that and she is very wise. Beneath his outward aloofness, I am sure he must love you as every child loves its mother."

"If Derek has feelings, I have yet to discover them," complained his mother. "He is callous and cruel to me, and a disgrace to his name." Then she made an odd little grimace and did an about-face. "However, the right woman could do much to improve him." She picked up her tea and smiled anew. "I'll be frank with you, my dear. Derek needs to marry wealth. But beyond that he has much to offer his bride. With a little money, his estate in Suffolk could be renovated to its former distinction. And his lineage is highly distinguished. The Deveauxes are related to the dukes of Warminster, as well as a score of other eminent families. And *I* am one of the Earl of Worthmere's daughters. I was Lady Winifred Purley before I was wed, and everyone knows the Purleys go back for centuries. Any girl would be grateful to ally herself with us." Her quelling gaze challenged Stacia to disagree.

"Gracious," said Stacia, "but surely there is more to marriage than land and lineage. There is affection to be considered. And"—she blushed a little—"you speak as though your son has made me an offer, which I assure you is not the case."

"But what if he does?" There was a pouncing quality to the question.

A drum was pounding in Stacia's temple. "I'm sure it is very improper for me to discuss this," she said weakly.

Lady Winifred frowned. "I will not see him wed to some merchant's daughter, Mrs. Edwards. He must marry money, and most heiresses worth his notice are snatched up in their first Season. At any rate, they are too young to interest a man of Derek's sophistication. You are older, my dear, and more worldly than these chits just out of the schoolroom. You have been married already, so you know what it is that men expect." Her eyes skimmed over Stacia's figure. "You could hold him, I think. Your proportions are elegant and your countenance pleasing. And he has shown interest in you, which is more than Richard ever—"

Clearly embarrassed, she broke off and took too large a swallow of tea. Her hand jerked as she choked, so that the hot liquid splashed over the side of the cup and burned her fingers.

"Oh, ma'am, are you all right?" Stacia jumped up to take the cup from her shaken guest.

Lady Winifred gave a trembling sigh and wiped her hand with her handkerchief. "When am I ever all right? No, that is a stupid thing to say and I so dislike stupidity. I am well, Mrs. Edwards. As well as it is possible for me to be."

Stacia moved her chair a little closer to Derek's mother. "Lady Winifred," she said, "forgive me if what I say seems forward. Is there anything troubling you?

138

Would you care to speak of it? I would tell no one, I assure you. I am not one to gossip."

"That is good," replied her guest, losing most of her former acerbity. "Derek dislikes gossips." Her eyes met Stacia's with vague puzzlement. "The only thing you can do to help me is to marry my son. But it is good of you to be concerned. I did not expect it of you. Or anyone."

"Well, I *am* concerned. The sentiments you've just expressed tear at my heart, ma'am." Stacia paused for a moment, then said gently, "You see, I lost my mother when I was very young. She ran away from my father and left me behind, which pained me a very great deal when I grew old enough to understand. And my father forbade me to discuss her because she had betrayed him, which was very hard on me when I longed to know what I had missed. So I understand what it is to suffer, ma'am, and to lack a relationship with one who should have been there in one's life."

Lady Winifred lowered her head and for a moment Stacia thought she was going to cry. "There's nothing that can be done," she said abruptly. "It's too late to change. Derek loathes me and I have little feeling for him. His father . . . was the same. Richard always had time for his mistresses and his gambling, but never for me." She spoke bitterly, allowing the rancor from the past to flow into her speech.

In a spontaneous gesture, Stacia laid her hand over Lady Winifred's. "It is never too late to change," she urged. "I had a governess who used to tell me that. As long as there is breath in the body there is time to turn one's life around, to steer it in whatever direction one wishes. She taught me a great many things, though I confess I did not always follow her counsel. Another thing she used to say was that no person is exactly like another. Perhaps Derek is not so much like his papa as you imagine."

Lady Winifred gave her the closest thing to a real smile that Stacia had yet seen. "I like you, my dear. You are very sweet and very sensible. I should like to have you for a daughter-in-law. Perhaps my grandchildren would inherit your generous disposition."

Stacia stifled a sigh thinking it ironic that so many people would comment upon her generosity when in her private thoughts she was sometimes so shockingly selfish and wicked. Even now, she wished only to lie down, for her head felt as though it were being pummeled as much from the outside as within.

Such a wish was not to be granted, however, for at that moment Challow returned to announce a second visitor.

"Mr. Deveaux," he intoned as Derek strode into the room.

It would have been difficult to say which lady was the more discomposed. "Why . . . Derek," said Lady Winifred in the uncomfortable pause that followed, "whatever are you doing here?"

"I might ask the same question of you, Mama," he said tonelessly. "I saw your carriage in the street." He gave Stacia a bow that was faintly mocking. "Mrs. Edwards. I hope you will forgive the intrusion."

Stacia stood up. "It is no intrusion, Mr. Deveaux," she answered formally. "We were . . . that is, your mother and I have been enjoying a chance to further our acquaintance. Won't you join us?"

Lady Winifred hurried to her feet. "As it happens, Derek, I was about to leave. You will wish to stay, I daresay, so we can talk another—"

"On the contrary," replied her son coolly, "I would be happy to escort you outside."

Sensing Lady Winifred's unhappiness, Stacia made up her mind to try to pacify him. With a deep breath, she said, "I wonder if you might return after you do so? There is something I wish to say to you—if it is convenient, of course."

The line of Derek's mouth changed and something glimmered in his eyes. "Of course," he said, giving her another slight bow. "My time is always at your disposal, ma'am."

Chapter Ten

While waiting for Derek, Stacia curled into the corner of the settee, her elbow propped on its arm, her chin resting on the palm of her hand. Instead of rehearsing whatever speech she meant to make, she closed her eyes and concentrated on relaxing the muscles in her neck and face, a technique she'd found useful in combating the headaches of the past. As the tension eased from her body, the throb in her head immediately lessened to half what it had been, while a mind-dulling lassitude stole slowly through her limbs. Her breathing steadied and deepened, and it became difficult to fix on anything beyond the pleasant floating sensation which supported her like a soft, fluffy cloud. Her clearest thought was that if she were not careful she would fall asleep before Derek came back, and this only winged through her head for an instant, then faded to dreamless oblivion.

The darkness lasted until her chin slipped off her hand, a sharp movement sufficient to jerk her from her slumber. To her surprise, she found that Derek was sitting in an armchair not three feet away.

"How long have you been sitting there?" she demanded, a self-conscious blush springing to her cheeks. Considerably embarrassed, she straightened her posture and swung the foot she had tucked under her to the floor. "Why didn't you wake me, for pity's sake?"

"Because you looked tired," he said, regarding her lazily. "Tired and peaceful and . . . very lovely. I found it restful to watch you sleep. It's been only a few minutes."

She studied him carefully, noting that he did not look annoyed or cynical or any of those other things that made her feel vaguely uneasy. He only looked relaxed. Relaxed and rather amused.

"Well, um, thank you for returning," she said, fighting an attack of shyness. The room seemed very quiet. "Would you care for some sherry?"

"Not at the moment. I am content merely to drink in the scenery."

The unaccustomed warmth in his eyes gave Stacia a spurt of courage. "That does not sound very like you, Mr. Deveaux," she said demurely. "I fear you are making mock of me."

He cocked an eyebrow and the corners of his lips lifted in one of his rare smiles. "What a contradictory creature you are. I thought a compliment would please you. Did you not ask that I be nicer to you?"

"I? Contradictory?" Stacia widened her eyes. "On the contrary, it is *you*, sir, who are the most contradictory person alive. I never know from one day to the next what you will say." She hesitated, then said bravely, "And being nice does not necessarily mean paying compliments. It means being a friend, Mr. Deveaux. We could be friends if you would allow it."

"Could we?" His tone was rather odd and, when she said nothing, he inquired, rather quizzingly, "Is that what you wished to say to me?"

"No. Actually, what I wished to tell you was that . . . if you will teach me how to drive my phaeton, I shall be very much obliged to you." She rushed the words, getting them out before those penetrating eyes could unsettle her any further.

"A wise decision," he retorted. "We can begin tomorrow if the weather is fair." He stretched out one long leg and studied her with intentness. "Tell me something," he said abruptly. "Is your Christian name Eustacia?"

The question caught her off balance. "No, that was my mother's name. I am merely Stacia. I was told that she insisted on the shortened version. Apparently she felt there was room for only one Eustacia in this world."

Derek's eyes seemed to glitter in the fading afternoon light. "And only room for one Stacia, I'll be bound. Somehow I doubt there is anyone like you, ma'am. I've known a great many females, but you're the first who's expressed interest in being my friend." His mouth slanted humorlessly.

"How sad," she murmured, not comprehending the emphasis he'd given the last word. "No wonder you—" She broke off, thinking better of what she'd been going to say.

"No wonder I what?" he prodded.

"Well, if you must know, I was going to say that it is no wonder you have such a poor opinion of the female sex."

For a few seconds his gaze shifted to the carpet, then returned to scan her face. "What the devil did my mother say to you? Did she put that notion into your head?"

Stacia drew a deep breath, for some reason focusing on the scar on his chin. "No, you did," she said frankly. "If you want the truth, Lady Winifred told me you need to marry wealth. She went on about it at great length, in fact. She seems to see me as"—her color heightened—"prime candidate for that office."

He surveyed her through half-closed eyes, the heavy lids concealing whatever thoughts were in his head. "And what was your reply, if I may be so bold?"

The sudden silkiness in his voice made her swallow. "Well, I . . . I said you had not asked me. I told her I found the discussion rather pointless."

"Did you?" His voice grew velvety soft. "And if I did ask you to be my wife? What might your answer be, Stacia?"

Her heart slammed against her ribs. "Why I . . . I

would say I do not know you well enough to consider matrimony." Hoping she did not sound as agitated as she felt, Stacia moistened her lips and said vigorously, "But I've no interest in being wed for my inheritance, Mr. Deveaux. I'd rather dwindle into a spinster."

His eyes narrowed. "A spinster? You are a widow, ma'am."

"My marriage was of very short duration, sir," she said quickly. "It was merely a slip of the tongue."

Accepting this, he sat back, the fingers of one hand lightly drumming the arm of his chair. At length, he said, "How long were you married?"

"Not long," she answered evasively. "He . . . Frederick . . . had to report back to his regiment almost immediately."

"Ah, I suppose that accounts for it," he said enigmatically. "Had you known him long? How did you meet?"

"Well, I . . . we . . ." Under his scrutiny, Stacia's inventiveness floundered. "Are you *sure* you would not like some sherry?" she said instead. "It's really very good. Or perhaps you are hungry? Cook made some truly delicious little cakes just this morning—"

"You don't wish to talk about him," he cut in. "I understand and I beg your pardon. Your past is your past and no business of mine."

Relieved, Stacia changed the subject to something she'd been longing to mention. "The night we met at the hotel," she said hesitantly. "The note I found on my tray. What did you mean by it?"

His fingers stilled. "That note, Mrs. Edwards, is no longer of any consequence. I beg you will put it from your mind. I should not have written it." He spoke with constraint, his lips tightening into the hard, tight line she so disliked.

"And I should not have referred to it?" she asked in dismay. "I am sorry. I'm afraid I do not know the rules of these things."

He eyed her closely, then sighed. "You've done nothing wrong. It is I who did wrong. In the future, my innocent, I hope you will not accept or acknowledge impertinent letters from unknown gentlemen."

"Oh, so it *was* impertinent. I was almost certain it was. In fact, I thought—"

"You thought what?"

"I thought it meant you wanted to . . . be alone with me."

"It did," he said grimly.

"And now you don't?" The words were out before she could stop them, ringing with childish chagrin.

His dark brows snapped together. "Stacia," he said finally, "that note was wholly improper. Again, I ask you to forget it."

"And you have decided we must be proper." She tried to say it calmly, just as she tried to ignore the illogical swell of disappointment in her chest.

"Precisely," he agreed, at his most suave and cynical. "We shall dine at my godmother's en masse with the rest of the world. For the present, it will suffice."

Games of chance held no allure for Derek, for he could never forget how much his father had lost playing hazard, or how closely he had come to losing Camberley, their family estate in Suffolk. Camberley was the only unentailed piece of property in the Deveaux family— everything else had gone to Derek's uncle, as the elder son, including most of his grandfather's very considerable wealth. It was probably just as well; Derek's father's share had only been flung onto the hazard tables anyway. Upon Richard Deveaux's death, Derek had taken on the burden of his father's debt, but over the years, with careful management, he had managed to hold his head above water, slowly paying off mortgages and keeping the creditors at bay, saving bit by bit until he at last began to feel that he could breath again.

But though games of chance were anathema to Derek, he did enjoy games of skill. He liked carom billiards, for example, because it required a keen eye and a steady hand rather than an impassive countenance and a resource as sly and elusive as luck. He never played hazard, and only played cards when it suited his mood and purpose. He'd won the mare—Palatine's mother—in a game of piquet, but afterward suffered a sleepless night recalling the quantity of money he'd risked. His opponent's skill had nearly matched his own but he had wanted the horse very badly. He had *needed* the horse. And he had won, and from that mare had come Palatine.

However, this evening's game of billiards in White's club meant nothing more to him than an opportunity to relax. Ironically, he'd won the lag without effort, but he had not played well since, chiefly because he was thinking more about Stacia than on the angle of his aim. In fact, Derek was well on his way to being soundly trounced by Lord Andrew Carisbrooke.

"Mind on other things?" inquired his opponent, who had just scored seven points running.

Derek grunted. "You could say that. Have you spoken to your brother yet?"

Lord Andrew studied the position of the object balls, then sent the cue spinning for the eighth time. "Missed by a hairsbreadth," he groaned. He turned and smiled at Derek. "Such an old sobersides you are tonight. Yes, I've spoken with Alec, but I cannot answer for the results. He has promised to ponder the climbing boy issue, but the Lords in general are an unreceptive lot. Let us speak of something more pleasant. Tell me how things proceed with the rich widow."

Derek stepped closer to the rail. "Well enough," he said evasively. His cue ball made hard contact with Lord Andrew's ball but missed the red.

"She's a taking little creature," rattled Lord Andrew at more frivolous a pace than usual. "I rather fancy her myself. There could be benefits to having a pretty wife,

146

don't you think? One's children might be pretty, too. Think how pleasant it would be to spawn no hatchet-faced heirs. And then, of course, how delightful to cuddle up to a soft, warm body on a cold night without even having to leave one's own house." He watched the red ball roll to a standstill in the corner of the table. "Into the crotch," he added. "I might have known."

Derek said nothing, but if looks could slay, Lord Andrew would have dropped to the floor. Instead, the duke's brother yawned, and said, "By the bye, Sir Marco Ashcroft won last night. In Brooks's. It seems no doors are closed to those who pay their debts."

"How much did he win?"

"Faugh, I don't know. Two or three thousand, perhaps. He was playing faro. Aping the out-and-outers, no doubt. At least he don't lose all the time."

"It's a damned good thing," growled Derek. He watched Lord Andrew drive the ball out of the crotch on the first try. "What do you make of Mrs. Greaves?" he asked, a shade abruptly.

At once Lord Andrew grew disinterested. "Unquestionably a diamond of the first water," he answered carelessly, "but with a millstone of a chip on her shoulder. Are you contemplating a ménage à trois?"

Derek laughed. "Do I detect a trace of disapproval in milord's tone?" At the other man's expression, he made an exasperated sound. "Bedamned to you, Drew, I've no interest in your diamond. You can have her with my good wishes." The memory of Dominique prompted him to add, quite feelingly, "I've had my fill of brittle sparkle just lately. Stacia Edwards is more to my taste. She's an opal"—his dark head tilted to assess the balls' positions—"and I've always liked opals. They're all fragile and cool and soothing on the surface, but underneath there's fire."

Lord Andrew was staring at him in amazement. "So it's happened at last," he remarked. "Derek Deveaux has found a respectable woman who doesn't bore him." He sounded quite smug. "Own it, my friend."

Derek shrugged. "She hasn't yet, at any rate." He bent to take his shot, adding, "Do you realize that Stacia is introducing Mrs. Greaves to the Ton as her friend? No mention of the 'companion' business now. She's trying to find her a husband."

"So I'd heard. How eccentric of her."

Derek watched his ball fly across the green baize cloth. "I think your diamond is using my soft little opal," he remarked.

Lord Andrew's lips twisted. "An adventuress, per se. How vastly amusing. I cannot wait to hear the gossip when the truth comes out."

Derek's next stroke was vicious and accurate. The cue bounced off the red to strike Lord Andrew's dead in the center.

"Oh, but I can," he said, straightening suddenly. He glanced around to assure that they were still alone. "I think her brother is taking advantage of her, too. The cub can't possibly have the blunt to pay the debts he's incurring. Sir George Ashcroft was not that wealthy. I think it's Stacia who's tipping over the dibs."

Lord Andrew's brows rose. "Good God! Are you sure?"

"No. It's conjecture only. But it seems the logical conclusion."

"The bloody cur. How much do you suppose she's forked over?"

"In my estimation, somewhere in the neighborhood of ten thousand pounds." Derek's face was hard. "Between her brother and your adventuress, she'll be a pauper by the end of the Season."

Lord Andrew had lost his jocular mood. "And what a leveler that would be, eh?" he mocked. "Best marry her quickly, or you'll have to find yourself another heiress."

Derek had been aligning his next shot, but at this he straightened, his expression unpleasant. "*If* I marry Stacia Edwards," he said softly, "it will be for the sake of

148

her fortune. Remember that, Drew."

Lord Andrew met him look for look. "Oh, is that so?" he drawled. "How very comforting. You know, I'm still hearing the strangest rumors about you, my dear fellow. Bastards in the country, or something of the sort. For Mrs. Edwards' sake, I hope it's not true."

Derek shrugged and took his shot. "One would hope so, wouldn't one?"

"Damn it, Derek!" snapped his closest friend. "What the hell kind of an answer is that? Do you think I will betray your confidences?"

"No." Derek's face was a mask of indifference.

"It would serve you right if I did take Stacia away from you!" complained the other man in frustration. "I've no reason to believe you'd treat her well. Look at what you did to my cousin."

Very slowly, Derek lay down his cue stick. "What the devil do you mean? I offered Claire marriage. Didn't she ever tell you?" Observing his friend's expression, he swore softly. "You bloody fool, why the hell did you never ask me?"

Lord Andrew cursed him back, roundly and vividly. "I thought it none of my concern," he finished in an angry voice. "I know what a private fellow you are. I do try to be tactful, you know."

"Well, it's ancient history now. She didn't want me, Drew. Not with Telford panting after her like a rutting sheepdog. I couldn't compete with a rich marquess." Derek smiled cynically. "She was very apologetic, of course. In lieu of her hand, she offered me . . . her body. She thought it adequate recompense. I didn't."

Lord Andrew looked vexed. "Why that little—She told me she loved you. She claims she still does."

"Really?" Derek was indifferent. "I wouldn't believe her. It's Telford's money she loves. It's why she married him."

"He whose house is of glass should not throw stones," murmured his friend.

Derek flinched. "It is not the same," he stated. "I merely toyed with the notion, whereas Claire—" He broke off with an oath. "Confound it, Drew, if I choose to wed Stacia Edwards, I'll do it because—" Once more he stopped. "Damn it, let's get on with the game."

Lord Andrew sighed. "It's your shot," he pointed out, quite gently.

At ten o'clock on the morning of Lady Crackenthorpe's ball, Stacia's shiny new phaeton stood waiting and ready in the street outside her house. As she stepped daintily inside and settled herself on the plush seat, she could not help noticing how elegant it looked, and how glad she was that she had chosen it. In fact, she was now quite thankful she had not purchased the high-perch variety, for not two days past she had seen one nearly overturn.

As Derek dismissed the groom and climbed in next to her, she gave him a cheerful look. "I do not think this can be so very difficult. How many lessons do you think I shall need to become a good whip?"

Smiling slightly, he sent the horses trotting forward. "As many as it takes until I think you can drive without risk. It is no great hardship to take me along, is it?"

She raised her chin, gazing up at him from under her long red-gold lashes. "No," she said seriously. "Not as long as you are nice to me and do not snap my nose off if I say the wrong thing."

"Certainly not," he replied with what actually sounded like amusement. "Your nose must stay right where it is. As soon as we reach the Park, I will show you how to use that whip I gave you."

"It is very pretty," she said. "I did not expect you to bring me presents, you know."

"Naturally," he agreed. "And that is why I did it. They are all the crack just now so I thought it would please you."

Something in his tone made her glance at him doubtfully. The light little whip had been especially designed for ladies, he had said. Its crop was fitted with a small, gaily colored parasol too minute to be anything but a token symbol of the driver's femininity, but Derek had assured her that the whip itself was fully functional.

"Well, thank you," she said, a wistful note in her voice. "Do you really wish to please me?" She knew it was a bold question yet something within her compelled her to ask.

"Can you doubt it?" he answered suavely. "Is there something else you would like, my dear? Have I been negligent in some way?" He glanced down at her, his green eyes brilliant with the sun's light.

"N-no," she answered quickly. "It is just that sometimes it seems that you like me . . . and sometimes it seems that you don't. It is very disconcerting, you know."

"Do you *want* me to like you?" he inquired.

"Yes, of course I do. I want everyone to like me," she added hastily.

"I see," was all he said. "Well, as my godmother says, everybody loves an heiress. I daresay you've already discovered that."

Stacia's spirits sank. "You're doing it again."

"Doing what?"

"Being arrogant. Oh dear, that sounds so censorious, doesn't it? But you do have a distressing tendency to say what is most likely to put up people's backs."

"Oh?"

His tone was not encouraging, but she went on, defiantly, "For instance, your statement might lead one to conclude that no one could possibly like me for any reason but my fortune."

Stacia attributed his silence to the fact that he was negotiating his way around two carts, but when it continued halfway down an empty street, she began to grow worried.

151

When he finally spoke, his words were not what she expected. "I like you a great deal, Mrs. Edwards, and for reasons which have nothing at all to do with your fortune. However, since my mother has most thoughtfully planted the notion in your head that I am after your wealth—"

"No, you did that yourself," she corrected.

He made a slight grimace. "I suppose I did," he said wryly. "Forgive me, then. I am not a tactful person. To put it bluntly, I am not averse to pumping a little money into my estate, but I have no intention of choosing a wife based on what she can bring me. There are other factors to be considered."

Stacia's heart nearly stopped. "I should hope so," she uttered in a voice gone suddenly breathless. "As for myself, I consider mutual affection to be of primary importance." She was not quite brave enough to say love.

"And shared goals," he surprised her by adding. "There is more to wedded bliss than a crazed longing for the sight of one another's face. There are certain basic issues that both partners should agree upon. It decreases discord."

Stacia turned this over in her mind. "I am sure you are right," she responded. "So what is it that interests you, Mr. Deveaux?"

"Ladies first," he parried as the phaeton rolled into Hyde Park. "I'd like to hear more about you, ma'am. What is it that you want of life?"

No one had ever asked her so personal a question, and for an instant Stacia was on the brink of pouring out her soul to him. However, common sense quickly intervened and she settled on a part of the truth.

"Well, I used to think I wanted my freedom," she said reflectively, "and I still do, I think. Freedom to make my own decisions and to act as an adult woman with a mind of my own. My father was too protective of me, you see. Until I came to London I lived my whole life on his estate in Lancashire and . . . I really didn't go anywhere

152

or . . . or do anything exciting at all." She was not quite successful in keeping the resentment from her voice.

Frowning heavily, Derek brought the horses to a standstill along the side of the carriage way. "But surely he sent you away to some sort of finishing school?"

Stacia could not prevent herself from flushing. "No. My father felt that I should stay at home. I had a governess when I was younger. When I grew older, he said it was because he could not do without me. I kept the household running smoothly," she added in a subdued voice.

"Then how did you meet your husband?" Derek's eyes were suddenly too shrewd for comfort.

"Oh, well, he was . . . he was one of Marco's friends," she prevaricated. "We had but a short acquaintance."

"Ah. A whirlwind romance. And your father approved of the match?"

Stacia struggled to think of a reasonable reply. "He did not object," she said at length, "because Frederick was from a good family. Please could we not talk about him anymore?"

Derek sent her a probing glance, but said only, "Very well, ma'am. Let us begin your lesson."

An hour later, Derek was forced to conclude that whatever cow-handed leanings Sir Marco possessed had not been passed to his sister. Not only did Stacia display a natural affinity for the ribbons, her simple pleasure in her achievement was both refreshing and infectious. Under normal circumstances, when he strove to please a woman—often an exertion directly proportional to his desire to take her to bed—Derek could be as flirtatious and personable as the next man, but such charm was deliberate and frequently required more effort than he was willing to expend. Where Stacia was concerned, however, the process was as enjoyable as it was effortless, and though he would have given his right arm to make love to her on the spot, each of her smiles was in itself a reward.

Seeking another glimpse of her bewitching dimples, he related the story of Viscount Petersham, who, in a public proclamation of his devotion to a certain Mrs. Brown, drove around town in a brown curricle drawn by brown horses with a groom dressed in brown livery.

Stacia found this as amusing as he'd hoped. "But what do you suppose he would have done if her name was Mrs. Green?" she asked, holding the horses at an even trot.

He studied her profile, noting the dusting of freckles on her pert little nose and the soft yet obstinate mouth. "Oh, well, I suppose he could have the curricle painted green—"

"But the horses, Mr. Deveaux? Are you suggesting he would paint them green, too?" She glanced at him, her lips quivering in the most fascinating way.

He smiled. "Well, ma'am," he responded, "you have me there." Perhaps it was only the twinkle in her brown eyes that made it seem so diverting, but he laughed, then went on to tell her about Viscount Palmerston and his wife.

"They both favor gray horses," he explained. "Lady Palmerston drives about with four perfectly matched gray carriage horses, while Lord Palmerston has his own gray horse for riding. But he is the despair of his wife. Can you guess why?"

Stacia's head shook, her underlip caught between her teeth in an unconsciously provocative pose.

He kept his face perfectly straight. "Because she lives in dread that someone will think he is riding one of hers."

He watched Stacia's face as the ridiculousness of the tale hit home, filled with secret satisfaction at the way her eyes widened and the corners of her mouth trembled on the brink of laughter. And then that laughter spilled out, a silvery sound as sweet as the ripple of a mountain stream.

"And that would never do, I suppose?" Her warm eyes

sought his as easily as though they had known each other for years. They weren't flirting, he realized with a jolt. They were conversing, laughing together, sharing in a way he had never done with a woman.

"Exactly," he agreed. "Appearance is far more important than speed or stamina to a great many people."

"But not to you," she guessed, smiling up at him. "You are not to be deceived."

"I try not to be," he acknowledged. "I dislike artifice as much as I loathe dishonesty and deception."

Suddenly Stacia's beautiful smile faded, and her lashes lowered to conceal her eyes. "Perhaps," she remarked, "there are times when a person feels that dishonesty and deception are justified."

Derek wondered what she was hiding and concluded that it was probably something to do with her brother's gambling losses. "I suppose one might feel so," he allowed, "but it is usually not the case."

He hoped his statement would induce her to confide in him, but instead her expression clouded even more. For approximately half a minute Derek stewed in silence, debating ways to reverse the damage his own tongue had wrought. He finally chose the most appealing course of action, a maneuver that had long ago proven tried and true.

"Halt the horses for a moment," he said. He watched with approval as she slowed the phaeton exactly as he'd taught her to do, then took the reins from her hand.

"Look at me," he commanded, and when her head turned, he bent and kissed her on the mouth.

It was brief but amazingly pleasant, what he considered a light, preparatory kiss, a hint of things to come. Stacia looked startled, but made no protest, so, encouraged, he slipped his arm about her waist and kissed her again.

Her lips were unbelievably soft and pliant, while her skin was fresh and clean, and smelled of scented soap. She was sweet and unresisting, and without any

155

conscious decision he increased the strength of his ardor. Desire welled in his throat, supplanting caution, overwhelming judgment an reason in a way he'd never have believed possible. Forgetting where he was, scarcely knowing what he did, his hand went to her breast, his thumb sliding over and around its tender tip in small, teasing circles. When she gave a small moan the ache in his loins ignited, a hard burning that was not altogether dispelled when she cried out and thrust her whip in his face.

"Mr. Deveaux," she choked, pushing against his chest so that the whip butted his neck, "please stop. What are you doing? We are in the Park, for God's sake!" Her breath was coming in uneven gasps, those shapely breasts rising and falling, their taut peaks pressed tantalizingly against her light muslin gown.

"No one saw." He said it raggedly, quickly, glancing around to confirm his own words. "Look around, Stacia. There's not a soul here but the birds."

"But there might have been!" Her eyes were dark with reproach. "Why did you do that? You have been so nice until now."

"I beg your pardon," he said with sudden stiffness. "You did not seem to be objecting overmuch."

"Well, I do object!" she said fiercely. "This has all been a ruse, hasn't it? You let me believe you were my friend when all you truly want is to dishonor me! I can see I should have listened to Angeline."

"Nonsense," he replied, taken aback. To own the truth, he was shocked by his lack of self-control, but all the same, she need not behave as though he had ravished her. After all, what had it been but a kiss? She had been married, hadn't she? She knew what it was all about, even if her marriage had not been of long duration. "You're making a great piece of work over a trifle," he added irritably.

"Yes, I daresay it *is* a trifle to you," she accused. "Well, I am much more worldly than you think, Mr.

156

Deveaux. I know all about men like you!"

Recapturing his suavity, Derek caught hold of her wrist, his voice smooth as cream. "Worldly or not, my sweet, you know nothing about me. And there is *no one* like me, though it may sound arrogant to say it. I am unique and so, may I add, are you. So don't pitch me any of that fustian, for I'll not swallow it."

She flushed. "I know more about you than you think, Mr. Deveaux. I know that you are insensitive and overbearing—"

"And I know that you are impetuous and over-generous," he countered. "So where does that leave us?" Though her assessment made him furious, he mastered his rage and released her wrist. "Strange as it may seem," he added, "I have no intention of dishonoring you. In fact, quite the reverse."

"Indeed?" She sounded contemptuous, but he noticed her hands were shaking. "And what might that mean?"

Derek's simmering temper battled his sense of caution. "I hardly think you are in any state to hear what it means," he said testily.

"Indeed, I am!" she countered. "And I demand that you explain your remark."

She looked so small and fiery and vulnerable at that moment that he longed to take her in his arms and finish what he had begun. Dominique would have been only too eager, he thought humorlessly. But Stacia was as different from Dominique as light was from dark.

"If you must have it then, my intentions toward you are entirely honorable." He paused to clear his throat. "I wish to make you my wife, Mrs. Edwards."

As a proposal, he knew at once it wasn't much, and if the expression on her face was anything to go by, it was even worse than he thought. He'd obviously managed to make the devil's own mull of it.

In fact, Stacia had gone quite pale. "*Now* who's talking fustian?" she asked scornfully. "Are you pretending to be in love with me? If so, you insult my intelligence, Mr.

157

Deveaux. I think our acquaintance has been a little too short for that."

He dug a deeper pit for himself with his next words. "No, I'm not in love with you, but I believe we should suit. I find you damnably attractive—"

"Why not speak the truth?" she cut in. "You find my fortune attractive, isn't that it? As for my person, I'm sure I ought to be flattered that you can endure to kiss me, but I've not the slightest interest in—"

"Devil take it, Stacia, listen to me! I apologize if I insulted you. I did not mean to do so." He stared down at her, not knowing how to explain. "I own I expressed myself clumsily—"

"You've expressed yourself clumsily since the moment we met!" she informed him in scathing accents.

Derek's mouth twisted. "Perhaps I should try again, then." To his own ears, his voice sounded curiously strained. "Mrs. Edwards, will you do me the very great honor of accepting my hand in marriage? I will do my best to care for you in every way I know how. Your comfort—and that of our children—shall always be my first concern. I will not squander away your fortune, but will employ it for the betterment of our home and our family—"

"It's too late for pretty speeches," she fired back. "I would be the greatest fool on earth to be duped by such talk. You are such a great one for frankness, so I'll be frank." Her voice wavered, her face a picture of distress and agitation. "I thank you for the driving lesson, but as for your declaration"—she drew a deep breath—"I would not wed you if you were the last man in England!"

Chapter Eleven

On the whole, Stacia's first ball proved to be more ordeal than pleasure, for she was too depressed to enjoy it and too proud to let her wretchedness show. For the past three hours she had laughed and talked as though she had not a care in the world—when all she really wanted was to throw herself down and weep. For her own peace of mind she tried not to think about Derek's devious attempt to make love to her, but it was etched as deeply into her thoughts as her own unpardonable, unblushing acceptance of that effort. How could she have permitted him to touch her like that? And how could she shunt the memory when he was standing only a dozen feet away from where she was participating in the quadrille with another man as her partner? Even if she did not look in his direction, the knowledge of his presence kept every nerve in her body taut and quivering.

The preball dinner had been a disaster, chiefly because Lady Crackenthorpe had placed her next to Derek. Oh, on the surface he had been polite; she doubted whether anyone else had noticed the chilliness beneath his veneer of formality. And as each succulent dish had been delivered and removed, Stacia's despondency had grown. To keep from bursting into tears under more than three dozen pairs of interested eyes, she'd had to remind herself again and again that Angeline had been right, that

159

Derek was only seeking a source of capital for his estate, and that his kisses had only been a tool to that end. But though this hard reminder staved off the tears, it rubbed salt in a raw, sensitive place.

And it was not even what hurt the most.

His brutal admission that he did not love her had been the most painful cut of all.

Well, at least he had been honest about it, she thought glumly, which was more than her father had ever been. But that hardly qualified as a comfort, did it? Papa might have been insensitive and selfish, but he had never twisted and pummelled her emotions in order to achieve his own ends. On the other hand, hadn't she known from the first that something like this might happen?

Yes, from the beginning she had sensed that Derek would wreak havoc in her life, but had she taken any precautions or mounted any defenses? Had she been wise enough to avoid him? No, she had not.

And why not?

At this point in her musings Stacia always reached a very solid point-non-plus. She had spent the afternoon deliberating the question and had not come up with any answer other than that she, Stacia Amaryllis Ashcroft, was a complete and utter fool. A fool who had not even enough wit to throw away Derek's note. A castle-building fool who dreamed of conquering his heart like some princess in a fairy tale. Fool.

Fearing her distress might show in her face, Stacia peered quickly at her current dance partner but he seemed unaware of her tension. Since dinner it had been better, for in the midst of dancing and music it was easier to focus on other things. Despite her pose as a widow, Lady Crackenthorpe had forbidden her to waltz until one of the patronesses of Almack's gave her the official sanction to do so, insisting that the proprieties be observed just as thoroughly as if she were an eighteen-year-old girl in her first Season. Not really caring, Stacia had submitted to this stricture, but it had not been long

MORE PASSION AND ADVENTURE AWAIT... YOUR TRIP TO A BIG ADVENTUROUS WORLD BEGINS WHEN YOU ACCEPT YOUR FIRST 4 NOVELS ABSOLUTELY *FREE* (AN $18.00 VALUE)

Accept your Free gift and start to experience more of the passion and adventure you like in a historical romance novel. Each Zebra novel is filled with proud men, spirited women and tempestuous love that you'll remember long after you turn the last page.

Zebra Historical Romances are the finest novels of their kind. They are written by authors who really know how to weave tales of romance and adventure in the historical settings you love. You'll feel like you've actually gone back in time with the thrilling stories that each Zebra novel offers.

GET YOUR FREE GIFT WITH THE START OF YOUR HOME SUBSCRIPTION

Our readers tell us that these books sell out very fast in book stores and often they miss the newest titles. So Zebra has made arrangements for you to receive the four newest novels published each month.

You'll be guaranteed that you'll never miss a title, and home delivery is so convenient. And to show you just how easy it is to get Zebra Historical Romances, we'll send you your first 4 books absolutely FREE! Our gift to you just for trying our home subscription service.

BIG SAVINGS AND FREE HOME DELIVERY

Each month, you'll receive the four newest titles as soon as they are published. You'll probably receive them even before the bookstores do. What's more, you may preview these exciting novels free for 10 days. If you like them as much as we think you will, just pay the low preferred subscriber's price of just $3.75 each. *You'll save $3.00 each month off the publisher's price.* AND, your savings are even greater because there are never any shipping, handling or other hidden charges—FREE Home Delivery. Of course you can return any shipment within 10 days for full credit, no questions asked. There is no minimum number of books you must buy.

before the ever-amiable Lady Cowper attended to the formality.

So it was that when the musicians struck up a waltz, Stacia accepted Mr. Matravers as her partner without a qualm. He might be a fortune hunter, she thought, but at least he treated her with courtesy.

"You are so very lovely," he murmured, flirting with her much more openly than before. His fingers squeezed her waist. "When I arrived here tonight I had no notion that I would be able to hold you thus in my arms." His voice lowered to a whisper. "I am enslaved by your beauty, my dear Mrs. Edwards."

Of course, the remark was highly improper, but Stacia, her tender ego still bruised, drank in the compliment, as she had the others she had received that evening. Let Derek see how other men treated her, she thought defiantly. Mayhap he would learn something.

In many ways the scenario resembled her fantasy ball. Yet it was also a cruel parody, for that one special gentleman who ought to have been leaning against a wall with his eyes pinned to her face was instead pointedly ignoring her. And, of course, she was sharing the limelight with Angeline, whom the young men swam around like a school of gaping fish.

Marco, of course, was one of the fish, but at least that meant she knew where he was. That he'd remembered his promise to escort them this evening had been a relief, but this was largely due, she suspected, to his knowledge that Angeline was to attend. Just lately she'd been wondering whether her brother's infatuation for the girl had waned, but tonight it seemed very much otherwise. On the way to Lady Crackenthorpe's he'd been unable to take his eyes off her, while the majority of his statements had been sprinkled with compliments and boasts. In an attempt to impress, Marco had described in tedious detail a high-perch phaeton he'd purchased from one of Mr. Denchworth's cronies. That he had carefully avoided his sister's eye while doing so suggested that he had not

161

forgotten the money he owed her, but at that particular instant Stacia had been too absorbed in her own troubles to care.

However, as the last strains of music drew to a close she abruptly recollected the purchase. She gave Mr. Matravers an absent smile as he bowed, but as soon as he was gone, a frown appeared in its stead.

"I fancy you are looking a little tired this evening," her next partner informed her with a smile, "so I thought we might sit out our set." In his hand, Lord Andrew Carisbrooke held a crystal wine goblet. "I've brought you some punch. Would you care to step out upon the balcony? Cool air can be so reviving, I have found."

Stacia darted a quick peep at Derek. He had not done much dancing, but if those two young matrons hanging onto his sleeve were anything to go by he was certainly not suffering either. Suddenly, the sight of his dark head bent attentively over the shorter of the two ladies filled her with rage. First, she thought furiously, he'd ruined her day by making that infamous proposal of marriage, then he'd ruined her dinner by making chilling remarks, and now, to add insult to numerous injuries, he was *flirting* in her presence! Those two women were conducting themselves quite shamelessly, of course, but he was still very much at fault. Stacia particularly disliked the one with the scandalously low bodice who kept thrusting her full bosom under his nose.

Fuming inwardly, she gave Lord Andrew her most brilliant smile. "By all means, my lord," she said warmly. "Some cool air would be perfectly splendid." She placed her hand on his arm and made sure not to glance at Derek again as they approached the open French doors at the end of the room.

The balcony was empty, partly because it was too small to extend much hope of privacy and partly because it only offered a view of the alley behind the house. Nevertheless, Stacia's nerves steadied as she drew in a long, deep breath.

"Actually, this *is* what I need," she confessed. "How kind of you to realize."

Lord Andrew propped an elbow on the iron balustrade and watched her sip her drink. "You had your first driving lesson this morning," he stated. "Did it fare well? Or was Deveaux in one of his stiff-rumped moods?"

"Oh, well . . ." Embarrassed, Stacia raised a shoulder and stared over the railing into the shadows below. Two floors down, sounds from the kitchen drifted up to mingle with the musicians' tune. "Mr. Deveaux behaved much as usual and"—she paused, affecting an airy attitude—"and as for the lesson, I fancy I've learned all I need. Tooling a phaeton seems to be a simple business."

"Ah," he replied, gray eyes glinting, "things did not go well. I thought as much from the way the pair of you have been so carefully avoiding each other."

For a moment Stacia merely pressed her lips together, but the temptation to vent her frustration was too great. "As a matter of fact, my lord, your friend is the most detestable man alive!"

"Is he?" Lord Andrew's voice was dry. "That must be why all the ladies adore him so. I always wondered."

"Do they?" Stacia took another sip of punch. "I hadn't noticed."

"Now that, ma'am, I find difficult to believe." Lord Andrew straightened, his dryness replaced by amusement. "I saw those dagger-looks you gave Lady Saville and Mrs. Westmont. Mrs. Westmont, by the way, is the lady with the daring décolletage. It is one of her quirks, one might say. And yes, she is very good Ton, in case you were wondering."

"Mr. Deveaux certainly found her interesting," she said bitterly.

"Jealous?"

"Indeed not. Why should I be?"

Lord Andrew turned to face the ballroom, his back to the rail. "Deveaux is not as bad as he seems. I've known

163

him long enough to know. What did he do to offend you?"

"I really don't think I can talk about it." She rubbed the rim of the goblet in a nervous motion.

"Did he kiss you?"

She hesitated. "My lord, what transpired between Mr. Deveaux and myself is rather personal."

"Yes, of course." There was a moment of silence. "Would you like a piece of advice? Or is that too presumptuous?" His voice was lazy now, yet it held a thread of seriousness.

"I don't know," she said uncertainly. "What is it?"

"Give him another chance. Derek's a good man. Whatever he has done, for whatever reason, give him another chance. There's something about you that draws him, something that sets you apart from other women—"

"My fortune—"

"Something more than that," he corrected. "He's difficult, I'll grant you that. And I do sympathize. I've wanted to plow my fist into his face any number of times. But I still count him my friend, for all that."

Stacia shook her head. "You ask the impossible, my lord. He only wants my fortune. He does not love me. He . . . he even said so . . ." Her voice drifted off as she realized the unwitting admission.

Lord Andrew made an exasperated sound. "The silly ass. No wonder you've been looking blue-deviled."

"How can you say that?" she protested. "I've been smiling so much my cheeks ache."

"Yes, I noticed. That's what made me wonder. You're normally such a grave little thing."

"Am I?" Stacia considered this. "Well, I don't think it's my natural disposition. My life until now has scarcely been one of merriment, so I suppose that must be why. I'm not used to laughing."

"Yes, I'd forgotten about your husband's death. I do beg your pardon." He paused for a moment. "Tell me

164

something. If Deveaux falls in love with you, what will you do?"

The words brought her chin up. "What do you mean?"

"Will it matter to you?" he said intently. "Would you spurn him?"

"I hardly know how to answer that—"

Lord Andrew's teeth flashed white in the dull light. "Allow me to explain. Despite his faults, Derek is my friend. I'll not help you to destroy him, but if you are the lady I think you are then I know I needn't worry."

Stacia regarded him doubtfully. "I'm not sure what you're asking, my lord."

"Revenge," he said succinctly.

Her eyes widened. "Well, of course I would not. I would never deliberately hurt any person or creature." Her low voice vibrant, she glanced back through the open doors into the brilliantly lit room. In an effort to convince, she said, "When I was a child, I used to rescue insects that had wandered into the house. Ants, spiders, that sort of thing. I always worried they'd be stepped on."

Lord Andrew chuckled. "A tender-hearted lass, no less. By God, that's what Derek needs, not one of these hard society women with hearts of flint."

"And low bodices," added Stacia, without thinking.

"Precisely," he agreed, a quiver in his voice. "So let's form a plan, shall we? Perhaps we can goad him into admitting his feelings."

Stacia swallowed. "Do you really think he has any?"

"Feelings?" Lord Andrew looked surprised. "Dash it, ma'am, of course he does. They're only buried under a dozen layers of cynicism. Protective layers, you know. So someone can't come along and, er, step on him."

Stacia could not repress a giggle. "Oh dear," she said helplessly.

"We'll start with the theater," he mused. "We could make up a small party and see *Merchant of Venice*. I'm told Kean's rendition of Shylock is superb."

Stacia brightened. "I should like that very much, my

lord," she said shyly. "And I'm quite certain that Angeline will also."

"How comforting," he answered, in a rather ironic tone.

Out of the corner of his eye, Derek saw Stacia and Lord Andrew reenter the ballroom. He'd been gritting his teeth the entire time they'd been out on the balcony, and the knowledge of his own annoyance had made him even more annoyed. Chloe Westmont and Melanie Saville were prattling on about something, each of them quite unaware that he was no longer paying them any heed. Their coy smiles had long since made it clear that they had each selected him as their next lover, and for the past fifteen minutes had been subtly vying for his favor with innuendo and thrusting cleavage as their weapons.

If he had been in a better mood, he might have appreciated the situation, but he was in far too vile a mood to be amused. He'd been in a black humor since the morning or to be more accurate, since he'd had the felicity of having his proposal of marriage hurled back in his teeth. He'd also spent the past several hours watching Stacia laugh as though the rejection had been nothing and, unaccountably, it hurt.

Damn her to hell, anyway!

She was vain and fickle and shallow and he didn't in the least want to marry the little wretch. There was no need for him to marry money. He had already clawed his way out of debt, and he had done it on his own. Though he could scarcely be called flush in the pocket—in this crowd he would be considered poor—his estate had finally begun to show a decent profit only this year. And then there was Palatine. After the Newmarket races, the stallion would be worth his weight in gold as a stud.

No, he didn't need Stacia's money.

He needed Stacia.

It hit him then, at the exact moment Mrs. Westmont

166

let out a high-pitched trill. Had he said something amusing? He had been murmuring automatic responses to her remarks, but he hadn't the remotest notion what he had said. However, since Lady Saville was wearing a sour expression, he concluded that Mrs. Westmont had scored a point.

Unable to bear another moment in their company, he excused himself and headed in Drew and Stacia's direction. What he was going to say he had not the faintest notion, but something had to be said. He could no longer bear the tension.

Lord Andrew solved his problem. "Ah, Derek, there you are," he said with suspicious joviality. "Do come and tell Mrs. Edwards you'll join us. She wishes to see Kean at Drury Lane, so we thought to make up a small party and have a merry time of it. What do you say?"

It was not quite what Derek had in mind, yet such an outing was not without possibilities. Noting that Stacia did not seem to be regarding him with hostility, he said cautiously, "It would depend on the night. I leave for Suffolk at the end of the week. Palatine's trainer is a good man, but I like to keep an eye on things myself."

"Palatine is Derek's racehorse," Lord Andrew told Stacia. "A first-rate animal. Prime blood. You ought to see him."

"I'd like that," she responded, in a shyer voice than Derek was used to hearing. "I'm very fond of animals."

Lord Andrew smiled. "She used to rescue ants and spiders as a child, Derek. Can you credit such tender-heartedness? I confess *I* used to catch them and pull their legs off. I was such a malicious lad."

"I find that very difficult to credit," Stacia said warmly. "I am sure you must be bamboozling us, my lord. No one as kind as you could ever have tortured a spider."

They could have been flirtatious words, yet Derek knew she wasn't flirting. But Carisbrooke *was,* he thought grimly. Very well, then. He would give the fellow a taste of his own medicine.

"Mrs. Greaves is certainly in looks tonight," he said casually. He had the satisfaction of seeing Drew's eyes swivel to the far end of the room, where a dozen lovestruck beaux were admiring his diamond's facets from every available angle.

"Yes, she seems to be enjoying herself," his friend agreed, a trifle shortly.

"She deserves to enjoy herself," put in Stacia. "Poor Angeline has not had a great deal of happiness in her life."

Derek's eyes narrowed. "Not everyone introduces her companion to the Ton," he said. "I wonder why you did it?"

"I did it because I am fond of her, Mr. Deveaux. And I hope you will respect my wish that her employment in my household be kept a secret. She is as genteel as I am and has as much right to be here as any of us."

Concealing his skepticism, Derek shrugged. "If my godmother invited her, I suppose she must be acceptable. Eh, Drew? Why don't you ask her to dance? She must be bored with all those puppies at her heels."

To his surprise, the suggestion won Stacia's approval. "Oh, yes, my lord, please do. Angeline needs to learn that you are not—" She stopped. "I mean she needs to learn how kind you are. Oh dear. That was the wrong thing to say."

"Yes, she seems to cherish a rather poor opinion of me," said Lord Andrew wryly. "And I'm dashed if I know why."

Stacia looked unhappy. "It is not *you*, sir, I promise. I can say no more, but pray do not take her comments amiss."

"Very well, ma'am. If it pleases you, I will go and offer myself as a partner, though I doubt not the lady's card is already full." He gave Derek a very bland look. "If I don't return, take Mrs. Edwards in to supper for me, won't you?"

*   *   *

168

When Lord Andrew was gone, Derek gazed down at Stacia, trying to think of something tactful to say, something that would please her and make her think well of him. While he pondered, she took a swallow of punch, her nose wrinkled slightly as if in distaste.

"What do you think is in this?" she inquired.

Derek removed the goblet from her hand and sampled it. "Mostly champagne," he answered. "Don't drink too much of it."

Her eyes flashed. "Don't dictate to me, Mr. Deveaux. You've no right."

He felt his mouth tighten at the oblique reference to her refusal of his proposal. "No, I don't," he said evenly. "So will you get yourself foxed just to prove it?"

"Of course not," she said. "What a poor opinion you have of me."

He took the glass from her hand and handed it to a passing footman. "That ought to be my line, shouldn't it?" he said coolly.

She flushed. "You really don't have to stay here with me if you don't wish to. There are plenty of gallant gentlemen who are willing to treat me with courtesy—"

"Like Paul Matravers?" he interrupted, jealousy driving his objective from his head. "He's a ramshackle fortune hunter, Stacia, one of Croxton's set, in case you didn't know. Good family, but like me, he's poor as a church mouse. Of course, the Earl of Lindon has a sizable fortune if you've a fancy to be a countess. And then, of course, there's Drew. He's only a second son, but nearly as rich as his brother thanks to his maternal relatives. Perhaps you might set your cap at him—"

"I'm not setting my cap at anyone!" she blazed. "Why are you being so horrible? Can't you ever be pleasant to me? Is it completely beyond your capabilities?" Stacia's voice shook with suppressed feeling. "Lady Crackenthorpe told me you had a difficult childhood, but I don't think that's any excuse. I didn't have a happy childhood either, but I don't go around insulting people because of it! At least Mr. Matravers and Lord Lindon and half a

169

dozen others here tonight have made me feel like an attractive woman, which is more than you've ever done!" One lone tear rolled down her cheek and she swiped at it angrily. "You have ruined my first ball, Mr. Deveaux. I trust you are satisfied."

She was struggling so hard not to cry that she missed his incredulous, sick expression. The mere thought of Stacia as a small child, hurting, perhaps suffering as he had suffered filled him with fury and pain and amazement.

"I think we should discuss this somewhere less public. I see that I have"—for once he remembered to pick his words carefully—"that I have made some mistakes."

"Mistakes," she echoed bitterly. "Yes, and so have I."

Another few seconds passed. "I'd like you to forgive me," he said finally. "Do you think that's possible?"

"One can always forgive, Mr. Deveaux. It's the forgetting that can be difficult."

"Some people find the forgiving equally hard."

"I would forgive and forget if you would allow it," she told him. "I would even be your friend if you would let me."

"Let me take you into supper," he said quietly. "Drew won't object. I promise not to say anything to distress you."

"Mr. Deveaux!" Her bodice dipping lower than ever, Chloe Westmont stood not three feet away, tapping her dainty foot and glaring at him in a pointed manner. "Mr. Deveaux," she repeated. "I am waiting."

"Waiting, ma'am?" Derek looked at her blankly. "For, er, what?"

"I was engaged to you for the supper dance," she replied in a stiff, outraged voice, "which you might take the trouble to notice is now at an end. Therefore, sir, I am waiting to be escorted to supper. I am quite famished."

Derek's eyes shut for an instant. Damn, damn, damn! So that was what the silly woman had been looking so smug about. One of his own automatic responses must

170

have landed him into this mess.

"I have turned down several other offers," Chloe went on, enunciating distinctly, "because I believed I was already promised." She glared at Stacia, plainly blaming her for the whole mix-up.

Stacia gave Derek a troubled look. "You must certainly honor your obligations, Mr. Deveaux," she said. "We can continue this conversation another time."

Aware that "forgetting" his commitment must make him look reprehensible in Stacia's eyes, Derek bowed at Mrs. Westmont. "Forgive me, ma'am," he said, trying not to sound as antagonistic as he felt. "I seem to be guilty of many transgressions this evening."

Yet, suddenly, hope loomed on the horizon. "Ah, here's Drew," he added. "His mission appears to have failed." He tried not to sound too happy about it.

Lord Andrew, in fact, was wending his way back through the throng in their direction with a neutral expression on his face. Upon his arrival at their side, his brittle smile encompassed them all. "Good evening, Chloe, my love. You look younger and lovelier than ever."

While Mrs. Westmont preened, Derek sent the other man a silent plea to take the woman off his hands. However, either Drew failed to comprehend or he was not in an accommodating mood.

"Dear me, how is it that you have two ladies and I have none?" Drew's eyes gleamed with mischief. "This is not at all fair. I believe I must steal Mrs. Edwards back from you, Deveaux." The deviltry in his eyes made Derek long to strangle him. "After all, she was mine with which to begin," mocked his closest friend.

There was nothing left for Derek to do but offer his arm to Mrs. Westmont.

Marco was desolated. Despite his compliments and gallantry, he had failed to win Angeline as his supper companion. She had not even agreed to dance with him, and he derived only a small amount of consolation from the fact that she had not danced with that arrogant Carisbrooke fellow either.

Her natural modesty notwithstanding, his angel had been surrounded by a dozen others, and it was one of these, a namby-pamby fellow named Sheldrake, that she had chosen to take her into supper. In consequence, Marco lost his appetite, not only for food, but for the ball. It was clearly a waste of time; other than Angeline, there was nothing of interest to be found in such a place. There was a great deal more sport to be found elsewhere.

He knew exactly where he meant to go. Reggie Denchworth had told him about a cozy little hell called The Pigeon Hole, a place where the play was very high and one could win a great deal. Dench had even promised to lend him his lucky pair of dice, and that, combined with his trick of stripping off his coat and turning it inside out before he made his bet, was bound to assure him success.

Marco's confidence had been running strong ever since he'd won the other night in Brooks's. His luck had changed ever since he'd learned the trick about the coat. Another fellow had told him about it and by Jove it had worked. Nothing could stop him now.

Marco took a last look around the ballroom where he'd hoped to woo Angeline. She'd be more impressed with him after he won himself a fortune. She'd favor him then, by God. After he won his fortune.

Chapter Twelve

"Please, Drew, promise you will introduce me tonight." Lady Claire, Marchioness of Telford, gazed pleadingly at the cousin she called her favorite, her rouged lips set in her prettiest pout. "Of course she will be at Almack's. It will be the perfect opportunity."

Lord Andrew Carisbrooke shifted his weight in the delicate needlepoint chair, his idle glance sweeping the sumptuous saloon. "Yes, but for what purpose?" he inquired. With startling suddenness, his gaze swung back to the lady's clear-cut features. "Why this fascination with a woman you've never met?"

"Must I really explain?" The lovely young marchioness sighed and leaned forward, hands clasped, her blue eyes fixed imploringly on his face. "Very well, then. I had it straight from Melanie Saville that Derek was engaged for the supper dance with Chloe Westmont. And he left her standing there, poor creature, while he flirted with this Stacia Edwards woman. So you see, I *must* see what she is like."

"So you see her as a rival." He did not sound surprised. "Claire, need I remind you that you are a married woman?"

She made a moue of distaste. "La, how can I forget? Four children in five years, my figure all but ruined . . . and all for the sake of giving Telford his stupid heir!"

She jumped to her feet and began to pace. "Well, he has his heir now, Cousin. After three silly little girls he finally has a son. I have done my duty," she added, with an unloving glance at the family portrait above the fireplace. Sir Thomas Lawrence had outdone himself, but she saw only the children, four little golden heads who were nothing but a reminder of those months of misshapen misery.

"And now you intend to take your pleasure elsewhere." The disapproval in her cousin's voice was unmistakable.

"Can you really blame me?" she demanded. "It is quite all right for me to take a lover, so you needn't look so stuffy about it. Telford himself does not care so long as I am discreet."

"Perhaps. But don't count on Deveaux jumping to your call. He won't do it, Claire."

Lady Claire's bosom rose and fell against the soft blue cambric of her gown. "How do you know? Have I become so unattractive? Has all this child-bearing robbed me of my looks?" To convince him otherwise she spread her arms and twirled, a rotation as graceful as a bird in flight.

"Not at all," he disclaimed with politeness. "I believe there are any number of gentlemen who find you quite delectable. But Derek is not one of them."

Her arms dropped like broken wings. "Did he tell you this?" she faltered. "What did he say?"

He looked at her sternly. "Derek told me he offered you marriage, Claire, and that you refused. You flummoxed me into believing he never came up to scratch. You told me he broke your heart, for God's sake."

"He *did* break my heart! Oh, you do not understand!"

"Then make me understand. Why did you refuse him?"

Her voice took on a throbbing note. "Oh, Drew, how could I wed a man whose father had gambled away nearly everything he possessed? How was I to know Derek

174

wouldn't be the same?" A large tear slipped silently down her pale cheek. "You know me. I could never be the wife of a poor man. But it broke my heart to refuse him."

Lord Andrew was unmoved. "Derek might have been poor," he corrected, "but he was never a gamester. And he has gradually pulled himself out from under the load of debt his father incurred." He paused significantly. "I could have told you he would, if you had asked me."

"Yes, yes, but he is still not *rich*," she wailed, dabbing her eyes with a wispy square of muslin and lace. "I could not have born it, truly I could not."

"So." Lord Andrew sat back, his contemptuous gaze clamped on her face. "You turned down his offer and countered with an offer of your own."

"He never told you that!" she gasped, her face aflame. She had never quite recovered from the indignity of that episode. Not in a thousand years would she have wished her sophisticated cousin to know that she had begged a man to take her . . . and that she had been refused.

Lord Andrew misread her distress. "Never fear, neither Telford nor the gossip-mongers will get wind of the tale. Derek would not have told me had I not goaded it out of him." With a trace of impatience, he tapped the gilded arm of his chair. "And the truth is, Claire, that I don't care."

She chewed her lip for a moment, the seed of an idea entering her mind. "You don't care that one of your closest friends stole my innocence? That he took what ought to have been my husband's?"

Lord Andrew called her bluff. "If that had been the case," he said with lethal accuracy, "then, yes, I might have taken some exception. But that's not quite how it was, was it?"

Her flush deepened. "You are horrid, Drew! As horrid as Derek! I vow I believe everything the gossips say of him."

"Do you?" he said flippantly. "I'm not surprised."

"Sally Jersey says he is as shocking a rake as his uncle!

And Mrs. Drummond Burrell says he is no better than Croxton's set."

"And if you believe everything those harpies tell you, my dear, then you're touched in the upper works. They're only piqued because he won't set foot in their precious Almack's, though they send him vouchers year after year." His dryness held a pensive note. "Derek is simply different from other men. That doesn't make him less honorable."

Lady Claire's chin jerked defiantly, sending the crimped blonde curls bouncing. "Fine words, indeed! But what of that French courtesan he was flaunting? Dominique whatever-she-calls-herself? Oh, you needn't fold your lips at me in that priggish fashion. I hear all the worst gossip, you know."

He sighed. "Yes, I can see that you do."

"And he is horrid cruel to his mama," she went on. "Poor Lady Winifred! I do feel for her so."

"Lady Winifred creates her own troubles. Derek gives her a great deal more than she deserves."

Provoked, the marchioness sought refuge in her original pout. "I can see you are determined to be disagreeable and disobliging, so I will find someone else to introduce me to this Edwards creature. I suppose Derek wants her for his new mistress," she added pettishly.

"No." Lord Andrew crossed his legs and smiled an infuriating smile. "No, my love, I don't believe he does."

"No?" Her fingers linked and tightened on a spurt of hope. "Are you certain?"

"Quite certain," he assured her, withdrawing a snuff-box from his pocket. "He wants her for his wife."

"*What?*" She gaped as he flipped it open, her jaw hanging in astonishment.

With a maddening lack of haste, Lord Andrew took a small pinch and raised it to his nose. "And if you dare to interfere," he drawled, "I shall use my influence to see that Telford has you banished to the country." He inhaled the snuff and smiled again. "With your children," he added softly.

"Really, Angeline, I've tried so hard to understand you, but I don't. You persist in turning Lord Andrew down, yet you cannot name a single reason other than that he is his father's son." Stacia surveyed her companion in frank bewilderment, ignoring the botch of embroidery threads in her lap. "You refused to dance with him at Lady Crackenthorpe's ball and you refused to drive out with him these past two days running. And now you say you will not go to Drury Lane simply because you wish to avoid him! I think you are being monstrously unfair to the poor man."

Her back rigid, Angeline kept her eyes on her needlepoint. "On the contrary, ma'am," she said tonelessly, "his lordship invites me only because you wish it. He seeks to wheedle himself into your good graces. Can you not see that?"

"I don't believe that for a moment," Stacia replied firmly. "And you're being unfair to me, too. I wish you to go the theater and to Almack's too!"

"I would rather not. But as your companion, I will, of course, do as you request."

Stacia studied the beautiful, stiff mouth. "You know," she said suddenly, "I think you are far less averse to him than you pretend. I think you feel something for him, something favorable."

The busy fingers stilled. "God help me, ma'am, I fear you are right." Angeline's head bowed and her hands gripped the embroidery frame as though it were the answer to her troubles. "I'm too much like my mother," she whispered. "I'm weak. The attraction is there, and I cannot fight it." Her shoulders hunched; she looked weary and defeated.

"Then stop trying," Stacia said bracingly. "You'll go with us to the theater and that is that. And tonight, at

177

Almack's, if Lord Andrew invites you to dance you absolutely *must* accept."

"Must I?" Angeline smiled for the first time in several days. "What a despot you have become, ma'am. You used to be so hesitant. You have changed."

"Have I?" The words triggered a shift in Stacia's mood. "Mr. Deveaux wishes me to continue my driving lessons," she said abruptly. "He claims I am not yet ready to tool my phaeton through the busy streets."

"Well." Angeline pursed her lips. "Do you agree with him?"

"I suppose so." Stacia lifted her hands. "Oh dear, it is so much easier to see what is right for others than it is for oneself. Common sense tells me to avoid him at all cost, yet my emotions are as tangled as these stupid threads." She tossed her needlework aside in disgust. "When he visited us the day after the ball, I swear I have never seen him so polite. Yet yesterday, when he called again, he glowered as much as usual and scarcely stayed twenty minutes."

Angeline's lip curled. "Ah, but the first day he was the first caller. Yesterday was different. Remember how Mr. Matravers kept leaning over your chair and touching your shoulder? And then there were six other gentlemen vying for your attention at the same time. And no ladies save for you and me, ma'am. I rather fancy Mr. Deveaux did not like that."

Stacia's brow furrowed. "But most of them had come to see you, Angeline. And there was nothing I could do about Mr. Matravers. He was a little bold," she acknowledged, "but I'm sure I did nothing to encourage him."

"That would not matter to Mr. Deveaux. He probably blames you." Angeline's tone was derisive. "Men are so unreasonable."

"None of us are behaving reasonably," Stacia reminded her a little sharply. "I suppose he is quite right about my driving. I have been stubborn about it."

"What I should like to know," said Angeline, quite suddenly, "is what the rumors are about."

"Rumors? What rumors?"

Angeline set aside her work. "Don't you remember what Lady Jersey said? About Mr. Deveaux? She would not grant him a voucher for Almack's because of certain shocking stories that were circulating. He must have done something truly dreadful, ma'am, and we ought to discover what it is. After all, it may damage your reputation to be seen with him."

"Oh, but that was only Lady Jersey. Lady Crackenthorpe says she is the worst gossip in town. We ought not to give credence to anything she says."

Angeline was not convinced. "Where there's smoke, there's fire," she declared. "Mr. Deveaux is the sort of man to possess a shocking reputation. I don't think you should drive out with him at all."

"Lady Crackenthorpe would have warned me—"

"Lady Crackenthorpe dotes upon the man. Of course she would not warn you. She wants you to wed him, ma'am. It's perfectly plain."

Stacia raised her chin. "I won't listen to gossip, Angeline."

"Well, if you won't, then I will," retorted her companion decisively. "And Almack's ought to be just the place to hear it."

Almack's Assembly Rooms were located in King Street, very close to St. James's Square. From the worshipful way people referred to it, Stacia had been expecting it to be the most marvelous place in existence, and was therefore disappointed to find that the interior was as unprepossessing as the exterior was plain. The ballroom was large but undistinguished in any way, and the refreshments were (as she heard one gentleman mutter) perfectly wretched. In fact, there was nothing to indicate why the place should be deemed the seventh

179

heaven of the fashionable world.

However, if the surroundings were far from splendid, the people were interesting. A great many of her newly formed acquaintances were present, as well as Lady Crackenthorpe. Lord Andrew was also there, which for some reason made Derek's absence all the more noticeable. Wondering what Derek could possibly have done to cause such an uproar, Stacia resolved to ask Lady Crackenthorpe about the matter. Her ladyship would give her facts, not whatever distorted rumors Angeline would dig up. More likely than not, she thought wryly, Derek had simply put his foot in his mouth once too often.

But she was hardly likely to learn the truth from the lady with whom she was conversing. Her name was Lady Claire and she was excessively pretty, but for some reason Stacia did not like her. Pale blonde hair curled about her heart-shaped face, her features were even and dainty, and her blue gown exactly matched her cornflower blue eyes. However, if her appearance was charming, the direction of her discourse was considerably less appealing.

"This is primarily a marriage mart, you know," Lady Claire was saying. She spread her pretty fan over her mouth as though to mask the sound of her voice. "It doesn't have to be showy. The Ton provides for its own entertainment." She laughed, a rippling little sound that was unaccountably annoying. "You and I are fortunate. We can afford to look down our noses"—she touched Stacia's arm—"at these poor little chits in their first Season. We are experienced women and they, poor things, do not even know what it is like to be kissed." She paused, her eyes scanning the dancers who took part in the cotillion. "Or at least they shouldn't," she added, her tone soft and conspiratorial, "but *I* certainly did at their age. Do you remember your first kiss?"

Instantly, Stacia's mind flooded with the memory of Derek's warm mouth on hers. "Er, yes," she mumbled, "as a matter of fact, I do." She had a sinking premonition what was to come next.

"So do I." Lady Claire sighed reminiscently. "I was eighteen and he was older, and very suave and sophisticated." She leaned closer, her mouth near Stacia's ear. "I should not tell you this, I know, but 'tis too delicious not to share. His initials, my dear, were D.D."

Stacia's color heightened. "Oh?" she replied, quite flatly. She forced her expression to remain calm, yet every muscle in her body was tight with foreboding.

"Yes," continued the lady with nauseating coyness. "I must be discreet, of course, but if you wish to try to guess?"

Stacia longed to turn and run away, but of course there was no question of that. "I doubt I could do that," was all she said, with nothing more than civility. "Doubtless there are many men with those initials."

The fan fluttered for a moment. "No doubt," agreed the marchioness. "But this particular D.D. has the most shocking reputation, and though I am a married lady I must guard mine." Once more her voice lowered to a breathy whisper. "However, I know I can trust *you*, my dear, for you have such a prodigious trustworthy face. You see, there are the most dreadful rumors going about. I daresay you may even have heard them."

Stacia shook her head. "I don't pay much attention to that sort of thing," she replied. Part of her recoiled from such confidences, yet her curiosity was caught, trapped by the marchioness's cleverly wrought cage.

The fan poked at Stacia's arm, then spread to hide the pink, malicious lips. "They say he is a shocking womanizer. They say he has fathered a number of children, one for every mistress he has had. And they say he has a house in the country where he keeps them hidden away."

Stacia's first thought was that it was too ridiculous, while her second was that the lady's horror seemed stagy

181

and artificial. "And I suppose he has murdered a vast number of people, as well?" she said aloud. "What do they say about that, madam?"

The other woman stared for a moment, then blinked several times. "Ah, you think I am jesting, but I assure you I am not. You see, I have good reason to know," she added with a suggestive smirk. "La, now you look pale, my dear. Why, 'tis natural, after all. Men will ever need mistresses, and"—she gave a prosaic shrug—"bastards are often the result." Her voice transformed to its formal coyness. "But I thought I should warn you, you see, in case you happen to form an acquaintance with my D.D. Old habits die hard, my dear, so beware." She allowed her voice to fade into significant silence.

"I have been in town long enough to know that there is always gossip," Stacia replied firmly, "but that does not mean I'm going to listen to it."

"But, my dear, you just did," said the marchioness gently.

"Good evening, ladies."

Lord Andrew had not exactly crept up on them, but Lady Claire started as though he had done so. "Oh!" she exclaimed. "Drew, I . . . I thought you had decided not to come." Her fan waved jerkily. "You are uncommon late tonight."

From a purely visual standpoint Lord Andrew's smile was as affable as ever, but his voice held a definite flinty edge. "And in my supposed absence," he said, "you found someone to introduce you to Mrs. Edwards." He turned to Stacia and bowed over her hand. "Pray excuse us, ma'am. Claire is my cousin. We have known one another since childhood." He surveyed the marchioness through his quizzing glass. "That shade of blue becomes you, my love. And where is Telford? Did the lady patronesses deny him admittance?"

Lady Claire looked rattled. "Nonsense, Drew. You know he and I never attend functions together. In fact I—" She broke off with an odd expression. "I don't

182

believe it," she muttered, staring past him toward the door. "It's Derek. Derek is here."

Following Lady Claire's gaze, Stacia's breath caught in her throat. Derek was indeed present, and if what she had heard was true, then he was setting foot in Almack's for the very first time. As he made his way forward, pausing here and there as his attention was claimed by one person or another, she watched him with unconscious feminine approval.

Like the other men he was wearing knee breeches, but there was no doubt in her mind that he wore them better than anyone else. He sported no pins, fobs, seals, or watches, but his white waistcoat and claret-colored coat were certainly no less *de rigueur* than any others in the room. Of course, his cravat did not match Sir Cuthbert's in height or complexity, but it was modish enough to suit Stacia's taste. And she liked the way his black hair was combed, neatly and not crimped into the ridiculous curls that Sir Cuthbert affected.

"He is a handsome creature, is he not?" Lady Claire whispered in her ear. "One is almost tempted to stare."

Refusing to acknowledge the gibe, Stacia raised her brows in unconscious imitation of some of the more imposing dowagers. "Is one?" she murmured haughtily.

It seemed an eternity before Derek reached them and by that time Stacia was jittery with nervousness. Why was he here? What would he say? And how was she to behave naturally with Lady Claire's shrewd eyes on her face?

When at last he stood before them, Stacia's stomach was tied into knots.

"Mrs. Edwards," he said, bowing, "and Lady Claire. What a surprise." Though his expression had not changed, Stacia wondered at the disapproval in his voice. "Evening, Drew. What transpires here?"

The two men exchanged a long look, then Lord Andrew shrugged. "'Twas none of my doing," was his cryptic reply. "What transpires with you? You have stunned all

183

London with this unprecedented visit."

Derek's arms folded over his chest. "Have I?" he said indifferently. His gaze swept the room, encompassing everything and everyone in it. "So this is what I've been missing, eh?" His tone implied that it had not been very much.

"If you dislike it so much, why did you come?" Stacia had been too flustered to remain silent, but when Derek's eyes shifted she wished she had not spoken. Something in his face warned her that he was in an unpredictable mood.

"To dance with you, of course," he responded, as the musicians launched into a lively German waltz. He bowed and held out his hand. "Will you honor me?" He was all courtesy and polish, the very picture of the well-bred gentleman, yet the green eyes were challenging and deliberate.

Aware of the marchioness's slicing gaze, Stacia gave him an awkward smile. "Well, I am already promised for this waltz. And . . . and all the other sets, too, I'm afraid."

"That's not an insurmountable problem," he answered. "To whom are you promised?"

Stacia consulted her card, her fingers shaking only the tiniest bit. "Oh, ah, Mr. Matravers."

"In that case," he said briskly, "strong measures are required." In one swift movement, he confiscated the card and shoved it into his pocket.

Stacia was astonished. "What—" she began, but as he caught hold of her hand she realized what he was about. "Just what do you think you're doing?" she exclaimed. "I told you this is Mr. Matravers's waltz."

"Matravers isn't a suitable partner for you." The curt remark was accompanied by a persistent pull on her arm that she would have resisted had she not, by pure chance, caught Lady Crackenthorpe's eye. Several yards away, her ladyship's quick frown reminded Stacia of their surroundings and the consequences a scene might en-

184

gender. This was Almack's, after all. And the truth was that she did not wish to resist.

As they wove their way among the other dancers, Stacia was enormously conscious of Derek's hand at her waist. All her indignation vanished; everything but the music faded—the room, the voices, the watching eyes— and she and Derek were alone in a dream that was not a dream, waltzing gracefully through a night without end or beginning. The warm spread of his fingers ignited emotions she had only dreamed of, yet the reality of his closeness intensified them tenfold.

How had he managed it?

Somehow, without her permission, he had vanquished her protests, buffeting them aside by the sheer dominant force of his personality.

And what if he had?

This was her defiant voice, the one that had always rebelled against Papa's dictates, the one that had persuaded her to come to London posed as a widow. Why should she care, it whispered, when everything that was feminine inside her cried out that this was right?

He was real, she thought wildly. Derek was no dream, no blurry invention born of loneliness and isolation. He was here, holding her, and she knew only that at this instant she wanted it to go on forever, to freeze the moment in time as something to cherish for all eternity. Indeed, the composite of everything about him—his form, his smile, his bearing, his countenance—it was all so relentlessly masculine that Stacia could scarcely believe it was she in his arms. And then, as she stared up into his emerald eyes, she came to a shocking conclusion.

She loved him.

The knowledge exploded within her, sending tremors of longing spiraling throughout her body. Despite his poor manners and rude remarks, she had fallen in love with this man. Dear God, why had she not realized it sooner? Only once before had every nerve, every fiber of her body been so quiveringly awake and that had been the

185

day that he had kissed her in the Park.

How handsome he was! Every detail pleased her—from the line of his jaw and the shape of his nose to those absurdly long, black lashes and the handsome curve of his ears. In many ways, she thought, it was a hard face, yet there was kindness in it too—though others might not be discerning enough to see it. Even the tiny scar on his chin seemed precious beyond measure, for it reminded her of Lady Crackenthorpe's tale of the pain he had suffered as a child.

Lady Claire's stories must be lies, she decided. She simply could not believe that the man she loved was as callous and irresponsible as he was portrayed. Since the day she had met him she had feared he was like her father, but she knew now that she had long since rejected this notion. Her heart told her this man could love—and that made him as different from her father as porridge was from cream.

Once, long ago, her beloved governess had said that in truly important matters one should listen to one's heart. Well, right now her heart was shouting that Derek was nothing like Papa. Derek had admitted to making mistakes. Derek had asked for her forgiveness, albeit in a rather gruff manner. These two facts alone were testimony enough, for Papa would never have done either. Derek was a good and decent man who simply needed to be healed of the wounds his mother had inflicted. A wounded dog will snap at those who try to help it, she thought, but with love and gentle handling its trust could be won.

Derek was studying her just as intently as she had been studying him. "What's going on in that mind of yours?" he inquired.

Stacia swallowed. "I was thinking that you are completely unscrupulous," she lied, "but upon reflection I have decided to forgive you."

"Have you now?" His expression fluctuated, betraying surprise. "What's brought this on? I thought you'd be spitting like a cat by now."

She peeped at him through her lashes, emboldened by the knowledge that this chance might never come again. "Don't you like cats, Mr. Deveaux?"

"Are you trying to flirt with me, Stacia?" He sounded amused. "Or are my preferences really of interest to you?"

"Well, of course I'm trying to flirt with you. Can't you . . . can't you tell?" She tipped back her head and smiled bravely.

His eyes gleamed with appreciation. "Oh, I like cats very well," he replied in a lazy, intimate way that sent a shiver down her spine. "As long as they don't scratch, mind." His hands tightened, and, infinitesimally, the gap between their bodies shrank.

Stacia knew she was blushing, but the conversation was far too exhilarating to abandon. "I don't scratch," she said breathlessly. "Not anymore, that is."

"Indeed." Derek's voice sounded a little thick. "And what brought about this change, may I ask?"

Now what should she say? Instinctively she knew that to confess her feelings would be the height of folly and the surest route to the destruction of her hopes. She must go slowly, carefully, feeling her way like a blind man in a crowd.

"It's quite simple," she told him hesitantly. "I have decided that you are"—she cast him a quick look—"a very agreeable person and that I . . . I like being with you."

"I? Agreeable?" Derek cocked a skeptical eyebrow. "That's doing it a bit brown, my sweet. I'm odious and horrible, remember? I never say anything nice."

"*Most* of the time you are quite amiable," she corrected. "Much nicer than Mr. Matravers." It was a finishing touch she thought would please him but instead his face darkened.

"What's that fellow done to you?"

Stacia blinked in confusion. "Who?"

187

"Paul Matravers, Stacia. Don't play innocent with me."

She raised her chin at him. "I'm not playing innocent, as you so ungallantly phrase it, Mr. Deveaux. And Mr. Matravers has done absolutely nothing, I assure you."

"He has not tried to kiss you, has he? Don't lie to me, Stacia. Your face will give you away."

Stacia grit her teeth. "Do you accept wagers, Mr. Deveaux? If so, I'd be willing to wager a fair sum that you are"—she took a deep breath—"that you are jealous!"

His smile flashed. "Perhaps I am, but I don't advise you to wager on it. I'll give you another piece of advice. Never wager more than you are willing to lose. A rather obvious rule of thumb, but few people abide by it. You'd be wise to pass it on to your brother."

For an instant, Stacia felt deflated. The last thing she wanted to think about right now was Marco's gambling. "I'm sure my brother knows that," she retorted. "I would never presume to tell him what to do."

She had hoped to close the subject, but he would not let it go. "I hope you would never give him money either," he said intently. "That would be the height of stupidity and you're not a stupid woman."

Despite these words, Derek's voice was not unsympathetic, and for an instant Stacia was tempted to pour her troubles in his lap. But that was cowardice and Almack's was not the place for such confidences. In an effort to distract them both, Stacia glanced around the room and was dismayed to see dozens of inquisitive eyes following their progress.

"Derek, everyone is watching us," she said, barely aware of using his given name.

His expression did not change. "It's because of me, my pet. All my doings are grist for the gossip mills, you know. And because you're with me—dancing the scandalous waltz, no less—you are dragged in." He paused for a few seconds, then said, in a peculiar, almost supplicating tone, "Do you care?"

188

She threw back her head and smiled at him. "No," she replied. "Why should I? I'm a grown woman. I'll dance with whomever I please."

"Ah, a woman of independent spirit. I like that." He paused. "So . . . I am to understand that you've, er, altered your opinion? About . . . er . . . me, I mean?"

Sensing his need for reassurance, Stacia met his eyes squarely. "Yes," she said in a soft voice. "I'm sometimes very pigheaded, but I usually come to my senses. I've forgiven you, Mr. Deveaux, and would like to continue my driving lessons, if you please." She hesitated. "If you dislike gossip so much, why go out of your way to court it?"

Derek was silent so long she thought he was not going to answer. "I'm a private man," he said finally. "I abhor having my personal doings aired and scrutinized and judged by every gossipmonger in town. But their lies and half-twisted tales of debauchery"—he spoke the word as though he despised it—"are preferable to me than—"

He broke off as the music drew to a close, but Stacia could not allow him to stop. "Than what?" she prompted.

Derek's mouth curved. "This is hardly a moment for confessions, little widow. I'm sure you've been regaled with all the latest and most sordid gossip about me, and if you haven't, you soon will be. Just know that I'm not as black as I'm painted." His head turned and, following his gaze, Stacia was almost certain his eyes fell on Lady Claire. "Nor am I a saint. But any good lie holds its measure of truth," he added enigmatically. "That's what makes it believable."

From the far side of the room, Angeline had been watching Stacia and Derek with distinct disapproval. Her admirers surrounded her like a swarm of locusts, and if male adulation had been all she desired, then she probably would have been satisfied. However, it was a hollow victory, for not only had Lord Andrew Carisbrooke *not* sought her out (so that she was denied the satisfaction of rebuffing him) he had not so much as glanced her way since his arrival twenty-two minutes before. And it was very difficult to wreak one's vengeance upon the object of one's enmity when that object would not cooperate.

In fact, it was difficult even to sustain that enmity when he was so unlike everything she had expected, or indeed what she had wanted him to be. (Sinister, dissolute, lascivious . . . that man Croxton better fit her image of what the villainous son of the Duke of Wight should be like. Failing that, she would have expected rudeness and crudeness, like that horrible Derek Deveaux.)

She had tried to convince herself that she did not care, but to no avail. Oh, she was weak. She had come to London to play a role, to present herself to the Carisbrookes in order to take advantage of her half sister's blood relationship, but at the crucial moment her courage had flown. She had stood before that huge town mansion where the family resided—and then she had walked away, hating them and hating herself for her own defeat.

While her three most ardent admirers fought for the honor of fetching her a glass of lemonade, Angeline's thoughts rolled back to that dreadful day and its even more dreadful conclusion. She'd walked the Mayfair streets for hours, unable to form a new plan or to think beyond her failure. Twice she had nearly been accosted, and then, exhausted, she'd found sanctuary in Green Park—alone and cold and frightened out of her wits. She shuddered, remembering how that night had seemed a thousand hours long, a nightmare of whispers and shadows, a test of her endurance. The real irony was that for the first time in years she had prayed, and with the morning sun those prayers had been answered. Stacia Edwards had come along—Stacia, with her warm smile and impetuous, generous nature.

She had watched Stacia's approach along the park's reservoir with desperate calculation, banking on the odds that it was kindness she read in those dreamy brown eyes. The tears, the heaving shoulders, the sad tale of her dead husband, the lover who had abandoned her . . . it had all been fabricated on the spot to win Stacia's sympathy.

The arrival of the lemonade returned Angeline's attention to the present. Well, she had won more than that, she reflected, her violet-blue eyes sweeping the crowded room. She had meant to take advantage of Stacia and look where those wicked intentions had landed her.

Almack's. Drives in Hyde Park. Beautiful clothes. Droves of suitors.

Employment with Stacia Edwards was like winning a lottery. And what had she done to deserve it?

Nothing.

Oh, in a mild sort of way she had tried. She had made an honest effort to mete out her worldly knowledge, attempting to warn her unsophisticated employer of the perfidy of men. Unfortunately, Stacia was too stubborn to listen and too innocent to believe.

It had been years since Angeline had listened to her conscience, but now, for the first time since her sister's death, she experienced guilt.

Bestowing a vague smile upon her horde of beaux, Angeline's thoughts centered on her benefactress. She owed Stacia so much; she must do something to cancel the debt. And the most obvious thing she could do was to save her from Derek Deveaux. By now she had discovered what the gossip was about, that Deveaux was an unreliable lecher with a multitude of bastards to his name. What would Stacia say when she heard? Angeline loathed the idea of telling her, but it would better if she knew. Stacia had already suffered the loss of her first husband and Angeline was prepared to do whatever was necessary to protect her from further hurt.

Angeline frowned suddenly. Perhaps—? No, what was

191

she thinking of? Lord Andrew Carisbrooke was not worthy of Stacia.

On the other hand, he was far more worthy than Derek Deveaux, and, as Stacia had pointed out, there was absolutely no evidence to indicate that he was a womanizer. In fact, she was beginning to believe that Lord Andrew had far more merits than deficiencies. He was handsome, he had a noble lineage, and could be exceptionally charming when he was not being top-lofty and arrogant.

More to the point, he was rich, whereas Derek Deveaux was an obnoxious fortune hunter.

And Stacia liked him, she mused. She did not love him, of course, but that was all well and good. Love could lead to all manner of perils.

Slowly, insidiously, the idea was taking root.

In comparison to that Deveaux oaf, Lord Andrew was a positive paragon of courtesy and sensitivity. And just lately had he not been growing more attentive toward Stacia? Had he not called at Upper Grosvenor Street every morning this past week?

Angeline's face clouded a little. Lord Andrew would make Stacia a most appropriate husband, she thought. All she need do was to prod Stacia in the right direction.

And if, from her own point of view, such a prod would entail a very great sacrifice, then that would be her penance for being so very wicked.

For she was now ready to admit that she was in love with him herself.

Chapter Thirteen

What the deuce had gone wrong? Derek stared at the crisp white sheet of vellum in his hand, reading and rereading the sentences writ in a neat, feminine hand.

If you have the least sense of decency, spare me the dishonor of your company tonight. I have a marked preference for Lord Andrew Carisbrooke and infinitely prefer his escort to yours . . . I find it unbearable and repulsive that people are linking our names . . .

What the devil sort of words were these from the lady who had so recently told him that he was "agreeable"? *Repulsive and unbearable*, he thought furiously. She'd said she enjoyed being with him, even *flirted* with him, for God's sake. Had it been but a cruel game?

Derek's brows drew together as another possibility occurred to him. Had it been an act, put on for Drew Carisbrooke's benefit? Granted, it was a common feminine trick to use one man to bring another up to scratch, but for Stacia to employ such a stratagem—! Frankly, he'd have thought it unworthy of her.

His face hardened as he considered this. Despite the heat of rage his insides were going unpleasantly cold, as though a thick, sharp slab of ice was pressing against his heart. He glanced down at the letter in his hand, feeling a little sick. Of course she preferred Drew. He'd simply been jackass enough to be gulled by a ploy as old as time itself. Christ's blood, he ought to have known Stacia would be as full of guile as the next woman. By his age, however, his skin should have been thick enough to withstand the disappointment.

Unfortunately, it wasn't.

He read the letter once more, his shoulders sagging. He felt disillusioned and betrayed, far more than he had when he'd discovered the truth about Claire. He also felt old. Yesterday had been so full of promise; because of Stacia the future had stretched out before him in a mist of golden possibilities. Even a few hours ago he'd been conscious of a sense of anticipation, for this was the evening he was to meet Stacia, Drew, Angeline Greaves, and his godmother at the Drury Lane Theater.

Of course, there was no question of his going now.

. . . unbearable and repulsive that people are linking our names . . . ! He'd known that the anomaly of his appearance at Almack's would cause talk, but he had not cared and thought she had not either. So people were talking, were they? Well, let them, he thought savagely.

Only yesterday he had believed in Stacia's sincerity and goodness, though he'd had other business to attend to and been unable to pay her a visit. Even in light of what he had unearthed this afternoon he had only thought her misguided and foolish.

However, now that she had sent him this insulting letter, he revised his opinion. She was a calculating, scheming little jade who deserved whatever she got. So let the tongues wag, he thought bitterly. Let them grind their grist for the gossip mills and if her reputation was destroyed he did not care.

He was sitting in his study with his feet on a stool, his long fingers wrapped around a glass of very decent brandy. Damn his impetuosity. If only Lady Cowper's last-minute voucher had not caught him in a weak moment—a moment in which he'd been thinking about Stacia in a way that was wholly improper and maddeningly addictive. Thanks to his godmother he'd known that Stacia would be at Almack's, and with the voucher's arrival had come that sudden, half-crazed impulse to make use of it. It had been an uncharacteristic urge, for until recently he believed that his self-control was supreme—and that women played but a small role in his well-ordered life. Derek's lip curled in self-mockery. Well, just lately he'd shot that philosophy to hell and made a fool of himself into the bargain.

To give himself credit, he'd at least had the sense to fight the impulse. He'd flung the voucher aside, paced around, and had a few drinks. He'd scowled and cursed and gazed out the window, damning women in general and Stacia and Emily Cowper in particular. He'd even spent a number of minutes wondering which courtesan of his acquaintance might be available for an impromptu romp in the hay. But neither Cecily nor Fifi nor Adoriana could have satisfied him at that indescribably frustrating moment, and as for Dominique, he'd rather have waded through a mire of offal than go to her.

No, it was only Stacia that he had wanted, and, blast his libidinous soul, even now continued to want. Only Stacia. The mere thought of her made him groan, and the knowledge that she was not *his* stung at him like a festering sore. It was maddening, baffling, crack-brained, and insane . . . and it was driving him positively dotty.

God's mercy, what was wrong with him? He kicked the stool aside and sat forward, his arms on his knees. He had far more important matters to worry about, he told himself harshly, than his own amorous cravings for a deceiving little witch.

He tried to relax and focus on nothing in particular, but his mind fought him, refusing to allow him any respite. He'd been planning to do something about Sir Marco Ashcroft's gambling—*not* that he should give a damn if the idiot threw away his sister's entire fortune. It would serve the vixen right. But he'd made his plans already, and to own the truth it would be pleasure to teach that idiot brother of hers a lesson.

Yesterday, a reliable acquaintance had given an eyewitness account of Marco Ashcroft's activities in Brooks's Club two nights past. It seemed that Sir Marco had lost five thousand at cards, then coolly doubled his wager and won. Even now, Derek's head shook in wonder and utter contempt. The fact that the bloody young fool had won had nothing to do with it.

However, such lunacy paled beside his next staggering discovery.

He'd been making inquiries about Sir Marco Ashcroft and by a stroke of rare good fortune discovered that the bank Marco and Stacia utilized—Herries, Farquhar and Co.—had been his father's bank. Old Farquhar knew him, and knew, too that he conducted his affairs with far more prudence than his father had ever done. And so, not three hours ago, he'd paid Mr. Farquhar a visit.

Derek's jaw hardened as he reviewed the scene in his mind. The interview had not been pleasant, for in his subtle way, Mr. Farquhar had made it clear that he recalled the devastation Derek's father had wrought. No one, the banker had asserted in a wheezy voice, disapproved of waste more than he did, and gaming was a particularly nasty vice! It was a simple statement, made in reference to Sir Marco Ashcroft, yet the memory of his father's excesses had hung between them like a rotten smell. Mr. Farquhar was well aware that Richard Deveaux's son was no gamester, but even that knowledge had not prevented Derek from feeling uncomfortable. He disliked discussing his father, and had had no wish to rehash the past with allusions, however vague. All he'd wished to do was discover the size of Sir Marco Ashcroft's fortune, and whether or not his gaming debts were being paid by his sister.

But this had not been as simple as he would have liked. Such information was confidential, the grizzled old banker had reminded him sternly. Why did he wish to know? Derek had hesitated, then explained that he was acquainted with Sir Marco and was concerned, but this had not been enough. In the end he'd had to spell out his intentions toward Sir Marco's sister as justification for his interest. Derek smiled mirthlessly as he remembered the subsequent scene. . . .

"Ah, so you mean to marry her," Mr. Farquhar repeated, peering at Derek over the rim of his glasses with surprise. "That puts another complexion on things." He leaned forward and cleared his throat. "An excellent choice, sir, and if I may say so, an excellent solution all around. Pray allow me to congratulate you."

"Congratulations are a bit premature," Derek admitted, "but I have little fear my suit will be rejected."

"Good, good." The banker beamed his approval. "No reason why it should be. You're a man of fine family connections—an excellent match." He hesitated, then brushed aside whatever wispy afterthought fluttered through his head. "Unless she is aiming for a title, of course, but let us hope she is not so imprudent. I would be less than honest if I said that all is well in that quarter. I had thought Miss Ashcroft a sensible girl when I made her acquaintance, but where her brother is concerned—" He shook his head in a mournful manner. "However, the money is hers by law. There is nothing I can do but advise."

Derek's expression had altered during the latter part of this speech. "Miss Ashcroft?" he said, his keen eyes suddenly narrowed. "Who is Miss Ashcroft?"

Mr. Farquhar stared. "I beg your pardon, sir? Is this not the young lady we have been discussing? Sir Marco Ashcroft's sister?"

"How many sisters does he have?"

"Why, only the one!" Mr. Farquhar looked indignant at Derek's clipped tone. "What do you mean, sir?"

Derek ignored the question. "To your knowledge, Mr. Farquhar, has Miss Ashcroft ever been wed?"

The banker lowered his bushy brows and absently rearranged a sheaf of papers on the desk in front of him.

"No, she has not," he retorted. "Unless she has done so since she came into her inheritance but I had not heard of it." His florid countenance looked disapproving. "I certainly hope she has not entered into any sort of clandestine arrangement. That would be beyond what anyone could condone—"

"No," cut in Derek a shade grimly. "I do not think that is the case." He frowned, thinking hard for a few seconds. "She has never made any mention to you of a Frederick Edwards, a man she claims was her husband, killed at Waterloo?"

The banker shook his head. "Should she have done so? Perhaps she has done so to her solicitor, but one would naturally think— However, young females will sometimes do unaccountable things. I know," he added gloomily, "I have three daughters of my own."

No, the man was not Stacia's solicitor, but if she had ever truly been wed, Mr. Farquhar should have heard of it. Even now, after mulling the matter over in the privacy and comfort of his lodgings, the whole thing pointed in only one direction. What it boiled down to was that either Stacia had been wed and never told the banker—or she had never been wed at all.

Which would explain a very great deal, Derek thought, caught between confoundment and a feral rage he did not understand. In the hours since the interview he had been stewing over the situation, trying to understand. He had told himself that some part of him had half-guessed the truth from the first: that Stacia was unwed and innocent and unprotected, a lamb in a city of wolves. No wonder she had been reluctant to talk about her husband! He had never existed! It would also explain that virginal quality she possessed, and why she had been so very shocked when he had kissed her in the Park.

Or had that, too, been an act?

Bloody hell! Too late, Derek realized this line of

198

thought was a mistake, for an instant later his body came alive with the memory of Stacia's lips, of her taste and light feminine scent, and of the incredible, sweet fullness of her breast where he had dared to caress her. She might be a shameless little deceiver, but he still wanted her as much as ever. Perhaps even more.

Derek set down his glass so abruptly that brandy spilled over his fingers. Seconds ticked by while he stared at the dark amber liquid, his teeth clamped shut with suppressed emotion. Whether Stacia was widow or unmarried girl, she was clearly not as up to snuff as she should be. Why, he thought angrily, she could not even recognize a man like Matravers for the slick-tongued rogue that he was! And if she had done as he suspected—foisted herself off as a widow before Polite Society for whatever deranged reason—and if Polite Society were to discover it had been tricked, there were going to be some unpleasant consequences. For a moment his lip curled with self-mockery. But why the deuce should he care?

Unfortunately, he did.

Lady Winifred Deveaux was feeling restless. She had spent the better part of the day with Sir Cuthbert, but now she was alone in her boudoir, and the silence stretched out before her like the years remaining in her empty life.

Sir Cuthbert Duncan was such a contrast to her first husband, she found herself thinking. Despite his gambling fever, Richard had been a sharply intelligent man, a man who should have known better than to gamble away his inheritance. On the other hand, Sir Cuthbert might be slow, but he was a thousand times more good-natured than Richard. And what did one need with intelligence, after all? She was done bearing children who might have been affected by such a lack-witted father.

She let out a sigh, thinking regretfully that an

intelligent father had done her sickly daughters little good. One by one her babies had faded away, quietly, peacefully, slipping into darkness until only Derek remained.

Derek, who bore his mama no more affection than she did for him.

Without warning Lady Winifred's face crumpled, and the tears came for the first time in a very long while. These were not the genteel tears she'd been taught to weep—they were hard and ravaging, racking sobs born of frustration and remorse for all that might have been.

No affection for Derek? No love for her only living child?

She tried to laugh, but all that came out was a hoarse, guttural sound. She'd been maintaining that foolish facade for so long now she almost believed it. Derek's behavior toward her over the last decade had become so indifferent, so cold-hearted, that she had come to believe the things she said, that she had loved her daughters rather than her handsome, glorious son. But the truth was that she loved him fiercely. Her heart's desire was to have him return that love, but it was something she only acknowledged in the dead of night, when some murky nightmare chased her sleep away.

Winifred's husband had wanted nothing to do with her, and she had taken out her hurt on her male child, rejecting Derek as his father had rejected her, casting blame on the blameless. She had become fussy and difficult, inventing palpitations and tremors that she had never felt, purchasing extravagances she did not need or want, and, in the more recent years, complaining and reproaching Derek almost continually as indirect punishment for not *seeing* what she needed. As his father had not seen or cared.

It is never too late to change.

The tears had dried now, but a stultifying sense of desolation remained. For a few seconds she dared to dream the impossible, to recall the simple words Stacia

Edwards had spoken. Was the young woman right? Was there something she could do?

She sat up, wiping her pale, blotchy cheeks with a handkerchief. If she and Derek were reconciled, then Sir Cuthbert's eccentricities would be so much easier to tolerate. Perhaps she might even be able to feel affection for the man were her emotions freed of the heavy load they carried. Perhaps she might learn to laugh again, and to see the humor in an amusing situation. Stacia Edwards had seemed to find Sir Cuthbert entertaining. Could she, too, learn to appreciate his good qualities? And what was the world coming to when the young were wiser than the old?

Lady Winifred's restlessness was suddenly too strong to contain; she leapt from the daybed and went over to her escritoire. She would bid Derek to come, but it must be phrased differently than her usual requests else he would ignore it. Frowning in concentration, Lady Winifred reached for her quill.

Much later the same day, Sir Marco Ashcroft progressed slowly along St. James's Street, quite unaware that a small, scruffy-looking stableboy was following him at a discreet distance. Though twilight had long since ended, the gas lamps kept the street well enough lit despite the layer of fog which hugged the ground. Tonight Marco walked alone, partly because his bosom companion, Mr. Denchworth, had been called out of town on a family matter, and partly out of choice. Solitude appealed to him when he was feeling glum.

For days Marco had done little but dream about that embodiment of feminine perfection, Angeline Greaves. He'd told no one, not even Reggie Denchworth, that it was for Angeline that he had been striving so desperately to win his fortune. Oh, to be sure, he enjoyed kicking up a lark at the tables, but there could be no denying that his first experience with heavy losses had taken a good deal of the fun out of it.

Marco's face shadowed with dejection and shame. Despite what Reggie thought, he'd never felt comfortable about borrowing money from Stacia; in fact, it made his stomach churn in a most unpleasant manner. But what the devil else could he have done? He'd *had* to win the money back. It was the only way!

However, the knowledge that his fortune was small—too small, he believed, to compete for Angeline's affections—had convinced him that gambling was an evil necessity. He had told himself a hundred times that if he could only win back what he owed Stacia, plus ten or twenty thousand more to plump out his pockets, Angeline Greaves would *have* to look at him differently.

For a long moment, he allowed himself to imagine the triumph of capturing such a beautiful creature as his wife. He would shower her with jewels, buy her a house in London, give her a different gown for every hour of every day in the year . . . anything she wished, so long as that fellow Carisbrooke learned that Sir Marco Ashcroft was not a fellow to be taken lightly!

Unfortunately, Marco was only too aware that his angel scarcely acknowledged his existence. Even his dashing new high-perch phaeton had failed to impress her—in fact, she would not even consent to go driving with him, as if that stupid, freakish accident was likely to recur.

Scowling slightly, Marco's lower lip pushed forward in a pout. Nellie Dawson had never made him feel this way, he thought peevishly. Back in Lancashire, the vicar's daughter had adored him, openly displaying her admiration for his manly attributes and superior wisdom. Angeline Greaves, on the other hand, only made him feel young and green and foolish—and that was not at all the way he viewed himself.

Briefly, he allowed himself to acknowledge his affection for Nellie. She could not compare with Angeline, of course, but she was a pretty girl, full of life

202

and vivacity, and simple in her tastes. As he turned to enter a narrow alley, Marco's chest expanded in a deep sigh mixed with nostalgia. Nellie had made him feel like the man he desired to be, he reflected.

By God, he rather missed little Nellie Dawson.

As it happened, Derek's manservant did not deliver Lady Winifred's letter when it arrived. He had long since been given leave to use his discretion in such matters, and since her ladyship's dispatches were invariably either requests for money or complaints concerning some spiteful piece of gossip concerning Derek (which she always seemed to believe), Digby's decision was to withhold the missive until his master's mood grew less irascible. So it was that Digby waited until sometime after the dinner hour before screwing up his courage.

Derek's humor, however, was not noticeably improved by that time. Not only was Stacia's letter still eating at him, but the afternoon's post had brought a worrying letter from Palatine's trainer. It seemed that the stallion had strained his left hock, an injury that could hardly be called trifling when one considered the imminence of the Second Spring Meeting. Under normal circumstances, Derek would have been in Newmarket these two weeks past, but he had allowed his preoccupation with Stacia and her concerns to supercede these plans. Well, no more. He would be on his way to Newmarket by dawn.

Stifling a yawn, he stared into space and tossed off the remainder of his drink. He was not far from being foxed, but what the devil did it signify? He had nowhere to go and nothing to do until he heard from the boy. He'd tossed Stacia's letter beside his mother's, the latter's faint lavender scent pervading his nostrils despite the heavy smell of brandy.

For hours he'd been ignoring that second letter, but now he picked it up, his hard mouth twisting with distaste. What was it going to be this time? A lecture?

Demands for money? A reprimand for his conduct at Almack's? After a short hesitation, he threw the envelope back on the table, knowing he was too tippled to deal with it. His mother could wait, he thought savagely. It would serve her right for being such an unloving—

"Forgive me for disturbing you, sir,"—Digby's silent approach would have startled Derek were his reflexes not so dulled with drink—"but the boy is here." The manservant's face was wooden, but Derek noticed the quick, curious look he gave the empty brandy bottles on the floor.

Derek scowled and glanced at the clock, which showed it was nearly midnight. "It's about time," he growled. "Send him in."

A few seconds later, a small boy of about nine trudged into the room. Though his clothing proclaimed him a stableboy, Derek knew he had spent his first years in the slums of St. Giles, learning to pick pockets. Since he had come into Derek's employ, however, he'd been well-fed and happy, and had grown so devoted to his employer that he would fly into a fury if anyone gave him the least cause to suspect that Derek was being maligned.

"Well, Sammy?" said Derek, his voice stern.

Unquelled, the boy shifted his feet, a wide grin splitting his small, homely face. "I done as yer said, guv'nor," he said with obvious pride. "I kept me ogles on the young gem'man all evenin', I 'ave."

"And?"

Sammy's eyes rolled down to take in the brandy bottles, then returned to Derek's face.

"Well," he began, scratching his nose, "'e didn't go out as early as yer said 'e might. 'Twas 'ard ter watch 'is house so as I kept walkin' up and down the street 'til 'e come out—"

"What time?"

Sammy shrugged. "Gawd's truth, guv'nor, I dunno. Proper dark, it was. Follows 'im all ther way ter Pall Mall, I did, though 'e kept dawdlin' so as I 'ad to keep duckin' into doorways. Goes up one street and down ther next 'til I thought 'e was bleedin' lost. Then 'e turns an' walks down the first alley as goes through ter King Street."

"And?"

Sammy's head cocked. "'Bout halfway down 'e stops an' stands fer a bit. Then I 'eard 'im knock and after another bit I 'eard a door open. I weren't able ter see nuffin more, but 'e went in, all right. If yer was ter ask me, guv'nor," he added, his eyes bright with wisdom, "I'd say 'twas a topping 'ouse."

"No doubt," replied Derek grimly. "Very well, Sammy, you may go. There's mutton and pudding in the kitchen and then to bed with you. You've done well."

Sammy grinned and saluted. "Thank yer, guv'nor!"

His stableboy's cheeky behavior would normally have amused Derek, but by this time nothing so trivial as amusement could have surmounted his wall of rage. His brain felt racked, fogged with drink and strong emotions that threatened to rip loose the less civilized aspects of his character. His first inclination after Sammy's departure was to smash the nearest object into a thousand smithereens, but as this happened to be his half-finished bottle of brandy, he instead tipped it to his lips and drained it, effectively completing his journey down the road of inebriation.

As it happened, he was acquainted with the alley Sammy had described. Like many others of its kind, it was mean and narrow, serving only as a connecting route between two more respectable streets. His father had visited such alleys often, for they inevitably contained the seats of vice for which his gambling fever thirsted. This particular seat of vice—or topping house, as Sammy had called it—was a snug little trap run by a Mr. Septimus Leach and his son, a former prize fighter.

As Derek recalled, it was an inferior gaming hell, kept shut up during the day and well-shuttered even at night. Visitors could enter the outer room without difficulty, but the inner recesses were guarded by a burly porter who scrutinized them carefully through an aperture before allowing them entry. Those not meeting his approval were told that there was no play going on. No one got in without permission, for these hells were known for their sometimes nefarious methods of fleecing the wealth from their victims and were thus in constant danger of being shut down. Why anyone went to them at all, Derek was at a loss to understand.

He took a hackney to the corner of Pall Mall and walked the rest of the way. His gait was commendably steady considering the quantity of drink he'd imbibed, yet when he attained Mr. Leach's establishment he made sure to lurch and slur his voice when the eye appeared through the peephole. However, the precaution proved unnecessary; the door swung open without the least hesitation.

As Derek's eyes grew adjusted to the dim light he strove to conceal his distaste for the place and everyone in it. The rooms were crowded and overheated, and stank of cheap gin, sweat, and the contents of the chamber pots in the corners. As he expected, the game of hazard appeared to be the principal draw, but he did not see Marco Ashcroft. There were several men he did recognize, but their eyes were riveted upon the circular table in the center of the floor and the rolling dice on its surface. The noise of the betting was uproarious.

Ignored, Derek searched the shadows for signs of Stacia's brother. Some demon inside him longed to catch Marco in the act so that he would have suitable justification for throttling the fool. But where was he? Then a shout went up as someone nicked the main, and the horde of bodies shifted enough to reveal the probable answer.

Derek threaded his way through the milling assembly to the door leading to another room. Like the primary room, it was lit by oil lamps set in wall brackets, but they did nothing to dispel its gloomy atmosphere. Its apparent purpose was to provide a place for visitors to abandon any lingering hold on sobriety, for there were six or seven small wooden tables wedged against its grimy walls. There was even a waiter, he observed, a weasellike creature bent under a load of mugs and bottles.

To Derek's disgust, Marco was sharing a table with none other than Sir Joshua Croxton, the lecher who had tried to paw Stacia the day she had ventured into Tattersall's. Neither Croxton nor Marco had noticed him yet, for they were hunched over a pair of dice. Derek could not see Marco's face, but his hair was as wildly disheveled as though he had been pulling on it. Joshua Croxton was smirking.

Derek went over and slid into the unoccupied third chair. "Mind if I join you?" he inquired, a vicious glitter in his eye.

Croxton's smirk turned to an ugly contortion of facial muscles. "What the devil do you want, Deveaux?"

Derek bared his teeth. "To observe," he replied. "Do you object?"

"You're damned right I object—" began Croxton, only to be interrupted by Marco, who was clearly as inebriated as Derek, if not more.

"Evenin', Deveaux," he muttered. "Nonshense, Croxton. Why should you object? *I* don't! The fellow's my shister's friend. It's all one to me if he wants to watch." His moronic grin failed to conceal the familiar sick look of the loser.

Derek studied him. "What are you doing here, Marco?" The question was softly put, for he did not want to startle his quarry too soon.

Marco looked glum. "This fellow"—he waved a hand at Croxton—"has been beating the pants off me. 'Just a few friendly wagers,' he said. Bloody hell, Deveaux, I can't lose anymore—"

"Then stop," snapped Derek, his voice like the crack of a whip. "Stop, you bloody fool."

Marco gulped but said nothing, a pathetic expression on his face.

Derek's gaze moved to the dice lying inert on the table. Croxton intercepted the look, but could not move fast enough to prevent him from sweeping them up.

"What do you think you're doing?" he demanded with consummate loathing.

Derek smiled. "Fulhams are the surest way to win, aren't they, Croxton? If not the most acceptable."

"You're drunk," sneered the other man. "Drunk and lacking in manners. But then, considering the rumors I've heard, I should hardly expect any better. They're Ashcroft's dice, you fool." He laughed, pushing himself to his feet. "By the bye," he added, with a new surge of malice, "I've a horse entered in the Second Spring Meeting. He's going to win it, Deveaux. Black Devil can run circles around your Palatine."

"Indeed?" Derek's eyes were glacial.

"I heard your horse strained a hock," continued the other man with a laugh. "Such a pity. My Black Devil is in perfect form."

Derek rose to his feet. "But you won't be," he warned, "if I find you troubling young Ashcroft again. Is that understood?" He opened his palm, displaying the dice. "Now I suggest you hand over any vowels Sir Marco Ashcroft has given you on this or any other night."

His paunchy cheeks empurpled with rage, Sir Joshua Croxton reached into his pocket and threw a scrap of paper onto the table.

Derek glanced at Marco. "Is that it?"

Marco stared up at him uncomprehendingly. "Aye, that's all. But—"

"And the other set of dice?" This was to Croxton.

There was a long hesitation before Croxton handed them over.

"Very well." Derek's voice sliced the air like a knife. "You may leave, Croxton. Ashcroft and I have much to discuss."

Chapter Fourteen

Stacia was dreaming something pleasant when the noise set in. It penetrated her sleep and for a few seconds became part of her dream, a sharp brass-upon-brass rapping that blended with the will-o'-the-wisp phantoms of her slumber. She lay still, ignoring it, but the rapping went on, angry and insistent, demanding attention she did not want to give.

It was the front-door knocker, she realized groggily, but the crack between her curtains showed that it was not morning. In fact, the sky looked black as pitch save for whatever light the gas lamps in the street threw up. Good God, it must be the middle of the night. Who in the world would come to the door at this hour?

Marco. It could only be Marco.

She sat up abruptly, horrifying possibilities crashing through her mind. He had come to tell her that he had gambled away the rest of her inheritance. He had lost it all, every farthing of it, and they would have to go back to Lancashire. Or perhaps he had had an attack of guilt and decided to flee the country instead. She would not let him, of course, but Marco had always been unpredictable. Or perhaps—Stacia's heart thudded as an even worse thought occurred to her—perhaps he had only come to tell her he was going to blow his brains out! Angeline said that men did that sometimes as a sort of coward's escape from severe pecuniary difficulties. Would Marco do such a thing? Considering this, Stacia was gripped with a new fear. Perhaps he had already ended his life, and someone had come to tell her the ghastly news . . .

She was out of bed now, her shaking fingers fumbling with the sleeves to her dressing gown. Her room was at the front of the house, so that the knocking—now it sounded more like the crash of a fist upon wood—was directly below her windows, two stories down. Groping for her slippers, Stacia thanked heaven that Angeline's room was on the back of the house. Whoever it was, whatever news they had brought, she wanted time to absorb it without having to listen to Angeline's acidic remarks.

Telling herself not to panic, Stacia felt her way down the dark staircase just as her butler entered the vestibule. He was wiser than she, for he had taken the time to light a taper and brought the footman along as a precautionary measure. The disgruntled footman, who was suffering from a severe cold, had forgotten to remove his nightcap, but Challow looked every inch the imperturbable butler, even in dressing gown and slippers.

"It might be my brother," she told Challow as she reached the bottom of the stairs. While her butler inserted the heavy brass key into the lock, Stacia waited, nervously chafing one hand up and down her other arm.

"Let me in. I must speak to your mistress."

It was not Marco. The rough, authoritative voice wrapped round the heavy door to send a whisper of fear pricking at her chest. Something *had* happened, she thought. Derek would never come to her house like this unless something had happened to Marco.

Her butler was hesitating, clearly aghast at the impropriety of Derek's presence on her doorstep at such an hour. "Are you aware of the time, my good sir? It is past two in the morning!"

210

"Let him in." Stacia took an urgent step forward. "Let him in, Challow!"

Her butler still balked. "Are you quite certain madam? The gentleman does not seem to be . . . himself."

"Don't worry." She gave the elderly servant a smile that was meant to be reassuring. "The gentleman is my friend. I'll be quite safe."

Yet as Derek stalked into the hall, Stacia nearly revised her opinion. Good gracious, he looks absolutely furious, she thought in astonishment. Granted, the queer glitter in his eyes might only be due to the flickering candlelight, but his mouth—surely his mouth had never been so twisted and hard? Was it something to do with Marco? Or could such bitterness possibly be directed at her?

Stacia's hand crept to her throat. "Would you care to step into the morning room?" she asked nervously. "Challow will see that we are not disturbed so you may tell me what the trouble is." Pride forbade her to mention his absence at the Drury Lane Theater that evening, or her own agonizing disappointment at the defection.

Derek bowed—mockingly, she thought. "Wherever you like, ma'am." he said ominously. "One room will serve as well as another for what I have to say to you."

The butler's posture was rigid with disapproval. "Do you wish to have the fire stoked up, madam?"

Derek answered. "By all means, and fetch us a drink while you're at it. Brandy for me and something nicer for the lady." He gave a short, harsh laugh. "This is purely a social call, you understand."

Dismayed, Stacia said quietly, "I don't want anything other than the fire, Challow. As for the gentleman, I think he could benefit from some coffee."

Her heavy-eyed servants scurried to obey—Challow went off to the kitchen to fetch coffee, while the red-nosed footman hastened to the fireplace. "We must

211

speak quietly," she warned Derek. "I do not wish Angeline to know—" She moistened her lips. "I mean I do not wish to disturb Angeline's rest." Still nervous, Stacia selected an armchair not far from the hearth, one hand gripping the other in her lap.

"Oh, perish the thought," drawled Derek. "We must certainly not disturb Angeline."

Slow, uncomfortable minutes passed as the servant kindled the blaze. Derek, rather than sitting, had chosen to prop his shoulders against the mantelshelf so that he could observe both the footman and Stacia in conjunction. This flustered Stacia, but it threw the footman into such a frenzy that it took the poor man twice as long as necessary to do the job before he was able to make his escape, losing his nightcap in the process. The moment he was gone, Challow trudged in with the coffee, but a look from Derek sent the butler retreating just as hastily.

Derek ignored the coffee. "Alone at last," he remarked. "I can't tell you how much this means."

Stacia flinched at the sarcasm, but before she could form a reply he swaggered over to where she was sitting, his gaze roving over her in an insulting manner. "Yes, you'd be well-advised to hold that thing together," he mocked as she clutched at her dressing gown. "Though I've no objection to a display of charms. That sash seems a trifle loose, my dear. Is that deliberate, perchance?"

Stacia stared at him in shock. "What—?"

"No, of course it is not," he went on. "How stupid of me. You could scarcely wish to attract so repulsive and unbearable a fellow as myself." He bent down, a hand clamped on either arm of her chair, his face thrust so close she could smell the telltale brandy fumes. "Tell me, my sweet, are you really as innocent as you look? Or is that all part of the act?"

Her head moved in faint, bewildered denial. "I agreed to let you come in because I thought something had happened to Marco and that . . . and that you had come

212

to tell me." She drew an uneven breath. "I see I was wrong."

"No, little jade, you weren't wrong." His mouth curved into a hateful smile, then swooped down, vulturelike, to brush against hers.

Stacia jerked back. "You're drunk, Derek. Please don't—!"

There was silence for a moment, then he straightened, but the proximity of his body kept her trapped in her chair.

"I'm not half as drunk as your brother was," he said, "when I found him dicing with Croxton this evening." His gaze scoured her face as though trying to see into her mind. "They were using loaded dice."

Stacia's brow furrowed. "Loaded—?" she repeated, not understanding. "With Croxton?"

Derek stared down, his green eyes boring into hers. *"Loaded,* my love, means that they were false. There are various ways of achieving that. They can be drilled and 'loaded' with quicksilver. They can be filed, or have a hog's bristle buried in one of the corners. There are all kinds of ways to cheat, Stacia, but suffice it to say that—"

"Cheat!" she gasped, as his meaning grew clear. "Are you suggesting that my brother was— You must be out of your mind! Ashcrofts don't *cheat!"* Filled with indignation, she attempted to rise, but he stood unbudging, solid and unmovable as the Rock of Gibraltar. Frustrated, she tried to push him away, her fingers splayed helplessly against his lower torso.

Derek laughed and captured her wrists. "Ashcrofts don't cheat," he mimicked. "Ashcrofts don't lie." Without warning, he hauled her to her feet. "Let me tell you something, my little firebrand. Your brother is one of the biggest fools I've run across, and you're almost his match. You've been paying his gaming debts, haven't you?"

"No!" Stacia twisted, trying to pull free. "Let me go, Derek!"

"Liar." Hot green fury shone in his eyes—incomprehensible fury as far as she was concerned. "I'm going to help you, though," he murmured, his voice going soft as a kitten's fur. "I'm going to marry you, Stacia, whether you like it or not." Despite her struggles, his arms were tightly coiled around her body, his strength crushing her body against his. "Next time big brother comes begging for a handout he'll have to deal with your husband."

"Your proposals become cruder each time you make them," she lashed back. "If you don't let me go I shall scream, and then Challow and the servants will come—"

"And Angeline," he sneered. "That *is* daunting, I admit. But you won't scream, Stacia, for if you do, I shall tell everyone who counts that Sir Marco Ashcroft cheats."

Stacia froze, her heart hammering crazily. "You wouldn't," she whispered. Something deep inside her was profoundly, inutterably shocked that he would threaten such a cruel thing, even in the throes of drunkenness.

Derek's brows rose in exaggerated surprise. "Of course I would. The gossips are right, you know. I haven't any sense of decency." Before she realized what he was doing, his hand slid under her dressing gown to stroke her through the thin lawn nightdress. "Such lovely curves," he taunted. "I'm glad you've been married before, my love. I like a woman to be past the stage of maidenly blushes. I want a wife who knows how to please me."

At once she renewed her struggles, sobbing with sheer impotent outrage. "Let me go! How dare you say such horrid things!" His fingers shifted suddenly, provoking her to gasp, "I won't marry you! All you want is my money! And Marco would never cheat."

He released her so abruptly she fell back in the chair.

"Perhaps the evidence will convince you otherwise," he remarked as she glared up at him. There was a deadly quality to his voice, as though he had passed beyond rage into some emotion infinitely more terrible. One hand plunged into his pocket, then withdrew and opened to her view. "Look at them," he commanded. "Go ahead. Touch them if you like."

Stacia surveyed the dice with a mutinous expression. "So? They look perfectly—"

"Normal? They aren't." His tone mocked her angry protest. "They're your brother's, my pet. You may confirm that tomorrow at your leisure. He's been trying to win his fortune to impress your precious Angeline. The greenhead fancies himself in love."

"No." She rejected this numbly. "Marco wouldn't cheat, not even for Angeline. I don't believe you. You're foxed. You're making it up to force me to marry you." She took the dice from his hand, examining them closely. "There's nothing wrong with them."

Derek's face loomed over her, dark and menacing as some predatory creature. "Very well, then. Let's find out if I'm lying. If they're normal dice, then you'll have a fair chance."

"A fair chance—?" Her eyes flew up.

"To escape me," he finished in a hateful drawl. "I'll give you five shakes. If I win them all, you will marry me without protest, when and where I wish. If not"—he smiled unpleasantly—"you can have Drew, if you like. If you can bring him up to scratch, of course."

Stacia's heart plummeted. "You wish me to wager on *marriage?*" she asked incredulously. A moment before she had been furious, but now that anger was gone, buried under an avalanche of despair. *He could not possibly be serious. Please God, let none of this be real . . . let it be a dream or a cruel joke . . .* But the sardonic curve of Derek's mouth convinced her he was in earnest.

"Why not?" was his flippant response. "What better way to win a bride? Especially one with such an alluring"—the green eyes flicked over her figure—"dowry."

"Well, I won't! You must be mad to think that I would!"

He dragged the nearest chair close to hers and sat down. "In that case, I'll be forced to carry out my threat." There was no trace of pity in his eyes, nothing but that wild green glitter. "By tomorrow your brother will be an outcast, Stacia. Society forgives every sin except cheating. In their eyes, it is worse than flagrant adultery, even murder—"

"No, no, no!" Stacia gestured convulsively. "You could not . . . you must not be so cruel! I'll . . . I'll wager with you if that's what you want. If the dice are truly Marco's, then I know they cannot be false." She opened her hand, staring down at the innocent-looking white cubes with frank revulsion.

"Such trust," he marvelled. "If you had such faith in me, my love, we might have a sporting chance." He leaned over to take them away from her. "I want your word, Stacia, that you will wed me if I win."

She gave him an anguished, wavering look. "Oh, very well. What . . . what are you doing?"

He drew a second set of dice from his pocket and placed them in her hand. "Normal dice," he said. "So you may test your claim." There was a jeer in his voice. "If they're both true, the odds will be the same, won't they? Don't worry, we'll play by simple rules. High total wins, and in the case of a tie, doubles take precedence. A tie with no doubles must be replayed." When she hesitated, he pointed to the small table beside her. "Just roll," he ordered. "You've got five chances. If you win even one out of five, you'll be free of me."

Casting him a dubious glance, Stacia obeyed, her heart pounding. *Was she mad?*

"A three and a five," said Derek. He threw a pair of fives with Marco's dice and smiled grimly.

Stacia frowned. "What did you do? Did you cheat?"

216

"How could I?" he taunted. "These are not false dice, remember?"

On the second throw, she rolled a three and a two, which he easily topped with a six and a five.

"Your turn, my sweet."

Stacia's mouth was dry. She was conscious of fatigue, dark and heavy, dragging on her eyelids despite her raw, shuddering nerves. Above them, in the drawing room, the clock tolled three o'clock. The only sound was the soft crackle of the fire.

"This is insane, Derek," she muttered, launching the little cubes. A pair of twos stared up at her like twin, mocking eyes. Derek defeated them with a four and a six, but did nothing discernable to achieve that win. They must be ordinary dice, she prayed. She would beat him on the next throw. But the tears sprang to her eyes when she lost, a six and a one to Derek's pair of fours. Oh God, what if he was right? What if Marco was guilty? Teeth clenched together, Stacia shook the dice between cupped hands, determined to win the last toss so she could vindicate her brother. She threw a five and a six.

"There!" Despite her exhaustion there was triumph in her face. "You'll never beat that."

Derek leaned forward, so that the rollicking firelight shone weirdly upon his face. "Never say never, my dear Stacia," he replied, very softly. "Didn't anyone ever tell you not to tempt providence?"

He took Marco's dice and rolled them between his palms for a number of seconds. Then, with an unwavering look, he flicked them across the polished wood.

The room was blanketed with silence. "Providence had nothing to do with those sixes," she accused. "You cheated, Derek! You must have!"

His eyes narrowed. "Ah, but you can't have it both ways," he reminded her silkily. "If I cheated then so did your brother."

Stacia bit her lip. "Are they . . . truly false?" She tried

217

to control her voice, but it fluctuated and broke. "For the love of God, tell me the truth!" She scooped them up, her shaking fingers explored the tiny corners in an attempt to discover a flaw.

"Of course they are," he snarled. "Those are high fulhams, guaranteed always to roll a four, five, or six. It takes practice, however, to roll just the combination one desires." He paused, then added gloatingly, "I won, Stacia. You'll have to honor our agreement."

Stacia could feel the blood draining from her cheeks. "How can you speak of honor?" she whispered. "You've just proved you can cheat as skillfully as any man."

Derek's breath hissed out. "My father taught me a great many things when I was young. This was one of them. To know when one is being cheated, one must understand the cheater's methods." His head turned toward the fire, his voice harsher than she had ever heard it. "My father did not put these methods to use, you'll be relieved to know. He lost the family fortune with his honor intact. As your idiot brother has been losing yours."

Stacia swallowed. "Was my brother cheating?" she asked, "or was he not?"

Something in Derek's posture suggested he was as weary as she. "It's doubtful," he said in a tired voice. "'Twas Croxton who was winning. But they were Ashcroft's dice. He claimed they were a gift from Reginald Denchworth, who told him they would bring him luck. Then Denchworth left town, leaving your brother on his own. Our friend Croxton recognized the dice for what they were and took advantage of the situation. Fulhams can be employed much more skillfully with a dice box." He shrugged as though indifferent. "Your brother was too full of gin to realize what was happening."

"So he *wasn't* cheating." On the wake of Stacia's relief trailed a backwash of anger. "So you lied, Derek, and that means our agreement, as you called it, is invalid. Now I

218

suggest you go home and—"

She uttered a cry as he reached out to grasp her chin, his eyes narrowed to slits. "On the contrary, you'll marry me, Stacia, and you'll do it when and where I wish. You gave me your word. Or is your own honor worth so little?"

She struck his hand away. "How dare you! It is you who have no honor, for you led me to believe Marco was guilty when you knew he was innocent—"

"Yes, I deceived you," he cut in. "Which is no more than you have done to me. And to society as a whole, I might add."

"What do you mean?"

"Need you really ask—Miss Ashcroft?"

Somewhere in the distance a floorboard creaked, but neither of them paid any heed.

"Well, so what?" she said rebelliously. "What does it signify if I am no widow? What difference does it make?"

"Unmarried young ladies of birth and breeding," Derek ground out, "do not waltz around town on their own. *Virtuous* young ladies have more conduct than to live without a *proper* chaperon, nor do they visit places like Tattersall's, nor do they take up with the likes of Paul Matravers—"

"Take up with," Stacia repeated, stunned by the injustice. "What are you suggesting?"

"What I'm suggesting," he thundered, "is that you have been behaving like a hussy. And if it becomes common knowledge that you are unwed, your reputation will be in shreds. Not even my godmother will be able to help you, Miss Ashcroft. You will be as shunned as a leper, and it will last the rest of your life. Is that what you want?"

It was too much. She was too tired and too overset to check the tears that coursed down her cheeks.

"So you will hold that over my head to get what you want," she choked. "Perhaps you really are as black as they say. Do you indeed have a house full of children in

219

the country? Is it true that you've fathered a . . . a child by every mistress you have taken?"

"The term is by-blow," he corrected. "Or bastard, if we really wish to be crude. And I shan't deign to answer that, my love. When you're ready to come clean with me, then I'll pay you the same courtesy."

"Courtesy!" Racked with sobs, Stacia buried her face in her hands. "Since when have you been courteous? From the moment we met you disliked me. You always seem to be angry with me and I don't have a notion why. I don't know what I have done that is so dreadful or why you despise me so utterly—"

"*I* despise *you?*" She could not see his expression but his voice was very queer. "Stacia . . . darling . . . where in the blazes did you get that idea?" He sounded genuinely perplexed. "I thought we had reached an understanding the other night. But that letter you sent was the most confoundedly wounding thing I've ever—"

The door to the morning room slammed open, causing them both to start. *"Get out!"*

Black hair streaming, Angeline Greaves stood in the doorway with a poker clutched in her hand. "I said leave!" She spat the words at Derek, her eyes glimmering with loathing. "Leave her alone, you lying, drunken sot. Can't you see she doesn't want you?"

"Angeline!" Stacia rose to her feet, her tear-soaked eyes wide with dismay. "Please go back to bed. Mr. Deveaux and I were only—"

"I heard," uttered Angeline, gliding slowly across the rug. "I know what he was doing." The violet-blue eyes fixed on Derek. "You have been trying to take advantage of this angel"—she gestured at Stacia—"since the day we met you. You have used almost every foul means available to coerce her into marriage, even to barging in here in the middle of the night. But what you were about to do is the lowest, shabbiest trick of all."

"What I was about to do—?" Derek crossed his arms over his chest and gave her a disdainful look. "I fear I do not take your meaning, Mrs. Greaves."

Angeline sneered. "You've tried everything else, haven't you? Everything but the cruelest, most despicable trick."

"What are you talking about?" Stacia's gaze winged from Angeline to Derek. "What does she mean?"

Angeline brandished the poker at Derek. "A man like this has no qualms about dallying with your affections, ma'am. To gain his object he will use endearments and honeyed promises—even passion." Her voice vibrated with emotion. "Words like darling and sweetheart, they are nothing but tools, a means to gain his self-serving, contemptible end—"

"Enough!" Derek exploded. He reached for the poker just as Angeline swung it at his head.

Dear God, no! Stacia's cry was a strangled whimper of pain, of agonized loss before any loss had occurred. Then instinct took over and she threw herself forward, but Derek was quicker than either of them.

In fact, he had already wrested the poker from Angeline and was holding it before him as a horizontal shield to fend off her blows.

"Beast!" yelled Stacia's avenger, trying to punch him in the face. "Coward!"

Derek backed toward the door. "Your companion earns her keep far better than most chaperons," he said dryly. "But she is too late. I will hold you to your word, Stacia Ashcroft."

He gave her the look of the victor. "Our betrothal will be announced tomorrow."

Chapter Fifteen

After Derek's departure, Stacia adamantly refused to discuss him with Angeline, much to that damsel's chagrin. Angeline, of course, had a great many aspersions to cast upon Derek, but Stacia's sharp and furious reprimand proved effective in halting the flow from Angeline's lips.

Stacia did not realize she was shaking until she reached the sanctuary of her room. Her bruised emotions had just weathered a storm of mammoth proportions and Angeline, though she undoubtedly meant well, had only managed to compound her distress. Knowing she could not possibly sleep, Stacia sank into a chair near the window, her brooding gaze angled upward at the inviolable skies. Fatigue notwithstanding, she wanted to think about Derek and she wanted to do it alone, without interference and certainly without Angeline.

The window was open a few inches, and the cool night air rushed in to mingle with her thoughts. What in the world was she to do? There was no sidestepping the fact that she was now honor-bound to wed Derek. She had foolishly, recklessly, given her word, and if there was one thing she had been brought up to believe, it was that one's word was sacrosanct. One did not give it lightly, nor did one break it without life-threatening cause. Both her father and her governess had agreed upon that.

So for pity's sake why had she given it? Granted, Derek

had goaded her cruelly, but she could have refused. Marco had made his own bed; she could have let him lie on it.

Never, drummed a voice in her head. She could never abandon her brother, but that was hardly what this was all about, was it? Wasn't this to do with her own needs, her own aspirations? Wasn't this to do with her desire to win Derek's love? That goal might have seemed more remote than ever—except for the fact that he had called her his darling. The contradiction gave her an anchor of hope.

Yet the memory of Derek's rage sent a chill down her spine. She had not understood it at the time, and she did not understand it now. He had treated her so cavalierly, touched her so intimately, insulted her so brutally—and yet she had agreed to bind herself to him. And if the truth were to be told, if she were absolutely honest with herself, she knew she would abide by her word, not because he had forced her to it, but because she wanted to be his wife. Come what may.

Never wager more than you are willing to lose.

Stacia's eyes scrunched shut in a surge of self-loathing. She was mad. Totally and irrevocably mad. Perhaps insanity ran in her family, she thought. Perhaps that was what had provoked her mother to run off with her lover, abandoning her only child to a father who felt nothing for her. Whatever the case, in matters of the heart she had neither luck nor pride nor sense.

Depressed by the notion, she opened her eyes to stare up at the stars, watching them blink and fade as the dawn slowly shaded the sky with soft, muted colors. Was she truly willing to give up her freedom for Derek, knowing that he did not love her? She had dreamed of winning his heart, but right now that appeared an impossible task. Two nights ago she had believed herself to be within reaching distance of that goal, but since then something warm and lovely had slipped away, and she was shivering from its lack.

But he had called her darling!

223

Did that mean nothing? Was it something men said simply to manipulate, to control? Or could it possibly have been a betrayal of his true feelings, the feelings she'd told Lady Winifred he kept hidden? In an agony of indecision, Stacia cuffed the sides of her head, dragging her fingers through her hair with enough force to cause physical pain.

This was killing her. It was the worst form of torture, this slow eating away of one's hopes and dreams, this always being filled with self-doubt, always wondering what Derek was doing, what he was thinking, the niggling uncertainties about his past. But she could no more shut it off than she could deny the link between them. Even if Lady Claire's stories contained some remnant of truth she would still be drawn to him, like a flower lured to the light. No matter what he had done she would forgive him and yearn for him, even if he had fathered a hundred illegitimate children. As for the marchioness's insinuation that she had been one of Derek's mistresses—Stacia sniffed at the claim. Somehow she felt sure that Derek would be more discriminating than that.

If only Angeline had not meddled just at the point when it seemed he'd been going to explain! It was so horribly frustrating. What in heaven's name had he been about to say? Straining to recall, Stacia felt the crushing weight of her weariness infiltrate her bones. Her body was crying out for sleep, even as her heart cried out with the need to comprehend Derek's anger. He had said she had wounded him with . . . a letter?

What letter?

Pondering this, Stacia at last abandoned the window to seek the comfort of her bed. At the first opportunity she would ask, nay, *demand* an explanation.

As her eyelids grew heavy, the thought skipped through her head that she would have to tell Marco about her betrothal. She wondered drowsily what he would say or whether he would mention Croxton or the false dice. Though it pained her to admit that her brother could be so foolish, she could not, in all conscience, overlook the implications of Derek's story. Whether Marco confessed or not, she intended to give him a dressing-down he would not soon forget. Derek had been right; she had been as big a fool as her brother, but all that was going to change. It was time to put her foot down, for if she did not, Marco would continue as he was and things would only grow worse. And she loved her brother too dearly to allow that to happen—no matter what the consequences.

Unfortunately, there was only one female of her acquaintance whose words had any real influence upon her brother and that was the vicar's daughter back in Lancashire. Little Nellie Dawson would have known exactly what to say. Stacia only wished she did also.

Lady Winifred was the first to learn of the betrothal, for Derek paid her a call as soon as he arose—despite the fact that his head felt as though it had been put through a threshing machine. From the feel of it, he had obviously been more drunk than he'd realized; he knew he had not gone directly home after he left Stacia's house, but no twinge of memory told him where he'd gone. Vaguely, he recalled falling down a number of times before he'd had the felicity of landing atop his own bed, which no doubt explained why his body felt as though it had been pummeled by one of those newfangled mechanical contraptions he had bought to increase the productivity of his land. He was fortunate his valet was large and strong, else he'd have spent the night—or what little remained of it—in his clothes.

It was nearly noon when he mounted the steps of the small, attractive house off Berkeley Square where his mother resided. She had not yet come down, but the butler, upon inquiring, informed Derek that Lady Winifred would receive him upstairs in her boudoir. Derek's head throbbed painfully as he climbed the stairs, but the force of sheer habit kept his face impassive as granite.

He was dreading the interview, of course, but

everything connected with his betrothal to Stacia Ashcroft must be carried out with rigid regard to propriety—and that included informing his mother of his forthcoming marriage. He hardly dared acknowledge the faint hope that she would be pleased—or to be more precise, that she would decide to simulate that emotion. Real or feigned, in the eyes of society he wanted his mother to appear his ally.

He found Lady Winifred seated on a striped satin couch with a cup of chocolate in her hand. Her peignoir—an exquisite lace and satin confection designed to harmonize with her surroundings—was far more lavish than the one Stacia had worn the previous night, and the thought passed through his head that Stacia would have looked bewitching in such garb.

His mother set down her chocolate and touched a handkerchief to her lips. "So you came," she remarked, her dark eyes fixed on him with some strange emotion. "I did not think you would." Her voice was low and lacking in astringency, a circumstance so unusual it aroused his suspicion.

"You seem in remarkably fine fettle, Mama," he retorted, his voice guarded. "Has Sir Cuthbert declared himself at last?"

"Cuthbert?" Her laugh was oddly genuine. "Gracious, no, Derek. Why on earth should you think that?" When he opened his mouth to answer, she said, "Come and sit down. 'Tis disconcerting to be towered over like this. And you may as well be comfortable. We have a great deal to discuss."

"Do we?" Since he felt like the devil he did not argue, but settled himself next to her with a weary sigh. "Forgive me for being obtuse, Mama, but I fear I do not follow."

She shifted to face him, her eyes burning with an intensity he found unnerving. "Then you did not read my letter. I thought perhaps you had."

Confound it, he had forgotten all about her letter!

"Well . . . ah . . . to own the truth, I did not," he confessed, cursing the ache in his head which made it so difficult to think. He buried a hand in his pocket and braced himself for her vitriolic blast, but when nothing of the sort occurred he said stiffly, "I'm sorry, Mama. Was it important?"

"Indeed it was." Averting her face, Lady Winifred twisted her handkerchief. "I truth, I hardly blame you," she said, almost humbly. "Things have not gone well between us for a long time. By and large, it has been my fault. I have been deliberately difficult."

Unable to believe his ears, Derek stared at his mother. Inside the pocket, his fingers curled in his characteristic fist, while long-buried emotions struggled to the surface of his mind. His mother never spoke in such a way. What the devil could be her purpose?

"Despite of what you think—what I have no doubt led you to believe—I harbor no ill feelings toward you. You are my son and I am proud of that." She read the disbelief and distrust in his eyes. "Yes, the deaths of your sisters made me bitter. I . . . I cannot deny that. But that time when you were little—" She stopped, her face working with emotion.

For God's sake, why now?

The muscles in Derek's jaw tightened painfully, but his voice, unlike hers, was controlled and even. "That was long ago, Mama. There is no need to rake up the past."

"But there is!" Lady Winifred strained forward, her gaze locked on his face. "As you know, my marriage with your father was arranged. Many such marriages work out quite satisfactorily, but ours"—she paused—"I'm sure you know ours was a disaster. Your father tormented me with his strings of mistresses, but barely acknowledged *my* existence. I was lonely, Derek. Horribly lonely. And that was why I took a lover."

Derek said nothing; he could only sit and listen and struggle to preserve an indifferent facade. Within his

227

pocket, his fist tightened.

"Back then I was still in love with your father. Perhaps I did it out of spite, but the man involved—John was his name—was good to me and I . . . I valued that. That day you saw us together I was frantic. I did not want your father to know and I panicked, Derek." A single tear rolled down her sunken cheek. "I realize now that I frightened you. I thought you were old enough to keep a secret. In so many ways you were adult and mature, such a little man that I thought—But of course I was wrong. Of course you told your papa, and I no longer blame you for that. I . . . I stopped blaming you years ago."

"You struck me," Derek uttered, with a total lack of emotion. "You slapped my face and called me the devil's spawn. You said I was selfish and cruel, unworthy of a mother's love." He kept his voice idle, as though the charges were of no more account than the weather, but his stomach cramped with the memory. "I was five, Mama," he added.

"I know." His mother was weeping now, her face ugly and contorted with grief. "There is no excuse, my son. I do not expect forgiveness, but I thought perhaps if I explained . . . You see, back then I suffered from uncontrollable bouts of temper. Some women have them, but mine were worse than most. They came each month without cause, regular as nature and . . . and just as violent." Her voice choked with regret. "I could not fight them, Derek. I swear I tried, but when they were upon me I was helpless. I would lash out at whomever was there, be it your father or a servant or . . . you."

Derek studied the Aubusson rug beneath his feet. "And that is what the letter said? You wished to lay this open now, more than twenty-five years after the event?"

Lady Winifred's head bowed in a jerky nod. "I suppose that is what it amounts to. I used to try, you know. Long ago. But you hid from me when I visited the nursery. It soon became obvious that it was no good, that I had already lost you. It was Nanny or your father you wanted, not . . . not me. So I stayed away from the

228

nursery and mothered my resentments rather than my child."

Derek looked at her then. Somehow, the full impact of her suffering came through to him with that statement.

She went on, "I suppose it seems ludicrous at this stage to apologize. That young woman—Stacia Edwards—put the notion into my head. She said that it is never too late to—"

"You discussed this with Stacia?" His inquiry was sharp and tinged with displeasure.

"Not . . . not all of it. Not what happened that day when you were five." She paused. "I like that young woman, Stacia. She is kind. One does not see much of that in women of our class."

Several seconds slipped by before he answered.

"I'm pleased to hear you say that," he said in a clipped voice, "because she and I are to be married. That is what I came to tell you. It was decided last night."

His mother did not look as startled as he'd expected. "I am glad," she said, in the gentlest voice she had used in years. "You are in love with her, I apprehend?"

Derek found the suggestion disquieting. A pretty pass it would be if he were, he reflected. The girl was a lying jade, a shameless deceiver—albeit a highly desirable one. Still, could that be the source of his anguish over Stacia's letter? It would certainly explain his half-crazed actions of the night before, and, God help him, that spontaneous and utterly insane dice game.

Striving for impassivity, he said, "I thank you for your concern, Mama, but that is something I prefer not to discuss." He withdrew his hand from his pocket, hesitated, then shoved it in again. "The purpose of my visit was to enlist your help," he added abruptly. "I have to go to Newmarket this afternoon. There is no getting around it and I will be gone several days. I need you to send in the announcement of our engagement to the newspapers and to stifle whatever gossip arises as best you can."

His mother's brows rose slightly. "Your godmother

229

could do that far better than I," she said dryly. "Diplomacy has never run in our family."

"True, but I'm asking *you*, Mama. I'm depending on you."

She was obviously moved. "Very well, Derek. I will do what I can. It is a good match."

Torn with indecision, Derek hunched forward. "There are circumstances, Mama, that may require a delicate hand."

"A delicate—" Lady Winifred peered at him anxiously. "My son, what have you done?"

His dark brows drew together. "Not what you are thinking. My bride-to-be is quite chaste, I assure you. That, er, is the crux of the matter."

Derek hesitated, wondering how much he should divulge. He was always uncomfortable with the notion of revealing anything at all about himself or his affairs—particularly to the woman who was his mother. Such a step was too foreign, too new, and besides, he did not trust her. Something within him was stirred by her apology, but a lifelong rein on his emotions kept him cautious. How long would this new attitude last? She seemed sincere enough, but he'd always thought her a shallow woman, lacking even the rudiments of sensibility. Was she capable of change? Of caring? As for him, the scars of childhood ran very deep; they were not going to disappear overnight.

No, the full measure of his foolishness would remain a secret, but perhaps she might be told a portion of the truth. After all, if the true story of Stacia's marital status leaked out, then Lady Winifred must be prepared to deny it. No matter what their relationship might be, Derek wanted no taint attached to his future wife's reputation.

Suddenly, the last vestiges of self-delusion melted away. What a damned fool he was. Of course he was head over heels in love with Stacia Ashcroft. Why not admit it? She had brought down his defenses as easily as the sun breathed life into the earth. Her very smile, for God's sake, was enough to keep him floating above the ground like some half-crocked phantom.

Fool.

For an instant, he allowed himself to dwell upon the hurtful message in her letter. Well, he thought sourly, if love and trust were meant to go hand in hand then he'd have to learn to separate them. He intended to marry her, but it would be a long cold day in hell before he trusted her again.

Later that morning, Stacia received a coolly worded letter informing her that Derek had left for Newmarket. She recognized her future husband's bold scrawl at once, but unlike the missive from their first meeting (which was still tucked carefully among her most personal belongings), its contents lacked any hint of warmth or apology. It was both formal and terse, and contained no reference to the previous evening other than the intelligence that his mother, Lady Winifred Deveaux, would see to the announcement. He had wasted enough time in London; the needs of his racehorse now took precedence. He trusted that Stacia could keep herself out of trouble while he was gone. As if this were not injury enough, his curt postscript proved even more ungracious. *Don't even think of reneging on our agreement*, he had written. *You know what will happen.*

Fuming with indignation, Stacia crumpled the letter and flung it into the grate. As though she would go back on her word! How in the world was she ever going to teach this man to love when he would not even trust? She paced the room in a seething rage, nourishing her grievances. No word of when he would return! No apology! Nothing but insolent, dictatorial commands! His horse was more important than she was. She was mad to have promised herself to such an utterly disagreeable man.

Her ill humor firmly established, Stacia donned a shawl and set off to pay a long overdue call upon her wayward brother. Twenty minutes later she was ushered into his parlor by a servant, where she was kept waiting a full thirty minutes before Marco wandered in, attired in a red brocade dressing gown.

Stacia did not bother to rise. "You look dreadful," she said baldly. "Your face looks positively bilious, Marco."

Indeed, the young baronet had obviously just risen from his bed. His ash-blond hair was standing virtually on end and a most unattractive puffiness underscored his bloodshot eyes. Moreover, there was at least two days' worth of stubble on his chin. If his glum expression was designed to arouse her sympathy, however, it failed dismally. Rather, the entire effect could not better have brought home to Stacia the shocking reality of the manner of life her splendid half brother was embracing.

"What in Satan's name is so urgent that I must come dashing down here before I've had my breakfast?" he complained. Looking disgruntled, he threw himself into a chair. "You know I ain't much for prittle-prattle at this hour of the morning."

"I have not come to prittle-prattle," Stacia informed him frostily. She opened her reticule and withdrew the two ivory cubes that had cost her so much. "Are these yours?"

Marco took them from her hand. "How the devil should I know?" he retorted, examining them testily. "Where did you get them?"

"Mr. Deveaux gave them to me," she replied. "He claims they are the same set of dice you used last night when you were gambling with Sir Joshua Croxton."

He stared at her. "Why would he tell you about that? And why the devil would he give them to you?"

"If they are yours," she said steadily, "then you must surely know they are loaded."

"The deuce they are! Why would Dench give me loaded dice? He said they were lucky. Dash it, I don't cheat! Never have and never will. Ashcrofts don't cheat."

Stacia sighed with relief, a great load lifting from her

shoulders. "That's what I said," she retorted. "I am sorry to have insulted you, Marco, but I had to ask. You see, they *are* false dice."

Marco's bemused gaze went to the dice. "Did that Deveaux fellow think I was cheating?" he said incredulously. "He must have windmills in his head."

She smiled faintly. "No, I don't think he really believed it, and yes, he definitely has a few windmills in his head." This led nicely to her next revelation so she took a deep breath and said, "He wants to marry me, Marco."

"Oh, he does, does he?" Marco said wrathfully. He shoved the dice in his pocket and readily took up this new topic. "So when is he going to ask my permission? Not that I'm at all sure I would allow the match. His birth is good, but there's some dashed offensive rumors about him flying around."

"I don't need your permission to marry," she reminded him. "I am three-and-twenty, Marco. And as for the rumors, I don't set much store by them."

"You don't, eh? Well, that don't comfort me, my dear sister. And that reminds me of another thing. That fellow Matravers has been hanging onto your sleeve lately and I don't like it. The fellow's a member of the Hell-Fire club, and don't ask me what *that* is, for I don't mean to tell you."

"You sound like Derek," she said irritably. "I've only driven out with Mr. Matravers once or twice and danced with him a handful of times. And though he comes to call nearly every day, I'm quite certain that it's Angeline he comes to see. She ignores him, of course."

Marco's shoulders slumped. "Angeline," he repeated in a despairing voice. "Oh, God, Stacia, what am I to do? I've tried everything I can think of to make her notice me. I tried to win a fortune, and look where it's landed me, for God's sake! I owe my own sister thousands of pounds, and where is the honor in that?" His head dropped to his hands, his fingers buried in his hair.

Stacia reached over to pat his shoulder. "The best way you can repay me," she said firmly, "is to stop gambling. And as for Angeline"—her voice gentled so as to inflict the least pain possible—"she's not right for you, my dear. Her difficult life has turned her into a complex person with deep prejudices. Whatever man she chooses will have to be very strong. You don't have that kind of strength. She would make you miserable."

His head raised, his face full of bewildered hurt. "But she's so beautiful," he protested, as though that were all that mattered.

"Marco, she's in love with someone else."

"Who? No, don't tell me. It's that hoity-toity Carisbrooke fellow. God, how I dislike the fellow."

Silence followed.

"Tell me," Stacia said carefully, "do you ever think of Miss Dawson?"

"Nellie?" Marco looked surprised. "Dash it, of course I do." Suddenly, he flushed. "You think I should go back to Lancashire and become a country gentleman like Father."

"You might consider it," she pointed out. "Papa's estates are your responsibility now. And Nellie is there."

Marco stared frowningly off into space. "I might do that," he said abruptly. "But I've a mind to see the races at Newmarket first. And I mean to have it out with Dench about those damned dice." He struck his fist into his palm, then fixed his gaze on her intently. "Are you going to accept Deveaux's offer?"

Stacia forced a smile to her lips. "I already have," she confessed. "I gave him my word."

Chapter Sixteen

Stacia's next call was on Lady Crackenthorpe. Derek's godmother had been dealing with some correspondence, but when Stacia was announced she put down her quill and greeted her visitor with a smile. Stacia had not known precisely what she would say, but one sympathetic look had her blurting out everything. The entire story spilled out from start to finish—Marco's gambling, the loaded dice, the circumstances of her betrothal and Derek's humiliating accusations—it all came out, along with a bout of tears that left her in hiccups.

Murmuring gently, Lady Crackenthorpe waited for the storm to pass before touching upon the one issue that Stacia had avoided. "Poor child. You're in love with him, aren't you?"

Stacia flushed. "Yes, I do love him, ma'am, but he does not care for me." Her voice was very low. "He thinks me a liar and a hussy. He said so."

"My dear girl, how can you be so sure he does not care?"

"Because of the way he speaks to me! He accused me of encouraging Mr. Matravers, while in the same breath insinuating that I have my cap set for Lord Andrew!" Stacia shuddered. "He seems to think me capable of anything."

Lady Crackenthorpe grimaced. "Has it ever occurred to you that he is jealous?"

Stacia looked down. "No. At least, yes, it occurred to me, but how is it possible to be jealous when one does not care?"

"Precisely." Her ladyship's tone was wry. "I rather suspect that my godson cares very deeply for you. I should have given a great deal to have witnessed that dice game."

Stacia's blush deepened. "But if he cares for me, ma'am, then why go to such pains to hide it? It almost seems as though he is trying to make me fall *out* of love with him." She looked down at her fingers, twisting the fringe on her shawl. "When we waltzed at Almack's he was so different. I honestly thought I had broken through his reserve, but then overnight he changed. I told you he was foxed and angry, but I forgot to mention what else he said. He spoke of a letter he had received, supposedly from me. It was evident that he found whatever it said contemptible." Her brow furrowed. "But I did not write it."

"Did you tell him so?"

Once more Stacia was swamped with frustration. "Well, I would have, but that was when Angeline burst into the room. So I thought I would do so today, and instead I receive *this!*" Reaching into her reticule, she withdrew Derek's letter, wrinkled and filthy from where it had lain in the grate.

The older woman scanned it in amazement. "Goodness, you are quite right about him being in a dudgeon! But why? Could he have misinterpreted something you said? Or perhaps this mysterious letter was from some talebearer who wished you ill."

"The only person who might wish me ill is Lady Claire. I met her at Almack's and I do not think she liked me one bit."

"Yes." Lady Crackenthorpe looked thoughtful. "I suppose she is capable of doing such a thing. I have always thought her a singularly unpleasant young woman. I would have preferred that you and she had not been introduced."

"She is Lord Andrew's cousin."

"She also came close to being Derek's wife," returned Lady Crackenthorpe tartly. "He was in love with her once."

The news came like a blow to the stomach. "Indeed?" Stacia managed.

"Oh, my dear, don't look so stricken. That was years ago. I don't know the details about what happened. Derek does not discuss her. As for the lady"—she said the word dryly—"she likes people to think he broke her heart, but between us, my dear, I doubt she possesses one. Unfortunately, her claim has contributed to Derek's reputation as a heartless libertine. I try to be charitable, but I have a hard time forgiving her for that."

Stacia stared at her fingers, hardly daring to form her next question. "As to that, ma'am, have you heard the rumors? I don't wish to be indelicate but if you know anything about the rumors concerning Derek and . . . and . . . children, I would very much like you to tell me."

Lady Crackenthorpe sighed. "I have heard, but I have certainly not taxed Derek with the matter. I don't believe them, if that's what you're asking. Derek loves children, Stacia. It is one of the things that makes him most human."

"Does he really?" Stacia considered this. "But where would such a rumor come from if it has no truth?"

The other woman gazed at her wisely. "My dear, how can anyone say from whence a rumor arises? It can come out of truth or lies, and it is up to each of us to decide whether we will listen or not. I have always opted for the attitude that we are all of us human, subject to the same errors and temptations as the next person. Derek is a good man, my dear. That is all I can tell you. Anything beyond that must come from him."

Stacia returned to Upper Grosvenor Street mulling over this advice, but once there she found she could not sit still. Perhaps she would go shopping, she thought recklessly. Since she was to be a bride, she would need bride clothes, wouldn't she? But no, she must stop procrastinating; there was something else she must do first.

Angeline answered her summons immediately. "Yes, ma'am?" she said in a subdued voice. Though as beautiful as ever, she wore a look of suffering that gave Stacia a pang of guilt.

"I did not see you at breakfast, Angeline."

The other girl's chin tilted proudly. "I have packed my bags," she replied. "I will be leaving within the hour."

Not for a moment had Stacia considered the possibility that Angeline would feel obliged to leave. Feeling guiltier than ever, she said carefully, "Gracious, Angeline, surely this is unnecessary! The rift between us is not so great as that. And besides, where would you go?"

Angeline shrugged. "Back to the country, perhaps. There is nothing for me here."

"Lord Andrew is here."

"He was supposed to have been for *you*, ma'am," she retorted. "I wanted you to have him."

Stacia studied the flawless face in astonishment. "But that is fustian, Angeline. He does not want me, nor do I want him. He has a pleasing disposition, of course"—she forced a wan smile—"but I am betrothed to Mr. Deveaux. As you know."

For an instant it seemed that Angeline would burst into tears. "Listen to me, ma'am, I beg! There is still time to cry off. I heard enough last night to know he does not love you. You deserve better! He will only make you miserable!"

Stacia controlled her expression despite the coldness trickling down her spine. "I told you last night that you should not have been eavesdropping," she said evenly. "It was an invasion of my privacy that I trust you will not repeat. However, I have not the least intention of allowing you to leave for such a foolish reason. You are my friend, Angeline. And I hope I am yours."

Angeline looked shaken. "You are more than a friend

to me, ma'am. You are my savior." Her voice trembled with emotion. "You are the most perfect angel alive."

"What flummery," said Stacia in exasperation. "I am no different from anyone else, Angeline. Now, I wish you will talk no more nonsense. Why do we not go shopping? You look like you could use some air and I have things I wish to purchase."

Somewhat to her surprise, Angeline made no objection, her sole statement being that she was of course at Stacia's disposal. If it seemed that she had decided to control her tongue, this hope was banished when they were settled into the Ashcroft coach.

"You never drive your phaeton. Do you regret the purchase?" Her voice was void of slyness, yet it contained a whisper of criticism, a reminder of that episode at Tattersall's and everything that had happened since.

Stacia gazed out the window of the coach. "No," she said with a sigh. "I do not regret it." Rows of houses stared back at her with blank, accusing windows.

Was Angeline right? Would she be miserable? Should she jilt Derek before it was too late? But no, she had given her word. Ashcrofts always kept their word.

Aloud, she said only, "I shall learn to drive it properly once I am married. Derek will instruct me."

Angeline's silence was eloquent.

They did not speak again until they reached Oxford Street, and even then it was of trivial topics. Stacia directed her steps toward a dressmaker's establishment she had visited before, where she spent a good thirty minutes debating which of several exquisite bolts of fabric was suitable to be her wedding dress. All the time she was conscious of Angeline at her elbow, silent and grim as a prison sentinel.

As they stepped out of Madame Giselle's into a billowing wind, the first person they set eyes upon was Lord Andrew Carisbrooke. He was emerging from a jewelry shop two doors down, and looked as disconcerted to see them as they were to see him. Nevertheless, his stride checked, and though his smile had a rather forced quality, there was nothing lacking in his courtesy as he greeted them.

"Good day, ladies," he said, tucking a small package into his pocket as he came over. "Rather windy, is it not? I do think we're in for a spell of rain." He gave them an elegant bow.

Conscious of awkwardness, Stacia murmured a civil reply and gazed meaningfully at Angeline, who perversely said nothing. The rumble of carriages and pedestrians' voices did nothing to fill the great chasm of silence.

"I, er, see you have been to Madame Giselle's establishment," he put in with false heartiness. "She does elegant work. My mother makes a great many purchases here."

As they exchanged several more, equally banal remarks Stacia made a decision. "To own the truth, Lord Andrew," she said with a bright smile, "I am glad we happened upon you, for I have a favor to ask."

His eyes settled on her face as though seeing her for the first time. "Anything in my power, ma'am," he said promptly. "Ask and ye shall receive."

She sent him her prettiest smile. "Could you be so obliging as to escort Mrs. Greaves back to Upper Grosvenor Street? I fear she is tired today. It was most thoughtless of me to have dragged her along." She gestured airly. "But I have some particular purchases I wish to make before I return."

At best, it was a clumsy effort, and Stacia held her breath on the fear that he would refuse. Lord Andrew's manners, however, were nothing if not impeccable.

"I would be delighted," he responded after a short pause. His eyes rested on Angeline's face with a curious gleam. "Is that acceptable to you, ma'am?" he asked gravely.

"It is . . . acceptable." Angeline's eyes were cast downward, her beautiful face betraying nothing.

One corner of Lord Andrew's mouth puckered wryly

as he offered her his arm. Then his gaze swept back to Stacia. "And what of you, ma'am?" he said, glancing around. "Have you no footman or maid?"

Stacia met his gaze squarely. "No, I . . . I did not bring either of them." She cursed the tinge of pink that was creeping into her cheeks. "Any purchases I make can be delivered," she added, as if that were an end to the matter.

His eyes narrowed. "If you don't mind my saying so, ma'am, Derek would not approve of you going about unescorted. Perhaps you should leave your shopping for another day."

"Mr. Deveaux does not care sixpence what I do," she responded, "nor do I care what he thinks. I am a widow, sir, not some young, inexperienced girl. I can take care of myself."

"Can you?" Lord Andrew sounded skeptical. "Derek does not think so."

Good grief, were the silly man's brains addled? Could he not see what she was doing for him? Here was his chance to woo Angeline, for heaven's sake, and all he could think of was propriety!

Her color heightening even more, Stacia focused on the lapel of his coat. "The truth is, sir, that there is someone I am planning to meet, er, privately. He will see to my safety, I assure you." Her lips did not form the lie easily, and for an instant she thought he must see through it. But no, the faint twisting of his lips told her he was fooled. Doubtless it was her deep blush that made the story plausible.

"I see," he said dryly. "Very well, ma'am. I will see to Mrs. Greaves."

Stacia watched them walk away with less satisfaction than she expected. 'Twas a pity she had to lie, she thought uncomfortably. But then, what did it signify if he thought she had made an assignation? What did his good opinion matter? What truly mattered was that he and Angeline had an opportunity to straighten out their troubles.

241

Perhaps he would tell Derek.

Though she tried to dismiss it, the notion made her uneasy. Well, and so what if he did? It would serve Derek right for the Turkish way he had treated her!

Starting off down the street, Stacia tried her best to ignore the curious stares of passersby. In this she succeeded very well until, three minutes later, two gentlemen strolled past with their quizzing glasses raised. A moment later a third gentleman gave her a lecherous smirk and actually tried to address her, but she managed to depress this presumption with a freezing stare.

Stacia's heart thumped nervously. There was obviously some merit in the dictum that a lady of quality required an escort, though she disliked the idea of being so constrained.

Unfortunately, Upper Grosvenor Street was too distant for her to reach on foot, and she still had an hour to fill before her coach was due to return. She now regretted that she had not kept her coachman waiting in the street as was the common practice, but it had seemed inconsiderate when the poor man had obviously caught the footman's cold. She glanced up and down the street with a sigh. There were scores of shops for her to browse through, including a great many who catered to the necessary and unnecessary in female clothing and fripperies. There were linen drapers, *plumassiers*, silk mercers, perfumers, haberdashers, and furriers. There were warehouses selling stays and corsets, ribbons and bonnets, muslin and shawls, and even ready-made linen. And there were a number of establishments—called manufactories—which sold goods made by hand on the premises, including patent thread, umbrellas, buttons, straw hats, and all manner of fancy trimmings.

Most young ladies could have spent half their lives in Oxford Street and had a perfectly splendid time, but Stacia was not one of these. She did not want to shop.

She wanted to be with Derek.

Blast him for leaving London. She could understand

242

that his horse was important, but what she could not accept was that he had not come to bid her farewell—at least as a courtesy, if not because he really wished to see her. Was this what their marriage would be like? she wondered forlornly.

As this thought was going through her head, every nerve in her body tensed. Sir Joshua Croxton was approaching. He was walking in her direction on the same side of the street, swinging his cane in a negligent fashion.

Instinct made her turn, her hand reaching for the nearest door without consideration for what was behind. It was very dim inside, but Stacia was so frantic she scarcely glanced around the shadowed interior. Inside, the powerful smell of tobacco clutched at her like a strangling hand. Unfortunately, she had chosen the worst place to hide, for there was something in its scent that always made her feel ill and lightheaded. *Hurry, Sir Joshua, hurry. For pity's sake, the man should have passed by the window by now.*

"Mrs. Edwards? Is that indeed you?" Though she had not been conscious of movement, Paul Matravers was suddenly at her elbow. Behind him hovered the proprietor of the shop, a gaunt, bespectacled man who wore a look of mild apprehension.

"How charming that we should meet," he went on with a beguiling smile. "I think about you so often."

"Oh . . . ah, good day, Mr. Matravers. I had no notion you were in here." She was trying not to breathe too deeply, trying not to inhale more of that wretched smell into her lungs than was strictly necessary.

His smile broadened. "I should not have expected you to have known," he answered urbanely. "We must thank fate for bringing us together."

"On the contrary, it was the merest chance," she corrected. "I only stepped in here to avoid meeting someone I very much dislike."

"Ah." His lashes lowered, hiding whatever his eyes

might have betrayed. "Would you care for my escort, ma'am? I promise to protect you from this person, whomever he is."

Stacia was about to refuse when, to her dismay, Sir Joshua Croxton entered into the shop. As his beady gaze crawled over her, she stepped close to Mr. Matravers.

"Well, well," drawled Croxton, not missing the move. "Have you been keeping secrets, my friend? You did not tell me about *this* conquest."

"How could I? I did not know of it myself," replied Matravers, deliberately permitting the other man to retain his false impression. Ignoring Stacia's gasp, he tucked Stacia's hand in the crook of his arm. "Is this the person you referred to, my dear? Or do I misread the expression on your lovely countenance?"

"Yes, it is he," she answered curtly. "And if you mean to make good your promise, sir, you may do so by finding me a hackney coach. I wish to go home at once. I need . . . air."

The blond brows arched. "So soon? My dear ma'am, I beg you will not run away. I have a much better notion. Let's spend the afternoon together, you and I. I know of a capital place where we can become better acquainted. Just the two of us, eh?" His fingers tightened over her hand.

Though the invitation was shockingly improper, it was actually the tone in which it was issued that set off warning bells in her head.

Stacia would later deem her response goosish, but at the moment she felt too ill to think logically. The two men seemed a menace from which she must escape at all cost, and the fact that Croxton was blocking her exit and the shopkeeper had retreated appeared ominous, at best. As Matravers's fingers moved up her arm, Stacia's imagination took over. Visions of abduction, seduction, and murder leapt to the fore, but the tobacco on his breath proved the finishing touch.

Oh, God, he was going to kiss her!

Like an animal fighting for its life, she kicked out at him, her mouth opening on a cry that never reached completion.

"For God's sake, don't scream!" Matravers's hand covered her mouth. "Damn it, Croxton, you said the girl was a doxy! What the devil does she think I'm going to do? Rape her?"

He was blocking her mouth and nose so that she could not draw a full breath. Vaguely, she knew the two men were arguing, but the sound was superceded by high-pitched bells pealing inside her head. The face above hers swam until all that was left of its features was a formless blur. Then the scene was shimmering, changing, dimming to pinpoints of light in a velvet black void. With a last flail of her arms, Stacia slipped quietly into a spinning vortex, a place where emotions could not follow.

Lord Andrew, meanwhile, was attempting to make the best of the situation into which he had been maneuvered. His curricle-and-pair were standing exactly where he had left them, and as he assisted his fair damsel into her seat, he decided that this was as good a time as any to say what he wished. Happily, Angeline made no demur when he dismissed his tiger, which he hoped boded well for things to come.

"As a matter of fact, ma'am, I have been wanting to have another conversation with you." A flick of the reins sent the well-sprung curricle surging over the cobbles. "This occasion is not of my contriving, but perhaps it may serve us well."

"Oh?" Her voice was unencouraging. "I cannot fathom what we might have to discuss, my lord."

Andrew grit his teeth. *Hell's teeth, did she expect him to grovel?*

Though he had no trouble dealing with women as a whole, Andrew had never made a proposal of marriage before and had not the least notion how to go about it. In fact, until very recently he had considered himself a confirmed bachelor, for as a duke's second son he was free of the responsibility to beget heirs for the Carisbrooke dynasty. He was a sophisticated man, a man who had had a great many women, yet for some reason this icy beauty had him sweating like a schoolboy. Derek had called her a brittle diamond, but then what the devil did *he* know? If the damned fool knew anything about women, Stacia Edwards would not be doing whatever it was she was doing.

He closed his mind on that thought and said aloud, "On the contrary, we have something quite important to discuss." He gave her a sidelong glance. "Us," he finished succinctly.

Angeline did not even blink. "You cannot be serious," she said in a dampening tone.

"I am perfectly serious. I have felt from the first that there is an attraction between us. Or perhaps it might better be deemed a connection, of sorts." He cleared his throat. "I felt it the moment I clapped eyes on you." *God, what a greenhorn he sounded.* "It, er, occurred to me that perhaps you did not understand," he went on with unconscious arrogance. "So I thought that if I explained my sentiments—"

"Your sentiments," she repeated with disdain. "What has sentiment to do with anything?"

He cast her a startled look. "Why, a great deal, I should think." Baffled as much by her remark as by his own lack of polish, he reached into his pocket and pulled out the small packet he had collected from the jeweler's. "This is for you, Angeline." Cursing inwardly, he thrust it into her hand.

Her eyes swiveled to his, then fell to the packet. "What is it?"

When he did not answer, her fingers moved to part the brown paper wrapping. Beneath, a small jewel case lay in her lap. She touched the exterior.

"Open it," he ordered.

She obeyed without comment, yet when his gift lay exposed, her violet-blue eyes regarded it without expression. Nestled on black velvet, the magnificent diamond-and-sapphire necklace was as perfectly crafted and as delicate as Angeline herself.

"Do you like it?" he inquired, rather too eagerly.

Disappointing seconds passed, then she snapped shut the box and handed it back to him. "It is very pretty," she said, lashes still lowered. "But you have not fooled me, my lord. I know perfectly well this necklace was not intended for me."

"It certainly was!" he protested, completely taken aback.

Never in his wildest fancies had he anticipated such a reaction. In his experience, females blushed and giggled when they received gifts, and though he was glad she did not simper foolishly, he had not bargained for such blatant ingratitude as this.

"Then you took far too much for granted," she retorted. "I cannot accept such a gift without compromising my reputation, and that, my lord, is something I am not prepared to do, even for you."

As discouraging as this might have sounded, her last three words rejuvenated his hopes. "Is that all that concerns you?" he inquired in relief. "Pray cast aside your scruples, my dear. I see I have not made myself clear. I am asking you to be my wife, Angeline."

To his utter astonishment, she rounded on him with fury. "Why? Because you fancy yourself in love with my face? Or is it a case of simple lust for what one cannot have?"

"Lust has nothing to do with it!" he shot back. "Or at least very little," he amended, his eyes roving over her hungrily. "Naturally I find you desirable. You are the single most highly finished piece of nature I have ever encountered."

Her lip curled. "Ah, now the truth comes out. You are

247

another such as your father—a womanizing scoundrel with an eye for a pretty face. Well, you very much mistake the matter if you think I should desire such a man for my husband."

The injustice of this stung him like a lash. "From your point of view, ma'am," he said with asperity, "I can see nothing but advantage in the match. Perhaps it has escaped your notice that marriage with me would elevate your station in life considerably. You would not have to work for your living, nor should you be expected to, as the daughter of an Oxford-educated country squire—"

"How do you know about the squire?" she cut in. "You arrogant coxcomb, did you pry into my background before making me this so-flattering offer? Well, let me tell you something, my lord high-and-mighty. When you were eight years old, my mother met your father, and he was very much taken with her. Ah, you did not know about that, did you?"

"What are you saying?" he said evenly.

Her eyes seared into him. "I am saying that your father seduced my mother and that two months later she found herself with child. Think about it, my lord, and then tell me if you still wish to marry me."

Suffused with shock, Andrew nearly steered his horses into a lamppost. "My God," he said hoarsely, "are you saying you are my *sister?* I don't believe it!"

"Why not?" she replied, her tone brutal. "It is perfectly possible. I would hardly be unique, either, since by all accounts your father littered England with his bastards."

Feeling ill, Andrew focused on his driving and slowly gathered his wits. They were halfway to Grosvenor Square, he realized in confusion. How had they come so far without his being aware?

"If it is as you say," he said wearily, "then naturally this puts things in a different perspective." *Hell and damnation, that was the understatement of the year.* "If you are indeed my . . . half sister, ma'am, then . . . I suppose

248

I must assume responsibility for your well-being."

"Oh, do you mean you will acknowledge me?" she mocked. "How noble. But I fear I must decline the offer—if that is what it is. I have taken care of myself all my life, and I shall continue to do so."

Very much at a loss, he inspected her miserably. "You don't look like my father." It was all he could think of to say.

"I am said to resemble my mother almost exactly."

"Then I can understand why my father did what he did. Though, of course, that doesn't mean I condone it."

They drove the remainder of the way in silence, but upon reaching Upper Grosvenor Street, he said, "I cannot leave the horses standing alone, but if you wish to talk some more—"

"I do not."

Her previous vehemence was gone, replaced by a ragged passivity. As Andrew helped her out of the carriage, he noticed her hand was trembling.

"I'm very sorry to have caused you pain," he said carefully. "But I want you to know this: no matter what my father did, I will always love you, Angeline. And I do mean *you*, my dear. Not your face."

She had already started to walk away, but upon these words she turned. "What did you say?" Her black-fringed eyes were wide, her cheeks as pale as a daisy's petals.

"I said I love you." Andrew was nigh to exploding with grief, but he stated it as calmly as he was able. Then, unable to bear another second of the exchange, he climbed back into the curricle and picked up the reins. He was halfway down the street before he looked back and saw that she was crying.

"You fool, give her air! That is no way to treat a swooning lady!"

The voice which penetrated the fog surrounding

249

Stacia's brain sounded suspiciously like Joshua Croxton's but if that were so, the concern of the sentiment made no sense.

"Here, here!" A second, very indignant voice wafted past her ears. "I say, I say, sir! This is most improper! Winifred, do you see this? I told you the little heiress came in here, and, by George, Winifred, I was right! Cuthbert Duncan knows what he knows, by George, and don't let anyone tell you otherwise."

"I never doubted you for a moment, Cuthbert," replied a third voice with a warmth that disappeared in its next utterance. "Pray allow me to inform you, Mr. Matravers, that clutching Mrs. Edwards to your bosom accomplishes nothing. The girl has fainted, for pity's sake. And you, Sir Joshua. Stop gaping like a stock and fetch us a chair." The voice was moving closer. "Some men are so ineffectual," it complained. "And where, pray, is the shopkeeper? Cowering in the back, I expect."

Stacia jerked back as smelling salts were thrust under her nose. "Ugh," she moaned, her eyes flying open. "Lady Winifred, please. I need . . . air."

"You swooned, my dear. Thank goodness I had my vinaigrette with me." Derek's mama recapped the vial of salts and stuffed it back into her reticule. "Open the door, Cuthbert," she commanded. "Thank you. Ah, here is a stool. Sir Joshua has at last made himself useful. Put it there, near the door, if you please."

The wind that gushed in did much to clear Stacia's head. She suddenly realized that the object against which she was languishing was none other than Mr. Matravers, and though she still felt woozy she pushed away from him with a strength born of absolute loathing. When she staggered slightly, it was, surprisingly, Sir Cuthbert who stepped forward to lend his arm.

"Allow me, ma'am. Not too steady on your pins, eh? Must do as her la'ship says," he advised as she sat down. "Winifred knows what's best. Always does. Clever woman. You'll be right as a trivet in no time." He nodded sagely, then glared at the two men.

While Sir Joshua brushed lint from his sleeve, Mr. Matravers cultivated a hypocritical smile. "Forgive me, ma'am," he said to Stacia. "You took me quite unawares. I am not in the habit of dealing with swooning fits."

"Nor am I in the habit of having them," she told him coldly.

She would have said more, had her attention not been caught by Sir Cuthbert, who was peering through his quizzing glass at Mr. Matravers's neck.

"I say, sir," he said, a peculiar expression on his face, "what do you call that arrangement?"

Mr. Matravers shifted his feet. "I call it the Oriental," he answered in a sardonic voice.

His tone might have put off some men, but Sir Cuthbert was immune to nuances. "Well, it ain't," he said frankly. "Take it from me. *I* know. In fact, to put it kindly, it is an abomination. Yes, an abomination." He pronounced the word with delight, casting Stacia a conspiratorial wink. "Her la'ship taught me that word," he whispered from behind his hand. "Devilish handy, ain't it?"

Probably because Mr. Matravers looked as though he would make an uncivil reply, Lady Winifred intervened.

"Do you feel well enough to walk?" she asked Stacia. "Sir Cuthbert's carriage is not far."

Within minutes, Derek's mother had whisked Stacia out of the shop and settled them all inside the baronet's town chariot.

"Well, Cuthbert," she said, with grudging respect, "you certainly saved the day. Not only is your sense of fashion superior, you have extraordinary vision." She turned to Stacia. "I vow we were a score of shops away when he spied you through the crowds!" She paused, then added, "I saw Derek this morning before he left for Newmarket. He told me that you are betrothed. As my future daughter-in-law, I trust you will not make a habit of visiting the gentlemen's shops. It is most imprudent."

251

"You misunderstand," said Stacia unhappily. "I did not plan to go in. It was only that I saw Sir Joshua Croxton, whom I dislike excessively, so I ducked inside so he would not see me. Then I was overcome by the smell of tobacco and . . . and . . ." Her voice faded off as she sought to explain a scene which must have looked damning.

Lady Winifred cleared her throat. "You need not go on," she said. "I understand more than you think. However, what I do *not* understand is why you were without an escort. Derek would certainly not approve."

Stacia gazed at her fingers. "Actually, ma'am, I was with Mrs. Greaves, but she was not feeling well. Lord Andrew Carisbrooke escorted her home, but I had more shopping to do."

Throughout this exchange, Sir Cuthbert had been staring into space. "I did, didn't I?" he said suddenly. "By George, Winifred, I saved the day. Good eyes, y'know. Runs in the family. My mother had good eyes. My father had good eyes. My sisters have good eyes. All the Duncans have—"

"—good eyes," finished Lady Winifred with a tolerance that did her credit. Her eyes rested on the baronet with something approaching affection. "You are a hero, Cuthbert."

"A hero," he repeated, beaming. "I'm a hero. A great gun, by George. A capital fellow, in fact. A regular Trojan. An out-and-outer. A cool hand." His chest puffed with pride. Then, without apparent cause, his attention shifted to Stacia. "I say, you ain't really going to wed that stiff-rumped boy of Winifred's, are you?" He looked quite horrified by the notion.

Stacia met his gaze with an equanimity she was far from feeling. "Indeed I am," she said calmly.

Sir Cuthbert shuddered. "Brave girl. Dash it, I may be a hero, but I wouldn't be in your shoes for anything!"

Chapter Seventeen

Derek leaned on the door to Palatine's box, his eyes resting possessively upon the majestic creature within. Save for a pair of stableboys at the other end of the building, he was alone with the stallion, enclosed in a world of dampness and hay and pungent animal odor. The atmosphere was almost soothing enough to make him forget his depression.

"Damn this rain," he said softly. "You want to run, don't you? You want to stretch those great legs and fly, not be trapped in here like a bird in a cage."

The stallion whuffled in answer and the noble head swung down to nudge his hand.

Derek stroked the satiny nose absently. "Tomorrow," he promised. "You run as well in the mud as you do on dry ground."

Overhead, the fierce pelting on the roof seemed unceasing, while beyond the walls the rolling ridges of Newmarket heath swept out in a bare, desolate grayness that gripped the edges of the sky. Since last night, the turf had turned into a mire of mud, a circumstance that had thrown some of the other horse owners into high fidgets. Derek, too, was feeling on edge, but it had nothing to do with the rain.

Odd how he could not seem to concentrate. He had been here a little over forty-eight hours, and for most of that time his thoughts had centered, not on the race or its outcome, but on Stacia and everything that was to come.

Derek frowned. Had some part of him decided that Palatine's success was no longer critical? Had his betrothal to a wealthy woman impeded his desire to see his life's ambition through to the finish? No, Palatine's success was *his* success. Nothing must be allowed to interfere. Not even Stacia.

Derek's eyes darkened with self-inflicted torment. Until Stacia was his, bound in legal wedlock, a seed of doubt would continue to haunt him. Nay, why not be honest? His worry was more than a seed—it was a full-fledged, smothering vine curled round the neck of everything he had ever wanted.

Would she cry off?

That was the question that plagued him. The knowledge that his happiness lay in her hands was like a rat gnawing at his belly. What if she refused to go through with the marriage? What if she decided that her disgust of him outweighed the importance of keeping her word? Then all he yearned for would be lost. Everything. Even Palatine's victory would be without value, a mocking tribute to the crumbled ashes of his dreams.

Derek shook his head, as if it were possible to shake the misgivings from his mind. Why the devil would she wish to marry him? He'd never behaved with enough gallantry to suit her, and as for going to her house when he was drunk—! He'd been a bloody, mindless ass. What had he to give her but his name? Not much.

And why did he wish to possess a woman who openly admitted she preferred another man? Why could he not rip her from his mind like every other woman he had known? Look how easily he had forgotten Dominique, a stunning woman for whom he had cherished—briefly—a fierce attraction. Yet she had flown from his memory as easily as her predecessors, unlamented and unimportant, a trivial piece of his past.

Why?

Scowling heavily, Derek mentally reviewed the various women with whom he had been involved. On a superficial level, each had been more beautiful and sophisticated than Stacia Ashcroft. Some had been witty; most had been graceful; a few had even been intelligent. All had been skilled in the art of lovemaking.

This led to another line of thought. Was his desire for Stacia merely sexual? Was it because he had *not* bedded her that he could not forget her? Pondering this, Derek walked to the door of the stables and stared out at the driving rain.

No, it was more than that. By God, he was over thirty years of age; he ought to know the difference by now. All this soul-searching only reconfirmed what he had already known—he wanted to wed Stacia because he was in love with her, deeply, desperately, and completely. He wanted her by his side for as long as there was breath in his body. He wanted children, *their* children. And he wanted her to love him in return, enough to make an effort to understand his moods, enough to share her feelings with him, enough to want him in her bed. Enough to *want* to give him children.

She might not care for him now, but he intended to wed her anyway. After that, God willing, he would teach her to love him. If she would only give him her love there would be no limits—the whole range and length and breadth of his essence would be healed and replenished. If she would only learn to love him as he loved her, then he would be complete.

Such thoughts revolved in his head until his trainer returned to stay with Palatine. Derek then made his way through the rain to the inn where he was staying, which was filled with individuals who had already begun to gather for the upcoming race. He was acquainted with many, but his uncompromising expression put off all but the innkeeper, a jovial-looking man who hailed him as he was starting up the stairs.

"A message for you, sir," he said, waving a small

255

envelope importantly. "It come just after noontime. I would 'ave sent the boy to find you if I'd bin able to find the bleedin' lad, but what with the inn bein' full and me 'aving to do everything myself—"

"May I have it?" The authority in the cool question cut short the man's rambling.

One glance assured Derek that the letter was from his mother. He was not surprised; he'd instructed her to write if anything went amiss. A gigantic, bone-chilling wave of foreboding crashed over him.

He took the letter to his room, but forced himself to change into dry clothes before he opened it. Had Stacia refused to permit the announcement? Perhaps she still hoped Drew Carisbrooke would drop the handkerchief. His entire body tensed at the thought. By all that was holy, he'd not stand for that. He'd do something, anything, to prevent her from marrying another man. He'd show her no mercy. He'd . . . what?

Slowly, Derek's mouth curved in self-mockery. What would he do? What *could* he do if she chose to favor another? Not very much, when it came down to it.

What he would *not* do was carry out his threats. Though Stacia had not known it, his blackmail had been mere bluster, a weapon created out of drunkenness and desperation and anger at her deceit. Perhaps that was partly why he felt so damned blue-deviled. She'd believed his threats and that, unaccountably, had wounded him. Hang it, she ought to have realized that he would never do anything to hurt her, he thought illogically.

Cursing himself for a fool, Derek sat on the edge of the bed and opened his mother's letter.

My dear son, she had written. *Inasmuch as you have requested my assistance in the matter, I am taking the liberty of informing you of a Distressful Incident which occurred this afternoon. Your Betrothed has expressed the wish that you not be told, but I go against her desire because I believe it my Duty, and for no other reason. I had gone to Oxford Street with Sir Cuthbert . . .*

256

She'd not jilted him. The realization flooded through him like whiskey on an empty stomach, then changed to still, simmering rage when he read on.

. . . though she was upright she appeared quite unconscious, the whole of her weight being supported by Paul Matravers. That dreadful Sir Joshua Croxton was present, and none other, for the cowardly shopkeeper had crept away to hide in the back. It was fortunate, to say the least, that it was Sir Cuthbert and I who discovered your Intended in a situation which some might deem compromising. Luckily, Cuthbert is favored with the most excellent eyesight . . .

Bloody hell fortunate indeed, Derek thought grimly. At least the fool was good for something.

His teeth ground together as he pictured the scene— Matravers and Croxton leering, Stacia probably terrified out of her wits. Damn it, the girl needed a keeper! And why the devil had she been without an escort? And what had she been doing in a tobacco shop, for God's sake?

His mouth set in a forbidding line, he skimmed on until he reached the postscript, which gave him another pause.

I have also received word that your Uncle Rupert was wounded in a duel, which took place outside Paris under what I can only call scandalous circumstances. It has become the latest on-dit, of course, but what need concern us is that there seems to be some question as to whether he will recover. I'm sure I hardly need mention what it will mean to you if he does not, but the accuracy of the report has not been substantiated.

Derek considered this information with a mental shrug. The duel would have been over a woman, that much was certain. He knew his uncle well. 'Twas surprising he was not the victor of the engagement, but doubtless Uncle Rupert would survive. He always did.

Dismissing the matter from his mind, Derek shoved a hand through his thick black hair and returned to the problem at hand. There was really no reason why he could not go down to London on the morrow. His trainer and the jockey had things well in hand. Palatine's hock was mending nicely. The Second Spring Meeting was several days away. There was quite enough time for him to reach town, seek an audience with the archbishop in order to procure a special license, wed Stacia, and be back in Newmarket in time for the race.

Yes.

It was the only way he could retain his sanity.

Stacia had fared no better than Derek during his absence. She had been making a defiant effort to prove to herself that she was quite capable of enjoying life without her betrothed, however the attempt thus far had been a woeful failure. Without Derek, the entire social scene had become as flat and dull as Lady Crackenthorpe had once predicted it might. She'd attended two balls in two evenings, danced every set with men for which she did not care a fig, been complimented and feted so extravagantly that she no longer believed a word her partners uttered, and arrived home both nights with her spirits lower than they had been at the outset. As if this were not bad enough, her rest had been plagued with nightmares, so that when she arose she looked as though she had not slept in a week.

To make matters even worse, Angeline had been more exasperating than usual. Despite Stacia's broad hints, her companion showed no disposition to confide the outcome of her encounter with Lord Andrew, which seemed more than a trifle unfair from her employer's point of view. Not that Stacia wished to pry, if course, but it would have been rewarding to know that her mortifying experience in the tobacco shop had been worthwhile, instead of wondering whether she had suffered for naught. However, Angeline was disobliging enough to refrain from confidences. Her hours were filled with tasks that she invented for herself, while she worked her eyes seldom focusing on anything visible.

On the morning of the third day, when Stacia

descended to the morning room with dark smudges under her eyes, Angeline said, quite as politely as the previous mornings, "Good morning, ma'am. Did you have a pleasant evening?"

Until now Stacia had answered with equal politeness, but upon this occasion she decided to be frank.

"No, I did not," she said shortly. "You were wise not to go. I found it excessively tedious."

Angeline's brows rose in mild surprise. "Was it?" she responded. "I am sorry to hear it."

"Lord Andrew was there."

"How pleasant." It was stated with perfect calm. "Did you dance with him?"

Stacia's fingers curled in frustration. "Yes, as a matter of fact, I did. You, too, could have danced with him—had you been there."

"I suppose that's so." Angeline's tone did not fluctuate an iota. "But since you said it was tedious, I must be glad I did not."

The last threads of Stacia's patience snapped. "Good God, Angeline, have you *no* sensibility?" Her hands swept out in a wild gesture. "You once admitted that you cared for the man! What has happened between you? Has *anything* happened?"

For the first time, Angeline's eyes fell upon her with a focused look. "You must know the answer to that," she said quietly. "You contrived that I be alone with him. Obviously something happened."

"Well then?"

Angeline sighed. "Very well, ma'am. I suppose you deserve to know. First he offered me a gift—a necklace. I accused him of giving something that was intended for another, but he claimed that was untrue." She shrugged wearily. "After that, he proclaimed what he termed were his sentiments. I found him insufferably arrogant. He seemed to assume that I would fall on his neck with joy simply because he had . . . sentiments."

"I see. And then what?"

259

"To own the truth, I misjudged him. I thought that he wanted me for his mistress, but I was wrong." Wonder filled the low voice. "He asked me to be his wife."

Stacia had a sinking feeling. "Oh dear. You refused him, didn't you?"

Angeline looked at her hands. "Not in so many words. I asked him if he had fallen in love with my face . . .or if it was common lust that drove him to speak."

"Good God," Stacia said involuntarily. "The poor man."

Angeline nodded. "And that was not the worst of it," she said gloomily.

Stacia's eyes closed.

"I am not always wise," admitted the other girl in an unhappy tone. "My pride is my undoing. For so long I had wondered what he would say if he knew about my mother and his father. How would he react? Would he shrug it off? Would he care? It has haunted me, ma'am. So I . . . I told him what happened in a . . . in a manner of speaking."

"In a manner of speaking," repeated Stacia with foreboding. "What did you say?"

Angeline grew defensive. "I told him the truth—at least a part of it! I told him his father seduced my mother and left her with child. Then I asked him if he still wished to marry me."

"*No,* Angeline!"

"Yes." Angeline's face was miserable, her eyes dark with pain. "I let the experiment go too far. I allowed him to believe I was his sister. It was to be just for a moment, you understand. It was a test. His answer, I thought, would tell me what manner of man he was. But then, when I saw the horror in his face, I realized what I had done. I had acted despicably. It was I, not he, who lacked honor. And I was struck dumb by that knowledge."

Stacia groaned.

"I now know," continued Angeline, "that Andrew Carisbrooke is the most noble man alive! Even when he believed me to be his sister, he still insisted that he loved me and vowed to do anything in his power to assist me." She laughed wildly. "Love! Now, when it is too late, I find it for myself."

Stacia deemed it time to step in. "Surely the matter could be mended," she suggested. "Perhaps if it were handled very delicately, you could make him understand—"

"Never!" Angeline was extremely pale. "He must never know what I have done. I would to God I had not done it, but I did and now I must live with the consequences."

Stacia regarded the other girl sadly. Behind that exquisite face was a soul in torment, a human being as desperately in need of love as any other.

There had to be something she could do, she reflected. She could not sit by and allow these two to sacrifice their love for a lie. She would have to consider the situation very carefully, so that another mistake was not made.

Perhaps it would take her mind off Derek for a while.

However, this was not destined to be, for at that very moment Derek was striding away from the archbishop's mansion with a special license in his pocket. Regardless of the drizzle, he chose to walk, but it was in the direction of Drew Carisbrooke's house, rather than Stacia's, that he headed.

Lord Andrew was in his library, gazing moodily into the fire when Derek was announced.

"What the devil are you doing here?" Andrew demanded. "I thought you were in Newmarket."

"I was." Derek walked over and threw himself into the chair next to Andrew's. "Important matters demanded a brief return. I'm surprised to find you here," he added shortly. "I thought you meant to join me."

"I did," said the other man calmly, "and I still do. I have plans to leave on the morrow." Studying Derek's

261

damp hair, he reached for the brandy snifter at his elbow. "This will take the chill off," he added, filling a second tumbler nearly to the brim. "You should have taken a hackney."

"I needed the exercise." Derek accepted the drink and cleared his throat. "Drew, I came here to ask you something."

Andrew's brows rose inquiringly. "Then ask."

"It's a damned difficult thing to ask your best friend."

Andrew looked faintly sardonic. "We've known each other a good many years. Why fight shy now?"

"True," Derek conceded, a quirk to his lips. "Very well, then. Have you been dallying with Stacia?" Andrew's look made him shift uncomfortably. "I don't mean dallying, actually. I mean, have you given her any reason to suppose that you might be, uh, intending to make her an offer?"

"Why?"

"Because I want to know," he snapped, losing patience. "I want to know what lies between you, if anything. Not that it signifies—"

"Not that it signifies!" Andrew let out a hoot. "Faith, that's rich! You cock-brained idiot, it obviously signifies or you wouldn't be asking." He sipped his drink, and added, "Face it, you're jealous as hell. Though you've no reason to be, I'm thankful to say."

Unconvinced, Derek rubbed wearily at his temple. "No? I have reason to know that she prefers your company to mine."

"Perhaps because I don't insult her," replied the other man testily. "Nor do I insinuate that I'm after her fortune. And I especially don't tell her that I'm not in love with her."

The fire crackled in the heavy silence; Derek stared at the carpet. "So she confides in you," he said roughly. "What else has she said?"

"Very little. But I'll tell you one thing, and I'll say it

262

because I think you should know. She had an assignation the other day."

"*What?*"

Andrew nodded. "I don't know with whom. We met in Oxford Street and she asked me to"—an odd note of constraint entered his voice—"escort Mrs. Greaves home. When I protested her lack of escort she did a good deal of circumlocution, then blushed and admitted she was to meet someone privately. She added that *he* would see she reached home safely." He shrugged. "I suppose she might have meant her brother, but I doubt it. I'm sorry."

Something threatened to explode in Derek's brain. He stood up, staring blindly. "I'll see you in Newmarket," he said. "Palatine is in good form. Things are looking well."

"Are they?" There was a mingling of irony and restraint in the answer. "I'm glad to hear that. I'll be there, my friend. I wouldn't miss it for anything, you know."

"Nor would I," returned Derek in a very flat voice. "Come hell or high water, I'll see my horse win."

"The gentleman refuses to come upstairs," Stacia's butler informed her a short while later. The woodenness in his voice did not conceal his opinion of such unrefined manners. "He chose to wait in the morning room, madam, and insists on speaking with you alone."

Stacia had been sitting in the Yellow Saloon with a book in her lap, but at this she closed it and rose to her feet. "Thank you, Challow. I will go to him." She looked at Angeline. "I will be quite all right," she added in a low voice.

For once her companion's hands were idle; Angeline had done nothing but gaze into the fire all morning. It seemed as though all her militant energy was for once focused on her own affairs, for she merely nodded

263

expressionlessly and did not move.

Perhaps because it was the morning room in which they had had their last confrontation, Stacia found that her knees were shaking as she descended the stairs. "Wet-goose," she chided herself. "Derek is a man, not an ogre. Why should I be nervous?" Even so, she had to take a deep breath before walking into the room.

His back was toward her, but upon her entrance he turned and raked her with his eyes. Silhouetted against the window, he seemed one with the grayness outside, while at the same time dominating the room with his presence. A detached part of her brain noticed that his buckskins and top boots were splashed with mud, as though he had ridden or walked a great distance in the rain.

She eyed him in trepidation. "Won't you sit down?"

"I'd rather stand," he said coldly.

Stacia would have preferred to sit, but to have done so would have given him that much more of an advantage. "Very well," she said, squaring her shoulders. "What did you wish to say?"

"Come here." It was uttered quietly in a voice only a fool would disobey.

She approached him with caution, but when she halted just short of his reach, he stepped closer and lifted her chin with his fist.

"Whom did you meet in Oxford Street the other day?" he inquired, so softly that she felt a frisson of fear.

"What do you mean? I met a great many people."

The perceptive eyes narrowed. "Don't fence with me, Stacia."

She moistened her lips. "Obviously someone told you that I fainted, so there is no use pretending otherwise. But it was the merest nothing, Derek. There was no need for you to rush back on my account."

"I think there was," he countered, steel in his tone. "As my future wife, I expect you to behave with discretion. I also expect you to refrain from making assignations with other men. I will not play the cuckold when we are married, nor will I countenance such behavior now."

"Assignations?" For a moment, she was genuinely at a loss. "I made no—Oh. You've been talking to Lord Andrew."

"Whom did you meet?" The voice was as relentless as the fist beneath her chin. "Was it Matravers? Or someone else?"

She reached up to clasp his wrist, but his hand did not stir. "May we please sit down?" she quavered. "There has been a misunderstanding. I can explain. Please Derek."

The green eyes looked into hers, then his hand fell away. "Very well, Stacia. I'm willing to listen."

They sat in the same chairs they had used during the dice game.

"Now Derek," she began, her fingers locked nervously in her lap, "I did *not* have an assignation. I merely allowed Lord Andrew to think so. I wanted him to take Angeline up in his carriage, but he was being dreadfully obstinate and pigheaded about leaving me behind."

"So you told him you had an *assignation?*"

Stacia flushed at his derisive tone. "It was the readiest excuse I could invent," she said defensively. "You see, I believed him to be in love with her and I thought that if he were given the opportunity he . . . he might make her an offer of marriage."

Slowly, the hard suspicion in Derek's face faded to astonishment. "Is this the truth?" he demanded.

"Yes!" she cried heatedly. "Why can you not trust me? Have I ever give you reason not to do so?"

He ignored the question, yet his voice lost much of its bitter edge. "You little fool, did it never occur to you that Drew is quite capable of creating his own opportunities? If he wishes to drop the handkerchief—which I doubt— he'll do so without assistance from you."

"Well, you are wrong!" she flashed. "For he did

indeed make Angeline a declaration! Only . . . only she refused him."

"Good God." Derek's arrested expression afforded her a momentary surge of satisfaction.

After a long moment, he sighed. "Well, that's their business, but you are mine. As far as I'm concerned, we've only scratched the surface of your exploits. I want to know why there was no footman with you."

"Both my footmen had colds," she explained. "And so did my coachman, which is why I sent him home."

"And your maid?"

"It was her afternoon off," she said with resentment.

"Ah, of course. And why go into a tobacco shop, of all places?"

"To avoid Sir Joshua!"

"An obvious choice," he said sardonically. "The shop where he buys tobacco is the ideal place to hide."

"You don't understand. It was the nearest door, and I had no idea that he would come in, or that Mr. Matravers was inside—"

"No, of course you did not," he agreed.

Her hands raised in a gesture eloquent of frustration. "You don't believe me."

"Actually, I do," he said, much more mildly. "Only you, Miss Ashcroft, could behave with such extraordinary naivety. You clearly need a husband to take charge of you—and the sooner the better. That's why I've changed my plans." His eyes held a curious expression. "I've decided to wed you today."

Stacia sat perfectly still. "Today," she repeated. "How is that possible?"

Derek patted his pocket. "I managed to coax the Archbishop of Canterbury into granting me a special license. I'm taking you up to Suffolk this afternoon, where my parish vicar will perform the ceremony. You will remain at Camberley until after the Newmarket races, when I will join you."

"And if I don't agree?"

266

His mouth tightened. "I'm not offering you a choice, Stacia. You and I will be leaving within the hour. Our agreement was that you would marry me when and where I wish, remember?"

Feeling bullied, Stacia said stonily, "Well, I won't go without Angeline."

"Hang Angeline," he shot back. "Let her stay here."

But Stacia held her ground. "That was not part of the agreement. She comes with me or I don't go."

With a glance at the clock upon the mantelshelf, Derek stretched out his long legs and crossed them at the ankle.

"Then I suggest you go upstairs and instruct her to start packing," he said curtly. "We leave in one hour. Oh, and Stacia?"

She looked at him.

"Do be sure she leaves her weapons behind," he said dryly.

Chapter Eighteen

Stacia grasped the strap as the chaise hit a rut in the road. Her eyes moved to the window, and for the first time since Cavenham she scanned the passing scenery. Without much interest, she noted that the church spires and timber-framed cottages of the village in which she had been married had given way to undulating pastures filled with grazing sheep. It was charming and picturesque, and on any other day she would have admired it, but at the moment she was too preoccupied for it to make more than a passing impression.

Today she had been married. *Married.* The word sounded foreign, a meaningless jumble of letters strung together to signify something that was precious and holy. What would it be like to be wed to Derek? Would they be happy? Now that they were man and wife would he at last learn to love and trust her? Or would every step forward always be followed by two steps to the rear?

Her shoulders slumped at the thought of such a struggle. She had been worrying about it since London, and even more since Cavenham. Perhaps if she had been able to discuss it with Derek he might have laid some of her fears to rest, but he had traveled the entire journey as an outrider, aloof and inaccessible, while she was left inside the carriage with Angeline and her maid.

She was very depressed.

The wedding ceremony had been performed by the vicar of Cavenham, a kind, distinguished-looking man who had known Derek well enough to shake his hand and call him by name. It had been a short ceremony, almost disappointing in its brevity, but at least Derek had kissed her quite properly at the finish. Of course, it had been nothing like the kiss he had given her in Hyde Park, Stacia thought wistfully.

Her heart twisted at the memory. That kiss had begun quite gently, she remembered, then slid into something altogether different, something hungry and uncivilized and completely foreign to her experience. He had forced her lips wide, invading deep into her mouth until he grazed the very fire in her soul . . . and then his hand had gone to her breast and, in her shock, she had come to her senses.

Stacia shivered suddenly. To be kissed like that was what she needed now, more than anything in the world, but she was inside a carriage with two other women and he was outside, astride a horse, beyond her range of view.

Separated, when they should have been together.

Keeping her face averted from Angeline, Stacia pressed her lips together to still their ridiculous quivering. There was still the wedding night to come, she reminded herself. Would he stay with her? He had spoken of going to Newmarket directly, but surely he would not leave before the morning? Surely he would spend the wedding night with his bride? The mere thought made her grow warm and breathless, and a queer, fluttery sensation throbbed in the pit of her stomach.

Or perhaps he meant to leave tonight, whispered the voice in her head. Perhaps he no longer had any desire to kiss or touch her, and his yearning was strictly for her fortune. Perhaps he had a mistress, she thought, someone like Lady Claire or that beautiful woman who had clung to his arm the evening of their first meeting. And if that were the case, perhaps he meant to keep her a prisoner in the country like Papa had, out of trouble and out of mind. *Out of his life.*

Stacia dug her nails into the palms of her hands until the sharp pain dispelled the foolish lump in her throat. She told herself she has asked for this. After all, she had known that Uncle Travis's fortune would carry weight with her suitors. And Derek needed money.

However, no matter what happened she was going to conduct herself with the dignity befitting an Ashcroft. She was going to be very brave—every bit as brave as Sir Cuthbert imagined her to be.

Camberley Hall proved to be a Tudor manor house of noble appearance. It was built of red brick, with mullioned windows and two large towers flanking either side of the main entrance court. Roused to more curiosity about the place than she anticipated, Stacia leaned forward to examine it through the window.

To her surprise, it was Derek who let down the steps and assisted her out of the chaise.

"Welcome to Camberley," he said quietly. Then, more intently, "Do you like it?" He had not let go of her hand.

She gazed at him in surprise. "Very much so," she replied, her heart thumping. "It has a stately quality, but I can envision it as a home as well."

Stacia's spirits lifted at his pleased expression. He actually cared what she thought, she realized. Would he have such an attitude if he had married her for what she could bring him?

The next hour proved both a strain and a source of satisfaction, for Derek expected her to perform the time-honored ritual of meeting and greeting his domestic staff. Conscious of being the cynosure of all eyes, Stacia waited dutifully while the servants filed into the Hall and formed a respectful line.

He addressed the small assembly with his hand on her shoulder. "I have asked you to gather so that I may

270

introduce you to your new mistress. We were married only an hour ago. I trust that you will give her your loyalty and I ask that you obey her wishes as you would mine."

One by one, he introduced them—the butler, the housekeeper, the first and second footman, and so on down the line. It seemed to Stacia that they were fewer in number than the size of the house demanded, but each one acknowledged her with a bow or curtsey, and a few offered smiles and good wishes. During these moments, she saw Derek as his servants must have seen him: an imposing, aristocratic figure who was every inch the lord of the manor, a man worthy of his servants' allegiance.

The marriage had not been a mistake, she decided. Any man who knew the name of every member in his household down to the last scullery maid could not possibly be the hard-hearted libertine Lady Claire had described. She gave him a swift, sidelong glance, taking in the weary grooves around his mouth and the stark silhouette of his form against the wall behind him. He was tired, she thought, and yet he took the time to do this.

As the servants proceeded out of the Hall, she saw Derek look intently over her shoulder. "Excuse me for a moment," he murmured. Without waiting for her answer, he strode across the marble to the front door and disappeared outside.

Stacia would have liked to follow, but, unsure of her welcome, she instead pulled off her gloves and willed herself to relax, to be brave and calm, and to focus on the positive rather than the negative. She stood alone for no more than a minute, then he was back and she was turning to him, emotion welling in her breast.

"Derek." She spoke his name aloud, but it was hopelessly inadequate, a mere whisper of what she wished to convey. Before she could try again, his distracted air caught her attention.

"Stacia, I have to go out." The words sliced into her

hopes like glass into flesh. "My housekeeper will show you to your room. I hope it proves comfortable."

"Of course," she said in bewilderment. "Do as you please." She shrugged carelessly, her chin raised to a proud angle. "I shall go on very well without you."

The dark head tilted as he regarded her, his face brooding, his expression too cryptic to read.

"You will want to rest, I expect," he went on. "I'm not certain when I'll return, so ring the bell when you grow hungry. Someone will bring you a tray if you don't wish to eat in the dining room." He paused, then added in a placating voice, "You may dine with Mrs. Greaves, if you like."

"That would suit me perfectly." Stacia's voice was brittle with forced indifference. *Ask him where he is going,* demanded her inner voice. *You have that right now. You are his wife.*

But she hesitated an instant too long—by the time her mouth opened he had already turned and was almost to the door.

Coward, she thought. *Foolish, craven idiot.* Her mouth fell shut automatically.

The housekeeper, Mrs. Partridge, was waiting for her at the foot of the staircase.

"The state apartments are in the east wing," she told Stacia graciously. "If you will follow me?"

As they walked, Mrs. Partridge explained some of the history of the house. It had been built in the mid-fifteen hundreds, and had originally belonged to one of Derek's ancestors, a man by the name of Navenby. The main staircase had been replaced in the late seventeenth century, stated the housekeeper, along with the main chimney piece, which was very fine. The Great Hall contained a Minstrels' Gallery, she added with evident pride.

"But as you can see, it needs work, ma'am," she said frankly. "The master puts what he can into the house, but it hasn't been near enough." The obvious inference

272

was that she hoped "the master" had married money, but Stacia was not about to enlighten her. The woman would know soon enough how things stood.

"We shall certainly have to see what can be done," she answered evasively.

Mrs. Partridge went on talking until they reached the door to the apartments allotted to Stacia. From her observations thus far, it was clear that parts of the house had been sadly neglected, however, she was delighted to find that her bedchamber was not one of these. In fact, it was even more lovely than the one she had had at the Pulteney.

"The master had it redone recently," the housekeeper informed her stolidly. "I expect 'twas to please you, ma'am. 'Tis the finest room in the house."

Stacia's first thought was that it smelled of hyacinths, while her second was that with the exception of the four-poster bed and walnut wardrobe, everything within the room did indeed appear new. The hangings and counterpane, the draperies, the cushioned chairs and stools, the delicate wallpaper, the paintings, the Axminster carpet beneath her feet—it all had a fresh look, as though just painted by an artist's hand.

And the colors, she thought wonderingly. He could not have chosen colors which would have suited her more. Along with shimmering gilt and silver, there were blues—azure and Wedgwood and cornflower—and deft touches of primrose tossed in like brushstrokes to provide enticing contrast.

"It's beautiful," she said simply.

"In there, too." Mrs. Partridge nodded toward the opposite door.

The adjacent sitting room contained a writing desk, a small chiffonier, a pair of mahogany armchairs, a teapoy, and a sofa. As a whole, it matched the bedchamber in color, grace and tranquility, and Stacia found herself contemplating it with amazement.

Had Derek really done all this for *her?*

"All new," asserted the housekeeper, as if reading her mind. "You haven't seen the dressing room yet. And there's another anteroom, and beyond that, the master's chambers."

The master's chambers. The rooms where her husband slept.

"Where?" Stacia asked, without thinking.

The housekeeper stepped back into the bedchamber and pointed to another door. "Your maid is in there now, ma'am, unpacking your trunk. The other lady, Mrs. Greaves, has been installed in the west wing of the house. The guest wing, that is. This wing has always been for the family."

Stacia had forgotten Angeline. "If my husband"—the word sounded strange—"has not returned by eight, I should like to dine with Mrs. Greaves." She paused. "In her room, I think," she added with an eye to her surrounding splendor. "Can it be arranged?"

Mrs. Partridge bobbed a curtsey. "Certainly, ma'am. Anything you like. But don't you worry, the master will be back. 'Tis his wedding day, after all."

Stacia stared into the lengthening shadows created by candles and the flickering fire in the grate. The handsome clock upon the mantelshelf had just struck eight times. Mrs. Partridge would be here in a moment.

Where was he?

Over and over the question thrummed in her head until she thought she must go mad with it. She had tried every chair, gazed out every window, explored every inch of her rooms (and even ventured into Derek's, which were austere in comparison to hers), but nothing subdued the intolerable, devouring frustration of being abandoned on her wedding night.

Ironically, Stacia's crushing disappointment did not seem to have affected her appetite—a fact her rumbling stomach seemed eager to attest—and the discomfort exacerbated the fretful state of her nerves. Now that it was too late, she rather regretted her decision to dine with Angeline. Alone, she would be left to agonize, but Angeline's Cassandrian attitudes were bound to test her patience to its limit.

Yet when she was ushered into her companion's room, she was instantly ashamed, for she saw at once that Angeline had been crying. Indeed, the drooping figure huddled on the bed reminded her of the circumstances of their first meeting, though a second glance confirmed that the lovely face was considerably more tear-ravaged than it had been on that occasion.

Berating herself for forgetting the other girl's troubles, Stacia hurried forward. "There, now," she soothed, stroking the shoulder beneath the spill of loose, night black hair. "Shhh . . . don't cry. I'm here, Angeline." She gathered the weeping girl into her arms, murmuring soft reassurances. Angeline clung to her for a while, but eventually pulled away.

"Forgive me, ma'am," she said huskily. "I don't know what came over me. I ordinarily have more control." Despite her reddened nose and eyelids, Angeline looked hauntingly beautiful.

Before Stacia could answer the servants arrived, and the conversation halted while a portable table was brought in and their places set. However, as soon as they were served Stacia sent the servants away.

Angeline eyed the steaming food with distaste. "I do not think I can eat."

"You must." Stacia spoke firmly. "Food will give you strength. And while we eat, we are going to put our heads together and decide what to do to set your life to rights." Her nose wrinkled as she took first one, and then another sip of her effervescent drink, which tasted suspiciously like champagne.

Angeline turned to look at the fire. "My troubles are beyond remedy," she stated.

"That is nonsense, Angeline." Stacia's patience was

275

already beginning to slip; she raised her glass to her lips for a third time, before saying, "I'm beginning to think you enjoy suffering, for you will not make the smallest effort to help yourself."

"You do not understand," was the subdued reply.

"I understand very well!" Stacia retorted. "You talk of pride. Well, I have pride, too. But that is not going to prevent me from making an effort to seek my own happiness—which, by the way, *you* have done a great deal to be sure I do not find."

Angeline bit her lip. "On the contrary, I tried to prevent your marriage because I honestly thought it the right thing to do. But you married him anyway. He is either very greedy or in love," she added in a reflective tone, "for even the letter did not dissaude him from having you."

"Letter?" Stacia repeated sharply.

"I hoped it would work," she went on. "But since it did not, I suppose I must confess what I did."

Stacia sat back, her eyes fixed on Angeline's. "Yes, you certainly must!" she exclaimed. "Good God, I think I am beginning to understand."

Angeline's gaze fell to her lap. "I was sure he had never seen your hand, and so would not recognize the writing as mine." Her voice was lowered. "I cannot say exactly what I wrote, only that it was calculated to have given him, if not a disgust of you, at least some second thoughts regarding the wisdom of an . . . alliance." She paused, then added into the silence, "Do you think you can forgive me? I meant it for the best, truly I did."

Stacia's first emotion was anger, but this was quickly palliated by the reflection that at least she now understood why Derek had changed toward her. What a simple explanation it was, she thought, and how easy it ought to be to rectify. And since her relief was so much greater than her anger, she only sighed and said, "Yes, I will forgive you on the condition that you promise never to interfere between us again. And you must also promise to allow me to do what I can to reconcile Lord Andrew to you."

The blue eyes raised, wide and startled and once more wet with tears. "You would really do that after what I did? I have always known you for an angel and now you have proven it beyond all doubt."

"Stuff," said Stacia in a pragmatic tone. She picked up her glass. "Now let us eat and enjoy this champagne. I own I am beginning to like it after all."

They drank all the champagne, and for perhaps the first time met each other on equal ground, without reserve or hesitation or consciousness of misdeeds. They talked of men and marriage, of the trials and blessings of being women, of children and death, and of birth and love. Their friendship, which for some days had shown palpable signs of foundering, was shot with new life, blossoming to a level which was to last the many long years of their lives.

By ten, they were both quite tipsy. Angeline was worn with fatigue, but when Stacia would have left her to sleep, Angeline begged her to remain. And so Angeline lay upon her bed and Stacia sat before the fire, her feet propped upon the chair that Angeline had vacated. They conversed a while longer, but eventually the lag between sentences grew, and Stacia looked over and saw that Angeline was asleep.

By this time, she was too sleepy to rise. Someone would have told her if Derek had returned, so she simply sat and gazed blearily into the flames, her head swirling with mist. Vaguely, she realized she had had too much to drink, but it did not seem to signify. In fact, nothing signified at the moment; the worries that had plagued her earlier in the evening had all receded into the comforting, gossamer-soft shadows of befuddlement. And then exhaustion dragged her down and there was nothingness until, much later, she dreamed that strong arms lifted her

277

as though she weighed no more than the surrounding air.

There was a curious rhythm to the dream, as though she were being carried down long corridors by someone with a determined stride. The fabric beneath her cheek smelled deliciously of wind and smoke and horses, and she rubbed against it, feeling the solidity and heat of its wearer. Wispy images of Derek trailed through her head, and, grateful for such a pleasant opportunity to indulge her fantasies, she kissed the warmth as though it were he.

There was an immediate increase in the pressure about her slender body—a dream embrace with an amazingly tangible feel. It was so lovely that she kissed the warmth again, with the hazy notion of holding it, or absorbing it into herself.

"Watch yer step here, sir," someone cautioned softly. "There's a bit o' plaster on the floor."

The voice brought the dream to an end—or, rather, was enough to pull Stacia away from the muzzy belief that what she was experiencing was a dream.

It was real.

Not only was it real, it was dark, save for the light given off by a candle held aloft by a servant. The swirling in her head lessened as she blinked, but when she tried to rally her thoughts, it seemed a strangely demanding feat. All that was clear was that, for once, her dreams were reality, and she truly was in Derek's arms.

"Derek?" she whispered. "How long have you been back?" Oddly, her tongue found it difficult to wrap around the words.

"Not long." He glanced down, the play of shadow around his mouth suggesting amusement. "I'm sorry I'm so late, love. I'm afraid it couldn't be helped."

She reflected upon this with a small frown. "Why are you carrying me? I can walk."

"Can you indeed? How much champagne did you drink?"

"I don't remember." Her voice was faint. "A bit too much, perhaps."

Derek's head lowered so that he spoke against her temple. "I suppose I deserved this. Just for the record—you didn't get yourself foxed on purpose, did you?"

Stacia surveyed him with indignation. "I'm not foxed, Derek. How dare you suggest such a thing."

A sardonic look entered her husband's eye. "My dear wife, I dare suggest such a thing"—he mimicked her slight slur—"because you most obviously are."

Unable to devise a suitable reply, Stacia simply relaxed against him in what she felt to be a dignified silence. At once her eyes drifted shut. *She was floating in a bottomless sea, a comforting, gentle sea whose waves cradled her, supported her, rocked her with soothing motion.*

This time it was the bounce of her body onto a mattress that jostled her awake. She was back in her bedchamber, lying square in the middle of the magnificent fourposter with its blue-and-silver hangings—whose counterpane and blankets had long since been turned down by her maid. Stacia's eyes fluttered open, then closed, then opened again as something nudged at her thoughts.

What had she wanted to tell him?

Derek stood looking down at her with a lazy smile. "I've sent your maid away," he said softly. His eyes flicked to the demure nightgown that Maisie had so carefully laid out in her absence. "I'm going to be your maid tonight."

Stacia returned his look with paralyzed fascination. In the glow of firelight he stood tall and forceful, a dark, shadow-figure looming over her like some ancient demigod. Mesmerized, her gaze wandered over him, taking in his physical attributes with an odd pride—black hair and brows, a face as fiercely sculpted as cut glass, eyes like glittering emeralds when it was not too dark to see their color.

Eyes she could drown in.

She watched from under her lashes as he removed her slippers and stockings, liking the feel of his hands as they skimmed over her ankles and calves. The mattress sank as he sat beside her, his body pressed against hers.

"I'm glad you've been with no one else," he murmured seductively. "I'll make you love me, Stacia. I'll make you forget Drew."

As he spoke, he reached forward and lifted her gently to a sitting position so that he might undo the fastenings of her gown. He did so with more swiftness and skill than she expected, and when her bodice loosened, she had just enough wit left to catch it before it fell.

"Why did you leave me tonight?" she whispered.

"There was something I had to do." His gaze rested on her lips. "Nothing which need concern you at the moment. But I think it *is* time I told you that I've no bastards tucked away. Not even one."

"I . . . never thought you did," she mumbled, as he reached to brush a red-gold curl from her brow.

Immediately, his fingers went to her cheek, then slid to the base of her throat where her pulse beat a furious tattoo.

He looked at the scrunch of gown in her hands. "Let it fall," he said hoarsely.

Obeying was not as difficult as Stacia might have expected, for her inhibitions appeared to have vanished along with her ability to think coherently. One by one her fingers opened, until she felt the cool air and looked down upon her own breasts, full and bare and glowing in the firelight.

As Derek's breath hissed out, her lowered gaze flashed to his face, then fell to his neck where his collar lay open. "You look nice," she said stupidly.

"So do you," he replied in a low, soft drawl. "Very, very nice."

All at once his arm was around her waist and he was pulling her slowly, deliberately, against his body. His face moved close, close enough for his tongue to touch her lips, where it lingered just long enough to make her restless. Then his mouth locked on hers, forcing her lips wide, delving deep, while his free hand seared her breast with its heat.

Shuddering seconds later he was pushing her onto the pillows, shifting his length so that he was half atop her, heavy yet not hurting, a solid warmth that tingled her flesh. Stacia's eyes shut as his lips wandered lower, following the line of her throat and down, down across the smooth, sensitive flesh that had never seen the light of day. Inside, she was singing with happiness, wanting it to go on forever, this wonderful touching that intermingled so easily with the dizzy spinning inside her head. Yet without warning it stopped.

"This is no good, Stacia. I can't take you like this." Derek's breath was shallow and harsh on her cheek, his eyes a glitter of darkness and hunger.

Stacia opened her eyes, very conscious of the unfamiliar male hardness still pressed against her thigh. She realized with surprise that she was naked.

"Why not?" It seemed a great effort to speak.

"Because you're intoxicated," he rasped, through teeth clamped shut with frustration. "Drunk as a wheelbarrow. Hang it, I can't take my bride to bed for the first time when she's tippled."

"Why not?" she repeated. It sounded funny, and she giggled. "Where else would you take me at such a moment?" She raised her arms over her head and stretched, languorous as a cat. "I want you to," she added.

"Do you indeed?" he murmured. "Well, you can be sure I'll remind you of that when I return." He kissed the tip of her nose and sat up.

"Return?" she repeated foolishly. "From—?"

"From Newmarket," he explained with uncharacteristic patience. "I'm leaving early in the morning. For the *race*, Stacia. The Second Spring Meeting is the day after tomorrow. I have to be there a day early."

"Oh." Her face fell. "Of course. I forgot."

For a long moment he stared speculatively down at her, then his mouth twisted in the old manner. "I

281

suppose I must be satisfied with the knowledge that you don't find me repulsive after all. You endure my kisses with commendable fortitude."

Stacia frowned as a brush of memory flit through the haze in her head, then vanished before she could capture it. There was something important she wanted to tell him. What *was* it?

"Take me with you," she said instead.

The dark head shook—reluctantly, she thought. "It's no fit place for you, princess. The Newmarket crowd is a rough-and-ready mix of high and low society. And my mind will be on other things. If I had to watch you the whole while—"

"I'm no child," she protested.

His eyes strayed to her body. "I'm well aware of that," he agreed, rather thickly. "Come, let's put this nightgown on you. I'm going to tuck you up now."

"Derek?" she said as he pulled the delicate lawn nightdress over her head. "Do you . . . I mean, you don't seem to take much notice of Angeline." Her head popped through the neckhole, and, with childlike submissiveness, she put her arms in the sleeves and lay back on the pillows. "She's very beautiful, you know," she added wistfully.

Sliding an arm under her knees to lift her hips, he pulled the nightgown down and arranged it about her ankles in a prim fashion. "Yes, she's a veritable Circe," he said dryly.

"But she doesn't affect you? You don't seem to—I mean, you never *look* at her."

Derek smiled crookedly. "Not in the way you mean. *You* affect me."

"Why? I'm not beautiful at all."

He looked at her with odd intentness. "Yes, you are. My God, Stacia, don't you know that?"

She shook her head. "Papa always said I was nothing in comparison to Mama. She was the first Eustacia, you know. She was very beautiful."

282

Derek frowned. "She abandoned you at an early age," he said harshly. "That doesn't sound very beautiful to me."

"She went with her lover. No one knows what became of them. Lady Crackenthorpe thinks they went to Australia."

He leaned down and kissed her lips. "Then I hope she remains there. As far as I'm concerned, her daughter is by far the greater prize. You're beautiful both inside and out."

Stacia sighed and closed her eyes. "That's the nicest thing you've ever said to me." Her voice was whisper-soft. "I'm sorry I got myself foxed. I didn't in the least expect it to happen."

"I'm sorry, too," he murmured, drawing the covers up to her chin. "Sleep well, love."

"Derek?" she murmured sleepily. "Thank you for the lovely room."

There was a long silence. "It was nothing," he said in a queer tone.

When she opened her eyes, he was gone.

Chapter Nineteen

Stacia's room was bright with sunshine when next she awoke. She blinked in surprise, and for the first few seconds was quite unable to recall where she was or how she came to be in such a beautiful room. Then, on the heels of the next instant, she remembered.

She was married and she was at Camberley, Derek's estate in Suffolk.

Her husband's home. *Her* home, too.

With a surge of energy, she pushed herself up, but it was too abrupt—the stab of pain in her head proved an all-too-effective reminder of the previous evening. Stacia dropped back onto the pillows with a groan, then shuddered as memory came.

She'd had too much champagne and fallen asleep before the fire in Angeline's room. And then Derek had carried her back, put her on the bed, and—

Oh, God.

With a low moan, she rolled over and buried her face in the pillow. Derek had wanted to make love to her, but been put off because she was vulgar enough to get herself foxed. How could she have done such a low-bred thing?

Seconds passed as she strove to recollect his reaction. For some reason it was easier to remember the images— his silhouette against the firelight, the contrast between his white shirt and the bronzed column of his neck, his eyes resting boldly on her body. Her face crimsoned at the knowledge that he'd seen her naked—naked and drunk, like a common trollop. Yet she did not recall feeling any embarrassment. How was that possible? She had actually liked him looking at her, enjoyed the feel of his lips and hands on her flesh.

Bit by bit his words came back to her, in patchy scraps rather than in sequence.

I'm going to be your maid tonight.

Once more the blood sprang to her cheeks as she recalled the soft, provocative voice in which it had been uttered. Before she could do more than blush, however, another phrase whisked through her head.

I've no bastards tucked away.

Well, she'd never really believed he had, but she was glad and relieved that he'd said it. It seemed a sign that he was willing to trust her with the truth about himself, which was what she so longed for him to do.

Trust her. And love her. Love and trust, trust and love. The two words bounced around in her head, until she forced them away by recalling the subsequent scene. He'd begun to make love to her and then . . .

The next flash of memory had her groaning into the pillow in mortification. After he'd drawn away, she'd asked him to continue, offered herself like a wanton, and still he'd refused. Oh dear lord, had the reason he'd offered been the true one, or was there some other reason? Had she not been pretty enough?

No, he had not found her wanting in that respect—the words he had spoken came back now with crystal clarity: *You're beautiful inside and out.* So either he did not see her flaws or they did not trouble him, and that was reassuring.

I'll make you love me.

Stacia's eyes unfocused as she cast about in her mind for his meaning. That was exactly what he had said. And if he wanted her love, perhaps, just perhaps, he loved her a little already. But as her excitement quickened there was something to spoil it, a gray veil over the blaze of light.

You endure my kisses with commendable fortitude . . .

It had not been a taunt. It had been a reference to his belief that she found him repulsive.

And then she remembered. Angeline had sent Derek a letter in her name, a hurtful, hateful letter designed to make him believe that she found him distasteful. No wonder he had behaved as he had. He must have received it sometime between their conversation at Almack's and that horrid dice game. It would certainly explain why he had been so insulting.

And though he had been gentle with her last night, he still did not know the truth. Fool, fool, not to have told him when she had the chance.

Agitated beyod logical reason, Stacia thrust back the covers and stood up, pausing only to clutch at one of the bedposts as a red mist formed before her eyes. She drew slow, deep breaths as it cleared, pushing aside the swell of nausea with monumental effort.

"It will wear off eventually," she said aloud. "Marco says it always does."

God, she would give anything to know what that letter had said. Could he possibly have kept it?

Feeling like an intruder, she entered Derek's room and commenced her search, working her way methodically around its perimeter. After about five minutes she found it, tucked inside a slender volume on new and improved agricultural methods. To her dismay, the letter's contents proved every bit as horrid as she'd feared.

Returning to her own room, she ripped it to shreds and tossed it in the grate. There! Now all that was left was to be sure Derek knew the truth. No, she had almost forgotten—there was one other important thing to be done.

Entering her sitting room, Stacia slid gracefully into the chair by her desk and took out paper and quill.

286

Frowning with concentration, she began a letter of a very different vein.

> *My Lord,*
>   *I hope you will not think me Impertinent to write to you upon a matter which is doubtless none of my affair. I do so only because what I have to say may well be crucial to your Future Happiness and I feel it my duty to speak out.*
>   *I have reason to believe that considerable Affection lies between yourself and Angeline Greaves, and that any hope of Natural Happiness resulting from this Affection has been thwarted. I, too, bear her much Affection, which is why I take the very great liberty of informing you that there is no Moral Reason why the two of you may not be wed. I fear she has led you to believe otherwise, and though it may seem very Wicked, I beg you to discover her reasons before you condemn her too harshly. I should like to add that, should you wish to renew your suit, I believe you will find the lady of more receptive mind.*
>   *I trust and hope that my Belief in yr. generosity is not Misplaced, and that my interference in this matter may result in a Happy Outcome.*
> *Yrs. Faithfully,*
Stacia Deveaux

Rereading it with a critical eye, Stacia decided that it was quite satisfactory. She then sanded the ink, addressed it to Lord Andrew Carisbrooke, and returned to her bedchamber to ring for her maid.

Maisie arrived instantly with her morning chocolate. "Good morning, mum. 'Tis a fine day today." She grinned widely at Stacia. "'Tis a pity the master had to leave," she went on, "but at least you had him for the night. 'Tis the first time I ever knew you to sleep 'til noon but a new bride has an excuse, and so I told that Mrs.

Greaves when she made so bold as to ask where you were. Which dress shall it be today, mum?"

Her cheeks pink with embarrassment, Stacia decided she could benefit from some air. "My riding habit, please. I daresay there must be something in the stables a lady can ride."

Forty minutes later Stacia was cantering across the fields on a spirited gray mare named Amazon. The previous day's rain had given way to unusually balmy weather, which induced her to ride longer and farther than she had at first intended. She explored every meadow, back lane, and copse she could find, savoring the glorious freedom she had never been allowed to enjoy when her father was alive. Sir George had never allowed her to roam farther afield than the edges of his own property or the nearest village, nor had he permitted her to go off without a groom as she had done today.

When she was ready to turn back, she was able to locate a track headed in the right direction, though it was not the one she had previously used. At length she was surprised to see what looked like the ruins of an old priory, tall and gaunt and beautiful against the Suffolk sky. Such a marvel fairly begged to be investigated, so at once she rode closer, surveying the flint buttresses and vast empty windows with interest. Its crumbling tower still boasted tapering pinnacles and elaborate flushwork decoration in its lower half, but there was not much left of the top, or of the main body of the church.

Sliding to the ground, Stacia tethered her horse and picked her way gingerly among the stones. It presented every appearance of a place long forgotten by all human souls, however the moment she entered the inner court she saw she was mistaken. A woman and a small boy were enjoying a picnic lunch on the square area of lawn which had once served as a cloister.

Loath to intrude, Stacia stepped back hastily, but she had already been seen.

"Hello," called the woman, waving her hand, "please don't feel obliged to go. We'd love for you to join us, though I'm afraid we've finished the food."

Stacia approached them a little shyly. "I do beg your pardon. I thought the place was deserted."

The woman looked to be in her late twenties, with soft brown hair framing a face whose refined features included a pair of twinkling blue eyes. "Well, Nate and I come here frequently," she replied, "but I don't know of anyone else who does. For a moment, I quite thought you were a ghost."

Stacia returned the woman's smile. "I assure you I'm not. What is this place called?"

"This is Leviston Priory, once the home of Augustinian Canons." She patted the blanket invitingly. "Do join us. 'Tis thick enough to keep out yesterday's damp, I promise. My name, by the by, is Clarissa Inglesant, and this is my son, Nate. He is two."

Persuaded by her pleasant manner, Stacia took a section of the blanket for herself. "I am Stacia Deveaux," she said.

Mrs. Inglesant looked startled. "Deveaux? But that must mean . . ."

Stacia blushed. "Yes. Derek and I were married yesterday."

"Yesterday," echoed the woman with a curious look. "I must tell you I know your husband rather well. Perhaps he has told you about me?"

A dozen possible replies swept simultaneously through Stacia's head, but the one which triumphed above the others was inspired solely by pride.

"Of course," she said, after only a split second's hesitation. "All about you. And Nate, too." She forced a smile, and looked toward the dark-haired little boy.

Nate had been wandering close by, gathering a bouquet

of grass and flowers, but at this point he tottered over and dropped it into her lap. "Wan' it?" he inquired.

Stacia's smile froze.

Those were Derek's eyes looking at her out of Nate's cherubic face. Luminous, glittering, and beguilingly innocent, and green as the grass on which they sat.

Mrs. Inglesant was flushing. "Yes, he has the Deveaux eyes. I thought 'twas a pity he did not resemble me more, because of the scandal." She sighed. "Nevertheless, I would not change the way he looks for anything. One loves one's children as they are, as I'm sure you will discover."

"Naturally," Stacia responded, through lips gone numb with shock. "He is a charming child."

"Your husband is such a good man," continued Mrs. Inglesant fervently. "How many of his class care enough to do what he has done? Not many, I'll wager. And he takes the time to visit the children, which is more than most would do."

"Exactly how many children are there?" Stacia inquired carefully.

Mrs. Inglesant's brow furrowed. "Well, counting the boy who just arrived, I think there must be twenty-three now. I'm afraid after the first dozen I started to lose count."

"Twenty-three!" repeated Stacia, aghast. "And my husband is responsible for all of them?"

"Yes, but do pray remember that he does it by choice, not because anyone expects it of him. I'm sure *I* did not expect him to provide for me and the child. 'Twas he who came to me, when he heard of my plight."

It was all Stacia could do to prevent her mouth from falling open. "I see," was all she could manage, in a rather choked voice. "How good of him indeed."

Mrs. Inglesant cast her an anxious look. "I hope you do not object? As his wife, I'm sure he must be greatly influenced by your opinions." As Nate came over, she reached out to touch him tenderly. "I beg you to remember that a great many depend upon your husband for their very existence. Perhaps you do not realize that such charitable efforts are few and far between. Oh, in London there are a few—the Foundling Hospital, the Magdalen House, and of course the Philanthropic Society, which has its houses at Bermondsey and St. George's-fields. But you must own that this is a different sort of thing entirely."

"Indeed, I do," said Stacia dully.

"Oh dear, I see you are not convinced. Is it last night's episode which troubles you? I promise we would not have sent the message had we known it was your wedding day. It must have seemed an unpardonable nuisance and I *do* beg your pardon for it. We never guessed that Derek would feel obliged to come himself, or indeed that he was in residence at all." Mrs. Inglesant hesitated, then made a helpless gesture. "But the poor man's leg was broken, you see, and Doctor Trent already engaged with a double birth over in Kentford. We did not know what to do."

Despite the leaden ache in her chest, Stacia was curious. "So what did Derek do?"

Mrs. Inglesant's brows raised. "Did he not tell you? I know he is shockingly modest, but I would have thought— However, it is none of my affair. He set the man's leg, of course, and made a fine job, too. The flesh is only a little inflamed around the area of the break."

Stacia blinked. "Derek set the leg himself? No, he did not tell me . . . that part of it."

"How odd." The woman shrugged. "Well, he is very secretive about his charity work, as I'm sure you know. He does not want people to know of the good he does, though why that should be so I cannot say. I must say it elevates him in my eyes."

"Perhaps he is embarrassed to be associated with such things," offered Stacia coolly.

"Embarrassed? Derek? I see you do not know your husband very well! Oh dear, I deserve a snub for that, don't I? It was a shockingly impertinent thing to say."

The woman looked so contrite that Stacia forced a smile. "Perhaps I do not. It is something I intend to remedy as soon as possible." She paused. "How far is Newmarket from here, would you say?"

"Oh, it cannot be above six or seven miles— Nate, do not pull on me like that. What is it?"

"Mama, I have to piddle," whispered the little boy.

Mrs. Inglesant looked rueful. "I see it is time that we went. I hope I have not said anything to overset you, Mrs. Deveaux. 'Twas kind of you even to speak to me after you discovered who I was. Your husband places such weight on speaking frankly that we are all in the habit of doing so. Of course, not all the folk around here are so generous, but they respect the Deveaux name enough to keep their feelings to themselves. I think they sympathize with your husband's desire for secrecy, which is why the truth about us is not widely known."

Not knowing what to say to that, Stacia rose to her feet and began brushing the grass from her skirt. Mrs. Inglesant bit her lip and folded the blanket in silence.

"I think you are a trifle shocked," the woman said finally. "I hope you will discuss this with your husband. It is not as bad as it appears. Many of the children are simply poor—not illegitimate. Here in the country, they are given the chance to breath fresh rather than sooty air. Instead of thieving, they are given a chance to learn an honest occupation. Instead of disease-infested alleys, they have the miles of countryside to enjoy."

Ignoring most of this speech, Stacia inclined her head and said, a little abruptly, "I certainly will discuss this with my husband. I bid you good day, Mrs. Inglesant."

As Stacia headed for Camberley, a tight, burning anger raged in her breast. Her initial impulse was to ride directly to Newmarket, locate Derek, and demand an explanation, however the obstacles to such a plan were obvious even to one in her tormented state. After a few seething minutes, she dismissed the notion as foolish, yet the desire to confront Derek instantly did not abate.

Nate's existence was something she could not dismiss as easily. He was clearly Derek's son, and therefore, whispered a voice in her head, her husband must have lied. The shameless woman had as much as admitted he was the father.

However, despite such damning evidence, something within her rebelled against this conclusion. True, she might not know her husband very well, but there were some things about him she did know, and one of these was that he always called a spade a spade. Derek was forthright to the point of rudeness, she reflected. In fact, she'd have judged him incapable of lying, and if that were so, then there had to be some other explanation. Yet what could it be? The child resembled him beyond the point of coincidence.

And *really*, she thought with a renewed spurt of indignation, twenty-three children and not a word to her about any of them! Of course she realized now that they could not possibly all be Derek's, but at first she had been utterly flabbergasted.

Obviously, however, Derek had not set up a private seraglio but rather some sort of charity institution for poor children and, in some cases, their mothers. For an instant her heart softened, but before she could embrace the image of her husband as philanthropist rather than philanderer, an insidious question wormed into her head.

How many of the twenty-three had green eyes?

Trust.

The word was a taunting arrow which found its mark on her conscience. How in the world could she expect him to trust her if she could not do the same for him? She'd fallen in love with him, she'd been willing to give him her body—she ought to be able to surrender her trust as well.

Stacia's shoulders straightened suddenly. Very well, then. She'd give it to him. For the time being, she'd

293

assume the child was not his. Derek had said he had no children, therefore he did not have any. There was some other reasonable, logical explanation. It was as simple as that.

Still, even if this assumption were true, he was not entirely off the hook. In fact, he had a great deal for which to answer, beginning with his failure to explain his departure yesterday evening. Stacia's eyes kindled with annoyance. If what Mrs. Inglesant said was true, Stacia was willing to grant that his reason had been valid, but that scarcely excused his insensitive style of exit. "I have to go out" was a trifle too abbreviated to count for much, she thought crossly.

For that matter, so was "Newmarket is no place for you." She was his wife, and if this race was that important to him, she ought to be there to witness it with him. She was obviously going to have to put her foot down with this man. She was going to fight for her happiness, and that meant forcing him to be more communicative.

By the time she reached this conclusion, Stacia realized that she was within sight of Camberley, though she did not recall giving her mount any direction since leaving the priory. She sighed and gave Amazon an absent pat on the neck. The horse had obviously known its own way home.

As she neared the stables, Stacia was surprised to see a familiar and very dashing high-perch phaeton standing nearby.

Seconds later she was hurling into her half brother's arms. "Oh, Marco, I'm so glad to see you! When did you arrive? And how did you know I was here?"

Though Marco accepted her embrace with every evidence of affection, his tone was irritable. "You may well ask!" he said huffily. "I called at your house yesterday only to be informed, if you please, that you had run off to be married to that Deveaux fellow! And never a word to me!"

"I am so sorry," she said guiltily. "But Derek gave me no time to do more than throw a few things into my trunk. We married by special license, you see."

"What the devil was the rush?" he demanded. "I thought you were going to post the banns, and so forth." His eyes ran over her figure suspiciously. "I say, there wasn't any, uh, particular reason for such haste, was there?"

"Reason?" Stacia said blankly.

Marco glanced around, then leaned closer to her ear. "You ain't breeding, are you?" he hissed.

"Of course not!" She eyed him reproachfully. "What a shocking thing to suggest."

"Then why the hurry?"

Not quite knowing what to say, Stacia affected a nonchalant shrug. "'Twas simply one of Derek's queer starts. He wanted to be married, and once he took the fancy into his head, there was no gainsaying him."

"Humph," said Marco, unimpressed. "Well, I still say someone should have told me. He's in Newmarket?"

Stacia nodded. "His race is tomorrow, you know."

"Of course I know," he said impatiently. "I'm headed there myself—everyone is! I came here, though, to see if you could put me up for the night. Every inn for miles is packed to the gills."

"Of course you may stay here." Stacia glared past him for a moment, thinking rapidly. "On the condition that you take me with you when you leave, that is."

Marco looked pained. "Oh, no! If Deveaux didn't see fit to take you, I'd be noodlebrained to go against his wishes. One don't cross a fellow like that if one can help it." He shuddered visibly. "He's got a devilish nasty way of putting things when he ain't happy."

"No, does he?" she said cordially. "*My* Derek? The Soul of Tact personified? Oh, don't scowl so! Of course Derek wants me there. He simply felt he would be too occupied to protect me properly. Please, Marco. I'm sure there could be no objection if you took me."

"Lord, I don't know, Stacia. I don't think I should. It's not a place for a woman."

They had been strolling toward the house, but at this point Stacia stopped dead and took hold of his arm. "Listen to me," she said steadily. "I need to speak to Derek about something and it cannot wait. Do you understand? I have not asked you to do many things for me in my life, but I'm asking this. Please escort me to Newmarket in the morning and help me to find my husband."

She could see that Marco was weakening. "Dash it, Stacia, if he cuts up rough about this, I'm going to tell him it was you—"

"By all means," she agreed, in dulcet accents. "Tell him it was me. Now do stop being so stuffy about it and tell me what you would like to eat."

Stacia attended with only half an ear as Marco continued voicing objections throughout the evening, however before bed, in the privacy of her bedchamber, she reconsidered her decision from every angle. It was definitely the right thing to do, she finally concluded, for the sooner she and Derek cleared up their misunderstandings, the better it would be for both of them. Why stay here and torture herself with idle speculation when she could go and ask him to explain? And surely he, too, would feel better if he were to learn that she had not written that vile letter? And if his horse lost, she would be there to console him. It was her duty as his wife. Moreover, the opportunity to deliver her letter to Lord Andrew might arise, for it seemed quite likely that he would be in Newmarket as well. If only Marco would cease being so dreadfully contrary.

By the next morning, however, Marco was still nurturing his doubts.

"Y'know, Stacia," he said, as he handed her into his phaeton, "it really ain't the thing for you to be traveling a public road in an open carriage like this. Deveaux ain't going to like it one bit. You wouldn't credit the raking-down he gave me over this 'widow' scheme of yours. He holds *me* responsible for the whole thing," he grumbled, "which is devilish unfair considering how you nagged and nagged until I—"

"Yes, it was *most* unfair of him," she soothed. "But traveling in an open carriage is not at all the same sort of thing. It is only a few miles, and besides," she added cunningly, "this is my first opportunity to ride in a high-perch phaeton. I've been quite *longing* for you to drive me, you know."

Her tactic worked. "Oh, very well," Marco replied, his face alight with gratification. "It's not such a great distance after all, and I'm a capital whip now. You'll see."

Thus it was that Stacia entered the town of Newmarket with her equanimity only a little shaken by Marco's driving skills. Unfortunately, he was not, as he had claimed, a capital whip. He had a shocking tendency to take his corners too fast, besides having an undesirable penchant for passing every other vehicle on the road, whether it was safe to do so or not. However, they had arrived and that was the important thing.

From her high vantage, Stacia scanned the faces of passersby for Derek, much in the way she had done on the busy London streets after their first meeting, but her efforts were in vain.

"Where do you think we should look for him?" she asked Marco anxiously.

"What? Oh, you mean Deveaux?" Marco scratched his nose absently. "Well, the heath, I suppose. It's on the other side of the town, to the west, near Devil's Dyke. Shouldn't be difficult to find him. That stallion of his is heavily favored to win—Thunder and turf!"

This exclamation was accompanied by a sharp jerk on the reins that had Stacia clutching the side of the seat. "What is it?" she gasped as the phaeton dived into an extremely narrow side street and lurched to a stop.

297

"Reggie Denchworth," said Marco succinctly. "Never had the chance to talk to him about those dice." He thrust the whip and reins into her hands. "Here, hold these until I come back. I won't be long."

As Marco strode back toward the wider street, Stacia craned her head around to see where he had gone. To her vexation he had already disappeared.

Teeth grit together, she sat stewing for approximately five minutes before a hay wagon entered the alley from its other end. Despite the fact that there was obviously no space to pass, it plodded inexorably toward her, as if determined to clamber right over the obstacle in its path. At last it paused, its driver regarding her with as much sullen resentment as his job-horse seemed to regard Marco's matched pair.

The driver spat tobacco before addressing her. "I 'as to get through, Missy."

"It was most foolish of you to enter this street when you could see your way was blocked," she informed him in a severe tone. "You must be able to see that I am waiting for someone."

"Can't wait 'ere," he said stubbornly. "This is a public street. Ye'll 'ave to move."

"Oh, very well." Sighing with exasperation, Stacia pulled gently on the reins. Step by step, she backed the phaeton out of the alley, but this created a great deal of furor among the male drivers of vehicles moving down the main street at precisely that moment. When a gentleman in a curricle gave her an irate stare and shouted at her to move on, she resigned herself to the knowledge that she would have to do as he said, particularly as the phaeton was not (as she had intended) positioned close to the edge of the street, but was protruding out into traffic at a highly inconvenient angle.

"Oh, Marco," she murmured wrathfully. "How the devil do you manage to put me into these situations?"

Fortunately, Stacia remembered enough of Derek's teachings to be able to whip up the horses with a fair degree of composure. Resolved to do no more than take them around the block, she steadfastly ignored the stares from the other drivers and held Marco's pair to a steady trot. They were inclined to be fidgety—perhaps because they sensed a different driver—but with strict attention to the reins she kept them under control. At the first large intersection, she handled the turn with more expertise than Marco had ever done, sweeping around the corner in an arc that was neither too sharp nor too wide.

Stacia was conscious of a thrill of exhilaration. No wonder Marco felt so dashing when he was driving one of these. This was fun! If only Derek could see her now—though perhaps it was as well he could not, she amended. He would certainly say she ought not to be driving such a dangerous vehicle in heavy traffic.

She completed her journey around the block and was nearly back to the point where she began when the accident occurred. A vegetable cart emerged from the same alley where Marco had abandoned her, while at the same moment a curricle swerved to avoid the cart. This in itself would not have been an insurmountable problem had not a beggar child dodged out in front of her, presumably to scoop up the few peppers and onions that spilled onto the road with the cart's abrupt halt.

She had a fraction of a second to make her decision. She could either hit the child or veer hard to the right and risk ramming the curricle. Choosing the latter as the lesser of two evils, Stacia yanked the reins with every ounce of her strength.

To her shock, the world tipped, and for the briefest of instants she felt disembodied, unattached to the seat cushions or to any other earthly force. Then the cobblestones came up and whacked brutally at her body and she knew no more.

Chapter Twenty

Marco actually saw the phaeton go over. He had just stepped out of a coffeehouse—having rung a very satisfying peal over Reggie Denchworth, who in turn had apologized for his gross misappraisal of what Would or Would Not be Acceptable to an Ashcroft—when the frightening incident occurred. Helpless to intervene, he witnessed Stacia's gallant attempt to avoid the child, his handsome features freezing with horror as she pitched to to the ground.

In the length of a heartbeat, a hundred images from childhood flashed through Marco's head: Stacia, following him around the house like a shadow; Stacia, taking the blame when he'd stolen cream puffs from the kitchen; Stacia, comforting him when some small thing had gone wrong in his life. Only his *half* sister, as Father had so often pointed out. Hell, forget the "half." She was his sister, and by God he loved her with all his heart.

Somehow he reached her side before the others, but the sight of her lying so still and pale nearly made him throw up. He barely noticed when several onlookers had the presence of mind to attend to the struggling horses, whose piercing whinnies added a gruesome element to the scene.

"Here, now, young man," someone cried as he lifted Stacia's limp hand. "Do you know this woman?"

300

"She's my sister," he replied in a cracked voice. "For God's sake, someone fetch a doctor."

"What the devil was she doing driving a phaeton on her own?" demanded another gentleman in critical accents.

Marco glanced up, his eyes like two chips of glacial ice. "It's my fault," he said. "I left her to hold the reins. It's my fault," he repeated. "Not hers."

Miraculously, someone recollected having spoken with a physician in one of the shops down the street, so that within minutes a Dr. Browning was kneeling by Stacia's side. After a brief examination, the doctor declared that though she had obviously struck her head, he could discern no serious injuries which would make moving her dangerous. "Of course, we must find somewhere close by where I can examine her more thoroughly," he told Marco.

Marco eased Stacia into his arms with the utmost care and followed the doctor down the street to the nearest hotel, the Rutland Arms. The news of the accident had already drifted inside, so they met at the door by the landlord himself.

"We must thank God her neck was not broken," commented the doctor, as the landlord's wife clucked her tongue and conducted them down a corridor to her own bedchamber.

"We've no empty rooms," she apologized, "but yer quite welcome to use mine and the 'usband's fer a bit. 'Appen I won't 'ave time to do more than bustle about all day anyway. God bless the young lady."

Marco placed Stacia gingerly on the bed. "Her husband is out on the heath," he choked out. "I should fetch him at once."

The doctor's brows raised. "I think that would be an excellent idea. By the time you return I may have some notion of the extent of her injuries. I must say I have a great deal of hope. Some of her color has returned, and both her breathing and pulse are normal." He looked at the landlord's wife. "Perhaps you, ma'am, might assist me while the gentleman is gone?"

The landlord's wife nodded. "Don't you worry, sir," she said to Marco. "We'll take care of 'er like she was our own. You can borrow my 'usband's nag, if yer own ain't able."

Marco nodded his thanks. "I'll be back as soon as possible."

In preparation for the race, Derek had moved Palatine to a temporary shed near the racecourse. For the first time in weeks there was no thought of Stacia in his head; every ounce of his concentration was focused on the stallion and what lay ahead. Eyes narrowed against the sun, he gazed down the treeless hill for signs of Lord Andrew, whose arrival he expected to be imminent.

"Don't you worry, guv'nor," said the jockey for at least the tenth time that hour. "'Is only real rival is Croxton's Black Devil." He walked over to pat the stallion's neck. "'E's a proud, aggressive beast. 'E wants ter win as bad as you want 'im to, and 'e don't like that Black Devil none at all."

Palatine's ears flicked as though he knew what they said. One hoof lifted an inch, then pawed at the ground.

Several minutes later, Derek caught sight of two familiar figures cantering up from the road leading back to the town. Recognizing them, he frowned, for though one was Andrew Carisbrooke, the other was almost certainly Sir Marco Ashcroft. He watched in irritation as Marco whipped at his mount, a common-looking beast whose heaving sides suggested it had been taxed well beyond its endurance.

When he was within twenty feet of the shed, the young baronet hailed him aggressively. "Deveaux! Thank God I found you! Met Carisbrooke on the way. Said you'd be up here."

Derek shoved his hands in his pockets and regarded his

wife's brother with faint mockery. "More problems, Ashcroft?" he inquired. "The duns on your heels?"

The remark was ignored; Marco was breathing hard. "It's Stacia," he said emotionally. "She's been hurt. You've got to come at once."

"*What?*" Derek went rigid. "Where?"

"In town. There was an accident. My phaeton tipped over and she was thrown—"

Derek swore vividly. Something threatened to explode inside him, while at the same time his lungs felt constricted, as though some deadly weight deprived him of air.

Lord Andrew slid down from his gelding. "Take Cato," he advised, holding out the reins. "I'll see to Palatine."

His acceptance consisting of a nod, Derek was on the gelding in one smooth movement. "*Where?*" he repeated, more roughly than before. "Where is she, Ashcroft?"

"The Rutland Arms. I'll show you . . ."

But Derek was already galloping down the hill. Fortunately, Drew's mount possessed the necessary speed and stamina to carry a man of his weight all the way back into town at such a pace. Even so, Derek demanded more of the creature, for once oblivious to everything but the mind-numbing need for haste.

As he rode, he told himself fiercely that she would be all right, that she *had* to be all right because anything else would be an unthinkable wrong in a world that was only beginning to be as it should. He would not allow himself to speculate upon why or how it had happened; he would concentrate only on what needed to be done, not on the dread that clawed at his throat like some raging animal.

It seemed to take forever to reach the Rutland Arms, and when at last he rode into the cobbled courtyard, the gelding was lathered in sweat and shaking from fatigue. Tossing the reins to a flunky, Derek strode inside, his forbidding expression enough to bring the landlord running.

303

"Sir?" queried the host, a tankard in each hand. "Is there aught I may do to assist—"

"My wife," interrupted Derek in a flat tone. "Where is she?"

"The lady who was injured?" He nodded toward the rear of the taproom. "Through that door, sir, and down the passageway to the end. 'Tis my own set of rooms, sir. My wife was there with the doctor, but she 'ad to go down to the kitchen fer a bit. I'd escort you m'self if 'tweren't so busy—"

"I'll find it."

Seconds later he was walking into the room where Stacia lay. Barely conscious of the doctor, he approached the bed, his eyes fixed on the gentle features which had become more beloved to him than life itself. Hang it, she *was* his life, he thought suddenly. Existence was worth nothing without Stacia—she was everything he had ever wanted and more.

He sank to his knees and pressed his brow to her hand, the muscles in his face working with emotion. He might not deserve her, but she was his love and his heart and his soul, and nothing, *nothing*, was going to be allowed to change that.

A discreet cough reminded Derek that he was not alone. He forced himself to look up.

"How is she?" he said tonelessly.

He was favored with a portly bow. "Dr. Browning, at your service, sir. You must be the lady's husband."

"I am." He reached out to touch Stacia's cheek, then possessed himself of her hand. "How is she?" he repeated.

Before the doctor could answer, he felt the slim fingers move.

"Stacia," he said urgently. "Can you speak, love?"

Her pink lips parted and closed, then, "Derek?" It came out as a whisper.

"I'm here, love. I'm right here with you."

She squeezed his hand in response.

"Sir, it is my professional opinion that your wife is not seriously harmed. There are no broken bones, and I can see no indication of other injury. As far as I can determine, she simply struck her head against the cobbles and was rendered unconscious. It is quite possible that there is no concussion."

During this speech, Stacia's eyes had opened. "Don't remember." The murmured words were soft and muzzy, as if she had been asleep.

Derek frowned anxiously. "You don't remember what happened?"

"No." Her head shook a fraction of an inch. "I remember . . . driving Marco's phaeton." She smiled feebly. "I was . . . cutting a dash, Derek . . . wishing you could see me."

"Does your head hurt?"

"Feels like . . . someone hit me with a poker." With her free hand, she reached up to touch the side of her head. "What happened?"

"I'm not sure. Your brother mumbled something about the phaeton overturning—"

Her eyes widened. "How—?"

"A beggar child ran out in front of you," inserted Dr. Browning in a benign tone. "I had the whole story from the landlord's wife, who heard it from someone who witnessed the incident."

"And . . . the child?" She sounded stricken.

"Quite unharmed, ma'am," imparted the doctor. "Thanks to you."

Still holding her hand, Derek stood up. "Is my wife well enough to be moved?"

"I see no reason why not. I very much fear she cannot remain here, since this is the landlord's room. The races have brought in so many that I do not know where—"

"Oh, Derek, the race." Stacia's voice gained a little in strength. "Did . . . your horse win?"

Derek gazed down at her, amazed that he had forgotten about it. "It's not been run yet," he answered lightly.

305

"Don't worry, Drew is there in my stead. Right now I'm going to take you back to Camberley."

She looked vaguely puzzled. "But, Derek, you must not miss the race on my account."

He tightened his grip on her hand. "Do you think," he said gruffly, "that I care about that now, when you are like this? Do you think I would leave you, even for a moment?"

Her soft brown eyes clung to his, but before she could speak, the physician said with approval, "By all means, sir, take her home. She should rest as much as possible. I shall administer some laudanum before you leave, but you should have your local physician examine her later. And if you have it, some ice applied to the head would not come amiss."

"I shall see to it," Derek replied. After a pause, he said, "Dr. Browning, do you know anyone who would be willing to lend me a carriage? Something fairly well padded, so she will not be jostled."

"You may take mine," offered the physician. "I consider it quite comfortable, though not in the first style of elegance. I rode all the way from Northampton in it without suffering annoyance."

Derek inclined his head. "You have been most kind," he said. He drew a five-pound note from his pocket. "Allow me to reimburse you for your services."

After a brief hesitation, the doctor accepted the money. "My best wishes to you both," he said warmly. "It is so gratifying to see a married couple with so much devotion for one another. It does my heart good."

Derek's gaze returned to Stacia. "Mine also," he said quietly.

Stacia slept the whole way back to Camberley and on into the late part of the afternoon. When at last she awoke, the sun hung low in the sky and the room was full of shadows. She lay quite still, noting thankfully that the pain in her head had nearly subsided.

"Maisie?" she called. She felt groggy from the laudanum.

"Right here, mum." Maisie moved quickly into her field of vision. "How do you feel?"

"Better. Thirsty. Is my husband here?"

Maisie poured water into a cup and smiled. "He's been sitting right there"—she pointed to a chair by the bed—"until a few minutes ago. He went down to the hall to greet some unexpected guests."

"I had an accident, you know."

Maisie nodded soberly. "Yes, mum, we all heard. Sir Marco arrived an hour after you and the master. He saw the whole thing happen." She shook her head admiringly. "I must say, the master was in a rare temper with Sir Marco—" She broke off as Stacia pushed herself up. "Here now, mum, should you be doing that?"

"Yes, Maisie, I must," she replied, reaching for the cup. "I want to see how my head feels. Anyway, how can I drink if I'm lying down?" She took several swallows of water and passed it back to the maid. "Who is here?"

"'Tis Lady Winifred and Sir Cuthbert Duncan, mum."

"I see." Stacia digested this as Maisie bent to plump up the pillows. "Could you please send a message to my husband that I wish to see him?"

"I'm here."

Stacia's heart skipped a beat as she turned toward the door. She had not heard him arrive, but he was there, leaning against the jamb, tall and controlled and intensely, achingly masculine.

Her husband.

"Derek." She said his name softly, then without knowing why, she started to weep.

He was across the room in two strides, enfolding her into his arms before the first tear slid down her cheek.

"Stacia, Stacia, my love, don't cry," he murmured, as

Maisie quietly departed. "My sweet, sweet heart's desire, don't cry."

Still sobbing, she clung to him, feeling his warmth and strength, gradually absorbing his endearments as their bodies nestled together. After a few moments, she raised her head from his shoulder.

"*What* did you call me?" she said breathlessly.

He rubbed his cheek on her hair. "I called you my heart's desire," he replied, in a voice gone ragged and tense, "because that is what you are. Lord, Stacia, I don't know what to say to make you love me. I didn't marry you for your money but I . . . I don't know how to convince you of that. I don't give a damn about your money. It's you I want. Only you."

Stacia hiccuped. "But I do love you," she protested. "I've loved you practically from the day of our first meeting." She hiccuped again and wiped her tears on his cravat. "I love you quite desperately, in fact."

He drew back an inch, a question in his eye. "Then why send me that damnable letter?"

"I *didn't!*" she retorted on a watery laugh. "Oh, Derek, I can't believe you thought I did! *Angeline* wrote it. I didn't even learn of it until our wedding night, after you had gone. And then later, when I should have told you about it, I . . . I forgot."

Derek swore. "That companion of yours has got to go!" he exclaimed. "Of all the interfering, contemptible things to do—"

"Yes, it was, Derek, but do try not to be too angry. Angeline feels very sorry for what she did and has promised not to do anything like that ever again." Her arms slipped round his neck to knead his tense muscles. "I found it in your room and I burned it."

"Good," he said, scowling savagely.

In an effort to divert his mind from his anger, she snuggled closer and said, against his shirt, "When do you expect to hear about the race?"

His muscles rippled with his shrug. "When Drew

arrives. It ought to be soon."

"I'm so sorry you had to miss it," she added in a small voice. "I still don't remember the accident at all. Can you tell me what happened?"

His arms tightened. "I will, but not now. I've a doctor waiting downstairs. I'm going to send for him now. And why are you sitting up? You ought to be lying down."

"I'm perfectly all right," she objected.

"Yes, well, I intend to make sure of that," he said, rocking her gently. "I've a great respect for Dr. Trent. He's taught me a thing or two in the past."

Such as how to set broken bones? It was just one of the questions she longed to ask, but the time was not yet ripe. He had declared his love for her—she would be satisfied with that.

The earth must be broken a clod at a time.

To Derek's relief, Dr. Trent's diagnosis concurred with Dr. Browning's. After a prolonged examination, the wise little man pronounced that, other than striking her head, Stacia had managed to avoid any injury beyond a few scrapes and bruises.

"Your wife is an extraordinarily lucky young woman," he told them. "I think I should warn you, though, that she may never remember the accident or the events which preceded it. 'Tis not unheard of, you see, for people to lose hours, or even days, after such blows to the head. The important thing is that there does not appear to be any injury to the skull, and for that we must all thank the dear Lord."

Derek escorted the doctor outside to his carriage. As they stood by the gig, he said quietly, "Did you manage to take a look at Dowling's leg yet? Clarissa will have told you what happened by now. I did the best I could, but—"

"You did well," replied the doctor, clapping a hand to his shoulder. "You would have made an excellent physician, Derek. Now go back to that wife of yours and

309

make her happy. She's a pretty little gel. I'm pleased as punch that you finally took a wife. Maybe *she'll* be able to convince you that all this secrecy is nonsense."

Derek shook his head. "I don't care about the gossip," he said brusquely. "I don't want people prying into my affairs. You know that."

"That was acceptable before," lectured the doctor, "but what you do affects her now. Remember that, my lad." With a hefty sigh, he climbed into his gig and drove off, leaving Derek to stare thoughtfully into the dusk.

Thirty minutes later Lord Andrew arrived at Camberley, tired, thirsty, and only a little depressed. It was, he considered, a vast improvement on his state of mind from the day before, but he was still thoroughly disgusted with himself. What was Angeline Greaves after all? Just another beautiful woman. He had seen beautiful women before. He had taken a good many of them to bed, too, and in the dark they had all been very much the same. So why did he continue to hanker after Angeline like some love-besotted idiot in a poem?

Derek received him in the bookroom, wearing a look of such blithe insouciance that Andrew was annoyed. As he eased himself into an armchair, he could not resist the temptation to toy with his friend.

"By jove, it's been a wearying day," he said with a yawn. "I could use a glass of sherry, or better yet, a bottle or two of your best French brandy."

When Derek seemed ready to oblige him in this or any other matter, Andrew silently marveled. How the deuce could the man prevent himself from mentioning the race?

Then he remembered the accident.

"How is Stacia?" he asked guiltily.

By the time Derek finished telling him, Andrew had a pretty fair notion why his friend was looking so complacent. The man was obviously head over heels in love with his own wife, who had narrowly escaped serious injury this very day. He had a right to be content.

Envying the other man's happiness, Andrew swallowed hard. "Curse it, aren't you the least bit curious?" he complained. "How the devil can you sit there and not *ask?*"

Across from him, the dark face was inscrutable. "All right, then. Tell me," Derek said calmly. "I thought I was gratifying you with my forbearance."

Andrew gave up. "Well," he said with a crooked smile, "Palatine did it!" His irritation disappeared as Derek's face lit with relief. "By God, he won by more than half a length," he enthused, "with Shiny Penny in second, and Wickham's Pride, third. You can collect your prize money tomorrow, if you like. It ought to be well over two thousand guineas."

"And Black Devil?"

"Fourth. He broke stride near the finish. In my opinion, 'twas the jockey's fault, but Croxton blames the horse. By God, Derek, I would you could have seen his face!"

"Croxton's?" said Derek lazily. "Or the horse's?"

Andrew stared at him for a moment, then burst out laughing. Knowing he could sustain his good humor as long as he talked about the race, he did so in detail, bestowing his own, very satisfying *coup de grâce* upon the finish.

". . . so I offered to take the beast off his hands. Croxton was so disgusted with the creature that he agreed to my first offer—before a host of witnesses, too! He'll make you a good breeder, Derek. He's to be my wedding present to you and Stacia."

"Good God!" Derek was obviously moved. "You cannot mean it, Drew."

"I assure you I do." Andrew paused to clear his throat. "It's good to see you happy, my friend. You not only found a woman who doesn't bore you, you fell in love with her as well. I congratulate you with all my heart."

311

Derek surveyed him thoughtfully. "Thank you. I wish I might say the same of you." His smile faded as he reached into his pocket. "This is addressed to you," he went on, extending what looked to be a letter. "I found it in my wife's reticule. I've no idea what it says, but"—he paused briefly—"I trust her enough to give it to you."

Puzzled, Andrew leaned forward to accept it. "Stacia wrote to me?" he muttered. "I wonder why—?"

Derek's voice was quite steady. "So do I. But that does not oblige you to share its contents with me, of course."

"The devil it doesn't," Andrew murmured beneath his breath.

As he spread open the single sheet, he saw Derek turn away to pour himself a drink. Picking up his own glass, Andrew focused his eyes on the neat, feminine writing. *My Lord,* it most properly read, *I hope you will not think me Impertinent . . .*

He skimmed through it cursorily, then reread the entire thing in a daze. No moral reason why he and Angeline could not be wed? Could it be true? A third reading had him reeling through a gamut of emotion: incredulity, relief, anger, bewilderment, and wild joy mixed with a powerful dose of indignation.

When he looked up, he saw Derek watching him.

"Your wife," Andrew uttered, enunciating carefully, "is an angel. Never, never forget it."

He dropped the letter into Derek's lap and left the room.

Stacia, meanwhile, was entertaining a visitor in her bedchamber. "And you are quite certain the phaeton can be repaired?" she asked Marco in an anxious voice.

"Aye, but once that's done I intend to sell it and buy a more sober conveyance." Her brother flushed slightly. "Something a country gentleman might use. Something Nellie will feel safe in."

Stacia was pleased. "Ah, so you do intend to offer for

312

Miss Dawson! I am so very glad. I have always thought her such a pleasant, amiable girl."

Marco's blush grew. "Well, I intend to make her a declaration, but ten to one she won't have me." He shifted uncomfortably. "Uh, there's something else I've been wanting to tell you."

Stacia's brows lifted. "What is it?"

"Uh, I want to . . . to thank you for putting up with me all these years." He hunched forward. "I know there's been times when I've been selfish and disagreeable, but, well, I wanted to let you know that I've always been fond of you. Devilish fond, in fact." He cleared his throat. "You're my sister and . . . I love you."

"Oh, Marco." Stacia's lips trembled. "You're so sweet. I love you, too, so very, very much."

Marco looked gratified. "Aye, well, I also want to say that I hope this Deveaux fellow is going to make you happy. If he don't, now, mind you let me know. I realize I ain't exactly been dependable in the past, but from now on things are going to be different. I'll deal with any problems you may have."

"And will you promise never to gamble again?" she inquired with a twinkle.

"Oh, well, as to *that!*" Marco's grin flashed. "Never more than I can afford to lose, at any rate. But first I mean to repay every penny I borrowed from you. It's like to keep me busy for years."

"But you really do not have to—"

His raised hand cut her short. "Yes, I do," he said firmly. "Every debt is a debt of honor. And I am more in debt to you than anyone else I know. In more ways than one."

Derek's arrival put a hasty end to the interview.

"I'll take my leave of you, now," said Marco, edging toward the door. "Evening, Deveaux. Er, I'll talk to you later, eh? Sure you must want to be alone with m'sister."

Derek bowed slightly. "How good of you to understand," he said, with only the slightest sardonic inflection to his voice.

When Marco was gone, Stacia turned laughing eyes upon her husband. "What in the world did you say to him, Derek? I swear he's terrified of you."

Derek sat on the bed. "Use your imagination," he teased, pulling her slender body up and into his arms. "That's what I was forced to do on our wedding night— beyond a certain point, that is."

Stacia turned pink. "So you would put me to the blush after all I have suffered," she complained. She slipped her arms around his waist with tingling delight. "How prodigious ungallant you are, sir."

He looked amused. "And what a meddling little matchmaker you are, my love. I gave Drew your letter."

"You found it?" she said in surprise.

"Yes." He hesitated for a moment. "Your reticule fell open when I threw it on the carriage seat. I noticed it then." There was a short silence. "I wanted to open it," he said with difficulty. "Instead I put it in my pocket and tried not to be jealous. And I found that . . . when you are in my arms I could not doubt you. Something inside me felt that there had to be some innocent explanation, even though I could not think what it was."

Her heart thumping, Stacia tilted her head back and said, "Nor could I think of a reason why Clarissa Inglesant's son should have your green eyes."

She could feel his start.

"You saw Nate?"

"It's one reason why I was coming to find you." Her stomach knotted, but she went on, bravely, "I know he cannot be your son, Derek. But all the same it was a shock. I realized it was time we talked, and . . . I decided it could not wait. That is why I came to Newmarket."

She saw the wonder flood his eyes. "Thank you for trusting me," he said quietly. "I was a fool not to have told you sooner. I thought I was sparing your sensibilities. You see, Nate is my uncle's son."

"Your uncle?"

314

"Rupert Deveaux, Lord Jettington." His lips twisted. "I'm afraid he is a libertine in the true sense of the word. Nate is his son, as are two others in the orphanage. The rest are a mixture—the flotsam of our society, you might say. The refuse nobody sees because if they did they'd be sick."

"Tell me more," she said softly.

He rested his chin on her head. "There's not much to tell. The idea came to me years ago, when a five-year-old climbing boy came down my chimney by accident. He was badly burned and crying, as well as filthy and undernourished. It reminded me—" He broke off, glancing down at her ruefully. "You did not have a happy childhood either, so you'll understand when I say that I felt great empathy. Not that I was deprived in a physical sense, but—" He cleared his throat. "Anyway, I went to the master sweep, who insisted that he took great care of the child. Stacia, I swear I have never felt more fury than I did at that moment." His face tightened to a cruel hardness. "But for a price, I was able to rescue the boy. Jason was my first 'child.'"

"And now there are twenty-three?"

"Not nearly enough," he said bitterly. "There are thousands of them out there, Stacia. I can't help them all. I haven't the money, and there is this house to maintain and the surrounding land."

She peeped up at him. "But you married an heiress. Think how much we can accomplish with my money."

"That is not why I married you," he said sternly.

"I know. But we could do it, Derek. We could help so many."

"You would really be willing to do that?"

"Of course I would be willing," she retorted. "But I would have people know the truth about you, Derek. No more vulgar gossip about . . . well, *you* know!"

"Yes," he agreed with a sigh. "I'll have to come out of the closet."

"And speaking of money, this room must have cost a

315

great deal. I could have done as well with a simple furnishings, you know."

He spared the blue-and-silver decor a brief glance. "No, my charity does not extend to depriving my wife of her comfort. I'll admit it was a gamble at that particular phase of our, er, courtship. But the prize money from Palatine's win will cover it, while his value as a stud should supply us with—"

Stacia's head jerked up. "Your horse won! But how wonderful, Derek. I am so happy for you."

He smiled. "I know you are, love. You have the kindest heart in the world."

"I don't think we are so very different," she ventured. "We both take in strays."

"I suppose you mean Angeline."

"Yes, I do. I know you do not like her"—she saw his expression—"but in a way she is much like your Jason. If you knew what she has suffered, how she was mistreated and made to feel miserable, well, I do not think you would condemn her as severely as you do."

He frowned. "I am sorry for it," he replied. "I had no idea that was so. It simply seemed to me that she was using you—"

"I suppose we all use each other in some way," Stacia said wisely. "That is part of being human."

Derek's mouth curved, but his eyes remained sober. "Speaking of human, you must realize you are not the first woman in my life. I can't change the past, but, praise God, the future offers no such barriers." He looked deep into her eyes. "I love you," he said, "and I could never, ever want anyone else."

He lowered his head to kiss her, but was interrupted by a sharp rap.

"Yes?" said Derek in a resigned voice.

Mrs. Partridge put her head around the door. "I do beg your pardon, sir," she said, looking very much harassed, "but dinner has already been put back twice and Cook is in a taking because the duck is overdone. And Lady

316

Winifred begs me to inform you that Sir Cuthbert is famished."

Derek sighed. "Very well, tell them my wife will have a tray sent up, but that—"

"No such thing," put in Stacia. "Tell them we will both be down directly. I am feeling a great deal better."

"Oh no you don't!" ruled Derek, forestalling her attempt to reach the bellpull. "You are going to rest."

This seemed as good a time as any to depress his dictatorial streak. "I'm quite tired of resting," she said firmly. "Do you mean to keep me on gruel and water, for pity's sake? I'm hungry!"

"You cannot be strong enough to walk so far."

"Well, then *carry* me," she said mutinously. "That is as far as I am willing to compromise."

For a long moment Derek stared at her, then suddenly his lips twitched. "Well," he acknowledged, "Trent did not forbid it. If you are certain you are well enough—?"

"I'm completely certain," Stacia replied, knowing she had won the encounter. "Don't coddle me, Derek."

"Very well," he said, smiling wickedly, "as long as I'm allowed to *cuddle* you . . ."

True to his word, Derek carried her all the way to the withdrawing room, where, under the interested gaze of three pairs of eyes, he deposited her onto a couch as tenderly as though she were an invalid of eighty.

Ringlets swinging with enthusiasm, Lady Winifred hurried over to kiss Stacia's cheek. "My dear, dear daughter-in-law," she said, with gushing warmth. "Welcome to our family! To be sure, 'twas most contrary of you to wed in such a hasty fashion, and so I have told Derek! There will be *such* talk, but of course Constance and I will do our best to repress the gossip." She squeezed Stacia's hand and added, "I am so very, very happy for you both."

"Winifred," interposed Sir Cuthbert with a cough,

"good time to tell 'em, eh? About us, I mean. You know, er, our Decision?"

"Very well, Cuthbert." Cheeks flushing, Lady Winifred turned and faced her son with a trace of defiance. "Sir Cuthbert has made me an offer," she stated, "and I have accepted him. We are . . . In Love."

"In Love," nodded Sir Cuthbert with a blush.

Derek's gaze shifted to the twitching baronet, then returned to his mother's rosy countenance. "Then I wish you both very happy," he said mildly. He nodded in Sir Cuthbert's direction. "Accept my felicitations, sir."

Sir Cuthbert blinked. "Thought you'd object. Thought you didn't like me."

"Not at all," said Derek gravely. "Whatever can have made you think that?"

Her ladyship's dark eyes were full of intensity. "Do you really wish us happy, Derek?"

Derek glanced at Stacia, who sent him an encouraging smile. "Yes, Mama," he said, "I really do."

"For God's sake, Winifred," hissed Sir Cuthbert, behind his hand, "there's no point in pressing the matter. Ask him when we can eat!"

Before her ladyship could do so, however, Marco introduced a new topic. "I say, Deveaux, any news of the race?" There was a certain degree of wistfulness in his tone.

Derek surveyed his brother-in-law. "As a matter of fact, there is. Drew tells me that Palatine won first place." As Marco exclaimed, Derek added, "Where the devil is the fellow, anyway? Are we never to eat our dinner?"

As if on cue, the drawing room doors were flung grandly open. "Lord Andrew Carisbrooke and Mrs. Greaves," intoned the butler in his most impressive accents.

Everyone turned. There on the threshold stood Lord Andrew, with Angeline's hand on his arm. "My apologies for the delay," said Andrew urbanely, "but I fear it could not be helped. Something rather important"—he glanced down at Angeline—"cropped up."

"What could be more important than dinner?" wondered Sir Cuthbert.

"The race," suggested Marco, rather irritably.

"Nonsense, Marco," objected Stacia, entering the conversation. "It is obvious that something of consequence has taken place. Angeline?" she prompted.

Across the space which separated them, Angeline's eyes linked with hers. "Lord Andrew has honored me with a proposal of marriage," she answered in a clear, quiet voice. "And I have accepted with happiness."

Stacia sighed with relief. "Well, thank goodness!" she said, which made Lord Andrew laugh.

There were a few minutes of general exclamations and handshaking, then Lady Winifred was claiming the floor.

"Before we dine, I have one more announcement to make," she uttered. She looked at Derek, her voice so serious that everyone grew quiet.

"It is the chief reason why Cuthbert and I came up to Camberley today," she went on. "I received some very sad news in this morning's post," she went on. "Derek, your Uncle Rupert is dead."

There was a long moment of silence.

"Makes you a baron," Sir Cuthbert informed him kindly. "Kept it a secret all afternoon. Told you I could keep a secret, Winifred."

"You did very well, Cuthbert," assured his betrothed.

"I'm quite a fellow, y'know."

Lord Andrew was gazing at Derek. "This means a seat in the House of Lords," he said softly.

"Yes, I'm well aware of that," Derek answered. Disregarding the company, he walked over to the sofa and scooped Stacia into his arms. "Well, Lady Jettington?" he said tenderly. "Shall we dine?"

Stacia slid her arms around his neck. "An excellent notion, my lord."

Author's Note

Dear Reader,

I hope you enjoyed reading Stacia and Derek's story as much as I enjoyed writing it. Writing is a far cry from what I have been trained to do—engineering—but I have come to feel that it is what I'm destined to do, and what I do best.

I love writing. It is hard work, but nothing worthwhile comes without effort. My goal is to create heroes you can fall in love with and heroines you can relate to. Have I achieved that? You, the readers, are the ones who decide.

I am always eager for feedback. Write to me c/o Zebra Books, 475 Park Ave. South, New York, NY 10016. SASE appreciated. Thanks and happy reading!

Julie Caille

P.S. Please watch for my next Zebra book, *A Valentine's Day Fancy* due out in January of 1992. My previous Zebra titles are: *The Scandalous Marquis* and *Change of Heart*.